# LEADING CONVICTION

*Conviction Series Book Six*

## GREER RIVERS

Blue Ghost Publishing, LLC
BGP Dark World

Cover Design: Cover Me Darling
Editing and Proofreading: My Brother's Editor
Diversity/Sensitivity Editing: A Book A Day Author Services and Blanca Sanchez

ASIN: B09VFYZ317
Paperback ISBN: 979-8-9861242-4-7
Hardback ISBN: 979-8-9861242-5-4

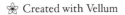 Created with Vellum

# LEADING CONVICTION

### *HAWK*

When my team called, I answered,
But I didn't know the cost.
I didn't know I would lose everything,
My fiancée, my best friend, my future...
All for a lie.
*Hannah was my world.*
And trusting the wrong people shattered my world.
Her father is hunting her.
My team is hunting *him*.
*But I found her first.*
I'll protect her no matter what,
*But can she forgive me for leaving her years ago?*

### *HANNAH*

When his team called, he answered,
Leaving me to fend for myself.
I thought I'd lost everything,
But one gift remained...
All thanks to a lie.
Hawk was *mi cielo*,
But trusting him darkened my sky.
Now my father is hunting me.
Only I couldn't outrun Hawk.
*He found me first.*
No matter what, I have to protect us,
*But can he forgive me for that night years ago?*

# A NOTE FROM THE AUTHOR

Leading Conviction is a second chance at first love, security firm romantic suspense with legal, military, and mature themes. It is the sixth—and final—book in the Conviction Series, wherein all the books contribute to an overarching plot, but there is no cliffhanger for the couple in their respective story. Please consider reading this series in order for best enjoyment. HEA guaranteed.

This series takes place in Ashland County, a small, fictional, southern county somewhere in the mountains of the Carolinas. Ashland County is full of steam and legal intrigue, and some characters may appear in other stories written in the same universe.

## TIMELINE

Leading Conviction concludes the entire saga of the Conviction Series. As such, new readers may be lost leaping in this late in the series. It's recommended that at least one preceding book be read first for better understanding.

## TRIGGER WARNING - PLEASE READ

While this book is not considered "dark romance," Leading Conviction has dark elements and should only be read by mature readers (18+).

Full list of triggers can be found at the QR code below.

Protect your heart, friends. Reader discretion is advised.

# THIS IS IMPORTANT

For information on human trafficking, go to
humantraffickinghotline.org.

\* \* \*

For information on sexual assault and crisis support, go to rainn.
org/resources.

\* \* \*

Never, ever forget: You are loved. You are wanted. You matter.

*To you, beautiful reader.*
*Thank you for loving this series.*
*I couldn't live my dream without you.*

# PROLOGUE

## One week ago

"On my count," Hawk commanded through his headset as he pressed against the wall. His team answered their confirmation, as did the FBI liaisons they were working with. He waited beside the stairwell door in the lobby, scanning to ensure he could give the all clear.

The private security firm owned by General Richard Smithers was a ghost town. Dead bodies and all. Other than the guards on the main floor, no one else had shown up for work. Whether that was because the General had ordered them to stay home, or whether the employees had known something was about to go down, Hawk didn't know. But fewer bystanders during a mission made their job a hell of a lot easier.

His heart thudded as he glanced around, but there wasn't a soul in sight. He swallowed once, clearing his head before entering the lion's den.

"Three," he breathed into his headset. "Two... one... *breach*."

The building tremored as the breaching charge set by their weapons sergeant, Draco, exploded the stairwell door the floor below them. Hawk waited for a beat, letting the dust settle within the stairwell, before cracking the still-intact door beside him to peer inside. His ears strained to hear any movements, but there was only silence.

*It's go time.*

"Clear," he reported before pushing the door open wide.

"Down the stairs and to the right," his teammate, Phoenix, offered over the headset as they ran. "We'll be entering a hallway —a straight shot, no cover—so be ready."

Phoenix had briefed the team on the way to their mission, so Hawk already knew what to expect when he got to the basement floor, including Phoenix and Callie's last kill during their escape.

He bent low, ready to fire if necessary as he advanced carefully through the busted entry and across the metal splinters that used to be the door.

Another dead man sprawled in front of the steel door at the end of the darkened hallway. Hawk clicked on the tactical light hooked to his gun and blinked to adjust his eyesight. His booted steps remained silent in the thick carpet as he examined their surroundings. Glossy mahogany paneling and sensual paintings lined the unscathed walls.

"I thought you said you burned this hellhole into ash," he muttered with a frown.

"The steel interior walls behind the paneling must've prevented the fire from spreading," Phoenix whispered behind him, following closely on his heels. "All the doors are mechanical, so we'll need to break them down."

They halted at a black door and positioned themselves defensively in case they were met with resistance from the other side. Two of his teammates, Jaybird and Devil, lined up on one side with a battering ram in their hands, and Phoenix and Special Agent Callie Castellanos took the opposite. Their other two teammates, Snake and Draco, were back in the van, coordinating with the FBI agents waiting for Hawk's "all clear."

Hawk aimed his weapon at the door, prepared to meet whatever waited for them. He always took point. This time would be no different.

"*Now*," he ordered.

Jaybird and Devil crashed the battering ram into the door. It caved inward instantly before collapsing to the ground. Hawk maintained a low stance as he barged into the room, preventing any potential center-of-mass shots that may come his way.

An acrid, familiar stench slammed into his nostrils before he could see inside.

*Burned flesh.*

He'd smelled it one other time before. That day still gave him nightmares.

The nearly pitch-black room only had a faint red haze emanating from the back corner. Apprehension crawled over his skin, but he shined his flashlight into the room anyway... and immediately wished he hadn't.

Dripping, charred corpses were piled in heaps throughout the large room. His foot bumped into one of the dead, and he barely resisted the urge to jerk away at the hill of bodies. It looked like that particular group had tried to escape through the door his team had just forced down. They'd been burned to a crisp, making it easier for the broken door to push them aside, allowing his team to enter.

What had once been the General's lush *playroom*, where he'd used sex trafficked victims to *entertain* clients, was now full of stinking death and soggy ash.

"Looks like the sprinkler system was too late to combat the fire," Jaybird pointed out as they investigated the scene.

"Thank fuck for that," Phoenix cursed.

A metal table in the center of the room had warped from the heat. Sharp edges gleamed on top of the table, and his flashlight revealed what looked like a stockpile of medieval weaponry and torture devices.

"That's what they would've used on me," Callie whispered behind him. "I was just a toy to them. A *thing* to be broken."

Callie had been a prisoner in the General's underground bunker for over two years. It was a miracle she'd made it out alive. From the looks of what those monsters had planned for her, she almost didn't.

Revulsion and anger coursed through his veins, and he tightened his grip on his gun.

"They died the way they deserved, then," he replied, taking in the way they'd seemingly tried to hide underneath each other to flee the fire that consumed their wretched souls. "Like cowards."

"That door in the opposite corner is open." Devil pointed to the red lighting Hawk could now see glowed dimly from the hallway. "But these fuckers baked in here. If it'd been open, wouldn't they have escaped?"

"Someone was here," Phoenix muttered.

"Or still is," Hawk countered, instantly on high alert again. "Eyes open. Phoenix, Callie, you come with me. Everyone else, see if you can find anything useful about these dead men."

"BlackStone crew, don't touch anything," Callie added. "The FBI will need to compile as much evidence as possible for this case."

As liaisons, the FBI had consented to Hawk's team entering the building first so long as Callie, one of their field operatives, was present. He wanted to think it was because they trusted his team of trained former MF7 spec-ops soldiers. But with all the bureaucracy he'd been dealing with lately as BlackStone's leader, he was more inclined to believe the feds wanted his team to take the brunt of whatever was thrown at them down there. Whether it was bullets or something that could result in bad press.

His team verbally confirmed both his and Callie's commands as he crossed the room toward the open door, with Callie and Phoenix following closely behind.

The hallway was a completely different story than the disaster they'd just left. It looked untouched with only a damp scent of wet concrete from the water sprinklers to speak of. Once they fully entered the space and found it clear, he hesitated a moment for Callie's directions.

"Right, then a left at the end of the hallway. The General's office will be the first door."

He followed her verbal lead, his eyes peeled for anyone coming their way. When he squinted at the end of the hallway, he could barely make out a lump on the ground. He tensed, bracing for a fight, but Phoenix's voice settled him.

"Dead. We took those two out when we escaped."

Sure enough, his flashlight illuminated two men slumped over each other against the steel walls. Blood seeped into the concrete around them.

"You guys didn't pull punches, huh?"

"Why would we, when they didn't?" Phoenix grumbled.

"Touché."

Phoenix and Callie had escaped the underground facility less than twenty-four hours ago. When his team had gotten the all clear to raid the General's headquarters for his sex trafficking ring, those two had jumped at the chance to join, despite having only just fought for their freedom. Hawk didn't blame them.

There was a lot of history between his team and General Smithers, the man who'd formed the MF7 unit before attempting to wipe it from existence. Not only had the General kidnapped one of Hawk's own men, Phoenix, but he'd tried to kill them all several times over. The burning need to make the bastard pay for everything he'd done boiled in Hawk's veins. To avenge Hawk's team—his *brothers*—not to mention the countless victims he exploited...

*And her.*

*No.*

The logical voice in his head—the wise one that sounded just like his old man's—told him to move on. He couldn't think about her now. It was hard, considering he had to work alongside Callie, who looked eerily similar, but he had to let it go.

What was done, was done. Nearly a decade ago, he'd made all the wrong decisions. Now he had to live with them. Besides, she was better off without him.

*But is she?*

Everything that'd come to light in the past forty-eight hours whispered over that voice of reason, growing louder as it guilted him into trying harder to find her. Two and a half months ago, he'd found out she was a part of a group of women who'd gone missing. That realization had rocked him to his core and he and Snake had been privately searching for her ever since. Before that, he'd thought she was safe. When he'd left her all those years ago, he'd never looked back, believing he and his best friend were making the right choice to both protect her and save the world. But now he questioned everything.

*Later. Figure this shit out later. Not right now.*

As he rounded the corner, more bodies clogged the hallway, lit by the bright fluorescent lighting in the open office.

Hawk's heart stalled in his chest, and his feet did the same as he paused to get his bearings. He couldn't see inside, and without knowing whether there was someone else down there in the bunker with them, he wanted to be sure before he led his teammate into danger.

He stepped carefully and silently around each dead man, trying to hold his breath. The cold basement had delayed decomposition, but the aftermath of death was already ripe and sweet in the air, mixed with the metallic odor of blood.

Finally, after painstakingly slow steps, he stopped outside the General's office and pressed his back against the wall beside the doorjamb. Not taking his eyes off the door, he held up his hand, signaling Phoenix to wait.

Hawk took a deep, steadying breath before rolling around the doorjamb to see who was inside—

No one.

The General's office was completely empty. Ransacked, burned, and wet, but empty.

"Clear."

Callie cursed as she and Phoenix entered behind him. "Shit, this place is a mess."

Hawk nodded. "Yup, but there might be something salvageable here to tell us where the General ran off to. Let's look."

"Phoenix and I tried to grab everything we thought looked important. Documents, flash drives—"

"—Polaroids of victims with names and dates on the back," Phoenix spat out, disgusted.

"Hey, *boss*," Devil grumbled over the headset. Hawk resisted rolling his eyes. He hated that nickname, but someone had called him that the day before and now he knew Devil wouldn't let him live it down.

"*Hawk* here," he corrected. "What'd you find?"

"Not much since we can't touch anything. Jaybird and I heard where you guys went over the comms and searched in the opposite direction. It looks like everyone's either gone, dead, or ash."

"Topside, we found some tire marks from someone peeling out of the back entrance," Snake offered. "We can try to match the treads with known makes and models. Perhaps get some answers there."

"Good find, Snake. Keep your guard up, everyone, just in case. We're in the General's office but we'll be giving the all clear to the feds soon so they can take evidence and bodies into custody."

"Copy. Devil, over and out."

"Let's check everywhere we can," he ordered Callie and Phoenix. "I don't want to miss anything."

Hawk trusted the feds as far as he could throw them, but he couldn't tell Phoenix that with Callie present. His team needed to get eyes on every scrap of information before the government took over and kicked them out of the investigation after all the hard work was done. It wouldn't be the first time his team had been so royally screwed over.

He, Phoenix, and Callie fanned out to examine the room. Almost everything had been incinerated, including the ostentatious desk filling a third of the room. Hawk peered through a window taking up one wall. Inside was a dark room, empty but for a chair, a box, and an open metal cabinet with the contents spilled to the ground.

"That's the room I was tortured in," Phoenix explained with an unnerving false cheer lilting his voice. "Nice decor, huh? I really like what they did with the place."

Hawk huffed a dry laugh even though protective rage boiled in his veins at Phoenix's words. He and his teammates were well versed in gallows humor, but Phoenix had perfected it in this hellhole.

Investigating behind the desk, Hawk noticed a small, square hole high in the wall with a wide-open door. A safe.

"You get everything from in there?" he asked, moving to stand underneath it.

Phoenix shrugged. "I think I did, but it was so high it was hard for me to see inside. Want a boost to double-check?"

Hawk shook his head. "Nah, I think I got it."

He tested the broken wood and metal that'd burned into a sturdy lump underneath the safe. Making sure it wouldn't break, he jumped from the ground. Catching the lip of the safe, he pulled himself up and balanced on the mound beneath him.

"Show-off," Phoenix muttered.

Emptiness stared back at Hawk from inside the four metal walls, until he realized the bottom was covered by a single piece of paper. He swiped it before hopping to the ground.

"What'd you find?" Phoenix peered around Hawk's shoulder. "Ooooh, a plain sheet of paper. Fancy."

Callie snorted as she approached Hawk's other side. "The General wasn't much for tech. I wouldn't be surprised if he had the secret codes to atomic bombs just lying around on parchment."

"Doesn't seem like you're too far off..." Hawk examined the string of numbers thinly scrawled on the back with a date above it. "These look like coordinates from... less than a week ago?" He turned the sheet over.

His heart stopped.

His breath ached in his chest.

His fingers trembled on the paper until Callie stilled it with her own hands.

"She looks like... *me?*" Callie gasped.

It was a close-up picture of a woman who—but for her obviously dyed blonde hair—indeed looked *just* like Callie. The woman's warm-olive skin glowed under the sun as she laughed outside a café at something—or some*one*—out of frame. Her brilliant smile, the one she only gave *him*, made Hawk's heart beat again, just like it did all those years ago.

Phoenix sucked in a breath and shook his head. "No... it's... holy shit. *Fuck.* Hawk is that—"

"Yeah... it's Hannah." He swallowed, his mouth suddenly dry with panic over what this could mean. "He found her."

# CHAPTER ONE
## Present Day

*"Es un día caluroso aquí en Truist Park mientras los Bravos de Atlanta juegan contra los Dodgers de Los Ángeles..."*

"I don't care how hot it is back in Atlanta. The Braves better beat them this time, that's all I've got to say."

*"¿Perdóneme?"*

At the sound of the female voice so close to her, Hannah's fingers tightened around her necklace and she jolted from her reverie, nearly dropping her newly dried T-shirt into the laundry hamper before she could fold it. Two elderly women, the only other patrons inside the *lavandería*, stood in front of her next to a large dryer a few machines down. One tilted her head at Hannah with curiosity, while the other's weathered brow furrowed, accentuating the wrinkles etched in her bronze skin.

Under the old woman's wary brown eyes, Hannah tucked her necklace back under her T-shirt and rubbed her sweaty hands on her jeans. Her cheeks heated as she explained herself.

*"Lo siento. Estaba hablando solo."*

An apologetic smile ghosted across Hannah's lips after she explained she was talking to herself, but the other woman's judgment didn't disappear. The two women held Hannah's stare for a moment too long. With only the sound of the machines running in the background, it was hard to focus on anything other than the awkward moment, making Hannah's muscles tighten with panic.

*Do they recognize me? Has someone asked about me?*

Finally, the scowling woman nodded once before returning to her laundry and muttering under her breath to her friend.

"*Chicana loca.*"

Hannah almost snorted at the woman's derision. A little over two years ago, she would've. But now, attention like that could be memorable and she survived on being forgotten.

Her stomach turned over at the thought of having to leave yet another city she loved, only to start all over again somewhere else in Mexico. Her little house was perfect this time around and had all the amenities she needed close by. There was a laundromat, a market, a café and a park to keep from going stir-crazy, and a post office where she could mail the artwork she painted for her online store to make ends meet. Mérida had been one of her longest stays yet, and the rich city was finally starting to feel like home.

*Don't overreact. They're just harmless old ladies. Busybodies, just like in the States, but harmless.*

She swallowed back the paranoia manifesting as a lump in her throat and continued to fold the clothes from the dryer into her hamper at a quicker speed. The laundromat had a small TV hanging in the corner and she'd planned laundry day around the Atlanta Braves baseball game so she could fold and watch at the same time. It'd already gone on several innings, much longer than she ever felt comfortable staying away from her house nearby.

Maybe it was time she left the city anyway. The more she stayed in one place, the more her body itched with anxiety over the fear she'd be discovered. It was a bizarre cat-and-mouse game, where she found more stability in the instability of moving around all the time, and less safety the more comfortable she became in her new home.

For the umpteenth time, she wished she'd been able to drop off her clothes and use the services the *lavandería* offered. But art commissions weren't a predictable income and now that her savings were running low, she needed all the clothes and money she had. If she'd used a laundry service everywhere she went, she'd have run out of both by now.

A loud *crack* resounded from the TV's speakers right before the announcer's voice increased in pitch and speed. Hannah glanced up at the screen just in time to see a Braves player slide into home. She subtly pumped her fist before she could stop herself, a simple celebration she'd picked up long ago and still a habit she couldn't break after all these years.

If the Braves won, there was a certain someone she'd have to answer to tonight, and she'd get to make sweet tea like the kind they had in the United States. It was a simple bet they'd had for the past two years, a way to bring a piece of home wherever they went, and she hoped they'd win because thanks to the Braves' losing streak, it'd been over a week and a half since they'd had the sugary beverage.

"*¿Viste al gringo caminando por el barrio esta mañana?*"

Hannah's eyes widened, but no longer focused on the TV in the corner as her heart froze in her chest. Her fingers stilled midair, clinging to a partially folded T-shirt, while her ears strained to hear the elderly woman's answer about whether she saw the white man walking around the neighborhood that morning.

"*Sí, claro que lo hice. ¿De verdad pensó que no lo notaríamos? Él estaba mirando dentro de nuestras casas.*"

*Yes, of course I did. Did he really think we wouldn't notice? He was looking inside our homes.*

Hannah's stalled-out heart kicked back into gear, racing in her chest. Before she could stop to think about how she might be putting them in danger by talking to them, she heard herself asking in Spanish whether they'd called the police.

*"¡Fue lo primero que hice! No podemos arriesgarnos después de que esa pobre mujer fuera asesinada la semana pasada."*

*It was the first thing I did! We can't take any chances after that poor woman was murdered last week.*

The woman's assurance translated in Hannah's head effortlessly thanks to her mother's insistence she learned her heritage and months now of actually living it. But the words made her heart twist.

The murderer who'd killed the woman a few *barrios* over still hadn't been caught and the crime had left a beautiful little boy an orphan.

*"Bueno. Gracias por eso."* Hannah's voice came out hoarse as she thanked the woman for protecting their neighborhood.

It was probably nothing. Mérida is one of the best tourist destinations in Mexico due to its history and culture, not to mention how safe it is. Those were the reasons why she chose the city, after all.

But she'd had it too good for too long, and her body had been on edge, waiting for the other shoe to drop. She hoped to God whoever this stranger was sniffing around their neighborhood, wasn't a bad sign.

*It's not a big deal. It's fine. We'll be okay.*

Even as she said it, even as she tried to convince herself, the words were useless against her anxiety. Instead of folding each article of clothing as she usually did, she bent to extract the entire pile of clothes out of the dryer and shoved them all in her laundry bag. She'd deal with the wrinkles later... if there was even a *later* to deal with.

As she packed up, the little old ladies kept talking about anything and everything, as if they hadn't just ignited yet another bout of terror Hannah somehow still hadn't become immune to.

She kept listening, trying to hear whether they knew anything else about the mysterious outsider. What he looked like, his height, whether he had an accent. Her small *barrio* was off the beaten tourist path, so newcomers in her neighborhood

rarely went unnoticed. Even her own Mexican American roots
didn't keep her as under the radar as she'd hoped since she'd
dyed her hair dark blonde. If she could've kept it the glossy black
she adored, she would've, but the man who'd been hunting her
had a type and she couldn't risk it.

So far, all she gathered from the women's gossip was that the
man was tall, blond, clean-shaven and *muy guapo*. The first two
descriptors could very well be one of the men that had been sent
to rattle her over the years. Granted, none of the ones she'd fled
from in the past could remotely pass for *guapo*, or good-looking.
The sudden appearance of an outsider after all this time of peace
still had her worried, though.

*Was this man one of his?*

She'd been running from him for two years and afraid of him
for longer than she could remember. If this was one of his men,
what would that mean for her this time? Would it be another
creepy present on the front porch? A letter in the mailbox?
Something as mundane as "I'm still watching you," or something
as terrifyingly soul wrenching as the dead hawk left on her
doorstep last year. It was as if they were truly playing a game of
cat and mouse and he was just fucking with her until he had her
right where he wanted her.

But what would he do with her once he finally decided to
catch her?

*That* was an answer she never wanted to find out. She'd
learned over the years he was a monster in his own right. That's
all she needed to know.

As soon as all the clothes were piled into the bag, she slung
the laundry over her shoulder, not bothering to close the dryer
door. The ladies wished her well, and she muttered "*hasta luego*,"
back as she power walked to the door.

"*Últimas noticias en la parte superior de la hora—*"

Something on the screen popped up in the corner of
Hannah's vision and she stopped in her tracks. Her eyes shot to
the TV as the news commercial for *Tele Yucatán* promised a scin-

tillating story after the Braves game. Her father's picture positioned in the corner of the screen was enough to make her gag, so much so she nearly missed the rest of the report.

"*Un poderoso miembro del ejército de los Estados Unidos, el general Richard Smithers, ha sido declarado desaparecido—*"

Everything afterward got lost in the excruciatingly loud heartbeat pumping in her ears. Her bag slid out of her hands seemingly in slow motion as she stared blankly. Its loud *slap* against the tile flooring knocked her out of her dazed terror, spurring her into movement.

And she ran.

# CHAPTER TWO

"It's hot as balls down here. I know you don't want to fade your ink, but I don't know how you can stand being in long sleeves," Draco grumbled as he tapped the car's air conditioning dial like that would make it blow harder, even though it was already at its highest setting. His lightly tanned skin was already flushed from the heat and sun.

"It's all about commitment, my man. I got used to it years ago." Hawk chuckled as he turned onto one of the smaller roads in a neighborhood outside the *centro* of Mérida, Yucatán, in Mexico. "Besides, we've had AC the entire trip. It's not so bad."

It'd been half a day of traveling, but they thankfully hadn't needed to drive the whole way or fly commercial. One of Black-Stone's wealthier clients owed them a favor and had offered their private plane from Ashland County's little metropolitan airport, so the trip to Mexico hadn't been nearly as long as it could've been.

The mix of colonial and modern houses adorned in vibrant colors and history looked exactly like the backdrop of the café Hannah had been sitting in when the surveillance photo was taken. The loud, bustling streets and rich aesthetic reminded him of the free spirit he knew nearly a decade ago. It was perfect for her, but back then, she'd never once mentioned wanting to relocate from Atlanta to Mexico. Something had to have prompted the move, but racking his brain over what that could've been made him sweat with dread.

A sharp, sudden sting in his lip had him wincing. He balled his hand into a fist and laved his injured bottom lip with his tongue to keep from compulsively tracing it with his fingers. Never before had he realized how bad the habit was, but his mouth was having a hard time withstanding all the thinking he'd been doing lately.

Why was she in Mexico? He knew her grandparents had emigrated in the fifties, but they'd died when Hannah was still a kid. If she was living in Mexico, why would her own father have to get coordinates to look for her? From what he could tell, Hannah and her father had always had a strained relationship, so if she finally cut all ties with him, why would he be looking for her in the first place? She was an art teacher who was fucking good at her job. Would she really pick up and leave everything behind just to escape her own father?

On second thought, that was probably exactly what happened. Hawk had only just learned the depths of the General's betrayal and depravity last week. What if Hannah had figured it out before they had? It wasn't hard for Hawk to believe she'd run away from her father after everything he'd learned about the monster.

Even though General Smithers had formed MF7, the military group organized to eradicate human trafficking all over the world, he'd been a thorn in their side from its inception. But it was only in the past week that his team had realized the man who'd recruited them, Hannah's father, was behind *continuing* the trafficking rings, not eliminating them. He'd used MF7 to take out the competition. Whatever survivors they'd saved, the General had forced them back into sexual slavery.

That truth gutted Hawk, but knowing Hannah was somehow connected made him sick to his stomach. He'd left her to protect her from all the powerful, evil men his team went after. What the fuck had happened?

*Was it all for nothing? Would it have been better not to leave at all? To risk going AWOL?*

"Looks like the news about the General is finally making global headlines," Draco grunted before he sat straighter. "Wait a minute..." He tapped his phone screen as he spoke, drawing Hawk from his thoughts. "This press statement just declares General Smithers missing? Is that really the only thing they're going to report on? They're making it sound like he's a victim."

Hawk dropped his finger from his worn lips and the damn cut he'd accidentally started messing with again. "That was the agreement the FBI, district attorneys, and BlackStone came up with."

Draco huffed. "So we're just going to leave out the whole running a sex trafficking ring in an underground facility where they had to clean out dozens of burned corpses?"

"Yup," Hawk answered as he rolled to a stop at an octagonal red sign inscribed with the word "ALTO."

His tall stature forced him to lean forward in order to glance underneath the visor and read the street numbers.

"Why?" Draco growled his question.

Between the two of them, it'd been comfortably quiet all the way from BlackStone. Draco had even napped on the plane. But it seemed like the silence had run its course.

"Because if we tip our hand to the whole world that the General is in charge of all this shit, then whoever else is aiding him could grow suspicious and go into hiding."

"You think a former United States Army general going missing wouldn't be enough to make his coconspirators suspicious?"

Hawk sighed. "It's all we've got right now. Hopefully, his investors and the men underneath him will believe he's just gone underground and they'll keep still and quiet, giving us enough time to come to them, rather than scatter and ruin everything.

For all we know, that's exactly what he's done, gone into hiding himself. But in either case, we have to find him before we let that cat out of the bag—"

"And before he finds Hannah," Draco finished for him.

Hawk nodded once and his voice broke over his answer. "Yeah. Before he finds Hannah."

"Why do you think he's keeping track of her?"

"I... don't know. But it can't be good. She and her father were never close, but I had no idea she'd cut him out of her life completely. I hope she's okay," he murmured the last bit under his breath.

Draco's dark-blue eyes bored into the side of his face, giving Hawk the feeling that the man was trying to read his mind. "I know you like her, and believe me, I know all about wanting to chase the girl. But if that is all this is, then we've got to go back home and tackle the rest of our problems head-on. We need to find General Smithers and that bald Russian fucker he always has with him. We can't do that if we're all over the continent. We're spread too thin as it is. That's why you've got me going instead of one of the able-bodied members of BlackStone."

Hawk flicked his eyes over Draco's body as he indicated himself. The blond Viking giant looked almost comical in the rented Ford Focus, his legs stretched out to the brink in the passenger seat. From the looks of his strong build, no one would ever guess he'd been in a coma for over a year after being shot by "that bald Russian fucker."

Since waking up, Draco had to resort to government-classified drugs to get back into shape. He was better than any normal civilian, but he was right about the reason he'd been chosen for this trip. BlackStone Securities, the firm Hawk founded to give his MF7 crew purpose after being kicked out of the military, needed their teammates to be in tip-top shape. While Draco was miraculously leaps and bounds more agile than he'd been just two and a half months ago, he was a far cry from the elite soldier he'd once been. He probably never would be again.

It was why Hawk had accepted Draco's offer when he volunteered to ride with him to check on Hannah. Unfortunately, like Draco insinuated, the entire trip was arguably something Hawk was doing to appease his guilty conscience. But there was more to it than that... wasn't there?

Hawk shook his head, trying to focus on the pitch he'd delivered to his teammates to convince them to let him—their own leader—go on this wild-goose chase of a mission.

"It's more than that. I'm not *chasing* Hannah. There's nothing between us anymore, not since I broke it off before entering MF7. But we don't have any leads on the General's or his henchman's whereabouts. The FBI and the rest of our team are still going through all the information Callie and Phoenix were able to get from General Smithers's HQ and everything you and Nora were able to retrieve from Gail Haynesworth's office at Charitable Technologies International. It's a 'wait and see what information we can piece together' situation and instead of sitting on my ass, I'm going to go after the one lead I can follow up on *now*. Not wait for someone else to tell me what to do. That's not my style."

Hawk's fingers had tightened more around the wheel with every word of his speech, anticipating having to continue to justify his decision with Draco. They were in Mexico already, sure, and allegedly only a mile away from Hannah's home, but if his team all felt like he needed to go back to Ashland County...

*No. Fuck that.*

"What if we can't find her—"

"Look," Hawk barked, unable to stop his frustration from deepening his tone. "If you want to go back, by all means, be my guest. But I'm not leaving until I find her. A megalomaniac sex ring trafficker is looking for her and missing himself. I left Hannah behind once for this team, and I'm not doing it again."

Silence crowded the air in the small car again, but instead of the usual comfort in their quiet, it filled the air like the humidity outside, making it hard for him to breathe.

"Well, shit. When you put it that way..." Draco muttered before finally taking his eyes off of Hawk and returning them to the busy road the Focus continued to roll down. "I've got your six, Hawk. Always. If this is what you need to do, we're doing it."

The air he hadn't realized he'd been holding leaked from his chest, escaping the viselike grip that fear had been clutching him with for the past two and a half months, ever since he'd recognized Hannah's picture among a group of missing women. He'd confided in Wes and the two of them had been looking for her ever since. It wasn't until they'd found the General's picture of her in his office that they'd gotten their first big break.

"Thank you," he answered roughly.

A few more moments of empty air filtered between them before Draco spoke again, "You never talked about her much after that first MF7 meeting with the General. I vaguely remember what happened then but I don't know what went down afterward. She was your girlfriend, right?"

*She was my world.*

Hawk swallowed. The answer should be so simple, but nothing was ever simple with Hannah. Especially when Eagle was in the mix.

"No," he finally admitted. "She was my fiancée."

"She was your *what?*"

"I proposed to her right before shit got serious in MF7." Hawk could feel Draco's judgment crashing into him.

"And then you, what? Just left?"

"As shitty as it sounds. It played out even worse. I'd talked the decision over with Eagle and at the time, I thought it was the best way to keep her safe."

"Wasn't Eagle friends with her too?"

Hawk snorted. "You've been hanging out with your girlfriend too much. What happened to the silent giant who minded his own business?"

"What can I say? My better half makes me better."

Draco shrugged before shifting in his seat. He extracted a

small case from his pocket and pulled a toothpick out before popping it into his mouth. The full-blast air conditioner wafted the light scent of peppermint toward Hawk.

"Hmm... I think a talkative Draco being considered *better* is a questionable assumption."

"Man, fuck off and answer the question."

"That's more like it." Hawk laughed but it drifted off the longer Draco stared at him.

The intensity in the man's gaze eventually forced Hawk to cave and fess up. Hell, it might be good to air it all out before he saw her right in front of him again.

"Hannah was always mine..." Hawk cleared his throat. "But back then? I think Eagle had wanted her too."

# CHAPTER THREE

## Nine years ago

"This is it, men. *This* is the team. MF7." Eagle grinned at his teammates, pride welling within him as he watched them take their seats around the base's conference table. They'd each just sworn their oath to the team, symbolically of course since their individual contracts were already signed weeks ago. The six of them were in it for the long haul now, whether their crazy asses liked it or not.

Hawk, his second-in-command. Snake, their comms sergeant. Phoenix, their pilot. And their two weapons sergeants, Draco and Jaybird. The best of the best Eagle had recruited for General Richard Smithers. Their team would defeat human trafficking once and for all throughout the world. It was a lofty goal, to say the least, but one he believed in all the same.

"Well, we *will* be MF7, as soon as we get our medic," Hawk pointed out, his eyes were narrowed and seriousness furrowed his dark-brown skin. "It's a good team, but until we get a medic, we're fighting with our hands tied behind our backs."

Eagle waved off his best friend's concern. "In due time. We'll be training for a while, and Snake can be our stopgap medic when we finally go on our missions. General Smithers has guaranteed me that the jobs we're working right after training will be a piece of cake so we can get our feet wet until we find the right person for the team."

A few of his teammates nodded, satisfied with his explanation, but Hawk and Jaybird still seemed skeptical. Or rather, Hawk seemed skeptical. Jaybird was pissed and had been ever since he ghosted his girlfriend to join the team.

The choice wasn't one Eagle would've personally made, but leaving without explanation was apparently the best the guy could do. Having to leave loved ones behind sucked, but that was the nature of spec-ops jobs. The missions they were about to go on would be dangerous and there was no way to know if they'd return.

Eagle and Hawk would have to do the same soon, albeit theirs would be a "goodbye for now" rather than the brutal disappearing act Jaybird had committed. Luckily, they were training in Atlanta, so they could put off their conversation until they actually had to leave base.

Then again, maybe Jaybird had the right idea. The extra time was bound to only make things harder.

"I've got someone in mind for the medic position. Name's Devil," Draco rumbled from the back, his mouth working around a toothpick.

"Is that the redheaded kid we worked with during that joint op? With the jump training out of helos?" Hawk asked. "He was a near prodigy at rappelling."

"Yup, one and the same. He's young, but good. Cool, icy calm under pressure. I trust him with my life."

Eagle's brows raised at the blond Viking's words, shocked the guy was chiming in at all. It wasn't every day the man spoke, let alone vouched for someone. After a stunned second, Eagle grinned his approval.

"Excellent. Reach out to him. Feel him out as to whether he'd be a good fit and would even want to join."

Draco grunted his assent just as the conference room door opened to reveal General Richard Smithers standing within the frame. Eagle's hand shot up to his forehead in salute, and all his men stood at once to do the same.

General Smithers had a not-so-subtle smile as he marched toward Eagle at the front of the room. It wasn't until the General turned with his hands settled behind his back and his perusal of the room was finished that he finally spoke.

"At ease. Take your seats."

At the command, Eagle's shoulders relaxed along with the rest of his team, except for Hawk. The man was always on alert at work. He'd be a great team lead for MF7 if it ever came down to it.

"Soldiers... welcome to MF7."

The men replied their thanks nearly in unison.

Eagle beamed at his new teammates as General Smithers continued, "Your training begins tomorrow. It will be brutal, but what I hear from your new team lead—Captain Greene, here— you can take it. The missions you're about to embark on will be dangerous, for you and any loved ones you've left back home. Take it from me. I've already had to distance myself from my own daughter in order to protect her. If you have any ties, it's time to cut them now."

Eagle's lips parted in shock. He shot his gaze to his new boss, but General Smithers's eyes were focused entirely on Hawk as he made the order. Hawk had been holding out on breaking the news to Hannah that he was leaving but breaking it off entirely had never been the plan.

"*Cut* ties?" Hawk spat out, as if the words were as bitter as the acrid taste on Eagle's own tongue. His best friend's burning charcoal eyes snapped to his. "Eagle, you never said anything about *ending* things. Delta Force doesn't even do that."

Eagle opened his mouth to defend himself, to assure his friend he'd thought it was just a goodbye, too, but General Smithers butted in.

"MF7 is a top-security clearance, off-the-books team. What you'll be doing is even more under the radar than Delta. That's why I wanted the best of the best. Cutting all ties, essentially being dead to the world as you know it, is how you'll ensure the safety of good citizens back home. The clandestine nature of this operation is the only way you'll be able to eradicate human trafficking outside and inside this country."

A *thump* resounded against the carpet as their pilot, Phoenix, dropped his chair back onto all four legs after sitting in it balanced on two.

"Wait, *this* country?" he asked. His tan face had paled slightly and he turned his ball cap backward as if doing so could help him see better. "As in the United States of America?"

General Smithers rolled his eyes. "Obviously, Officer Santori. And remove that godforsaken hat. Do you think I wore my uniform just to see you dressed like a slob?"

Even as Phoenix complied and tossed the hat onto the table, he scowled, muttering something about uniforms and being a secret organization.

But their comms sergeant, Snake, didn't let it go. The guy had black hair and looked like an even more buttoned-up version of Clark Kent. He even acted like the comic book reporter with his drive to learn everything.

Snake pushed up his glasses and frowned as he continued the line of questioning. "But the military doesn't engage in conflict on our own soil. Our job is to defend this country, not fight it. We're not meant for domestic affairs..."

"Of course *other* units aren't. But you will be." General Smithers sighed his annoyance, as if the smartest guy in the room hadn't just made an extremely valid point. "That's why I said your team is 'off-the-books.' This is the big leagues, boys. You've got the highest security clearance possible in the land. Human trafficking operations are insidious and can rot our very own chain of command. There will be no records kept after a mission is completed, and what will be documented will be doctored in all government accounts to show you were on routine jobs. Meanwhile, you'll be making and picking off enemies left and right, powerful ones that could lash out at all the people you love. Cutting loose ends is the only solution."

Anger welled in Eagle's chest and he opened his mouth to argue, but Hawk beat him to it. He leapt up from his chair, one hand balled into a fist at his side and the other pointing accusingly at the General.

"*Hannah* is not a 'loose end.' I know you hate the fact that I'm dating your daughter. You made it clear when I asked for your blessing."

*His blessing?* The phrase dropped like a stone in the pit of Eagle's stomach. He'd had no idea Hawk was going to finally pop the question. Eagle gulped back the urge to vomit and focused on the anger in Hawk's deep voice.

"You're a great soldier, Captain, but not good enough for my daughter. The fact you thought I'd ever bless a union between you and my Hannah was delusional. *No one* is good enough for my Hannah," General Smithers hissed.

Hawk shook his head and stepped back, dropping his hand to his side. Even with several feet between them, Hawk was formidable in his own right and still towered over General Smithers.

"Make no mistake, General. I only wanted your *blessing* to marry your daughter because it's the right thing to do. But, we don't need your permission. No matter what you said, I love her and I'm not fucking going anywhere. If this is your attempt at getting rid of me—"

General Smithers lunged forward to get in Hawk's face, or at least tried to. Eagle's friend had several inches and about thirty pounds on the guy. Hawk never flinched, but Eagle's adrenaline was off the charts. If Hawk fought his own commanding officer, what the hell would happen to him? To Hannah? She'd be left all alone...

The thought lit a forbidden flare of hope in his chest, but he snuffed it out. Hawk was lucky enough to have the type of love

Eagle had always selfishly pined for. Unfortunately, Hawk was also the very reason he could never have it.

"You think I'm fucking around?" The General stabbed his finger into his own chest. "That I won't be doing the same exact thing when one of these trafficking bastards tries to come after *me*? Don't be a fool, Captain Black. Your affiliation with MF7 will only endanger Hannah. You *will* end things with her. That's what you signed up for when you committed to this team. Backing out now would be desertion. Trust me, I'll be the judge, jury, and executioner in that court martial and you wouldn't like the outcome, soldier."

Hawk's eyes narrowed as he straightened his posture, looking down his nose at his own general. "I've taken an oath. I would never shirk my responsibilities or my love for this country, but trust *me* when I say I'll also never stop loving Hannah."

The General's pale face had already reddened and the rage welling inside him seemed to sprout through the perspiration on his forehead. He finally shook his head and backed up, returning to the center of the room, at ease with his hands clasped behind his back.

"Very well," he huffed. "Training begins tomorrow morning at oh-six-hundred hours. Captain Greene?" Eagle's shoulders tensed as General Smithers's still angry blue eyes met his. "I will be informing you of your first job before the end of the week."

"The end of the week? So soon?" Eagle blurted, unable to hide his shock. Normally special ops teams had to have years of training before they went out in the field.

Based on the uncomfortable shifting throughout the room, the rest of his teammates must've been thinking the same thing.

General Smithers's brow rose. "I don't repeat myself, soldier."

The urge to question his commanding officer made Eagle's lips open again, but what came out was automatic.

"Sir, yes, sir."

# CHAPTER FOUR

## Present Day

"General Smithers was insanely protective over his daughter, even against me and Eagle, two guys he chose for his own team. Then again, maybe he was more possessive than protective. Unless he was schmoozing politicians, he treated her like a toy doll, practically ignoring her until he needed to show her off at parties. Once we started dating I put a stop to that shit real fucking quick."

Hawk hoped like hell the General was just delusional and creepy and Hannah hadn't silently suffered worse from her father. She'd always been open with Hawk—or so he thought.

He shook his head. What she might have kept from him was something he couldn't think about without going insane.

"It was uncomfortable to see then, but now after all we know..." Hawk felt his face twist in disgust.

"Now it's even more fucked up," Draco finished for him. "Is that how you guys met? One of those parties?"

"Yeah. Hannah and I met at a military ball. It was love at first sight."

"How did Eagle feel about that?"

"It's funny, because I still wonder if he even knew how he felt about her, if it was a crush that grew gradually over time. We were all best friends. Anytime Eagle and I could go home to Atlanta after being deployed, the three of us were inseparable. We even hung out with Phoenix a few times when he could come up from Louisiana. It was that way until Eagle and I left for MF7."

"Hawk, man, I didn't know it all went this deep. If you loved her so much... why the fuck did you abandon her?"

The pang of regret and guilt collided with his heart and fell heavy like a rock into his stomach.

"Duty called," he answered simply. "I didn't realize duty meant I'd have to lose her. But when our jobs threatened her safety, too, I did what I had to do to keep her safe and at the time, I still believed we were a legit spec-ops team and the General could have me court martialed for desertion."

"Fuck, if you'd only known then that running away might've been the best choice for everyone."

Draco's words twisted the knife already carved in his chest, but he confronted the accusation head-on.

"I'm not a deserter, and I thought I was doing the right thing. Watching those towers fall on live TV did a number on me, Draco. It was my dream to go into the MLB after graduating high school, but 9/11 changed me into this... this..."

"Soldier," Draco finished for him.

Hawk's hands tightened around the steering wheel. "I thought I could have it all. Fighting in my country's name, saving lives all over the world, my best friend, my girl. But General Smithers stole everything from me the moment I signed on with MF7. When our enemies finally forced me to end things, Eagle and I made a pact to leave her alone and say goodbye. I broke it off with her, hoping it was enough to keep her safe, and moved on to MF7's base that night."

A vision of heartbroken tears streaming from Hannah's sweet-tea-brown eyes cut across his mind. He shook his head to rid himself of the awful memory.

"Everything's fucked, isn't it?" Draco mumbled.

"Yeah, and it took seeing all of you finding the women of your dreams to realize how badly I fucked up my chance with mine."

He'd wasted so much time for the good of a cause that had been a sham all along. It burned him up inside to know he'd lost the two best people in his life to an organization that not only tricked him and his men, but actively harmed innocents in the process. Anger welled in his veins, threatening to boil over, but he only allowed it to channel through his fingertips squeezing the steering wheel.

Draco finally fell silent again, seemingly sated with his questions. There was nothing more Hawk could say anyway. He'd made a mistake all those years ago and if the gorgeous, happy look on her face in the surveillance photo he found in General Smithers's office was any indication, she'd moved on.

That smile was one he'd dreamed about for years, the one she saved only for him. Who was she sharing it with now? The answer would no doubt gut him, but he had to move past it. Her safety was paramount. Whatever man had captured her heart better step aside long enough for Hawk to make sure she was safe.

They rolled through the neighborhood of apartments, duplexes, and small houses, all connected by colorful adobe, stucco, and stone. Children played on the sidewalks and people gathered around gates and doors, listening to loud music and laughing, like a block party in the middle of the day. The entire *barrio* seemed safe, eclectic, and friendly. It was perfect for Hannah and the tension in his muscles eased.

She was obviously trying to keep away from her father, but at least she was able to stay safe and her artistic soul could be sated while she did it.

"I think that's it." Draco squinted at his phone before pointing to a house with faded red stucco. "It's rented under a 'Paula Gomez,' but when Wes cross-referenced camera footage in the area with our facial recognition tech, he found a woman who matches our photo and frequents the café at the corner that *also* matches our photo. *Plus* there's a post office nearby that an online store uses to ship artwork like you've described."

Draco lifted his phone screen to show a gorgeous painting of a sunrise over a bright-blue Caribbean coast. A single bird flew in the top corner of the horizon, so small you could almost miss it.

They'd already been over everything multiple times on the trip there, but when he'd first seen it, the painting was what had convinced Hawk. That single bird was her signature on everything she did.

*My dove.*

No.

*She's not mine anymore. I did this. I have to accept it.*

"That's Hannah," Hawk said out loud and cleared his throat. "Paula Gomez isn't too far of a stretch from her real name, Hannah Paloma Smithers. Her mother was Gutiérrez before she married."

Hawk slowed the car and ducked his head under the visor again. Wes, BlackStone's tech wizard, had been able to find the house based on the coordinates from the back of the photo. And here it was, finally right in front of them. The pretty pink home with matching terra cotta roofing had bright-purple flowers growing on thick vines. They covered the bars around the two windows flanking the door.

He frowned. "Hmmm. The bars on the windows aren't a great sign. And I don't like that they're next to the door. Someone could easily break in."

"Hopefully you won't have to use that to your advantage. I sure as fuck wouldn't open the door for the bastard who left me in the dust nearly a decade ago."

Hawk snorted at the joke even though that pang of guilt gnawed at his heart again. "I'm not hoping for forgiveness. Only the chance to keep her safe."

"*If* she even needs our protection," Draco reminded him

while lazily pointing his toothpick in Hawk's direction. "She could refuse to come with us. This could all be for nothing."

"It could be." The words were dragged out of him, his instincts refusing to fully agree with the statement.

He shifted the rental car into park and unlocked his seat belt, gathering his courage with every movement.

"You want backup?" Draco asked. "I could just go to the closest bar if you need your space."

Despite the fact Hawk hadn't had a drink in years, he had half a mind to tell Draco to grab a seat and order a beer for him too, just in case she kicked him out before he could say his peace.

Draco was right. Hawk had no idea how Hannah was going to receive him, and he was more nervous walking into his ex's adorable house than he'd ever been on the other end of a bullet. He wanted privacy for their conversation, but what if she kicked him to the curb as soon as he walked in? What if, like Draco said, she didn't even open the door for him?

"Better stick around here... just in case."

Draco grunted and leaned forward to push all the vents toward him. "Okay, but I'm leaving the car and AC running. Good luck not melting in your black Henley. Hope your ink's worth a heat stroke."

*Hannah's never seen my tattoo...*

The realization kicked in, heightening the apprehension and excitement making his hands tremble on the wheel. Hawk studiously ignored Draco's scrutiny as his stare beat down on him hotter than any summer sun ever could.

He scrubbed his fade with his hand as he analyzed the best way to approach the house. There was only one entrance from this side, but while he'd been driving around the *barrio*, he'd thought he'd noticed a sidewalk on the other side leading to a back door—

"You're nervous," Draco finally stated.

Hawk opened his mouth to object, but he and Draco had

known each other for the better part of a decade. They'd fought together, killed together, and watched their teammate, Eagle, die for them all. There was no lying to the man, no matter how badly Hawk wanted to lie to himself.

"Yeah, I'm nervous." His voice cracked on the last word.

"Well, if it goes to shit, just give me the signal."

"What signal?"

Draco shrugged. "I don't know, man, I can't come up with everything."

"Sounds good, brother." Hawk huffed a laugh, thankful for the minor relief in tension. "I'll figure something out."

He expelled a huge exhale before exiting the car and leaving it running for his friend.

Loud music set him on edge as the beat gave off a sharp report, like arrhythmic fireworks. The noise had him reaching for his own gun, but no one else around him seemed worried in the slightest, instead singing along with the music and laughing.

*Fuck, I need to get my head on straight.*

He took in another deep breath, this time soaking in the mouthwatering scents of rich spices and smoked meats flooding from the houses and street fare down the road. It took him a moment to ground himself, but he focused on his other senses to quell his adrenaline so he could focus on the task at hand and not slide into some inopportune flashback.

As he rounded the hood, sweltering heat and humidity boiled him from the inside out thanks to the weather and the uncertainty warming underneath his skin. He walked across the street to enter the pink house's wrought iron fencing. Tiled sidewalk led to the door. It was cracked, but shone brilliantly under the sun in gorgeous orange, red, and green designs. Hawk couldn't help but smile at the thought of Hannah painting them herself. When he made it to the door, he stood there for a second, gathering his courage.

Without even looking, he knew Draco was watching his back, maybe even literally. Knowing he had someone on his team there, having his six, encouraged him to raise his fist to knock on the blue door. Heat radiated from the bright paint underneath his knuckles. Just as he was about to rap against the wood, a rustling inside made him pause.

He leaned closer to hear better. Sweat prickled his brow from the scorching sun's reflection on the door. When his cheek brushed against the sticky paint, he almost jerked back. The door cracking open had him pushing it wider instead.

The rustling inside stopped, but a grunt made his pulse quicken. A loud shout of pain had him springing into action. He snatched his gun from his holster as he burst the rest of the way inside.

# CHAPTER FIVE

Hannah's sneakers slapped the pavement as she sprinted down the sidewalk. She'd taken the street leading to her back door from the *lavandería* rather than face the bustling party that always seemed to be going on in front of her house. Her laundry bag bounced heavily against her back from the awkward way she held it. She should've just left it behind, but the two women had yelled at her through the doorway and openly judged her for being *loca* so she'd had to go back and pick it up.

*They might be right.*

Hopefully, this was all a big overreaction and she'd be returning to her perfectly safe house where she could then promptly forget her moment of panic ever happened. Even as she wished it, her mind quickly filed through all her options, just in case.

She hadn't tried to live in Tulum yet. It was a gorgeous town on the coast that had been perfect as the backdrop for one of her paintings. The scenery was beautiful, although the number of tourists could be both a blessing and a curse.

She'd learned hiding in plain sight among other expats from the United States could provide her with the cover she needed, but damn, American tourists were a train wreck when they came to Mexico. There were only two groups who visited: the respectful sightseers and the ones who got wasted. No in-between.

Over the past two years, Mérida had been the first place she'd felt truly at home. It was her *abuela's* hometown, and reminded Hannah of the few memories she still had of her *mamá*, the only person who ever loved her unconditionally and stayed. Until her heart attack, at least.

*Focus, Hannah. Get home. Get your duffel bag. And get going.*

She nodded to herself and increased her speed, pumping her free arm to help her go faster. Her calves began to sting, but as soon as her little pink house came into view, the blue back door with the two windows on either side—a mirror image of the front door—still intact, the tension in her leg muscles loosened and she slowed down.

"Okay, everything looks fine," she reassured herself out loud. "Maybe I was overreacting. I just need to check inside where everything will be perfect. Hopefully those *viejitas* don't gossip across the *centro histórico* about the *loca* down the street and I can stay here."

*You're talking to yourself again.*

"*Mierda*," she murmured to herself and groaned when she realized she'd said that out loud too.

It'd been a bad habit ever since she'd started painting. Art was a lonely passion, and for a while there, hearing the sound of her own voice was the only human interaction she had some days.

Once she got to the door, she fished her key out from her blue jeans pocket and unlocked it. She opened it slowly, holding her breath.

Nothing but the air conditioning's heavenly breeze greeted her.

"*Menos mal...* thank goodness," she whispered to herself

before clamping her hand over her mouth. The main female character in every horror movie she'd ever watched had died seconds after thinking the very same thing. Her heart thumped in her chest again as she strained to listen past the whooshing in her ears.

But still... nothing.

"Okay... *really*, thank God." She made the Sign of the Cross, like her mother taught her when she was a little girl and took a deep, steadying breath.

The delicious aroma from the citrus she'd used to prepare food that morning wafted toward her. There was no movement in sight as she entered the living room and plopped her laundry bag onto the blue-and-white tiled floor. Afraid to take her eyes off her surroundings, she closed and locked the door behind her without turning around.

The low hum of the air conditioner slowly began to overpower the staccato drumbeat of the blood pounding in her head. Its cool air kissed her sweaty skin, fluttering the baby hairs falling in her face from her messy side braid and settling her nerves.

She scouted out the rest of the open-concept living room and kitchenette, then worked through the remainder of the house. After checking inside the hall bathroom and her bedroom, she quietly peeked inside the door to the second bedroom. She could hear the tinny sound of the baseball game's announcer coming from his headphones. They were always way too loud, but she'd let it slide this time.

She closed the door silently, even though it wouldn't matter. Everything was as she'd left it. Safe and sound.

For good measure, she went through the main room to the small kitchen and peered out of the front window. There was only the lively music and hubbub on her street that she loved. Nothing out of the ordinary.

As she relocked the back door, she prayed the new dead bolt

her landlord installed would work this time. The last one allowed the door to drift open with the lightest of breezes.

After several more moments of relative quiet, the tension in Hannah's chest finally started to ease. She leaned against the wall to take a much-needed breath. Even if the *gringo* in question was just a tourist—the most logical conclusion, really—she still couldn't shake the undeniable terror that'd taken over her body at the thought she'd been found again. That, plus the news segment—

*Mierda.*

She'd almost forgotten the scariest detail of it all. Regardless of whether the person sneaking around their *barrio* was someone she should be afraid of, the man that actually instilled fear inside her down to her very bones was missing. If she couldn't keep tabs on him, could that mean he'd stopped keeping tabs on her?

*He could be dead.*

A confusing feeling fluttered in her stomach.

*What if my father is dead?*

She wouldn't have to worry about him anymore. She could stay where she was. Hell... could she go back home? To Atlanta?

Was there even anything to go back to?

She'd left her art teaching career behind over two years ago. Could she return to that life? Did she even want to?

*One thing at a time.*

She blew out a breath that trilled her lips. The sound made her pause one last time to see if anyone would appear to inspect the noise. Granted, with the loud commotion in the neighborhood and how effective headphones were these days, she could set off a bomb and none would be the wiser.

When she was met with silence, she pushed off the wall, accidentally bumping the canvas hanging beside her. The painting was the only one she'd had a chance to paint for herself since she'd arrived in the city. Although the hasty strokes weren't her best work, the blues she'd used for the sunrise and the ocean at the brink of the horizon had reminded her of home, so she kept it anyway.

She looped her necklace around her finger out of habit and straightened the painting with her other hand before going to the small kitchen. It was well past lunchtime. She could finish the laundry after whipping up something to eat.

"Nothing like running for your life for no reason to work up an appetite," she snorted to herself.

Her laugh died as soon as she saw the dishes—that *definitely* weren't supposed to still be dirty—mocking her in the sink. She shook her head with a huff before tucking her necklace back underneath her T-shirt, freeing both hands to wash and put the dishes away, no longer minding how loud she was being. If she interrupted the game at this point at least she'd get some help with the chores.

Unfortunately she wasn't so lucky. When she had finished the task all by herself, she left out a large pot for sweet tea and plates for the *panuchos de cochinita pibil* she'd prepared that morning.

Her mouth watered as she thought about eating the juicy shredded pork nestled on top of fried, black-bean-stuffed tortillas. It wasn't the healthiest of meals, but in her mind, feeding a picky eater with fried tortillas was healthier than starving them. Besides, they deserved a bright spot in their situation.

She put a pot of water on the stovetop to boil so she could make the sweet tea, hoping the Braves would keep winning and she wasn't counting her eggs before they hatched. Next, she used a washcloth to wipe off the plates she'd need for the *panuchos*. Up until Mérida, she'd used paper plates, but this home actually came with its own furnishings, including kitchenware, making it possible for her to cook the recipes her mother had taught her.

While she was drying off one of the gorgeous clay plates, something on the glazed surface caught her eye. She lifted it to the light to inspect the smudge. In the reflection of the bright-yellow sun painted in the center, a large shadow moved behind her and she whirled around.

A huge man stood in the middle of her living room in front of the cracked open back door with its now busted lock. She gripped the clay plate tightly and stepped away from the counter, her eyes wide.

"*Mierda*."

# CHAPTER SIX

The tall, blond man's face twisted in an evil grin.

She sucked in a breath and the plate dropped from her grasp, crashing to the floor. She jolted away from the cabinet to race for one of her guns, but an audible, *familiar* click stopped her in her tracks.

"I would not move if I were you."

She froze. His thick Russian accent reminded her of her father's right-hand man, Vlad. Was this one of their lackeys? The thought made her brain stall out, but she played the part just in time.

"*¿Qué haces aquí? ¿Quién eres? No hablo inglés.*"

"Do not act like you do not know English, Hannah Smithers. I know it is you, even with blonde hair. I come to finish job."

"J-job? *¿T-trabajo?*" She scooted infinitesimally to the side, gliding her hand over the knob of the drawer behind her. Her voice shook as she continued to pretend like she couldn't speak English, "*No sé de qué estás hablando.* L-leave... or I call *la policía*."

Over the years, she'd received threat after threat as her father made sure she never had the luxury of tricking herself into thinking she was safe from his reach. It'd been a terribly lonely, scary way to live, always running. Always hiding. After what he'd done to her over the years, she didn't even allow herself to imagine what he was truly capable of.

But even in her wildest, unbidden nightmares, it'd never been this. Her father's men had never actually approached her. Never entered her *home*. She'd take a thousand dead birds on her doorstep if it meant this intruder would leave her alone and never come back.

"Vlad says boss will not need you. You are a... loose end. Vlad does not like loose ends."

"*Vlad?* Vlad is calling the shots now?" she asked before she could stop herself. "I-I mean... *¿Quién es Vlad?*"

She knew she'd fucked up royally even before the Russian's smile grew wider.

"So you are Hannah Smithers. Good. I was hoping I had the right house this time. Not like last week."

*Fuck.*

Hannah gulped. The stalking had never risen to a deadly level, so it hadn't even occurred to Hannah that the murder of that poor single mother days ago had anything to do with her. But even as guilt and terror twisted her stomach, relief flooded her veins.

*At least her son was okay.*

She barely resisted the urge to glance toward the hallway leading to the bedrooms, and prayed to all the saints her mother had believed in that whatever happened next was quick, painless, and no one else would get hurt.

"It is only you he wants gone. Do not worry."

The man's smug voice had her anything but unworried. She focused on the intruder as he shifted out of her periphery. His gun and silencer were now raised at her face. She coughed as her fingers gently tugged the drawer away from the cabinet.

*Talk to him. Say something, anything to stall.*

"So... so, um, Vlad? H-he's in charge now? I-I thought he was just my father's drinking buddy."

The man snorted. "Drinking buddy? Vlad does not drink with the boss."

"But... but the General is still the boss, then?"

She analyzed him as they spoke. If she somehow escaped, she wanted to remember his face. He wasn't actually bad to look at, but his positively maniacal grin and eyes transformed him into something ugly.

*"Muy guapo," my ass. Not with those ojos locos.*

"Everything is different now," he boasted cryptically. "Everyone under old boss must be gone."

"No loose ends," she mumbled as her palm touched cool metal.

"Goodbye, Hannah Smith—"

Hannah collapsed to the ground to escape the gunshot, breaking the drawer as she took it down with her. The bullet whizzed by, just above her head, but she extracted her own gun from the broken drawer and lifted it with both hands, spraying shots at the intruder around the cabinet between them. Unfortunately, her haste and lack of practice made her miss him by a foot.

His shocked wide eyes and dropped jaw would've been comical if she wasn't on the verge of passing out from terror.

*Please don't come out. Please don't come out. Keep those headphones way too loud. Stay in your room.*

The inner thought repeated across her mind like a prayer as she aimed for the intruder again, just as he did the same. Their gunshots were deafening, despite his silencer, and she hoped to hell the noise-canceling headphones in the other room did their job.

*Focus—*

She rolled just in time to escape a shot that was way too fucking close for comfort. The bullet hit the wooden cabinet door behind her, splintering shards just above her head.

Before she could take aim again, the intruder ran around the cabinetry and pounced on her instead, scratching at her shooting hand to take the gun away from her. She grunted under his weight and tried to kick him in the groin, fight back, do *something*. All she could do was cling to the gun for dear life, knowing without a doubt her life was exactly what was at stake.

His focus on her gun was so single minded she was able to finally get enough leverage to knee him in the groin. He groaned and held tight to her gun with one hand and his crushed *cojones* with the other as he curled in a fetal position. His shifted weight enabled her to wriggle the rest of the way out from underneath him, and she used the counter beside the stove to get up.

That spurred him into motion. He tightened his hold on her gun while he used his other hand to yank the waistline of her jeans with such force she fell to her ass on the hard tile floor.

She bit her lip to stop herself from crying out. Before he could get on top of her again, she reached up blindly to the oven's burning top and snatched the pot off the eye of the stove, letting it clatter onto his head. The half gallon of boiling hot water gushed from the large pot, making his fair skin flush red where every blistering drop fell.

He shouted and dropped her to clutch his face. As he turned on his side, writhing on the ground, she scrambled to her feet, trying not to slip on the water. Just as she got her bearings, the front door slammed open.

The Russian's wild eyes snapped to the door, but her entire focus remained on him. She didn't bother to take aim as she quickly fired into the man's chest, emptying the pistol and praying like hell at least one round would be a killing blow.

His hands clutched at the hole near his heart as he collapsed limply to the ground. Crimson blood poured from his wound onto the pretty blue-and-white tile. The liquid flowed outward in little rivulets, guided by the grout between the tiling.

Somewhere in the back of her mind, her inner artist admired the beautiful way the deep, rich red painted the clay artwork underneath it before soaking into the mortar. But as she dodged a thick river inching closer to her sneaker, the realization of what she was actually marveling at finally hit her.

The life of a man she'd *killed* drained out in front of her, right before her eyes.

Disgust roiled in her belly up her esophagus, prompting her to swallow. But she didn't allow herself time to think about what she'd just done. Her hands trembled as she lowered her gun slightly.

When her would-be murderer's glazed eyes flickered toward her, he attempted one last lunge up to grab her, but a sudden spray of bullets peppered his abdomen.

She screeched and hustled backward into the corner of the kitchenette, unable to take her eyes off the man's body as it jolted with each gunshot.

Up until that point, she'd completely forgotten the door had opened, allowing someone else to witness the fight. When the gunfire was over, she whipped around and used both trembling hands to aim her empty gun at the new intruder.

Her whole body went numb and muscle memory in her fingers fought to hold on to her gun.

"*Hawkins?*"

# CHAPTER SEVEN

After all these years... Hawkins Black, the man who'd broken her heart by choosing strangers over her—just like everyone else before and after him—filled her doorway with his striking stature.

He was bigger than she remembered, and his sculpted muscles were hills and valleys through his thin, black, long-sleeved shirt. Sweat glistened against his dark-sienna skin, slowly trailing down his face, following the faintest creases that hadn't been there nearly a decade ago. His fade tapered right above his ears, but was slightly longer than his nearly buzzed military cut, and now had soft waves.

Those hard, charcoal eyes she still dreamed about, glared at the corpse on her floor, as if Hawk's angry gaze alone could send the man straight to hell. If anyone had that kind of ability it would've been Hawk.

For the past two years, she'd wished and prayed he had power over death itself. And here he was... *alive*. Making her wonder if her prayers had been answered or if she'd finally lost it.

"Was he the only one?" he asked, his familiar deep voice shocked her to her core after not having heard it in years, but the sharp tone was nothing like he'd ever used with her.

He glided into her living room, checking behind furniture while flicking glances toward her.

"Han? Was he the only intruder?"

*Other than you?*

She nodded her head as she slowly got her wits about her. "J-just him."

Hawkins slowly relaxed, lowering the weapon down as he turned to finally make eye contact.

A flurry of emotions washed over her. Cool relief, warm gratitude, hot betrayal, and burning lust. The very real, varying temperatures throughout her body sparked perspiration on her skin and she gripped the counter at the sudden wave of dizziness.

He was by her side in an instant, his worried gaze flitting up and down her body, seemingly checking for injuries. The disbelief that had frozen her to her spot finally began to thaw as her mind latched on to the fact her ex-fiancé was right in front of her.

"I knew teaching you how to shoot was the right move. Are you okay? Did he hurt you, dove?"

His full lips had been set in a grim line until they formed around his endearment for her. They'd curved slightly upward and her index finger itched to trace the soft pillows, to recommit the texture to memory so she could properly paint their perfection again. After all their time apart, she'd been afraid she'd almost lost the visual, but here he was, right in front of her again.

Hawk kicked the body to the side before towering over her again, giving her the distinct feeling he was shielding her from the rest of the fucked-up world. He ran his long, deft fingers over her body, searching for trauma.

*You won't find it there*, she thought as she resisted the urge to massage the sudden ache in her chest.

His touch was foreign and familiar at the same time, and a

shiver of pleasure rocked through her body despite her confusion. His thick, dark brows bunched in concern.

"Hannah, you're shaking. Did he hurt you? Did he touch you?" His voice had gentled and caressed over her like a balm.

She wanted to answer him, but she couldn't get her mind past one singular, prevailing thought.

"Y-you're... alive?"

He stilled at her question and his eyes locked on hers. Emotions she felt intimately herself swirled in his gaze as he swallowed.

"Yeah, dove. I'm alive."

Tears stung her eyes as she opened her mouth, only to close it again, still at a loss for what to say. Everything that had just happened couldn't have been more than a few minutes, but looking into his gaze felt like forever.

It always had.

Just as she was trying to gather her wits about her again, yet another person barreled through her door. Her heart nearly clawed its way out of her chest as a tall, blond, straight-out-of-Iceland-looking Viking of a man barged in with his gun pointed.

"*Mierd*—"

"It's okay, Han. You're safe. Draco's with me," Hawk reassured her and looked at the man whose sunburned face looked undeniably pissed off.

"Gunshots weren't the signal I had in mind, Hawk," the guy —Draco—muttered under his breath as he examined the scene with fierce, Atlantic Ocean–blue eyes. "People were scared shitless when they realized it wasn't music. The neighborhood's been cleared, but that means the police won't be far behind."

"Copy that. Check the body for any identifying information. I'll get her out of here."

"You... I was told you were dead," she insisted, waving her hands around. The words grated against her throat as she forced them out.

Hawk quickly disarmed her, removing the gun from her hand, making her realize she'd been pointing it around without regard.

"I'm not, Hannah. I swear I'm alive and real, and I swear we need to get the hell out of here before the cops show." He stuffed her gun in the back of his waistband and tilted his head at the dead assassin.

"Who was this guy?" Hawk asked as Draco bent to pat the body down.

"I... I don't know." She shook her head and pointed at Hawk. "How are you here? And who are you?" she asked, shifting her accusing finger at Draco, who didn't even bother to look at her as he kept going about his task. She glared at Hawk as her mind tried to connect the insane puzzle pieces she'd collected from the past ten minutes. "Are you guys with *him*?"

"With *him*?" Hawk's head jolted back as his thumb jerked toward the body on the ground. "You mean the guy I just helped you defend yourself from? The guy I shot?"

"No! I mean... yes. Wait." She massaged her temple. A raging migraine was already pulsing under her fingers. "I have to go. *You* have to go."

"What? Go where? We need to get you out of here—"

A whoop in the other room made all of them pause.

"Shit," Hannah muttered.

Hawk stepped in front of her, his back to her chest as he crowded her into the corner of the cabinetry.

"Stay behind me," he growled just as she heard the door of the second bedroom open down the hall.

"No, you *have* to leave. Now," Hannah hissed as she extricated herself from behind Hawk. She rounded the counter to preemptively block the entrance to the kitchenette and yelled toward the bedroom. "Stay in your room!"

Her gaze darted around the kitchenette and behind the counter, making sure Draco and the body in the kitchen couldn't be seen from the hallway. Hawk was suddenly inches away from her again, his gun still out.

She grabbed his forearm and whispered through clenched teeth, "Put your gun down. *Now.*"

The stubborn man from her past listened and lowered his weapon, just in time to hear the familiar voice that made this life of running worth it.

"Braves won! *Finally!*" The voice had the jarring quality of a person with their headphones on too loud. Sure enough, as soon as he appeared, she saw the knockoff over-ear headphones covering his ears. "That means sweet tea tonight—"

Hannah put up her hands to stop him from getting anywhere close to the kitchen, protecting him from what he could see on the ground. His eyes narrowed at her stance before they widened on the man behind her. That azure gaze darted back to her and he slid the headphones from his ears onto his neck.

When Hannah glanced back at Hawk, he'd stepped in front of the space between the wall and the *L-shaped* counter, further preventing the corpse from being seen. But instead of relaxing at the sight of the boy in front of her, at the realization there wasn't another enemy, his entire body had gone still as a statue. His biceps and chest were stone underneath his Henley, even as his breaths came out unevenly.

Hannah swallowed before turning around and settling her hands on the boy's shoulders. "*Mijo*, go to your room."

"Hannah, who... who is this?" Hawk's question came out rough and slammed into her back like a baseball bat, knocking the breath out of her with the vulnerability laced in his deep voice. Her heart pricked at the confusion and pain there.

"Yeah, who are *you?*" asked in the much younger and much higher pitch.

She held her breath before pivoting on her heel to Hawk and facing the awful mix of heartbreak and hope in his expression.

"Um, Hawk, this... this is Tommy." She swallowed as her still racing heart beat a million miles a second. Her gaze darted back to Tommy's curious one, and she ran her trembling fingers through his soft blond hair. She met Hawk's gaze again before admitting the rest, refusing to feel shame for the best thing that'd ever happened to her. "He's... my son. And he's also—"

"Eagle's son."

# CHAPTER EIGHT

The sight of the little boy in front of him made Hawk's calm pulse—his default setting whenever he faced an enemy—stutter to a stop. The boy's serious scowl and blue eyes were painfully familiar, and Hawk couldn't stop watching Hannah's slender fingers thread through the boy's thick mop of hair that was just like his father's.

Protectiveness rolled off her in waves as she stood proudly in front of Hawk. The blonde mixed in her dark hair suited her, especially with the gorgeous, wavy strands escaping her loose side braid. Flecks of brightly colored paint splattered her tight jeans and worn, baggy Atlanta Braves T-shirt that he could've sworn looked familiar. A blue speck dotted her cheek, and Hawk resisted the urge to wipe it away with his thumb.

"Fuck," Draco cursed, bringing Hawk back to the moment. "I'm, uh... I'm gonna canvas the neighborhood, make sure no one is calling the cops about the gunsh"—he coughed—"I mean *noise*."

"Hurry," Hawk muttered. "We don't know how long we have until we need to get out of here."

On the way to Mexico, Hawk had considered giving Hannah the choice of leaving or surveillance protection in her home. But if men were actively hunting her—and her *child*—then there was no way he was leaving them to the wolves.

Draco grunted and left through the broken door. The child's watchful eyes followed Hawk's teammate and widened again, no doubt having just seen the state of the door. When he returned his gaze back to Hawk, he took a step in front of his mother with a glare of determination on his face.

"Who are *you?*" he asked again, his voice carrying all the authority of a little man of the house.

Hawk's chest felt like it'd been carved open just so the kid could excavate his heart, stomp on it, and stuff it back inside. But pride warmed his chest at the protectiveness in the boy's stature.

"You're just like your dad," he murmured, his voice hoarse.

Tommy's wary eyes widened farther and shot up to his mother's before meeting Hawk's again. "You knew my dad?"

Hawk nodded. He cleared his throat to get past the emotion clogging it. "Yeah... I knew your dad. He... he was my best friend."

The admission brought on a coin toss of hurt. One that his best friend was gone, and the other, that the love of his life and his best friend had had an affair. Judging by the kid's age, apparently right before they left for MF7. Was it before he and Eagle had made a pact to keep her safe and leave her behind? After?

Did it matter?

Then there was the added realization that a piece of his best friend, the one he'd thought he'd lost forever, was still in this world. *Here* in front of him. It was taking every ounce of self-control not to pick the kid up and bear-hug him.

"Your best friend?" The wonder and hope in little Tommy's voice made Hawk swallow. "Did you help him save the world, too? Were you there when he died?"

*Shit.*

"Tommy!" Hannah scolded.

Hawk raised his hand to say it was fine, even though he didn't even know where to begin to answer this child's question about his father.

"Yeah, I... I helped your dad save the world."

It was a lie, but the truth was something that even he wished he didn't know. A child, especially *Eagle's* child, never needed to learn it.

"Cool." The kid grinned at him, showing off two big front teeth and a missing molar on the bottom right.

"Wait..." Hannah whispered, her voice pitched higher. "If *you're* alive—"

"No," Hawk interrupted her, vaguely breaking it to her that Eagle didn't make it. "I'm sorry."

Her eyes dropped to the ground, but not before he saw that flicker of hope snuff out entirely.

*Did she love him, too? How did I miss that?*

A far-off siren accompanied by hurried footsteps stiffened Hawk's spine with panic. He twisted woodenly to face the sound, but Draco's deep voice announced his entrance, making Hawk relax a fraction.

"It's me," Draco reassured, allowing Hawk to lower his already raised gun. "But the cops are coming. There's a gathering outside down the street and I don't know Spanish, but I know the word *policía* isn't going to end well for us."

The kid's tanned face paled and he sought his mother's with a questioning glance.

"Mom, should we go—"

"*Sí.* Get your bag, *avecito.*"

"Shit," Tommy cursed and turned out of her grip. Hawk's brow rose as he waited for Hannah to light into the kid for cursing, but she just rolled her eyes.

"You know the rules, *mijo*. No complaining until we're on the road. Now, *ándale*. We have to go."

Tommy groaned, but double-timed it to his room.

"I'll move the car closer," Draco mentioned before disappearing as he shut the front door.

Hawk was left with a dead body behind him, and the woman he killed for in front of him. He wasn't sure which one he dreaded dealing with more.

The sirens seemed to get closer, snapping them both into survival mode.

"Why are you here, Hawk?" Hannah whispered harshly. Her tone made him jerk back before answering.

"I came to save you."

"*Save* me?" She snorted. "*¡Que rico!* How rich. Well, I've been saved. You can go now. Tommy and I have been doing just fine by ourselves the past nine years, no thanks to your *boss*—"

"My *boss*?"

"—so if you don't mind, see yourself out so *we* can get the hell out of here. Or be here when the *policía* arrive, I don't care. Good luck figuring out what to say about your boss's dead hitman, though."

Stunned by her response, Hawk stood dumbly and watched as she spun away from him and crossed the living room with purpose.

She gathered her sketchbook, paintbrushes, and paint bottles from around the room without skipping a beat. Once she'd finished, she reached behind a side table to grab a hidden duffel bag and stuffed the items inside the already packed bag.

*She's been on the run.*

He'd suspected it since he'd seen the General's surveillance photo. But seeing her going through the motions of someone who'd been living this life for too damn long made his chest ache, and suddenly the need to comfort her was all-consuming.

"Hannah, take a breath and listen to me."

He followed her into the living room where he gripped her shoulders and turned her to face him. There was a dead body in her kitchen and she was obviously ready to flee for her life, but the panic he would've expected on anyone else's face, wasn't on Hannah's. Focus smoothed the faint beginnings of worry lines on her forehead, and she only looked annoyed that he'd stopped her.

But she didn't shrug out of his hold, which was a win in his book.

"What do you want, Hawk? Every second matters right now and I need to mentally go over my next steps, which don't involve you."

Her words stung but he pushed through the ache. "Come with me. I can keep you safe. I... *none* of us work for your father anymore. "

Her forehead wrinkled as she scoffed. "Are you out of your mind? So maybe you don't work for him anymore, but still, why on earth would I go with the man who *left* me to work with the very bastard I'm running from? You can't expect me to trust you after all this time!"

A bullet to the chest would've hurt less. But the sirens were getting louder and he didn't have time to convince her to go with him. His own plans flipped through his mind as he tried a different tactic.

"Okay, let me help you pack, then. What do you need?"

She glanced at him up and down, taking his full measure before her frown lessened.

He looked around to see if he could answer for her, but other than the scattered art materials she'd already picked up, there was hardly anything that said she lived there. Back in Atlanta, every inch of her apartment and the one he shared with Eagle had been covered with her masterpieces. But there was only one canvas hanging in the kitchen. He'd had to leave it all behind. Had she been forced to do the same?

Without thinking, he turned around, grabbed the canvas from the kitchen wall, and marched back to her.

"Hawk, what are you doing—"

Draco rushed through the back door, making Hawk's already racing pulse skyrocket. Hannah's resistance was distracting him, and the only option he could think of blared louder than the sirens outside the front of the house.

"They're here," Draco grunted. "Time to go. Car's out back."

"*Mierda.¡Avecito! Ven aquí!* Now, please, *mijo!*"

At his mother's summons, Tommy emerged from the hallway, a large duffel bag of his own slung over his shoulders and a baseball bat in his hand.

"Ready. But, Mom, what if the car doesn't start again?"

The question made Hawk's stomach flip and her answer made him nauseous.

"I-it will." Hannah tried to comfort her son before snatching the boy's hand. "It has to."

"That's it," Hawk growled and grabbed Hannah's duffel bag from her shoulder and caught her free hand in his.

"Hawk! What the—"

"We're leaving, Han. Trust me or don't, but you're coming with us. Draco, you take our six. Tommy, follow me."

"Let go of my mom!" the kid growled like a lion cub.

"Hawkins, stop! We're not going—"

The sirens suddenly cut off. Car doors opened and slammed and people yelled in Spanish outside the front door behind them. Indecision warred in Hannah's wide, frightened brown eyes before she finally nodded and turned to her son.

"Follow him, *avecito*. We have to go. I don't know if the car will work, but we can... we can trust him."

Hawk could hear the question in her voice. Judging by the kid's narrowed eyes bouncing from him to Hannah, so could he.

Hawk bent low to meet the boy's worried blue eyes. "Listen, I know you're the man of this house and you're used to protecting your mom, but I care about your mom, too. You can trust me to keep her safe."

Tommy held his gaze until he finally nodded.

"Good, let's go. Don't let go of your mom's hand, little man." Hawk squeezed Hannah's hand and led her out the door, checking behind him to ensure Tommy and Draco followed.

There was a grunt and a crash inside before Draco emerged. "Figured tipping the fridge in front of the door would buy us some time."

The yelling got louder and more adamant. Hawk ignored the commotion, beelining toward the rental car parked behind a beat-up car that looked older than Tommy.

He deposited Hannah's duffel bag into the rental car's trunk, ignoring the way she glared at him for being so overbearing. He didn't feel guilty in the slightest. There was no way her rust bucket would've survived as a getaway car.

Thankfully, she didn't object when he opened the door for her and Tommy to slide into the back seat. Hawk quickly rounded the hood and sat behind the steering wheel. As soon as Draco plopped into the passenger seat, Hawk drove out onto the street, fighting every instinct to step on the gas.

"Draco, tell our pilot to be ready when we get there."

When he rolled up to a stop sign, cops sped past them, leaving their car in the dust. Hawk glanced in the rearview mirror to watch them stop right in front of Hannah's house and run inside. No one followed him as he turned onto the busy street. Before he knew it, they were on the main road to the airport, out of danger.

Or at least, *they* were out of danger.

Judging by the icy sweet-tea-colored eyes glittering back at him, *he* was in major trouble with the woman behind him.

"A *pilot*? Just where are you taking us, Hawk?" she spat.

He met her gaze in the mirror before returning it to the street to navigate the traffic.

"Home, Hannah. I'm taking you home."

# CHAPTER NINE

"Hannah, this is my team." Hawk's calloused hand gestured around the large, modern, industrial-styled common room.

The black leather *L*-shaped couch held a surprising number of people. Ten sets of eyes—each varying in emotion—stared back at her as Hawk introduced everyone.

Of course, she'd already met Draco. Despite the hours they'd spent in the car, plane, and helicopter ride to the BlackStone Securities facility, his silent demeanor had made it impossible to get to know him. And she'd met Phoenix nearly a decade ago when she dated Hawk.

But Nora, Callie, Wes, Devil, Ellie, Jules, Jason, and Marco were all new faces. There were almost too many odd call signs to keep up with, and if it weren't for her years of teaching, she would've never gotten the names right. She was also able to piece together the few stories Hawk had told her before he left her for MF7. Now she was getting to meet the rest of his adopted family.

*His family.*

A pang of jealousy stabbed into her chest. She rubbed the tender spot above her heart, a wound she'd felt acutely ever since Hawk had told her who she'd be meeting "at home."

She'd always craved a big family. It'd basically just been her and her mother when she was a child. Every time her power-hungry father had gotten a promotion in his military career, he'd lug them around like two travel-worn carry-on bags. After her mother died from a heart attack, Hannah was all alone.

At one point, she'd thought Hawk would be her family. But this team—this *family*—had stolen all that from her.

*No... Hawk gave* me *up for* them. *It's not their fault.*

That reality had been needling her for nearly ten years. But that needlepoint had sharpened and grown to the size of a dagger with the evidence in front of her. It's easier to forget someone doesn't love you when you never have to face your replacement.

She inhaled deeply and raised one hand to the crowd. "Um, nice to meet you. I'm..." She paused for a second, realizing she could use her real name for the first time in the past two years. "I'm Hannah. This is my son, Tommy."

Hannah squeezed his shoulder lightly. He glanced up at her, obviously trying to read how he should be reacting to all of this.

*Hell if I know.*

"*Está bien, avecito,*" she reassured him out loud, instead. "*Podemos confiar en ellos.*"

*It's okay. We can trust them.*

"You call Tommy 'Little Bird?'" Hannah startled as Marco, the assistant district attorney Hawk's team worked with, interpreted her endearment for Tommy. "That's adorable."

Tommy frowned. "It's not *adorable.*"

A genuine smile lifted Hawk's lips. "It's actually really cool, Tommy. That's what we call our helicopter, too."

"Really?" Tommy asked, his face lighting up for the first time since he saw said helicopter.

But just as soon as the excitement flashed over his face, uncertainty replaced it, like he still wasn't sure if he could let his guard down. It broke her heart to see him be so distrustful at such a young age. He'd been through so much already.

"*Mi abuela es del norte de México. Cerca de la frontera con Texas,*" Marco spoke again, telling her his grandmother was Mexican, and from the Northern border near Texas. "*¿Tú?*"

"*Mis abuelos también eran de México, pero se mudaron a los Estados Unidos antes de tener a mi mamá,*" she answered, telling him her grandparents were Mexican, too, but moved to the United States before having her mother.

The stress in her muscles eased as they used their grandparents' native tongue. Hannah hardly ever spoke Spanish after her mother passed away. It'd become second nature once she sought refuge in Mexico and she'd picked up the different dialects as she traveled. The feeling of safety she'd associated with Mérida soaked through every word.

A handsome smile lit his bronze face. "*¿Ah en serio? La península de Yucatán es hermoso. Mi abuela me llevó cuando era niño.*"

*Ah, really? The Yucatán Peninsula is gorgeous. My grandmother took me when I was a boy.*

"*Sí, lo es...*" *Yes, it is*, Hannah replied carefully, finding peace in the interaction, but still wondering where he was going with this.

His grin lessened to a more serious expression, but the genuine, friendly connection of shared experience stayed strong between them.

"*Es verdad, lo sabes. Puedes confiar en ellos. Prometo. Soy fiscal y no trabajaría con ellos si no fueran los buenos.*"

*It's true, you know. You can trust them. I promise. I'm a prosecutor and I wouldn't work with them if they weren't the good guys.*

His words shouldn't have comforted her since she didn't know him from Adam. But something about speaking the same language her mother had taught her gave her security, and Hannah was beginning to suspect Marco knew that.

She nodded slowly before thanking him, "*Gracias.*"

When her eyes met Tommy's, he didn't seem as easily convinced. She attempted an encouraging smile, but apparently failed miserably. He scowled, setting his glare back on the group before stepping protectively in front of her and crossing his arms.

"Fuckin' *A*, he looks just like Eagle," Phoenix muttered.

A man with a scar showing through his short, pecan-brown hair—Jason—reprimanded his teammate, "Phoenix, man, you can't curse in front of a kid. They're like sponges."

"Hey, dude. I'm just saying." Phoenix raised his hands in surrender.

Despite his laughing tone, Hannah frowned at him. He was still in his signature backward ball cap, but the perpetual happiness that used to brighten his eyes had dimmed. There was a darkness there to him now that she didn't recognize. Even though they'd never really been close, it hurt her heart to see.

Tommy had tensed underneath her hand, so she cleared her throat to show him they could indeed trust Hawk's team. Hopefully, she wasn't wrong.

"It's good to see you again, Phoenix. Still no Braves hat, though, I see."

Phoenix cracked a smile. "I always said you gotta get me one. You know it's football all the way where I'm from."

"Mom, you know him?"

"*Sí, mijo.*"

"See, look at that serious little face. Are we sure he's not a damn clone of Eagle?" Phoenix continued. "The General's reach is practically limitless these days. Who knows what he's got in his back pocket."

Hawk had told her their team had cut all ties with General Smithers and they were now trying to take him down. But Hannah's back still straightened in panic at just the mention of her father. She was trying to ignore her anxiety when Tommy asked the question she knew had been on his mind since Phoenix opened his mouth.

"You knew my dad?"

Phoenix opened his mouth to answer but Hawk intervened.

"We all did, little man. Or almost all of us. Your dad fought alongside us when we were saving the world."

"Saving the world?" one of the men snorted. Hannah snapped her gaze to the redheaded giant appropriately nicknamed Devil.

"Yes," Hawk answered with authority that made Hannah's lower belly flip. "Tommy's *father* helped *save the world*."

Devil's cheeks reddened and she felt her own blood freeze with the cryptic implication. Something had happened during their time at MF7 that they weren't telling her. She'd known her father was a shady creep, but she'd believed Hawk long ago when he'd told her his team had the lofty goal of eradicating human trafficking. But from the heavy, tense undertones in the room, there was more to the story.

"Do you know how he died?" Tommy asked.

The words hung in the air like a guillotine waiting to drop. It was on the tip of her tongue to reprimand him for his blunt question, but she'd been dying to know the answer since the day her father taunted her with the news.

"You don't know?" the tatted, blue-haired Clark Kent–looka-like, Wes—or Snake, as he'd been called in MF7—gently questioned while pushing up his black glasses.

"I found out through the mail. I thought your whole team had—" Her voice was too hoarse to continue, so she cleared her throat to attempt to get rid of the emotion and anxiety clogging it. "It just said it was... 'in action.'"

*Killed in action.*

She couldn't bear to say that one word out loud. It'd haunted her for the past two years. She'd already been on the run when she'd received the ominous unofficial letter. It was left on her doorstep beside a dead hawk, one of her father's many twisted ways of intimidating her while she tried to escape from under his thumb. Every single day since, she'd worried if the team's death was somehow her fault. Maybe a punishment for disobeying some invisible rule.

Hannah's father had warned her something terrible could

happen if she didn't toe the line. Was there more she could've done to prevent his death?

"You don't know how he died?" Hawk asked low, those warm, charcoal eyes full of sympathy. His deep timbre had her lower belly fluttering, and she fought the urge to fiddle with her necklace as she whispered.

"No."

Hawk sighed heavily, his chest rising and falling with the weight of the world bearing down on him. He scrubbed the back of his head and glanced at his team before stepping closer to her.

As much as she didn't want to hear the details of how her friend died, she needed to know even more that his death wasn't her fault. A gnawing pit in her stomach quickly filled with dread as she waited for the truth, but Hawk shook his head slightly.

"I'll tell you later, dove. When it's just us. Right now, we need to get you and the little man settled in and figure out our plan of action."

"Settled in?" Callie, the woman dressed in all black with raven hair and a complexion close to Hannah's own narrowed her brown eyes at Hawk. "The General's daughter is staying *here?*"

The words themselves felt like an accusation.

"Yes." Hawk's own tone brooked no argument. "Hannah is a victim in all of this and as much a part of it as we are. I'm not sure what part yet, but we'll figure it out as soon as she gets some rest."

"Wouldn't it be better to get answers now?" The curvy woman dressed in a sharp business skirt suit crossed her arms. "If this missing madman is after her and we know he already has a vendetta against BlackStone Securities, shouldn't finding him be our first priority?"

The woman—Jules—was right, but weariness and fatigue were already soaking Hannah to the bone. Her *pobrecito* leaned against her, practically falling asleep standing up. Hawk had always been laser focused, though, forsaking all else for the *mission*. There was no way she'd be getting out of this one.

"Okay," she sighed, gearing up for the hours of questioning she'd no doubt have to endure. "But it's late, and I'd like to get Tommy into bed. After that, I'll come back—"

"No."

Everyone, including Hannah, snapped their attention to Hawk. His thick biceps strained against his long-sleeve Henley as they crossed over his broad chest. Determination hardened his jawline to stone.

"No?" she repeated.

"You're getting sleep, Han." The command in his voice made her spine tingle. "All this can wait until you're rested."

Wes cleared his throat. "But Hawk—"

"I said no." Hawk's large hand gently encircled her wrist as he murmured a command just for her. "Come with me. I'll take you to your room."

# CHAPTER TEN

In her bone-weary state, Hawk's own personal brand of rigid authority and soft touch made it impossible to resist his command. But, then again, she'd never been able to resist where Hawk was concerned.

She set her hands on Tommy's shoulders as she followed Hawk out of the living room, leaving confused and stunned looks behind them. It was probably for the best they left, since her own bewilderment was no doubt apparent on her face, too.

The past twenty-four hours had been a whirlwind, waking up to what had become a normal day on the run, learning her father was missing, fighting for her life, finding out the only man she ever loved was still alive, killing a hitman with said ex by her side, traveling from one country to the next, and capping off the day by meeting the team the love of her life chose over her.

And here he was, in the middle of a crisis, choosing *her* over *them*.

"*¡Por Dios!* I need a nap." She yawned.

Hawk stopped next to a door at the end of the long, wide, empty hallway and pointed to their bags that lay beside her painting and Tommy's baseball bat against the wall.

"Draco dropped your bags off here. It's my room. You can

sleep in here if you'd like. Our other rooms are taken at the moment."

At Hannah's nod, Hawk picked up both duffel bags, opened the door, and stepped inside. Hannah murmured her thanks and motioned for Tommy to grab his bat while she took the painting. She ushered him inside before following behind them both. Once she stopped to take in her new surroundings, her heart cracked.

It was barren.

No color, no memorabilia, no art. Nothing.

"You *live* here?" She couldn't help the confusion in her voice. Other than Hawk's faint scent, she'd never guess this was his room. It was nothing like the vibrant life he'd left behind nearly a decade ago.

"I won't stay here," he reassured her, obviously misunderstanding the basis for her shock. He turned to place their bags next to the small dining table, but Hannah caught the hurt wrinkling his brow before it was out of sight. "It'll be just you two."

"Where will you stay?"

"Don't worry about that right now. And I'm sorry it's not much." He pointed around the studio apartment that was bigger than the entire home she and Tommy had lived in for months. "But the bed is big enough for the two of you, or there's a couch if that suits better. The bathroom's there, closet there. I'll ask one of the women to bring you more clothes from their store."

Hannah paused from looking around his room. "Their store?"

"My men have all found their perfect matches and a few of them have a store they use as a front for a women's crisis center. Jules, Nora, Ellie, and Naomi run it and can get you anything you need."

"Right... well, I have my bag. It'll do for now. It's been enough for years." She picked up her duffel bag and left Tommy's side and laid it near the bedside table. "Tommy, go ahead and get ready for bed. And *don't* forget to brush your teeth."

"*Fine.*" Tommy dropped his duffel bag to the ground and

sighed heavily, like she'd told him to use his toothbrush to scrub the floors instead of his teeth.

Hannah ruffled his hair with a laugh before he disappeared into the bathroom, dragging his bag behind him. It wasn't until the door was closed that she realized it was only her and Hawk left in the room.

She shifted her gaze to his and her chest tightened at the concern marring his handsome features.

"What's wrong?" she asked with a frown.

"When we got discharged from MF7, I looked you up and saw you'd won teacher of the year. I didn't check back in because I didn't want to draw attention to you or put you in any danger. I only found out two and a half months ago that you were missing. But you... you've been on the run for *years*?" He shook his head and swiped his hand down his face. She could swear there was guilt mixed with the worry now.

*Good.*

Let him feel bad for abandoning her. It was literally the least he could do.

She didn't answer and instead waited for him to continue.

"What the hell happened, Han?"

His question annoyed her, but she shrugged her shoulders, feeling protective over the difficult decisions she'd had to make for way too damn long.

"How are you so shocked that I've been running? You haven't explained everything to me yet, but if my father is as bad as you're implying, why wouldn't I have run?"

"I've been looking for you for weeks, ever since I realized you'd gone missing. But I only just found out your father was behind everything we're investigating. He'd been watching you and finding a photo with your coordinates on the back was the first break I'd had about your location. That's why I went to find you first. I had to make sure you were safe."

"No! For the past two years, *I* did what I had to do to stay safe. I did. *Me.* Not you."

"I'm not trying to fight, I just want to know what happened." His brows furrowed in the center. "Talk to me. You were safe when I left with my team—"

Anger suddenly surged through her, lunging her forward until she stopped within a foot from him. She pointed at his chest, not daring to touch him, unsure of what her body would do if she made contact in her rage.

"That's right, Hawkins, *you* left *me*. That means *you* don't get the right to know *me* anymore. You can find out the details with the rest of your beloved *team* tomorrow."

Her fingers itched to rip him to shreds, but the sincere pain in his gaze made her traitorous heart want to hold him instead.

"I'm sorry, Han. At the time... at the time I thought it was the right move. I never wanted to leave." His deep voice cracked on the last word.

Sympathy pricked behind her eyes and she took a tentative step back, forcing much-needed space between them.

"Forget it. What time do I need to be ready in the morning?"

Hawkins blinked, obviously trying to catch up to her dismissal. "I, uh, I'll tell the team oh-eight hundred hours—I mean—eight in the morning."

The military time irritated her more than it should. She'd always hated it when her dad insisted on using it. Hawk knew that, but apparently he'd forgotten it like everything else they'd had between them.

*Petty, petty, petty... I'm being petty. All that matters is Tommy's safety and staying the hell away from my father.*

"Alright then." She sucked her teeth. "Guess I'll see you in the morning."

Hawk lingered, like he wasn't sure what to do next. It was strange to see the man who'd always been cool, calm, and collected, now stutter, backtrack, and second-guess his every move. Was that a new development thanks to MF7? Or was it new because of her?

She blew out a breath, determined not to read into things,

and walked past him toward the door. It hadn't been shut all the way so she opened it farther and gestured for Hawk to leave.

He scoffed. "You're escorting *me* from *my* room?"

"You escorted me across two countries. I figured it's the least I could do."

His steady gaze fixed on her, waiting for her to fold, but he had to know her better than that. It'd always been a battle of wills between them. The only time either of them gave ground was in the bed—

*No.*

A sudden flush of heat rose in her cheeks and she turned her face, lifting her chin toward the hallway. "I'm tired, Hawk. I'll see you in the morning."

She didn't look at him but she felt his heated stare. Did he see right through her? That she was trying her best to navigate this crazy, strained situation, while also attempting to bury her emotions along with her past?

Heavy footsteps made her heart race, knowing he was coming closer. She kept her relaxed posture, allowing very real exhaustion to show through. When his tall frame entered her vision his presence nearly overshadowed her good judgment.

He stopped in front of her, his chest at her eye level. After a moment it dawned on her he was waiting for her to look up. Despite her best efforts not to submit to his silent command, she found her chin lifting to meet his gaze.

His full umber lips were only inches away. She concentrated on steady inhales and exhales, and the gold necklace she wore underneath her shirt burned her skin. All she had to do was balance on her tiptoes and gingerly press her mouth to his, allowing herself freedom she'd been denied for years.

But she couldn't.

She opened the door wider.

"You can't do that anymore."

"Do what?" he asked with a frown.

"*This*." She waved in the thick air between them. "We can't be what we used to be. What we had required trust."

As if a new angle could help him see her point of view better, he tilted his head in that infuriating way that both annoyed her *and* made her itch to paint him. The position showcased the minute muscles in his jawline, the ones that were impossible to get down perfectly in portraits without him clenching his jaw right in front of her.

"Han." His defeated sigh made her blink away from those muscles and return to the conversation. "I know leaving ruined everything, but you can trust me in this. I only ever wanted what was best for you. To keep you safe." His chin jutted toward the bathroom where the sound of water rushing from the faucet leaked underneath the door. "And now, Tommy. After we take down the General and I know you're out of danger, I'll leave you alone."

That knifelike pain stabbed into her heart again. He was saying all the right things, but implying that it was best to leave her—*again*—somehow still felt like yet another betrayal.

"Good." She coughed to clear the wavering in her voice. "See you in the morning, Hawkins."

His charcoal eyes burned with the emotions still boiling between them, but he didn't say a word as he nodded and left the apartment. She refused to watch him walk away from her again, so she quickly closed the door and locked it tight. Some part of her still hoped he'd stop her, but he never did. He just left.

Again.

The knowledge that she was surely going to have her heart broken all over again gnawed at her stomach, making her hurt from the inside out. She tried to breathe through the pain as she went into mom mode, tucking Tommy into his side of the large bed before getting ready herself.

When she came out of the bathroom, she laughed softly at the sight of her son already sprawled out like a starfish across the mattress. Thankfully, it was the biggest bed she'd seen in a long time, and she still had plenty of room on her side. But as she finally slipped under the covers, that ache she'd been ignoring throughout the night—throughout the *years*, really—burrowed into her soul, keeping her up.

She lay for hours, trying to come to terms with her new reality as she stared at the blank ceiling. Bare, just like the rest of his apartment. When sleep finally claimed her thoughts, she turned over and inhaled deeply.

Leather. Pine. The dewy freshness of a spring morning.

She'd started over and over and over so many times, all by herself. She could do it again.

Couldn't she?

But as the scent and memories she'd tried to rid herself of for years soaked back into her skin, she wondered if she'd ever been free from them in the first place.

# CHAPTER ELEVEN

## Nine years ago

The rich combination of worn leather, earthy pine, and the dewy freshness of a spring morning. Add popcorn and stadium food on top of that and nothing could beat the smell of major league baseball opening day.

"Coming by you, Eagle."

Eagle leaned back in his seat, allowing Hannah room as Hawk helped her return to her seat between the two of them. A whiff of sugar and oranges wafted under his nose and he couldn't help the deep inhale.

Well, *almost* nothing could beat the scents of opening day.

"Thanks for keeping our seats safe, brother." Hawk lifted his chin.

"Sure. Yeah, no problem," he mumbled as he watched his best friends get settled in their seats again. "Did you guys come back empty-handed?"

"*Ugh*. I know Phoenix couldn't come because of some 'book club meeting,' but he'll have to wait until the next game to get his own damn hat. Maybe by the time he decides to actually see a game they'll have finally changed the branding. Then *he* can stand in the crazy long lines and get *me* all the memorabilia while *I* get to watch the game."

"Is that what took you guys so long? The gift shop?" Eagle chuckled.

"Yes! I thought Hawk was going to have a conniption." She poked Hawk and a cute smile curved her rosy lips. "But it's not like we're going to miss anything. Baseball games last *hours*."

Hannah laughed, but Eagle lost focus as he overanalyzed the way Hawk fidgeted in his seat.

Men like Hawk don't *fidget*, but the box in the man's pocket had to be burning a hole in his jeans.

After Hawk dropped the *engagement* bomb, time had simultaneously sped up and slowed down. Like the milliseconds after a baseball cracks off a bat and you're not sure if you have enough time to catch it before it hits you square in the nose.

He wasn't sure how he'd feel after Hawk proposed and he'd been trying to protect himself from getting smacked in the face ever since. Would it be a triumphant catch? Would he be happy for his friends? Or would it break him?

His new MF7 team had been his only solace, even as the actual work had been scary as fuck. When he'd agreed to start a new force with General Smithers, he'd thought they'd have months—or even years—of training, like every other military branch. But General Smithers had made them hit the ground running.

They'd already had quite a few missions against local sex traffickers. The takedowns were of low-level pimps, nowhere near what Eagle knew the General had in store for them. MF7 was meant to eradicate trafficking rings all over the world and his team was already getting a little frustrated they weren't going for the big guns at the top. They were risking their lives bunting fastballs when they should've been swinging for the fences.

Eagle got the theory behind it though. It was hard to train like every other Special Forces team when they *weren't* every other Special Forces team. They were technically paramilitary, off-the-books, and only answering to one man. The type of security clearance that made him wonder whether the president was even in on it. That was the only way to ensure American government officials answered for their crimes if they'd been compromised themselves. It was a lofty goal but his team was the best of the best. Every one of his teammates had been handpicked by himself with General Smithers's guidance.

The only person he and General Smithers disagreed on needing was Hawk. Eagle'd had reservations about including him on the team. Not due to his skill, though, far from it. He'd been one of the best Night Stalkers the Army had ever seen, an amazing instructor, a hell of a leader, and an even better best friend.

Thinking about their friendship was when Eagle's guilt crept in. He knew how heartbroken Hannah would be once Hawk inevitably had to say goodbye to her—whether the man believed he'd have to or not. It was true that asking the team to leave their loved ones behind was unprecedented even by special ops military standards. Hawk thought he could make it work, keep Hannah and the dream career, while Eagle was skeptical. Then again, if anyone could do it, it'd be him.

That was why Eagle was sitting in the stands on opening day for the Atlanta Braves, about to witness the biggest moment of his best friend's life, knowing the whole relationship would surely end in disaster.

Eagle wasn't even supposed to be there. When Hawk had talked about the details of the proposal, he'd confessed he'd grown nervous about the idea since the team had bypassed training and gone straight into missions. He'd questioned whether he should do something more low-key, but Eagle had seen it as *his* opportunity to shine.

He'd told Hawk he was overreacting because they'd only dealt with easy targets thus far. While that was true, in reality, Eagle wanted that big moment to finally act on his *own* feelings. To see if he truly loved Hannah, or if he just coveted the love between his friends. If it was the former, he'd have the balls to stand up and interrupt the proposal. If it was the latter, well, then he'd shut the fuck up and clap with the rest of the stands.

But then Hawk had metaphorically slammed the door on that idea when he told Eagle it would just be him and Hannah at the game. That'd been the plan at least.

Last week, Eagle and Phoenix had been playing video games when Hawk brought Hannah home to their apartment after a date. Hawk had invited Hannah to the game right then and she'd turned around and invited Eagle and Phoenix out of the goodness of her heart.

Phoenix had been able to get out of it, coming up on the fly with some fake-ass bullshit about a book club. But even as Hawk had silently shaken his head, Eagle had jumped at the chance and said he'd love to go.

Eagle glanced over at Hawk who was now compulsively staring at the scoreboard every time there was a lull in the game. Hawk likely waited with bated breath during every announcement, despite the fact he'd been given the exact time it would roll onto the giant screen. Poor guy was a wreck.

"Hawk, *mi amor*, you are a mess today. What has gotten into you?"

His shoulders lifted casually in a shrug, but his biceps were straining against the short sleeves of his Braves jersey and his knee looked like it was about to take off on its own if he didn't kneel soon. "Just watching the game, dove. No big deal."

Eagle snorted but Hawk's evil eye prompted him to clear his throat and straighten in his chair.

"Ah, give the man a break. It's a close game," he offered, only gaining Hannah's discerning eye.

"Mhmm... okay, the game's nowhere near 'close.' You're both being weird and you have been for weeks now. What gives? Is something wrong?"

"No, Han, nothing's wrong. I promise." A warm, encouraging smile stretched across Hawk's face and Hannah relaxed in her seat.

The way they gazed at each other sparked a jealous fire in Eagle's stomach. One he'd been able to ignore for years, but now burned him from the inside out.

He looked away, unable to keep watching them, and turned his eyes to the game.

Hannah was right, the Braves had this game in the bag. What Hawk had planned would be the cherry on top of a great opening day.

And Eagle wasn't sure he could bear it.

The ball cracked against the hitter's bat, drawing Eagle from his pity party. He found the foul pop fly high in the sky and followed its descent onto the field, directly in front of their seats, and right into a Braves player's mitt, and securing the final out of the inning. The crowd leapt to their feet and a figure darted across the stairs in front of their section.

Eagle frowned and glanced around, his senses kicking into high gear as he tried to find the person. He wasn't sure why it was important. The stadium was packed, so there were plenty of people crossing in and out of his vision. But something in his gut told him he needed to be on alert.

He absentmindedly clapped along with the fans, still searching as everyone milled around and left their seats during the inning change. When he didn't find anyone or anything suspicious, he slowly returned to his own seat. Taking advantage of the fact the elderly couple next to him had gotten up for refreshments, he feigned stretching in his seat so he could keep looking. But there was nothing.

Several chords blared on the speaker, making Eagle jolt. A large figure barreled up the aisle toward them. Eagle reached for the holster he'd snuck in underneath his Braves jersey... only to realize it was just a cameraman.

*Thank fuck.*

He and Hawk had been tricking the metal detectors to get into Braves games for years. It was nerve-wracking to hide his pistol right next to his dick, but underneath a brass belt buckle was the surefire way to fool the security guards when they had to resort to their handheld wand metal detectors after setting off the walk-through metal detectors. Once they were given the all clear, the two of them would then go into the bathroom and store their guns in their waistband holsters instead. Carrying at an MLB game was overly cautious, no doubt, but at least he knew he could protect himself.

*...from a fucking cameraman.*

Eagle shook his head at his own paranoia just as the speakers crackled, preceding a very cheerful announcer.

*"Ladies and gentlemen, I'd like to direct you to the scoreboard screen for a very special proposal."*

Eagle's thumping heart tanked into his stomach. He almost wished it'd been an attacker instead.

Still, the stress zapping through Eagle dissipated once he saw his two best friends still standing, all eyes on them. Hawk's brilliant smile gleamed in the stadium lighting and tears welled in his eyes. Eagle couldn't see Hannah's face so he turned to watch the show that was right in front of him play out on the scoreboard screen instead.

The joy on her face dissolved all of Eagle's jealousy. Hawk fumbled adorably as he attempted to remove the ring from its box. Once Hannah seemed to realize exactly what was going on, she gasped so loudly Eagle could hear it over the crowd. She covered her smile with both hands, but her rounded, sun-kissed cheeks gave away the fact she was still grinning wildly. When Hawk finally got the ring free, her gorgeous brown eyes widened.

Even though Hawk had invited Eagle to help pick the ring out, he still didn't know what it looked like.

Granted, "helped" was a generous word for the sulking and shrugging he'd subjected Hawk to that day. Hawk had already known exactly what Hannah would love, he just wanted company. He'd even thanked Eagle for being there, saying something about how he wished his pops was still alive to go with him, too.

Hawk's gratitude hadn't made Eagle more accommodating, though. Being in that goddamn store had been the last place Eagle had wanted to be. He'd been so shitty that Hawk hadn't even bought a ring. He'd gone back to pick one later without Eagle's salty ass. From the look on Hannah's face, he'd chosen perfectly, despite Eagle's best efforts.

She was obviously going to say yes, so if he ever wanted to say anything, to *confess* anything, then *this* was the moment.

But Eagle watched on in silence as his best friend proposed to the love of his life—the woman of Eagle's dreams. Part of him was even elated for them both, but he still couldn't muster up even half the excitement the strangers in the crowd showed. At least the harder he worked at keeping up appearances during the proposal, the harder it was to concentrate on the proposal itself. He was so preoccupied with schooling his face for the damn camera, the bright-neon question exploding on the screen was practically a blur.

Hawk enveloped Hannah's hand in his and slowly began to kneel. Eagle watched like an extra in a movie as the main character said those five life-changing words out loud.

"Han, will you marry me—"

A loud *crack* pierced the air. Eagle snapped his gaze to the field, expecting to see one of the players running the bases. But the players were looking to the stands, seemingly just as confused as he felt. When it happened again, screams ignited across the stadium.

In the next moment, the air was knocked from his lungs as Hannah was thrust into him. He fell to the ground, pinballing between the empty seats before his back finally hit the pavement in front of his chair. Hannah wriggled and cursed, fighting to get off of him, but his arms latched around her tight, refusing to let her go.

"Hawkins Black! Why the hell would you push—"

Hawk leaned over them both and cut Hannah off by pressing her farther against Eagle.

"Those are gunshots," Hawk grunted as he searched the stands with wide eyes.

Eagle had never seen the man look so panicked. But the way Hawk's gaze darted between Hannah and finding the shooter, Eagle realized it wasn't just Hawk's panic he was seeing for the first time.

It was fear.

Another shot rang out and the stadium ground underneath Eagle's back thudded as everyone stampeded to safety. Eagle could see people's heads bobbing over the rim of the seats as they fled, but even though fewer and fewer people remained, the bullets kept zipping just over their section.

Hawk ducked and shielded both Eagle and Hannah with his body. A chunk of the seat Hawk crouched behind scattered around them.

This wasn't just any shooter. *They* were the targets.

When Hawk leaned up again, Eagle shifted so Hannah was shielded between the two of them. Hawk yanked Eagle's Braves jersey collar and whisper-shouted in his ear.

"There's more than one. But the one I saw looked very fucking familiar."

Eagle's already racing heart stuttered. "One of the jobs?"

Hawk nodded, not needing to clarify that one of the bastards from their missions was now targeting them.

Alarms suddenly blasted over the speakers. Interspersed between three blaring warning tones was a prerecorded public service announcement.

*"Attention all patrons: there is a report of an active shooter in the stadium. Please calmly and safely—"*

Another crack of a gun made Hannah scream. Hawk stretched his broad body to completely cover her, further sandwiching her between them both. She tried to duck into Hawk's chest, but Eagle held her closer, fighting her instincts to seek out her boyfriend for safety.

Hawk pulled away and shot his own gun over the rim of one

of the green plastic chairs. A man screamed just as another bullet clipped the seat beside Hawk.

Hawk ducked and when the shots stopped firing, he pulled Hannah by the nape toward him and kissed her fiercely on the lips. Eagle felt her melt in his arms for another man, but before the jealousy could take root in his gut, Hawk broke it off and locked eyes with Eagle.

"Get her out of here and I'll draw them away. Once she's safe, I'll take care of them."

Eagle nodded and grabbed Hannah. Her formerly pliant body turned rigid as she tried to escape him.

"Hawk, no! Come with us! Please, *mi cielo*! Please!" Hannah cried out, reaching for Hawk.

He shook his head. "I love you, dove." Another bullet sliced through the green plastic chair next to Hawk's head like butter. His focused eyes found Eagle as he shouted, "*Go!*"

Hawk leapt from the ground and ran like hell, drawing gunfire his way. The stadium had nearly emptied out around them, so he had no trouble leaping, jumping, and crouching down the row.

After he made it to the next section of stands, Eagle did the same, ignoring Hannah's pleas and the scratches she made on his forearm. He picked her up and carried her, one arm around her waist, his pistol drawn in the other.

All hell had broken loose topside as the packed stands funneled through the much-too-small aisles and gates. Everyone was so concerned with their own safety no one even noticed the woman being lugged around, screaming her head off.

"No! We can't leave him!"

"Stop moving, or I can't defend us!" he yelled, but it was no use.

She tried to wriggle away and turn around, but Eagle halted his running to grasp her tighter. A bullet whizzed in front of him, right where he would've been if he hadn't stopped to grab her.

"Shit, that was way too damn close."

Out of the corner of Eagle's eye, Hawk raced from his shielded position behind a row of seats and picked off the guy that'd shot at Eagle. Before another shooter could take out Hawk, he leapt over one of the metal handrails on the stairs and landed into a crouch in an adjacent row.

"Come on," Eagle ordered Hannah. "We have to get out of here."

"But Hawk! What if he gets hurt?"

"Then don't let his sacrifice be in vain. Let's go!"

He didn't wait for her to respond. Instead, he hauled Hannah up and clumsily sprinted with her toward the closest exit. When he glanced back to check on his friend, Hawk's recklessness made Eagle's heart hammer impossibly harder in his chest.

The man who always played by the rules was breaking all normal protocol, not bothering to take cover as he shot out in the open, hopping dangerously through the rows, and obviously doing everything and anything he could to draw away the attackers to keep Hannah safe.

Eagle dragged his gaze away to focus on escaping and concentrating on getting them to the lower ground level. When he navigated Hannah toward the stairs, he whisked her down them, three at a time, and raced through the last rows.

A metal guardrail stood between them and the lowest level. Hannah yelped as he plopped her onto the other side without warning before leaping over the railing himself.

The ground-level exit was feet away, and he half carried her again through it until they ran smack into a stampeding crush of people trying to flee. Instead of fighting through the crowd toward the main exit, Eagle shoved across to a discreet employee exit on the other side, both thanking and cursing the fact that Hawk's paranoia panned out. Eagle had thought he was a lunatic for making them memorize all the exits, but he was sure as fuck grateful now.

A pang of guilt sparked in his chest. Eagle had been the one to convince Hawk to go through with the stadium proposal. He'd told Hawk it would be safe.

"Leave it to me to be wrong as fuck," Eagle muttered.

"What?"

He shook his head at Hannah's question. "Nothing. Come on, this way."

He tugged her through the door and pulled her to the rendezvous point, a bench on a sidewalk close enough to the stadium that the building provided cover. The small patch of pavement probably served as an employee break area, but it would be their sanctuary for now.

Once they arrived, he dropped Hannah's hand and crouched to his knees, trying to catch his breath and bearings.

This was all his fault.

The whole reason why Eagle had insisted the proposal be at the Braves game was because he'd promised himself this would be *the* moment. The do-or-die game-time decision where Eagle would either have the courage to stop the proposal and tell his best friend's girl *he* loved her, or he'd realize his feelings had nothing to do with loving the girl and everything to do with the dream of being loved.

Logically, he knew Hannah would never choose him. She'd been in love with Hawk from the day they'd met.

But Eagle wanted what Hawk had and Eagle had promised himself he would at least try.

And he hadn't.

He'd sat there, a torturous blend of happiness and despair swirling inside him as his best friend made his own dream come true.

"Who were those guys?" Hannah asked, still huffing for breath beside him. Her black hair had flown out of her side braid, and her forehead glistened with perspiration.

Eagle shook his head but Hannah didn't let it go. She was like a dog with a bone when she was onto something and she'd always been able to run all over him. Only Hawk could make her relax when she was riled up. Hawk was her port in the storm and Eagle was just the rocks keeping her from safety.

"You guys said they were a 'job?' What does that mean?"

Eagle cringed at her words. She might've been one of his best friends and now that she was potentially at risk in all this, she might've even deserved to know the whole truth, but instead of explaining it to her, he took the coward's way out.

*Like always.*

"You'll have to ask him, Hannah. Right now isn't the time."

Hannah fixed her angry eyes on him and frowned, but a siren on the other side of the stadium pierced the air, making her jolt. Her narrowed gaze widened as she seemed to recognize that they weren't out of the woods yet. Instead of arguing, she stared at the door they'd just barreled through, worry now replacing frustration.

"Do you think he's okay?" she whispered, twirling the brand-new ring on her left hand.

Its royal-blue sapphire emerald-cut stone was flanked on each side by a smaller aquamarine gem and a diamond. The sparkling combination of blue with the gold band complemented her gorgeous warm-olive skin. Beautiful and understated. Bright and unique. It was perfect.

Eagle's heart ached at the sight, but he had no way of knowing whether it was because the woman he loved was yet another step away from ever being his, or because the love of *her* life might be gone already, and he was doing jack shit to help.

*But if Hawk is gone, then maybe I have a shot with Han—*

"Thomas, please answer me. Do you think he's—"

"He'll be fine!" Eagle snapped, horrified at his own thoughts. Shock and hurt flattened her full lips into a thin line and he sighed. "Seriously, he'll be fine, Hannah. I swear."

That thought had been a fluke. A disgusting mistake of an idea only a total monster would think. He hoped to God he wasn't lying to Hannah and Hawk was fine. Eagle fought the urge to go back in and find his best friend, but if something happened to Hannah, Hawk would never forgive him. Hell, he'd never forgive himself.

The idiotic alarm still instructed civilians to "please calmly and safely" escape a fucking *active shooter*, but at least it was muffled behind the stadium walls. The one siren had become many and they now seemed to be all around them.

Stress bunched the muscles in his shoulders and his fingers gripped the gun tighter.

"Thomas, what if—"

Eagle shushed her just as the employee door *clicked* and cracked open. He grabbed Hannah's arm and slung her behind him before aiming the pistol.

A tall, broad figure emerged from behind the steel door and Eagle's shoulders slouched with relief.

"*Hawk!*"

"Han—"

Hannah sobbed as she shoved past Eagle and flung herself at Hawk, wrapping her legs around his waist. He clung to her and threaded his hand through her thick raven hair, holding her tight.

"You're okay, baby," he whispered. The obvious relief in his deep timbre tightened Eagle's chest. "You're okay. We're okay."

"Who were those people? Where are they now? Are... are they dead?" Her watery voice muffled as she snuggled farther into Hawk's embrace.

Hawk's eyes caught Eagle's over the top of her head. Resolve and heartbreak hardened Hawk's jaw.

"We'll talk about it when we get home, dove. Right now, we have to go."

"Don't you need to talk to the police?" she asked as she pulled away to search his face. The steady wail of sirens seemed to punctuate her question.

"I'll explain later," Hawk answered as he released her from his grasp, but he kept her hand in his as his focused gaze narrowed on Eagle.

"I need to get Hannah home. Call who you need to in order to get all this straightened out."

"Copy that," Eagle answered, not caring that his second-in-command was giving him orders.

He understood the sorrow and determination on his friend's face. The man's mind was made up and while Eagle understood what Hawk had to do, understanding didn't make reality less heartbreaking.

They were already in danger and MF7 hadn't even left the Atlanta base. General Smithers was right.

Hawk was trapped in MF7 until their contract was over, maybe even afterward, too, depending on how many enemies they made and how successful they were at getting rid of them. And General Smithers had made it clear he would press charges for desertion if Hawk quit or ran away.

Despite the new ring tying them together, Hawk would have to sever the cord to keep Hannah safe from their job.

Then, as much as Hawk would hate it, he would have to leave her behind. She would be a loose end.

And loose ends get cut.

# CHAPTER TWELVE

## Present Day

One of the things Hannah had to come to terms with when she went on the run was that her son snored.

*Loudly*.

She'd been fortunate enough to always find two-bedroom apartments and houses within her budget to rent. But those first few weeks of hotel hopping had been pure torture, in large part because she'd been exhausted as hell thanks to her little lumber-jack sawing logs in the same room.

According to Hawk's ancient radio alarm clock that Hannah suspected had belonged to his late pops, it was six a.m. That meant it was five a.m. in Mérida and from the way she'd tossed and turned, there was no way she'd slept more than three and a half hours throughout the night. She was practically delirious.

*Hawk's probably up, too.*

Her eyes widened at the unbidden thought.

*Now I know I'm delirious. Why the hell would I care about that?*

She frowned and shook her head before finally calling it quits and rolling silently out of bed. It wasn't like she'd ever wake up Tommy. The boy slept like the logs he sawed. But looking at the blank ceiling all night had sparked two ideas and she wanted to see them both through before Tommy woke.

The first was that she still owed him a batch of tea. She hoped the facility had the brand she liked, but she'd settle for any tea at this point. Tommy needed a sense of normalcy in this new home and she was hoping she could help him find it with a simple glass of sweet iced tea.

The second thing she wanted to do had been on her mind since they'd flown in and landed on the BlackStone Securities roof helipad last night. The facility was at the bottom of the Appalachian Mountains and they'd arrived too late to properly see the view, so she'd been itching to check it out.

Without making a sound, she quickly grabbed her duffel bag and went to the bathroom to get ready for the day. She changed into worn jeans and a simple T-shirt with a scoop neck so she could tuck her necklace underneath and braided her hair. She slid into a pair of sneakers and waited for one of Tommy's particularly obnoxious snores before opening the door and walking backward to sneak out.

After closing the door behind her softly, she smiled to herself at the little bubble of excitement in her chest. Without wasting another second, she spun around on her heel... and crashed into a broad man carrying a large bundle in his arms.

She opened her mouth to shriek, but the man lunged at her and cupped his calloused hand over her mouth. The movement made her stumble against the wall, bringing them both into the dim light.

"*Shiffft*," Hawk mumbled what sounded like a curse past a paintbrush he clenched between his teeth. He spit the stick out of his mouth into one of the many bags he'd shifted to hold in one hand so he could silence her with the other. "Shh, Han, it's just me, dove. Don't be scared."

At his assurance, the pounding in her chest immediately subsided. Whether he meant to, or not, his entire body had her flush against the wall. His scent overwhelmed her and she closed her eyes, letting her body relax underneath his touch, just like it used to.

Her breaths slowed and she opened her eyes again to see his lips lifting in a grin that didn't reach all the way to his eyes.

"There you go. That's it." He gently removed his hand from her mouth. "You okay?"

He didn't step back, and shock tingled her skin as she realized she didn't want him to. His strong chest rose and fell with hers as he searched her face for answers and his sturdy frame clad in his black long-sleeve Henley nearly eclipsed the light in the hallway. What shined through highlighted the muscles in his sharp jawline as they ticced with concern.

"Hannah?"

Her eyes shot up to his hooded gaze. "Yeah?"

"You okay, dove?"

The liquid velvet in his words made her lower belly flip and she dropped her gaze to the lush lips the delicious voice dripped from. It'd been so long since she'd been this close to any man at all, let alone Hawk, and her drained body had a mind of its own.

Hawk leaned closer, and she perched on her tiptoes. He balled his hand into a fist above her head as he caged her in, making her feel safe from the world. A plastic bag bumped into her breasts—

*Wait.*

Hannah jolted and pushed Hawk's chest lightly. It was only enough to put an inch between them, but he stumbled back.

"Sorry, I—"

"Damn, Hannah, I'm sorry—"

The blurted-out words collided between them and they both paused before chuckling.

"Sorry about that," she tried again. "I don't know what came over me. I think I'm still half-asleep." She chuckled awkwardly before continuing, "Old habits die hard, I guess."

"Yeah... uh, I didn't sleep very well either." A flicker of hurt wrinkled his face and then it was gone. That almost smile spread over his lips again, and her fingers itched to trace its ever-so-slight curve. "Then again, not all habits have to die, you know. Some are good for you."

His implication sent tingles up her spine, but before she could respond, he cleared his throat and laid the bags down beside the door.

"Been shopping?" she asked and grimaced. "I mean not right now, of course, the sun hasn't even risen yet."

"Yeah, actually. Ellie brought some clothes from the clinic in one of those bags. The other came from a craft store in town. I'm glad you woke up in time—"

"Woke up in time?" she murmured. Her eyes narrowed as she inspected the bags, opening each one to find clothes, paintbrushes, canvas—

"Hawk, did you buy me painting supplies?" Hannah's voice lilted in excitement as she sifted through the various colors of paint. "*Mierda*, these are some great brands, too."

"Really? That's good, that's good. I tried to remember the ones you liked but I double-checked online. And then I triple-checked with the associate at the store. There's also a bigger crafts store in the city—"

"*Hawk*." She straightened and walked toward him, trying not to giggle as she interrupted his rambling. The man's confidence was sexy, but she couldn't deny he was cute when he was flustered, too. It happened so infrequently, she almost hated to interrupt it. "Thank you. This was—*is*—amazing."

"Happy to do it." A shy smile spread across his face before he shook his head. "So yeah, uh, I checked and sunrise is in about fifteen minutes. Should give you enough time to set up."

*Sunrise.*

"You remembered?" Her voice was soft, even to her own ears. It was one of those things about a relationship that was so small, insignificant even, but it would have broken her heart to learn he'd forgotten.

*He brought back the ocean sunrise landscape canvas from Mérida... of course he "remembers."*

Disappointment stung her chest until he stepped closer and dipped his head to hold her gaze.

"I could go a thousand nights and never forget your sunrise, dove."

Emotion clogged Hannah's throat, making it impossible to speak. After a moment of heating up under his burning charcoal eyes, all she could do was nod her head and whisper her thanks.

"Happy to do it," he repeated. "I'll, uh—Do you want an escort up there?"

"No!" she blurted out. His brow rose and she bit back a wince. She hadn't meant to come off so strongly, but another minute with him was surely going to make her lose all her resolve. "I mean... no, *thank* you. I remember how to get there from last night."

"Got it. Well... I'll leave you to it. See you afterward for the meeting?"

"S-sounds good. See you then. Oh, wait—"

"Yeah?" Hawk asked, a hopeful look lifting his lips.

"Do you guys, um, do you happen to have sweet tea? The good kind?"

Emotion flickered over his face before his lips settled into an easy smile. "Yeah, we're all stocked up."

"Good." She nodded. "Thank you."

He lifted his hand to say goodbye and turned to the elevator in the center of the long hall. She couldn't watch him leave. The ache in her chest was too strong. So she gathered the supplies and quietly brought them into the room. When she closed the door behind her, she leaned against the steel and searched the dark ceiling for answers, trying to catch her breath.

More than anything, she wanted to run out of the apartment, catch Hawk, kiss him like mad, and then invite him to the roof to sit with her while she painted the sky, like old times.

But it'd been so long and there was so much unspoken between them. So much hurt. Hell, she'd believed he was dead until yesterday.

It was too soon, right? Was she crazy for wanting to wait? Or was she crazy for even wanting to try again?

Did *he* even want to try again?

The thought that this pull between them was all in her head made her stomach twist with nausea. He'd claimed he was all in before, and then he'd pulled the rug out from underneath her. That couldn't happen again. Especially since there was so much more at stake than her hurt feelings this time.

They'd been in their twenties when they dated. No care about anyone except for themselves and their careers. Now she had Tommy to think about. And Hawk still had his team as his number one priority.

Realization sank in like being dunked in an ice bath.

He still had his team. His *family*. He didn't need her before. He wouldn't need her now.

"Well, I don't need him, either," she said before catching herself. She snapped her mouth shut out of fear she'd wake her son.

But Tommy snored back at her, loud as ever, and she huffed a laugh to herself. She walked around the apartment, considering her next move and fiddling with her necklace until the alarm clock caught her eye. Six thirty.

Sunrise.

Her eyes drifted to the bags beside the door.

"They really are such good brands..." she reasoned with herself quietly.

It'd been ages since she'd had good supplies to paint with. Ever since she'd been on the run, her cache—if you could call it that—had been dwindling. Plus, she needed an outlet, especially since the meeting with BlackStone was bound to be stressful. *And* she hadn't painted a good Blue Ridge sunrise in a hot minute...

As she bargained with herself, she tiptoed toward the bags beside the door. From what she could tell when she searched them earlier, she had almost everything she could possibly need. Bright, shiny, and new, begging to be used.

It only took half a second more of Tommy's snoring for her to make up her mind.

She looped the bags around her wrist before opening the door and closing it behind her.

"First, I'll make tea. Then I'll test out the brushes... just a little," she murmured absentmindedly before reassuring herself one last time. "No big deal. No big deal at all."

# CHAPTER THIRTEEN

The sunrise shone brilliantly that morning as Hannah worked, color toning the canvas so the landscape would have a unifying base coat instead of boring off-white. She lost herself in the gentle susurrus of brush against the slightly coarse surface and the repetitive flick of the wrist. Only the rooftop asphalt steadily heating up underneath her made her realize how much time had passed.

She cursed her one-track mind before packing her easel and power walking across the hot roof.

"This thing really could use some earth tones to keep it from reflecting the sun and making it hot as a desert up here," she muttered before leaving the canvas and paints inside the roof's stairwell landing and racing back to the room to wake Tommy.

While he was getting ready, she had a few sips of the orange blossom sweet tea she'd set out to cool. It was the perfect combination of citrus and sweet, so she poured a mason jar on ice for Tommy and stored the rest of the pitcher in the refrigerator. Tommy drank the tea in one gulp before they both ran down to the first floor to meet with Hawk's team with only seconds to spare.

She'd seriously considered leaving him to binge on TV all day, but they'd just abruptly moved across countries yet again. He should have a sense of autonomy over their situation and the meeting with the team about why Hawk had insisted they move to Ashland County would be a good start to giving power back to both of them. Besides, leaving him all alone in a brand-new place with people he didn't trust was bound to lead to more psychological damage than their lives had already inflicted.

The BlackStone Securities facility was a modern, windowless industrial warehouse that had been fortified into a castle in desperate need of a pop of color. It was a high-tech fortress, too, if the room they were in now was any indication.

The *war room*—as Hawk called it—was a large conference room with the same staid, industrial aesthetic as the rest of the building. There wasn't much to it other than a massive conference table and a wall of computer monitors.

At the moment, they showed footage from the security cameras positioned around the facility—though not in her room, Hawk had promised—and other places around town. Wes sat at a desk in front of the screens and the rest of the crowd she'd met the night before—sans Marco, who was apparently working one of his other cases—stood or sat around a round conference table.

Once again, all eyes were on her and Tommy as the team waited for her to fill them in on the missing pieces of the last nine years of all their lives.

"So... from the beginning?"

"Are you sure Tommy needs to be here for this? My girlfriend Naomi could watch him—"

"He stays... for now at least." Her son frowned at the caveat, and she turned to speak to both him and the team. "Our lives haven't been easy, but I've promised my son he would be as informed as possible. He stays until there's something I feel like I need to filter for him."

"Fair enough. We'll keep it PG-ish as much as we can." Wes nodded.

"Good luck," Phoenix huffed.

Wes cut him an exasperated glance before continuing. "Start as far back as you think is necessary."

Her eyes cut to Hawk's, searching for guidance. But whatever he was thinking was carefully hidden behind his gaze.

She used to know every curve and line in each expression he had. The new fine wrinkles in his dark-sienna skin helped mask any emotion underneath.

What had he been through to have frown lines deeper than the laughing ones at the corners of his eyes? Would she ever know?

"From the beginning..." She trailed off and glanced at Tommy seated beside her.

His arms were crossed in that almost comically serious way he had. At least, it was comical until she remembered it was their fucked-up situation that'd made him that way.

Did she need to go back to the moment Hawk told her he was choosing all of the people in front of her over her? The cause—eradicating human trafficking across the globe—was something she'd supported in the grand scheme of things. But selfishly, it'd never made sense to her that he'd choose a pipe dream over the real-life love story he'd had in front of him. She'd actually begged him to quit and run away with her instead, something she admittedly wasn't proud of. She'd known it then just as she did now. If he had quit, her father would've ruined him, maybe even court martialed him. He'd said as much when she'd pleaded with him to release Hawk from the MF7 contract.

Over the years before she finally ran away, her father had no problem throwing it in her face that Hawk had chosen him and the military life over her. Of course, Hawk hadn't known the depth of the complicated relationship she had with her father. The fact that Hawk had no idea was her fault, not his.

She'd never been able to open up to him about the things in her past that she'd only recently come to grips with as abuse. Her head was in the sand about it back then. Over the past two years, though, she'd had no choice but to confront her demons—mentally, at least. Physically, she'd run like hell.

Hawk had said he was choosing her life and safety by staying in MF7 and leaving her behind. He'd claimed then that the shooting at the Braves game was caused by local traffickers his team had taken down. Later, the bastards who were caught had records a mile long, including trafficking, so the story had checked out.

But what would Hawk do when he found out that leaving her had been exactly what her father had wanted? And with her father in the picture, she'd never been safe.

She blew out a breath but felt no less stressed as she finally began, "I'll start at the party."

The pretty blonde with tan skin, Ellie, and the woman who looked creepily similar to Hannah, Callie, both piped up in unison.

"The Scholarship Fundraiser?"

"The party?"

Hannah nodded slowly. "Um, yeah. The Ashland County Scholarship Fundraiser. I am—*was*—an art teacher. Around two years ago, I got an invitation to go to a fundraiser that gave scholarships to bright and promising art students across the southeast. I received Teacher of the Year that year..."

As she mentioned her award, she didn't miss how Hawk's lips curved upward in a smile. The pride on his face made her chest light, giving her the courage to walk through the rest of the details.

"The invite was from some company—"

"Charitable Technologies International?" Wes asked.

"That's the one. I'd never heard of them before then, but I sure as hell know them now."

"Same here," Nora, the woman with purple curls and rose gold–framed glasses, mumbled across the table.

"Well, they invited me under the guise that I would present the award for an art scholarship. I was excited to go. Got a sitter and drove all the way from Atlanta to Ashland County. But once I arrived, I quickly realized something... *weird* was going on."

"How so?" Jules asked down the table, not looking up from her legal pad as she took notes.

"Well, for starters, when I got there and asked for instructions, no one knew about the scholarship I was asking about." Hannah chuckled wryly. "I stayed, thinking I must've gotten something wrong. But when I was about to leave, a big bald man called me into a room. I found out later his name was Vlad—"

"Motherfucker," Draco muttered behind Nora.

"Draco, the kid's *right* there." The one with the scar right above his left ear, Jason, pointed to Tommy.

Tommy shrugged. "I've said worse."

Hannah felt her eyes bug out as she turned on her hellion of a son. "*¡Ay! ¡Dios mio!* Oh my god, Tomás Hawkins! I know you didn't just say that." She narrowed her eyes into slits until the boy had the good sense to look chagrined. "You make it sound like I'm okay with you cursing like a sailor."

"Sorry, mom," he grumbled. The bright red in his tan cheeks almost made her smirk, but she returned her attention back to the rest of the room.

"I swear, he doesn't go around cursing everywhere. It's just a harmless way we blow off steam when *mierda* hits the fan..." She trailed off at the stark silence and shock on every face staring back at her. "Did I, um, say something wrong?"

She glanced around self-consciously until her gaze finally landed on Hawk. A flurry of emotions passed over his usually carefully blank expression.

"Tomás... Hawkins?" Hawk's voice broke at the end of his own name.

The air in her chest seized and she felt her cheeks heat.

"Yes," she answered simply, even though they both knew he wasn't really asking a question.

She held his gaze, her heartbeat thrumming in her veins. The regret was a palpable thickness in the air between them, and she wondered which questions he hated to dwell on the most.

Early on for her, the worst ruminations centered around that one night. What if Hawk had stayed? What if she hadn't opened the door when his best friend came to console her?

When she'd found out she was pregnant, she'd prayed it was Hawk's so she could have something to remember him by. Logistically, Tommy could have just as easily been his. If he had known, would he have stayed?

But any reality other than the one she'd lived meant she wouldn't have the Tommy she had today. And *that* reality was unacceptable.

"Tommyhawk, huh?"

Hannah's gaze snapped to Phoenix's, prepared to go to battle if the man said one bad word about her kid. But the smile he had on his face was genuine.

Tommy nodded as he watched Phoenix somehow balance on two of his rolling chair's four legs. She saw the gears turning in her mischievous son's head and read his mind when he slowly pushed back from the table to try to do the same. Before he could tip back, Hannah grabbed his hand and shook her head. He frowned back at her and crossed his arms with a slouch, but when Phoenix spoke again, the silent reprimand was forgotten.

"I like it, kid." He jutted his chin up. "It suits ya. Your dad would've liked it, too."

Tommy beamed. "Really?"

"Yeah," Hawk replied, his voice hoarse. "Like I said, your dad was my best friend. He would've loved that his son was named after both of us." Hawk raised his eyes to Hannah's. "Just like I do."

Relief flooded her body and the breath she'd been holding released from her chest. She'd never thought Tommy would meet his namesakes after she'd received her father's taunting KIA letter. Knowing Hawk approved of Tommy's full name made it all the better.

A throat cleared and Hawk's hold on her broke as she searched for the owner. Wes pushed up his glasses.

"You, uh... you were talking about Vlad?"

"Oh, yeah... right." She shook her head. "Sorry about that. Anyway, Vlad told me to follow him into a room designated for scholarship donors. But once I got there—"

A loud childish shriek broke the tension in the room as a small, redheaded girl in a green princess dress sprinted inside, followed by a woman who was clearly her mother.

"Wes!" The girl giggled and leapt into Wes's open arms. "Wes! You're it!"

Wes's shoulders shook with laughter. "I'm 'it,' huh? What're we playing?"

"Hideandseektagcuzthefloorislava. It's a game I made up. Hey, Wes, why is everyone in the bad room?" The little girl suddenly stopped and looked around like she was just now realizing where she was. "It's different than before."

Wes's face clouded. "You're right, Thea. The room *is* different. We fixed it and it's all better now. What happened last time won't ever happen again. You're safe here, understand?"

*What are they talking about?*

Thea nodded slowly before throwing herself around him and hugging him tightly.

"Thea, baby," her mother murmured. "Let's go back upstairs. Wes isn't playin'. He's in a meetin' right now."

"I thought this was a secure facility," Draco grumbled. "How is a child able to sneak up on us?"

"It only guards against people five feet or higher." Phoenix snickered. "That's why Nora can break in all the time."

"Hey!" Nora frowned before seemingly thinking it over and shrugging. "But, you know what? Fair, actually. You kinda have a point. Especially now that we've set up more tech and defenses since the bombing."

The hair on the back of Hannah's neck rose even as the rest of the room broke into unworried chatter. She rested her left hand on Tommy's shoulder and leaned to the right to quietly question Hawk.

"Bombing? What does that mean? Was this place bombed? Are we not safe here?"

"You're safe, dove. I wouldn't have you here if it wasn't," Hawk murmured low, just for her. "I'll explain later."

His hand spanned her jean-clad thigh underneath the table and his strong squeeze gave her comfort while the endearment gave her butterflies. It'd been nearly a decade since she'd heard it and he'd been slipping it in freely ever since he crashed back into her life the day before. Despite everything, her chest tightened at the sentiment.

She wanted to forget him. She'd tried to, at least. For years. Then she'd thought she'd lost him forever. Was forgetting him still what she wanted?

Her attention was tugged away from her thoughts by the little girl's high-pitched voice.

"Where'd you come from?" Thea asked Tommy.

"Mérida," he replied, his voice cut with a defensive edge to it. "Where'd *you* come from?"

"Upstairs." She giggled until something like recognition lit her face and she gasped, "You know Mary-duh? Mommy! Mommy! Mommy! This boy knows Princess Mary-duh!"

The woman laughed and picked the girl up even though she was almost as big as her. "The Mérida Tommy and Miss Hannah came from is a place, not a redheaded princess."

Tommy turned to Hannah with a furrowed brow, but Hannah shrugged, just as unsure as he was of who they were talking about.

"We're headed back upstairs. Sorry to interrupt y'all. She beat me in our tag-floor-is-lava-hide-and-seek mashup game." She bopped Thea on the nose with her finger as they both giggled. "We've stayed at the mountain cabin more than we've ever stayed here, but somehow this four-year-old knows her way 'round way better than I do."

"We're watchin' *Brave* if you wanna come," Thea offered, pointing at Tommy, whose scowl was back on his face.

"The Braves don't play today."

"Yes, it does," Thea insisted with her own face twisted in confusion. "I watch *Brave* whenever Mommy lets me."

"No, you don't. They don't play every day."

"Yes, it does."

"No, they don't."

"Yes, it *does*!"

"*No*, they don't!"

"*Yes, it—*"

"Whoa, whoa, whoa—" Naomi interrupted with a laugh. "I think there's been a slight miscommunication. Thea, the Atlanta *Braves* are a baseball team Tommy likes. Tommy, *Brave* is a movie about Princess Merida. If you would like to come watch that with us, we'll be watchin' the first fifteen minutes on repeat because that's this one's favorite part. But we can watch somethin' else, too, if you'd like. Did you happen to eat lunch? I can fix you a grilled cheese."

Nora looked at her watch and cursed, "Oh my goddess, it's already past noon!"

"We usually have a late lunch, so I'm sure Tommy wouldn't mind eating now. What do you say, *mijo*?"

Hannah studied Tommy as he thought over his options before finally shaking his head.

"I'm not hungry yet. Besides, we're having a meeting. I can't go watch a kid's movie right now."

His tone had a hint of regret, and Hannah's heart ached for him. Tommy was just an eight-year-old boy. He shouldn't have had to be so serious. After everything they'd been through together, she'd only thought it was right to include him in the decisions and meetings that impacted his own life. She'd been moved around like a rag doll most of her childhood, she wanted him to feel like he had some agency in his own life. But was she putting too much on him?

Thea rolled her eyes dramatically, making her red curls flounce around her shoulders.

"Grown-ups *always* have meetin's. I wanna *play*," she all but yelled the last word and everyone but Tommy and Hannah snickered in their seats.

"You can go, you know, *avecito*," Hannah reassured him. "You don't have to be here if you don't want to be, and I can tell you anything you want to know afterward."

Tommy shrugged his slumped shoulders. "Maybe I'll watch it later."

Thea's bottom lip poked out with disappointment, but when Wes piped in, her smile returned easily.

"Hey, Thea, just give us grown-ups a little more time and I'll be up there to watch *Brave* with you, alright?"

The way the little girl beamed at him made Hannah's chest tighten.

"Okay, but if you're late, I get to start it over." She dared a glance at her mother, testing her limits with her meager bargaining.

"I don't negotiate with four-year-olds, T." Thea went back to pouting, but her mother laughed and waved at Hannah. "I'm Naomi, by the way. I don't think we've properly met. Maybe we can chat sometime soon after all this slows down?"

After all this slows down... *what would that feel like?*

Hannah nodded, unable to ignore the hope firing in her chest. "I'd like that."

Naomi's smile widened before she addressed everyone else. "I'll leave y'all to your meeting. See you later. Come on, Thea."

She hoisted her daughter higher on her hip and left the war room to a chorus of "goodbyes" and "see you laters" from Hawk's team.

# CHAPTER FOURTEEN

When all the excitement left the room, silence floated in the air like a storm cloud.

Wes was the first to speak. "So... Vlad?"

The question brought reality crashing back down. She thought about telling Tommy to go follow Naomi and Thea. As a teacher, there were parts of this story she wouldn't dream of telling a child. But as a mother, she'd been through hell and back with her son. Even though she sugarcoated quite a few things, she'd *always* told him the truth. Today would be no different.

"He said he worked for my... um... the General and... he had a video. A live stream actually. Back on the house."

She nodded meaningfully toward Tommy, hoping the team would fill in the blanks that someone was surveilling him while she was out of town. Tommy definitely didn't need to know that not only was there a camera trained on him and his babysitter through the window, but a gun, too. She was banking on the team getting the picture so she wouldn't have to spell it out in front of him.

"And what did you see when you watched the video?" Wes's measured question made her wince.

"Their, um, *target*... in the crosshairs," she answered, referring to the fact Tommy was squarely pictured in the gun scope's camera video image.

Hawk stiffened beside her, his only overt emotion a twitch of his fingers on her thigh. His eyes heated with a rage she'd never seen. A few of the men shifted at the uncomfortable reality, while others muttered curses, despite Tommy being in the room.

"So the General threatened you?" Hawk clarified. "Why?"

The fact that Hawk didn't say "your father" was a blessing. As truthful as she'd been, she'd never outright told Tommy it was his own grandfather they were running from.

"Control," she answered with a sigh. "With him, it's always been about control. I just wish I'd realized it before that night."

Wes leaned forward in his seat. His forehead scrunched in thought before he spoke, "Did Vlad say anything to you?"

Hannah nodded. "It was cryptic and confusing at first, but it helped me put a few things together. He said, 'The General will cut all loose ends, even if they are close to him. Forget anything Eagle told you and do not be a rat.'"

"Eagle?" Hawk asked, his brows furrowed in the center. "What did he tell you?"

Hannah shrugged and shook her head. "Thomas didn't tell me anything."

"Nothing? What do you mean, nothing?" That protective fire she knew burned within him at all times glinted in his eyes as he turned his body toward her. "Did you guys talk about anything MF7-related whenever he asked about Tommy?"

Hannah shifted to hide her discomfort. "After you guys left... I never talked to him again."

"He—you and Tommy—" Hawk cleared his throat. "He left you both?"

"I had no way of getting in touch with him and he never contacted me again after..." Hannah gulped at the admission before continuing. "I only found out he was... *gone* after I got that letter on my doorstep."

"Shit. I'm so sorry, Han—" Hawk stopped, his voice breaking

before he subtly tilted his chin at an obviously bewildered Tommy. "So they never got to meet?"

"No." She cleared her throat. "I'm not even sure he knew about him."

A spark of understanding lit in Hawk's charcoal eyes. He closed them slowly and hung his head. When he finally lifted them again to meet her gaze, the certainty in his voice made her chest ache.

"He knew, Han," Hawk insisted. "We didn't know. But somehow, he did."

"He did?" she asked.

Before Hawk could continue, Phoenix interrupted. "He knew alright. Vlad said Eagle had two attachments that made him—"

"*Phoenix*," Hawk snarled as he whirled on his teammate. Callie elbowed him in the ribs.

"*Ow*, Jesus H. Christ, brown eyes. What'd ya have to do that for? All I was say—"

"Quit talking, 813." Callie's glare stopped Phoenix's retort before it began, his mouth snapping shut.

Confusion whirled in Hannah's mind but Hawk squeezed her thigh, bringing her back to him.

"I can explain later. But he knew, Hannah. He knew about his son and even though they'd never met, he loved him enough to make the ultimate sacrifice."

Hannah's eyes stung and she blinked rapidly to prevent any tears from spilling as she nodded. She didn't know all the facts, but knowing Thomas died loving his son was enough for now.

Wes cleared his throat, his eyes focused, but soft with compassion behind his glasses. "Did Vlad say anything else?"

Hannah shook her head. "No. He didn't say anything else, and I didn't need him to. After he threatened me, I ran to my car and drove as fast as I could to get home."

"Makes sense. Vlad's not really one for words," Callie agreed.

"You got that right," Hannah mumbled as she massaged her temples.

She could feel a tension headache beginning to take root behind her forehead. Every time she felt like she was catching up, something else threw her off, like the fact that she and Callie looked so much alike. They could've been sisters. Twins even.

With that thought, Callie's words finally registered and alarm bells went off in her mind. "How do *you* know Vlad?"

Phoenix fidgeted with his hat before removing it, revealing dark-brown hair.

Callie remained statue-still as she answered, her brown eyes carefully trained on Hannah, making her feel like they were the only ones in the room.

"There's a reason why I'm here, ready to go to battle against the General. And let's just say it's for the same reason you and I look alike."

Hannah's eyes widened and dread filled her veins like tar.

"What... what does that mean?"

"Nothing, Han. Come on, this meeting has gone on long enough as it is. Let's go get an early dinner," Hawk urged with another squeeze of his hand but Hannah brushed it away.

"No, tell me. What does that mean?"

Callie glanced at Tommy then around the room. "We shouldn't talk in front of—"

"Tommy can hear whatever you have to say."

"I don't think that's true, Hannah," Callie replied firmly. Her eyes were an angry storm but the rest of her face and her voice were carefully neutral.

While Callie was the picture of calm, Hannah was anything but, so much so that Tommy slipped his hand in hers and held tight.

"You okay, Mom?"

Guilt made her wince. She'd always wanted Tommy to be knowledgeable of their situation. He at least deserved that much after she'd uprooted his life to flee the country. But she'd never intended him to be the rock in their relationship. He was the son, the *child*, and yet she was the one he had to console at the moment. It was one thing to have him understand, quite another to have to share the burden.

"Yeah, *avecito*, I'm okay. But I, uh, I think I need a moment to chat with Miss Callie right now."

"Are you sure, Hannah?" Hawk asked. "It's already been a long day—"

"I need this," she interrupted him, leaving her gaze on his so he understood how important this was to her. He nodded once, and she turned back to Tommy. "*Mijo*, let's go back up to the room. We can get you an early dinner and then settled watching TV before I come back down—"

"But I don't want to go back to the room." Tommy frowned. "I want to be here. I get to listen. That's what you always said."

She grimaced at the accusation. "I know, *mijo*, but there are some things I need to hear first before I share them with you."

His little frown deepened. "But Mom—"

"Hey, little man. What if we go throw a baseball around?" Hawk asked.

He let go of Hannah's thigh before leaning around her to see her son.

"Really?"

"Sure. We'll get you something to eat first and then we can throw it on top of the roof. What do you say?"

Tommy did a small fist pump and his eyes lit up with so much glee it was almost painful for her to see. He'd missed out on so much not having a father around.

"Is it okay if I go, Mom?"

Her instincts told her he was safe with Hawk, but her mind still worried. The same flight response she'd been relying on the past few years pushed at the edges of her thoughts. But when she glanced at Hawk to make sure he was okay with being the distraction, the eagerness softening the hard muscles in his face made her decision easy.

"Sure, *mijo*. Just be careful and listen to—"

"Okay, okay! I'll be safe, I promise." The words rushed out of him as he hopped up from his chair.

Hawk got up just as quickly and mussed Tommy's hair.

"Come on, little man." Hawk's smile was wider than she'd seen it in a long time. "Race you to the roof."

Tommy didn't need to be told twice. He sped out of the room without even saying goodbye. Before Hawk left to follow him, he bent toward Hannah and whispered in her ear. Her hair fluttered from his warm breath, making her shiver.

"Come find me when you're done, dove."

She nodded and swallowed, trying to regain her composure as a flush crept up her neck. As soon as he left, she turned to face the rest of the room, only to see the four women whispering to one another. When they were finished, Callie glanced at her and looked around the room before speaking.

"I think this conversation should be just the women."

# CHAPTER FIFTEEN

Hannah expected the men to push back, but Phoenix simply nodded. "Agreed." He pushed off the table and twirled his finger in a small circular motion to round up his teammates. "Move out."

The rest of them listened without argument, but before Wes could leave, Nora called out to him. "Hey, do a little switcheroo with Naomi, will ya? She might be good for this."

"Will do," he replied as he disappeared through the door.

"Once Naomi gets here, Callie will explain everything," Jules explained with a soft smile.

As they waited, Nora chatted away about everything and nothing. Hannah couldn't figure out if it was anxiety or if the girl just loved to talk, but she nodded along, silently begging for someone to come clean with her already.

After an eternity, the auburn-haired mother from earlier in the meeting came into the conference room and shut the door behind her.

"I've been summoned?" Naomi joked before sitting down and passing out peanut butter and jelly pockets that had always reminded Hannah of pale, unfried empanadas. "What's up? I brought some of these Uncrustables. Hawk said y'all might need some sustenance."

"Yes! Uncrustables are a need." Nora snatched a sandwich and unwrapped it before stuffing it in her mouth in one move.

To be nice, Hannah unwrapped the one in front of her and took a small bite of the bland, crimped dough. She slowly set it back down on its plastic wrapper, hoping her friends wouldn't notice if she didn't touch it again.

"Hannah deserves a few explanations," Callie replied cryptically as she tore her sandwich apart into small pieces.

"Oh? Like…"

"Like why I'm here and why we look alike," Callie answered and popped the food into her mouth.

"Oh." Naomi slouched into her chair. "Shit… okay."

Hannah huffed and crossed her arms. "Can someone please just tell me what's going on? All this back and forth is worse than ripping off the Band-Aid."

"More like ripping off a limb," Nora muttered under her breath and crumpled her leftover plastic.

"Nora," Jules warned, her authoritative tone taking control of the room in an instant. She'd yet to touch her sandwich, making Hannah feel better for neglecting hers.

Ellie ate hers without complaint while Callie straightened in her seat and blew out a breath.

"Okay. Let's get right into it. Hannah, what I'm about to tell you is disturbing, but I have a feeling you won't be surprised. Are you ready?"

Hannah's brow rose at Callie's blunt delivery, but she found herself nodding that she was ready, even though she wasn't sure if she was telling the truth.

"Alright, here goes. I'm not sure how much you know. Hawk isn't typically like the others when it comes to their Neanderthal tendencies of protecting their women by keeping them in the dark, but it seems like he's adopted the habit just for you. So, here's what

I *know* he hasn't told you." Callie exhaled heavily again and met her gaze. "Your father is the head of an international sex trafficking ring. I was supposed to be sold in it, but he kept me instead."

All the air left Hannah's lungs, and she collapsed against the back of her seat.

"What the... he... he *kept* you?"

Callie nodded once with the same finality as the punctuation at the end of a sentence.

Heat bloomed up Hannah's cheeks at the information.

"But... but MF7. He started that organization. Hawk left because they were supposed to be eradicating human trafficking. I... I don't understand."

"It was a front, Hannah," Callie replied. "It was all a front so he could have highly trained operatives wipe out his competition. Once he took down other traffickers, his followers at a fake women's shelter told the victims they were going to be helped back into society when in reality, the General forced them back into the market."

"*Mierda*," Hannah muttered as realization set in. "So, how does BlackStone Securities play into this? Hawk's team now, they were once MF7. They were the ones who helped him. Are they going to get in trouble?"

"No," Jules answered. "None of it was their fault. They thought they were helping people too, but they were tricked just like those women."

"Oh, my... *Dios mio*. This is... this is disgusting. What the fuck? I always knew he was awful, but this? This is insanity." The words didn't feel like enough, but nothing would. She'd always suspected her father was a monster, but she'd naively thought his behavior stopped with her. "So BlackStone Securities is... what? Trying to make amends?"

"Well, it's a long story," Ellie conceded. "So here it goes."

What Ellie said afterward floored Hannah. Ellie had been kidnapped from a party just like the one Hannah had attended and Nora had been kidnapped soon after by Vlad. Both were meant to be sold, but Ellie's brother and the rest of BlackStone Securities were able to save them in time.

"They've been trying to take the traffickers down ever since, only to find out your father, their former general, was behind everything."

"They only found that out about a week ago. It's been a blow for them. Not gonna lie." Nora sucked her teeth. "Callie was able to provide us more information after the team raided his headquarters in Atlanta."

"Atlanta? Is that when he went missing?"

Callie nodded. "Yup. And that's where this conversation comes in. Your father kept me for a reason and he made it very clear why."

Hannah swallowed, afraid she knew what was coming. "Why?"

"Because I reminded him... of you."

Bile rose up in her throat. "Me?"

"He made remarks about being 'Papa' Do you know—"

*Papá*

Hannah gagged and rolled back in her chair. Saliva built in her mouth as her body began to ready itself to vomit. It'd been years since she'd called him that. Not since she came to terms with the fact that what she'd been through was abuse.

"Hannah... did your father..."

Hannah shook her head violently, trying not to think about what Callie was asking. But she knew deep down they—*especially* Callie—deserved to understand.

"He was... he was inappropriate with me. He... touched me, but not... worse than that."

"That's fuckin' bad enough," Naomi spat.

"I know that now. But when I was growing up, I thought I was the issue. As a kid, I knew I was uncomfortable, but it took me being an adult to realize what he did was wrong, and it took me being a mom to understand the abuse was so ingrained and so much worse than I even knew."

"Jesus. I'm sorry, Hannah," Jules murmured from across the table. "That's terrible."

"Callie." Hannah breathed through the nausea as she asked the question she absolutely didn't want to know the answer to. "Do you think... do you think he bought you because of—"

Thankfully, Callie didn't make her finish. The words were already hard enough to get out as it was.

"Yes. I know that's hard to hear, but I think he chose me because he was able to do things to me that he'd stopped himself from doing to you. I'm sorry you dealt with that monster as a child."

Hannah dug her hands through her hair and shook her head. She was messing up her braid, but she didn't give a shit. The women sat in silence as Hannah digested the information. She was grateful for their patience, even if the words going down were rancid.

All those years ago, she'd thought something was wrong, but he'd told her if she said anything she'd be taken away from her mother. After her mother died, compliance had already been so ingrained in Hannah that she didn't even consider reaching out to someone as an option.

But what if she had told? Could she have prevented all of this?

"I'm... I'm so sorry," she finally whispered.

"Sorry?" Callie's head jolted back. "What the hell are you sorry for?"

"If I'd told, maybe none of this would've happened," Hannah mumbled, refusing to meet the eyes of the women who'd been hurt by her father. His evil schemes and greed. Her own silence.

"Hannah..." Naomi's soft Southern accent drifted toward her. "Hannah, look at me."

Hannah slowly lifted her head to see warm-chestnut eyes looking back at her.

"You can't think that way, Hannah. You, Callie, Ellie... *y'all* are the victims."

"*He* is the guilty party," Jules offered. "Not you."

"I know... but what if I'd reported it?"

Jules shook her head. "You can't think that way."

"But—"

"*No.* You. Can't. Think. That. Way." Naomi enunciated each word as the other women nodded.

"Have you ever thought about what would've happened if you'd reported?" Jules asked.

"A little." Hannah sniffed. "Wouldn't he have been prosecuted or gone to jail?"

"That's always the goal in these situations." The fair skin on Jules's forehead wrinkled with concern. She brushed her honey-blonde hair off of her shoulder before using her hands to emphasize her words. "The thing is, we don't know and we never can know. Could he have gone to prison for the rest of his life and never hurt anyone ever again? Sure. Could he have murdered you and gotten away with it?" Hannah gulped audibly, but Jules kept going. "Also, a possibility. Considering what we know now about what he *is* capable of? Do you really think your nightmare would've stopped as a child if you'd simply told someone? Hannah... it could've been worse for you."

"Yeah, but because it wasn't worse for me, my nightmare went to other people."

"And that's *his* fault," Callie insisted. "Not yours."

Ellie reached across the table and took Hannah's hand in hers. "I'll be real with you. People who report are heroes. But the ones who make sure they're safe aren't monsters. The *monsters* are the monsters. They're the ones who are guilty. Not the ones who were just trying to survive. And that's what you were. You're the survivor. Never forget that."

Tears pricked Hannah's eyes. She wasn't sure if she could ever forgive herself for refusing to confront reality for so long. And she definitely didn't think she deserved that forgiveness from others. But getting it from these women who her silence had directly impacted was a salve on a burn that probably would never fully heal. A relief but only a brief one.

"Thank you," Hannah whispered and squeezed Ellie's hand.

Her soft smile lifted her face as she squeezed back.

Hannah massaged her chest with her hand, and Callie cleared her throat.

"I'm sorry to put all this on you. But things are probably going to move fast once the guys figure out where to look next for the General. I know you couldn't report when you were a child. But now, in the safety of BlackStone Securities... you could help."

Purpose welled in her chest and Hannah let go of Ellie's hand to sit straighter. As she did, Nora pulled out a laptop from a bag beside her and quickly set it up on the table.

"What can I do?" Hannah asked as she watched her get settled.

Nora looked around at Jules, Callie, Ellie, and Naomi before seeing whatever confirmation she was looking for. She faced Hannah, her fingers poised on the keys as Callie spoke again.

"Tell us everything you know about your father."

# CHAPTER SIXTEEN

The *pop* of the baseball hitting his worn glove was music to Hawk's ears. He retrieved the ball from the center of the leather and threw it back to Tommy.

Hawk didn't hold on to many tangible things from his past since he'd had to move all throughout his military career. But thanks to his pops's hoarding tendencies right before he passed, Hawk still had his favorite mitt, baseball, and even the binoculars his old man used to wear to games. Hawk hadn't been able to part with any of it after getting them out of storage two years ago. It'd taken a good amount of conditioner, new netting, time, and love to restore the mitt, but working on it took him back to late summer afternoons with his pops.

Apparently Tommy took his own ball, glove, and bat everywhere he went, too.

"Ever throw a ball on top of a roof before?" Hawk asked with a grin, but Tommy just shrugged.

Eagle's little mini-me was nothing like his father in that respect. Eagle had always had something to say and never met a stranger. But Tommy seemed much more cautious and reserved. Which was understandable considering what the little man had been through.

When Hawk suggested they throw the ball on the roof of the BlackStone Securities facility, the kid's bright-blue eyes widened with excitement. But as soon as the glow took over his face, it disappeared just as quickly, like life had already taught him to tamp down his emotions.

"PB&J used to be a food group for me growing up, but I'd never had an Uncrustable until tonight. They're pretty good, actually. Did you like yours?"

The kid had eaten three so Hawk knew the answer, but he was trying to make small talk until he felt like opening up. Tommy lifted a shoulder in answer, and it wasn't until they'd thrown back and forth several times that he finally spoke without prompting.

"So what do you think they're talking about down there?" Tommy asked as he caught the throw with practiced skill.

"Who taught you how to catch?" Hawk asked instead, hoping they could change the subject.

The kid frowned like he knew exactly what Hawk was doing, but he threw the ball back and answered, "My mom. I used to do T-ball until..."

"Until... what?"

"Until we had to start moving around everywhere."

The answer made Hawk's heart ache. Finding out Hannah had been living on the run had been such a shock. Now he craved all the information he could get about their circumstances, even if every word stabbed guilt through his chest like a knife.

"When was that?"

Tommy shrugged after Hawk's throw *thunked* into his glove. "I dunno. We left when I was in first grade. All I remember is waking up in the middle of the night, her putting me in the back of the car, then driving forever and ever. We had to change our names. She changed her hair a whole bunch."

A few more thumps of the ball passed between them before Hawk prompted him again.

"But she threw the ball with you?"

Tommy nodded. "I think she feels bad about having to move a lot."

Hawk felt his heart beat in time with each catch and throw thumping into his mitt, a rhythm from a past life. "How do you feel about it?"

"I dunno. I don't care. I miss T-ball. But going to new places is cool."

"Which one was your favorite?"

"Mérida," he answered without hesitation.

"How long did you stay there?"

"I dunno. The longest time out of any of them. But it was cool."

The little half answers Tommy gave forced Hawk to hold back a grin. He might not be quite like his dad in that respect, but Tommy reminded him a hell of a lot of his own awkward reluctance growing up. The ol' man had worked on it though, pulling back Hawk's layers every time he got in his own head.

If Tommy needed that kind of encouragement, well, then Hawk had learned from the best, so he knew what to do. Hell, if they threw the ball the whole time, he could do it all day.

After a few more throws back and forth, Tommy finally spoke again, "You like my mom, don't you? I've seen the way you look at her. You don't smile much but you do around her."

*Out of the mouth of babes... whelp, no use in denying it.*

Hawk chuckled. "You caught that, did you?"

"Yeah, it's pretty obvious." Tommy nodded before sighing dramatically. "Hate to break it to ya, but you can't like her."

"Oh, yeah?" Hawk tried not to laugh at the protective little man. "Why's that?"

Tommy shrugged. "Cause she's in love with someone else."

"Wh-what?"

Tommy's lazy throw came barreling toward Hawk's head as he stared in stunned silence. At the very last second, Hawk absentmindedly threw his glove up into the sky, barely catching the baseball.

"Yup. Sorry." Tommy shrugged again, evidently his go-to gesture. He readied himself to catch, like Hawk wasn't now gripping the ball for dear life, on the verge of a heart attack.

He shouldn't have been surprised. Hannah was perfect. It was naive of him to assume she was single, but it'd never crossed his mind that she was with someone else.

*Then again, it never crossed my mind that my best friend would sleep with her, either.*

Hawk cleared his throat, trying to regain some composure. "Do you... um. Do you like him?"

Tommy lifted his shoulders once again. "I dunno. Never met him."

"What? You've never met him?" Hawk couldn't hide his frown.

Tommy didn't seem to notice as he answered, "Nope. All I know is that she loved him before she had me. I used to think it was my dad, but she only ever called him Thomas or Eagle. Mom calls me little bird, but that's not near as cool a nickname as all you guys."

"Tommyhawk's pretty cool, though," Hawk countered.

"Yeah, I guess so." The boy tried to hide a smile as he shrugged again. "Anyway, I found the painting she did for him, too. That's when I knew she *loved* him, loved him."

Hope fluttered in Hawk's breaking heart. "A painting?"

"Yup. Here, I'll show ya."

Tommy tugged off his glove and put it under his armpit before running toward the duffel bag he'd brought to the roof. He knelt in front of the bag and shuffled through it. After a few seconds, Hawk began to seriously wonder if he was sweating because of the heat and his long sleeves or because he was having to wait so long to see evidence that the love of his life loved someone—

"Here it is! See, look." Tommy gingerly pulled out a carefully folded canvas and handed it to him.

Hawk knelt beside him and accepted the canvas with trembling fingers. His heart thudded harder and harder in his chest as he unfolded it and recognition sank in. By the time he'd laid and flattened the canvas out on the asphalt roof, his chest had tightened to the point of pain.

Gorgeous and rich reds, yellows, blues, purples, and greens rolled together to make layers of the most beautiful Appalachian sunrise he'd ever seen. And the most familiar. In nearly a decade, not a day had gone by that he didn't think about it. He'd made sure of that.

The tenseness in his muscles eased the more he recommitted the stunning landscape to memory. It'd been forever since he'd seen the painting in person. When he found the single, pretty white dove soaring through the sky, he couldn't stop himself from caressing it with the lightest of touches.

"See here?" Tommy asked as he pointed lightly to the dedication Hawk already knew was at the bottom right of the canvas. "That's how I knew she loved him."

"*Para mi cielo*," Hawk read out loud, trying to hold back the emotion rioting through him.

"It means—"

"For my sky," Hawk finished for him.

"Uh, yeah." Tommy's eyes narrowed. "How'd you know that? Do you know Spanish?"

Hawk shook his head slightly. "I learned that one a long time ago. Now it's one of those things I'll never forget."

"Well, she never puts this kinda stuff on her paintings. Not the ones she keeps, anyway."

Tommy gingerly took the canvas out from underneath Hawk's hands. As soon as the painting left his fingers, he stretched and balled them into fists to keep from reaching for it again. It'd been so long since he'd held it, but he let Tommy place it lovingly back into a side pocket in the duffel bag.

"This is your duffel bag, isn't it? Does your mom know you have this?"

"She thinks she lost it a long time ago. It made her sad to look at, so I took it during one of our moves. But I knew she wouldn't want to *actually* lose it, so I've kept it until she can look at it again without being sad." He snapped his head to Hawk and gave him a stern look. "Don't tell her I have it."

"I won't." Hawk held his hands up in innocence.

"Good." Tommy nodded once.

"How do you, um... how do you know she loves her *cielo*?"

"I just know. Her voice gets all soft when she thinks out loud about him and none of her other paintings are signed like that. Besides... she never paints those mountains anymore."

"She doesn't?"

"Nope." Tommy shook his head hard and stood, prompting Hawk to do the same. "Only skies over beaches and Mayan ruins and stuff."

"Do you know why she doesn't paint them anymore?" Hawk asked with a frown.

Tommy shrugged. "I asked her once. She said it's 'cause it hurt too much. It made her miss home."

Hawk's chest ached and emotion clogged his throat. This kid was unwittingly putting him through an emotional triple-header. First, there was the heartbreak of hearing that Hannah was in love with someone else, then the guilt and relief that came when he saw the painting, and now knowing she'd missed home.

*I missed home, too, dove.*

"She talks about him all the time. Or at least she used to," Tommy continued as he tugged his glove back on. He tossed the ball to Hawk before returning to his position in front of the helipad.

Hawk's arm stilled midthrow as he asked, "Used to?"

"Yup. She used to talk about him a lot, but she hasn't for a while. Not since we got that letter that said my dad died. I never read the letter, but I think the guy she loved died, too. When she talks about him now, she's sadder than she used to be."

*Not for long, if I can help it.*

Hawk nodded slowly and returned the ball. Eventually, they fell back into the even tempo.

"My pops and I used to throw the ball like this," he commented after a while.

Tommy's face soured. "I wish I had a pops."

*Shit.*

Hawk's heart dropped in his chest and he nearly stumbled as he caught one of Tommy's particularly hard throws. Possibilities of what to say ran through his head, but nothing helpful magically appeared. Nothing said would ever be enough.

"Me too, little man."

"It's okay. Mom said he loved me. He just had to finish saving the world before he could meet me. But then he died."

Hawk sucked in a breath before returning the ball. It wasn't lost on him that they were still casually throwing the ball around while also talking about the death of Tommy's father and Hawk's best friend. But he'd always found baseball therapeutic. There'd been times in his life when answers could only be found amid the steady cadence of throwing and catching the ball with someone he cared about.

Luckily for him, Tommy seemed to feel the same way.

"What was it like having a dad?" Tommy asked.

After a moment of trying to figure out the best words, he finally landed on the simple truth.

"My pops was my hero," Hawk answered and cleared his throat. "We loved this game together. He wanted me to go pro, but then nine-eleven happened."

"Nine-eleven?" Tommy frowned.

Hawk's jaw dropped, and he stilled with the ball in his hand. "You don't know what nine-eleven is?"

"Nope," Tommy answered. "So what was it?"

Hawk huffed a surprised laugh before throwing the ball back.

That moment had been so pivotal in his own life, it never occurred to him that his kids would have no frame of reference outside of a history lesson.

*Not that Tommy is my kid...*

A mix of regret and hope had him smiling to himself at the thought. He'd always wanted kids, had expected to have them, honestly. But he'd foolishly let life, duty, responsibility—basically everything else—get in the way.

*Never again.*

"Nine-eleven was one of the most important days in my life. The world changed and so did I. It encouraged me to go to the Army instead of playing ball. But I still love the game."

Tommy seemed to think for a second before throwing the ball back. "That was what my dad was in, too, right? The Army?"

Hawk chuckled. "Yup. I met him there. We were in the same unit and were best friends"—he threw the ball and snapped his fingers—"like that."

Tommy paused for a second and tossed the ball into his mitt a few times before returning it. "What was he like?"

A lump developed in Hawk's throat. He swallowed the emotion down so he could answer to the best of his ability. Hawk remembered the way he used to hang on his pops's every word. This kid had never met his father, so Hawk could imagine just how much weight words *about* Eagle would carry for Tommy.

There was so much baggage wrapped up in his history with MF7, and with what they suspected about their final mission— that Eagle might've been a reluctant double-agent for the General—it only added to the team's confusion about their former leader. It was a fucked-up situation that had left Hawk with some fucked-up feelings about his best friend. Not to mention the fact he'd only just found out Eagle had fathered a kid with the love of Hawk's life.

Bile churned in his stomach, threatening to come up at that last thought, but he clenched his jaw and focused on getting past his own personal feelings. Tommy didn't need to know any of that shit, and if it were up to Hawk, he'd *never* know about it. Kids should never have to learn their parents aren't heroes, especially if they're the villains.

"Your dad... Tommy, your dad was a leader. He was funny, optimistic, always putting his team and friends first—" His voice broke at the last because he was playing catch with a living, breathing example of how untrue the last sentiment actually was.

The fact Eagle had slept with his best friend's girl should've been something Hawk hated. But after nine years, he couldn't find it in himself to be upset when this cool-ass kid was the result. Hawk *was* mad at him for leaving Hannah all alone, though.

*But I did that, too.*

Guilt shocked through him, causing a phantom pain in his joints as his body tried to push back against the truth. But his conscience was right. He couldn't blame Eagle for doing the same exact thing he'd done. Tommy could've very well have been his if the time line was correct.

They'd caught the Braves game shooters, who'd confessed in a top-security clearance hearing that they'd been retaliating against MF7. That confession never saw the light of day, but the people got their much-needed false sense of security when the life sentences were doled out publicly. What that justice did for Hawk, however, was ensure that he was scared shitless.

Over the years, he'd seen what traffickers were capable of. Hacking and surveilling were child's play for many, which meant any amount of contact or interest in Hannah made her vulnerable. So he and Eagle had made a pact to leave her be and let her live her life.

When he'd gotten back, the BlackStone team still dealt with the same bullshit and evil, powerful men. He hadn't wanted Hannah anywhere near this life, and he'd foolishly thought after seeing the online news article about her Teacher of the Year award that she was thriving. He'd believed her father was still protecting her, up until two and a half months ago when he'd realized she was one of the missing women his team was looking for.

He'd told Wes everything in confidence, and together, they'd searched everywhere for her, trying not to alert any of their enemies that she was on their radar. Then they'd found out the General had been behind everything they were investigating. If they hadn't stormed the General's security firm, they wouldn't have found the photo of Hannah with the coordinates, and Hawk may never have seen her again.

Anger surged through him at the thought. At his naivety, and the willingness to put Hannah's safety in the hands of another man, let alone that monster.

"The things I'd do if I had a fucking do-over," he muttered.

"What?" Tommy asked.

*Kids and their insanely good hearing.*

"Nothing," Hawk answered with a quick shake of his head. "Okay, where was I?"

"Talking about my dad?" Tommy replied with a hopeful lilt in his voice.

"Right." Hawk blew a harsh breath. "Your dad worked hard. He was good at his job, too. He saved my ass a million times."

"My dad saved your life?" Tommy asked with a big, toothy grin.

"Hell yeah, he did. Too many times to count. Your dad was a hero, little man. I wouldn't be here without him."

A few seconds passed before Tommy's voice cracked again. "Mom said he loved me. But I think she's just saying that. I don't know if he even knew about me. Do you... do you think he would've liked me?"

A small sob broke at the end of Tommy's question and Hawk cleared the space between them in half a second. The boy swiped his face angrily, like his own emotions offended him. Hawk rested both hand and glove on his shoulders and met his eyes.

"Hey, little man, it's okay." The kid shook his head hard, but Hawk tightened his grip on the boy's shoulder. "Tommy, listen to me. Whatever you're feeling right now? It's okay, alright?"

He bent low to meet watery blue eyes. The kid's lips were flattened in a thin line, but they vibrated with emotion Hawk could feel rolling off of him in waves.

"I just wish I'd met him," he whispered so softly that Hawk almost couldn't hear him, but his whole body ached from the impact of his words.

"I know," he said simply. "But Tommy, I meant what I said downstairs. Your dad? He *loved* you. He would've given the world to know you, I have no doubt in my mind he did. Never ever forget he loved you, okay?"

At Tommy's tiny nod, Hawk pulled him into a bear hug. Small arms embraced him back instantly. Hawk's heart stuttered in his chest as the kid trembled silently in his hold.

He let Tommy pull away first. When the boy finally let go, he rubbed his blue eyes, so vivid now with the red rims around the edges.

"Don't tell my mom, okay? I don't want her to know I got upset."

Hawk frowned. "She loves you too, little man, and she's tough as nails. She can handle whatever you're feeling, alright? You don't have to hide from her. And you don't have to hide those feelings from me either. I miss your dad, too." As soon as he said it, an idea crossed his mind. "Hey, it's good to talk about how you're feeling, you know that, right?"

Tommy gave his noncommittal shrug, but Hawk kept going. "So if I ever need to talk about your dad, is it alright if I come talk to you? It'll feel good to get it off my chest. Maybe cry a little."

Tommy's brow rose. "*You* cry?"

"Absolutely. Crying helps me make sure I feel all my sad emotions so I can feel all my happy ones, too. You can't feel your happiest if you're afraid to feel your saddest."

The kid frowned before nodding resolutely. "Yeah, okay. Can I, um, can I come talk to you, too? Whenever I'm sad?"

Hawk resisted the urge to fist-pump. "Of course you can. Come talk to me anytime, with whatever you're feeling. You remind me of your dad, you know? It feels like I'm able to talk to him again when I talk to you."

His tan cheeks, rosy from the sun and tears, rounded as he smiled a big, toothy grin. "Yeah, okay. I can do that."

Hawk returned the smile as he placed the ball from his glove into Tommy's and walked backward across the hot roof. Thankfully, the summer sun might've been direct, but the open air and breeze above the building were a godsend. Without that breeze, they'd never be able to barbecue on the grill or hang out up there. It was also why they had the rooftop helipad, to easily lift the Little Bird they'd "permanently borrowed" from the government a few years ago.

Once Hawk got into place, Tommy called out to him, "Hey, stay there and I'll go all the way to the end of the roof! Then I'm gonna throw it as hard as I can!"

"Alright, let's see what you got, little man." Hawk hit the glove and waited as Tommy ran toward the end of the warehouse.

The rooftop was sparse, but for the helipad, large round turbine vents, a large AC unit, a toolbox on wheels, a huge tool shed near the roof stairwell and a grill. The rest was wide open space, with surrounding guard walls at chest height.

Theoretically, the height would make it easier for his team to hide behind and attack any intruders on the ground. They hadn't had any before Vlad bombed the facility months ago, or after. But they could never be too cautious, especially since the General and Vlad were still out in the world, presumably ready to strike at any moment.

"Stop there!" Hawk called out, making Tommy halt about three-quarters of the way across the roof. "Give it your best shot!"

Despite the fact there was no way for Tommy to fall off the side of the roof thanks to the guard walls, having him too far away still made Hawk anxious for some reason.

"Okay! Here I go!" Tommy yelled before pulling back and throwing his whole body behind the ball.

Hawk watched with widening eyes as the ball sailed through the air, quickly realizing he'd misjudged Tommy's abilities.

"Damn, little man! You've got one hell of an arm!" Hawk shuffled, then backpedaled faster and faster before he finally reached up. When he found the ball in the bright sky, he used the mitt's webbing to filter out some of the sun and guide the ball in, just as a small familiar voice squeaked behind him.

He collided with the newcomer and as soon as he caught the ball, he turned around to catch her, too. He wrapped his arm around Hannah's waist and tugged her curvy body flush against his before he accidentally bulldozed her into the stairwell. He caught himself at the last second by slapping his gloved hand beside the rooftop door. The position was useful for balance, but it ended with him caging her against the wall with his bare hand resting on her lower back.

The homey scent of sugar, tea, and oranges filled his nostrils and he looked down to see warm-brown eyes glittering up at him.

"Hey there, dove." He smiled down.

She swallowed and breathed hard against his chest. A tentative grin lifted the corners of her rosy lips.

"Hi."

# CHAPTER SEVENTEEN

Talking with the women of BlackStone Securities was one of the most empowering moments of Hannah's life. As a child, she hadn't fully understood that the way her father looked at her, talked to her... touched her, it was all wrong. It'd taken becoming an adult to fully realize the extent of the damage he'd caused, and becoming a mom to realize what he was capable of.

Out of fear, she hadn't reported him as a child, but she felt a strength and power doing it now. She didn't go into detail about what happened in her childhood. That wasn't necessary for herself or the case. The information she did share, though, would hopefully help take him down once and for all.

Homes, vacation houses, potential buildings in his name, favorite places... Nora even asked what foods he liked best—seafood, from what she remembered. Why that was important, she didn't know, but Nora said she, Naomi, and Wes were going to try to piece everything together with the information they'd gotten from suspects that had already been apprehended in the trafficking ring.

When they'd finally finished after hours of picking apart everything Hannah knew, Nora had called Wes to come back down. He'd confirmed that Tommy and Hawk were on the roof after eating the peanut-butter-and-jelly pockets for dinner. Although Hannah knew the way, Naomi had still insisted on walking with her, chatting about the team as they went.

Before they exited the elevator to enter the roof stairwell landing, Naomi pressed the "close elevator" button to keep the doors shut and gently grabbed Hannah's arm.

"Hey... before you go out there, I want to share somethin'."

Hannah felt her brow furrow with interest. "Okay... go for it."

Naomi inhaled and exhaled slowly before speaking. "I meant what I said before. You don't need to feel guilty about not reportin' him as a child."

Hannah felt her cheeks heat with the shame lingering in her chest, despite the women's assurances earlier.

"Thanks, but um, I don't know how I could possibly just forgive myself for not saying *something*."

"I know. I get that, I really do. I was in a situation... with my fiancé—"

"Wes?" Hannah asked, her eyes wide.

"No. God no." Naomi shook her head quickly. "Wes treats me like a queen. But my fiancé... he didn't. It took Jules, Ellie, Nora, and Wes to convince me to leave. But before I met them, I'd gone back and forth about whether I wanted to prosecute if I ever did escape him. Honestly, if I had tried it without Black-Stone Securities he might've found a way to kill me."

"*¡Dios mio!*" Hannah's hand jumped to her mouth as she gasped. "Where is he now? Are you safe?"

"Yeah, I'm safe, now. Let's just say my ex-fiancé got what was comin' to him, thanks to Callie. Wes and the guys have all made sure we're safe inside the facility and the team's cabin. It was touch and go there for a second after the bombin'—"

"Yeah, tell me about this 'bombing.' I keep hearing reference to it, and it's starting to freak me out."

"The General had Vlad bomb the place almost three months ago. But they were lookin' for someone BlackStone had in custody for this case. It's a long story." Naomi waved her hand

and continued, "Trust me when I say I wouldn't have Thea here if I didn't think it was safe. I've found this team is pretty damn good at their job."

"That's a relief."

As she said the words out loud, pressure released in Hannah's chest. She'd been worried ever since the *bombing* was hinted at, but another mother thinking it was safe made her feel better about keeping Tommy there. It also made her realize the extent of her father's reach.

If he'd gotten a one up on BlackStone Securities, she'd been a fool for thinking she could outsmart him all by herself. She'd never had a chance throughout the years. His stalking and her misery had truly been a cat-and-mouse *game* to him. The reality that he had sent a damn assassin made the decision to stay in a modern fortress that much easier.

A sliver of a memory from yesterday filtered through her mind. It'd all been so chaotic it went by like a blur and it was hard to keep track of the specifics. It already felt like it'd been years—not twenty-four hours—since she'd fought for her life. But there was something the guy had said...

*"Everything is different now. Everyone under old boss must be gone."*

Was her father the one who sent the hitman... or was it Vlad?

"Havin' a big broodin' leader sleepin' outside your door can't hurt, either." Naomi laughed.

Her words whiplashed Hannah out of her thoughts, and she frowned. "What do you mean?"

"Hawk slept outside your door last night. The guy apparently refused to sleep on the couch or in one of the spare rooms. It's sweet, if you think about it, although I'm sure the guy's neck is killin' him. Falling asleep upright against these steel walls can't be comfortable."

"He slept outside my *door*?" Hannah couldn't hide the incredulity in her voice, but Naomi just nodded with a knowing smile.

"Some of these guys still have some growin' up to do, but

not him. You've got a good one lookin' after you now. You don't have to just rely on yourself anymore. As a mom, I know how good that sense of security feels, so soak it in. You deserve it."

Those simple words were like a weight lifted off her shoulders. As Naomi continued, the conversation began to wash away the stress from the years of running.

"And this might be brutally honest," Naomi continued. "But in my opinion, it's not your responsibility to save anyone. In this life, you have to save yourself and not every situation makes reportin' better." Naomi squeezed Hannah's arm and her gaze settled on her with purpose. "Your father's sins aren't yours, and you don't have to atone for them."

"Thank you," Hannah replied with a nod as her chest loosened. "But what we did down there, it helped me. Now that Tommy and I are safe, I'll do whatever I can to stop my father."

Naomi lifted her finger from the elevator button, allowing the doors to open. "Believe me, honey. I get that. Thanks again for helpin' us, although it sounds like you're doin' it for yourself now, too."

Hannah nodded as she stepped out of the oversized freight elevator, ignoring the pinch of emotion in her eyes as the doors closed behind her.

"Go get your boys, Hannah."

"Oh, Hawk's not my—" She turned to see her reflection staring back at her in the steel doors. Even though it'd been on the tip of her tongue to deny Hawk was her *anything*, the hope in her eyes said differently.

She tried to hide her smile as she faced the stairwell landing and took a big, steadying breath before opening the rooftop door.

It took her a second to find them since the helicopter was the eye-catching feature on the spacious roof. She was about to call Tommy's name, but when she finally found them, the scene gripped her heart so tightly it stole her breath away. She froze, afraid she'd somehow interrupt them even though she was so far away.

Hawk sat on his haunches, his large body at eye level with Tommy's much smaller one, and Hawk's hands on Tommy's shoulders.

The tender moment brought tears to her eyes and a flood of emotion warmed her veins. She fidgeted over the outline of her necklace, still underneath the cotton of her shirt, as her mind wandered to that place where what-ifs were abundant but answers were few.

Would this have been what Tommy had experienced if his dad were alive right now?

What if Tommy had been Hawk's instead?

Would Hawk have stayed?

It'd been selfish of her to beg him to stay. Her father had loathed her relationship with Hawk, and he'd made no bones about doing his best to destroy Hawk if he ever got court martialed. She wouldn't have wanted that for him, but if Hawk had known about a child, would that have been enough to have him at least keep in touch? Or would that have made him stay farther away since he'd been afraid for her safety?

She shook her head and closed the door softly behind her before leaning against it. There was no use dwelling on the past. What had happened, happened, and she wouldn't trade Tommy for anything. If Hawk never forgave her for sleeping with his best friend, well, she wouldn't blame him. But she'd also never apologize for her son, and although she hurt Hawk by turning to his friend, she got the best little boy in the world for it. How could she allow herself to feel shame for something when she was so grateful for the blessing she got out of it?

She watched as Hawk hugged Tommy. Her son clung to him like a lifeline. Hannah blinked rapidly in a sorry attempt to make the tears threatening to spill over disappear. She strained her ears to hear, but like the game of catch they'd just bonded over, the breeze caught their words and pitched them into the wind, leaving the moment just for them. When Tommy let go, Hawk said something else, making the boy smile before they went back to throwing the ball.

Her rowdy child suddenly ran to the other end of the warehouse, past the helicopter and near the edge. She stepped away from the wall to stop him, but Hawk called out nervously before the mischievous boy got too close. Then Tommy stretched back and rocketed the ball as high and far as he could.

She was so mesmerized, watching it fly through the air, that all she could do was squeak her protest when the large man in front of her collided with her to catch it.

His strong arm enveloped her, tugging her in as he caught her too, ensuring she didn't fall as he propped her against the wall.

"Hey there, dove." His charcoal eyes burned down at her as his handsome smile glittered in the sun.

"Hi." Her heart leapt in her throat and she swallowed, unable to keep from returning his grin.

They breathed in tandem, her chest pressing against his. Little droplets of sweat prickled on his forehead and his scent wafted toward her in the breeze. Pine, morning dew, and leather, like an early spring baseball game.

Like the last opening day she ever attended.

That final thought made her chest clench in the spot right underneath her necklace, but instead of pushing him away, all she wanted to do was pull him closer, to cling to the past they could've had and the dreams she'd wished for them. To fall into his heated gaze and pretend like the years away had never happened.

He licked his lips, and his eyes flicked to hers. She leaned up on her tiptoes to reach him, wanting to know if he still tasted the same way—

"Mom?" Tommy's voice worked between them, shaking her from their shared reverie. Hawk straightened, pushing away from the wall and releasing her waist, leaving her bereft of his touch.

She tugged and straightened her T-shirt despite the fact nothing was out of place. He cleared his throat before they both turned toward Tommy.

The boy punched one hand into his mitt absentmindedly and his lips pursed, as if he was trying to figure out what was between them.

*You and me both, mijo.*

Hannah laughed awkwardly and took a careful step away from Hawk, providing much-needed distance if she was going to think straight. Hawk tugged his glove off and stashed it underneath his armpit before tossing his worn baseball to Tommy.

Tommy caught it with ease, but his eyes widened as Hawk spoke.

"Hey, little man, thanks for the game. It felt good to talk."

Her son nodded and Hannah swallowed back the lump of emotion in her throat at the sight of the small, proud smile curved on his face. "Yeah, thanks, Hawk."

"I hear you've already had dinner, *avecito*, so it's time to settle down for the night and get ready for bed. It might feel early but it's been a long day."

"Ugh, Mom, there's still light outside. I'm not even tired."

"I know, but we're in a different time zone here. To make sure you get back on a good schedule we need to go to sleep at the bedtime that fits here or we'll get tired too early tomorrow."

Tommy sighed. "*Fine*. Can I have some TV time before, though?"

She chuckled and ruffled his fine blond hair. "Okay, but only *one* show. I'm going to talk to Hawk for a minute and by the time I get down there, you better be in bed."

As soon as the words left her lips, Tommy's blue eyes lit up, and he did a subtle fist pump, no doubt at the prospect she'd take too much time and he'd get to watch more than one show.

"Awesome!" He pushed off his back foot and sped past her before confirming her suspicion. "Talk as long as you want!"

"Wait, Tommy!" But he'd already flown through the door. She

huffed a laugh and threw up her hands. "Well, I guess he knows his way around."

Hawk chuckled. "The kid has a way with direction already. Like his old man."

Hannah tried to hide her wince, but it was useless. He always saw right through her.

"Hey, you okay?" His large hands rested on both of her shoulders, keeping her straight so she had to meet the concern on his face head-on.

"Yeah, I'm okay. I just... is it weird for you?"

"Is... what weird for me?" Hawk asked, a frown on his face.

"This." She pointed between them and tilted her head toward the door. "You, me... Tommy."

Hawk shook his head. "Not weird at all. It feels good to have you both here with me."

She nodded, still unconvinced, but she didn't want to dig into it right then.

"I saw you throwing around with him. Did he... did he say anything?"

Hawk lifted his shoulder with nonchalance, but she could've sworn a sly smile ghosted across his lips before it disappeared.

"Nothing out of the ordinary. We talked about his dad a little bit. Eagle would've loved the little man. I wish they'd been able to get to know each other."

"Me too," she answered quietly, pushing past the ache in her chest. "I don't regret Tommy, but I do regret not being able to get in touch with Thomas... or you. I tried, you know. I tried to get in touch with you both, but I had no way of finding you. Once you guys left, it was like you disappeared—"

He winced. "I know, Hannah, I'm sorry. We were supposed to be dead to the world."

"At one point, I thought you were," she whispered.

"Shit." He shook his head before meeting her eyes again. "Hannah, I—"

Hannah waved him off, breaking eye contact with an

awkward huff. "No, I'm sorry, I really didn't mean to get into it."
She sighed. "I came to get Tommy for bed."

"Right." The hesitation in Hawk's voice made her stomach
leap.

*Stay.*

The thought came unbidden, but once she'd had it, she realized how much she wanted to say it out loud. She'd already
begged for it once before, though. There was no way she'd do it
again, no matter how much she wanted to. She couldn't bear the
rejection.

"Well, um, I guess I should be a gentleman and escort you to
your room, then," Hawk murmured and held open the rooftop
door for her.

The gesture would've made other women smile, but all she
wanted to do was slam it shut and pounce on him. Whether that
was to yell at him or kiss him, she didn't know, but the urge was
strong. Her emotions had always been overwhelming around this
man, and nearly a decade of yearning between them did nothing
to remedy that.

"Thanks," she said curtly, unable to hide her disappointment.

But as soon as she was about to walk through the door, a
strong, calloused hand tugged her back and spun her around.

This time, her sky came crashing down.

# CHAPTER EIGHTEEN

There was nothing tender or gentlemanly about the covetous way Hawk's lips slammed against hers. He devoured her the way she'd had to dream about for years with her hand between her thighs. His scent enveloped her, drawing her into him and she wrapped her arms around his neck. He bent to lay his glove on the ground and as he stood, he scooped her up underneath her thighs. She locked her heels around his lower back and held on while he carried her across the roof.

It was on the tip of her tongue to ask where they were going, but she forgot the question entirely as his own tongue pushed through her lips, insisting on entry before it dipped into her mouth. When that warm, slick muscle intertwined with hers, tingles zapped down her spine and she moaned into his mouth.

He cupped the globes of her ass and lifted her higher. Before she could register what was happening, he plopped her into the helicopter's pilot seat and threaded his hand through her hair, unraveling her braid. His large palm spanned the back of her head, cradling it as his tongue dove deeper into her mouth and his other arm curved around her hips to scoot her close until her core pressed against his upper abs.

"Goddamn, you taste like home, dove," he moaned against her lips. "Like sweet tea and oranges."

"Made my recipe this morning," she replied with a smile and pushed her center against him to find some friction. "Glad you like it."

"Fuck yeah, I do. I love it."

He was only talking about sweet tea, so why did those last three words make her heart race in her chest faster than it had in years? It was exhilarating to know he still had this effect on her after all this time. Exhilarating... and terrifying.

With one hand still tugging her hair, Hawk's other hand slipped underneath her T-shirt next to her jeans' button. His fingertips grazed the sensitive skin along her waistband. Her lower belly flipped but even as her legs tugged him closer, she stopped him with her hand on his wrist.

"Hawk, wait... I don't know."

He pulled away and nodded at her words.

"I know," he sighed. "It's too soon—"

"No, it's not that, it's just..."

How could she explain it? It wasn't too soon, not for her. She'd been missing this man for nearly ten *years*, two of which she'd thought he was gone forever. But before he left, they'd had a level of trust that she still needed now. She wasn't sure if she could give herself to him, not yet.

*But soon.*

His eyebrow rose along with his voice as he spoke, "Talk to me, dove."

"My life has been so out of control lately," she finally whispered. "Not knowing where I'll be living, who I can talk to, whether my art will pay rent. It's been uncertainty day in and day out. I want to trust you. But I don't know if I can give over what little control I have."

Understanding relaxed his handsome features. "That makes total sense. We can go back downstairs..." He trailed off as she shook her head.

"I don't want to stop. I just don't want to move forward yet."

Hawk frowned. "Okay, maybe I don't get it."

She groaned into a laugh. At a loss of how to explain it to him, her gaze flitted around her surroundings, to see if anything could help.

"It's okay, Hannah, seriously. I'll take what I can—"

"Get in the copilot's seat," she blurted out. His brows lifted again, wrinkling his forehead and she couldn't help but grin over his confusion. "Please? I have an idea."

Hawk watched her through the bulbous glass windshield with curious but wary eyes as he traveled around the helicopter. Hannah's inner muscles fluttered at the sight of Hawk's biceps flexing through the thin cotton of his long-sleeve black shirt. He grabbed the inside of the cockpit frame and pulled himself up into the copilot's seat in one swoop. As soon as he sat down, she crawled over the controls and handles between them, and strad-dled Hawk.

"Oh... I think I know where you're going with this," Hawk chuckled as he gripped her ass through her jeans.

She tsked at him with a smile, "Nope. I don't think you do. Not yet."

While holding one of his hands, she grabbed a shoulder harness with her free hand.

"Hannah," he grumbled in warning, but she shook her head.

"Please... trust me so I can trust you," she pleaded, allowing her voice to sound as desperate as she felt.

It was symbolic more than anything. But being in charge of her own body in that moment would go a long way to healing the hurt he'd caused her soul. Her heart pounded as she waited for this powerful man to agree to play along, hoping she still had as much of an effect on him as he did on her.

The helicopter cockpit faced the dying sun, but she didn't want to look at the view behind her when the man in front of her was so striking. Hawk's warm charcoal gaze had the sun's firelight in its depths. She nearly got lost in the colors as he searched her face and she waited with bated breath to see if he would refuse.

A slow smile lifted his lips, and relief lightened her chest.

"Alright." He threaded his arms through the seat belt restraints and held on. "Do your worst, dove."

Her pulse throbbed in her core as she strapped him in, making sure he was secure before she set her other plan in motion.

"You have to hold on the whole time," she commanded as she swiveled over the growing bulge in his pants.

"I will." His jaw clenched with determination. "Even if it kills me."

He hissed a breath when she ground against him, holding on to his sturdy shoulders for balance. The urge to take his cock out of his pants and have her way with him was strong, but if she was truly honest with herself, she wasn't ready.

She rotated her hips and rubbed her clit against his length in small rocking motions. Need built in her core as she found the perfect rhythm and her nipples pebbled underneath her shirt. Slowly, Hawk pushed his hips up and moved with her, creating a rhythm that made her inner muscles throb. Sunlight caught his tightening knuckles, making their dark-sienna shade shine and highlighting his need to let go of the seat belt restraints.

"You want to touch me, don't you?" she huffed her tease, but he drove up into her, hitting her clit through her jeans *just right* and she moaned through the ache.

"You know I fucking do, dove. I can't stand not touching you. But if this is what you need, I'll give it to you. I always will."

Her heart thundered in her chest at the sincerity in his gaze. Instead of confronting those emotions, she locked her fingers on his shoulders, ducked her head, and rocked faster and faster.

Her thighs burned with the motion and her clit grew more sensitive with each roll of her hips. Liquid arousal filled her panties and she couldn't help the whimper that escaped.

"That's it, dove, find your release," Hawk murmured to her

low, his voice thick with his own desire, encouraging her to go faster. "Damn, I've missed you."

Despite the fact they were still completely clothed, need rose up in her core, twisting and tensing with every pulse against his cock. She keened as her pussy climbed higher toward that peak from the friction.

"Fuck, you're going to make me come like this, Han. It's been a long-ass time."

That admission shocked her into pausing for a second and she opened her eyes, not realizing she'd closed them, to see his focused solely on her.

"H-how long?" she asked, worried about the answer, but curiosity got the best of her.

His eyes narrowed but a lilt of pride lifted his lips. "You know how long, baby."

*Not since me.*

The answer whispered sensually over her mind as if he'd said it out loud. Stunned, she swallowed at the revelation. Suddenly, the need to be filled was overwhelming. Her pussy ached for him, but deep down, she still knew her heart wasn't ready for that step. She couldn't go another second without at least feeling his touch, though.

"Let go," she whispered as she rocked forward again on the hard steel in his jeans.

"You don't have to tell me twice," he growled.

He let go of the restraints and slipped his hands underneath her T-shirt. His fingers spread wide, dipping inside the waistband of her jeans as he gripped her waist and hips. His calluses were rough against her skin, just like she remembered. In the small cockpit, with his large body in front of and below hers and his hands spanning her waist, she felt completely supported and secure.

He squeezed tight just above her hip bones and pushed upward with his cock. She moaned at the motion, wishing she'd give herself permission to not only let go, but let him inside, too.

But he didn't seem deterred by her boundaries. Not at all. Instead, he helped her ride him and moved her so quickly against his cock that the final crashing orgasm came out of nowhere.

"Hawk!" she cried out before devolving into full gibberish in Spanish and English. She didn't care what the hell she said as she exploded in ecstasy and emotion on top of him. Her eyes closed as she fell into her pleasure. She focused on the grip of his hands, the way his own harsh breaths mingled with hers, and the slight give the seat beneath them had, allowing them further range to grind against each other as she found her release.

Even though the climb was rushed, quick, and immediate, the fall was a gentle decline that lasted forever, leaving her keening and pulsing against his chest as she came down.

"Ah, *fuck*, I'm coming." Hawk thrust harder against her core until he wrapped his arms around her and trembled underneath her. She pulled back enough to marvel at the sight of his handsome face contorted in pleasure. His brow furrowed as he cursed through gritted teeth, ending with her name on a relieved moan.

When her body was just shakes and tremors of relief, her exhausted inner muscles quivering, she fully collapsed against Hawk's chest, giving in to his embrace and the pleasure of release. Their chests moved in sync and she shivered as his breaths fluttered against her hair. She snuggled into his neck, prompting him to clutch her tighter.

"I'm surprised we just got off like two teenagers in the back seat of a car. In a military-grade helicopter, no less." She giggled.

His laugh rumbled from his chest, vibrating against hers. "Best action this thing's ever seen, I promise you that."

After their breathing finally slowed, she pushed lightly against his hard pecs to sit up. His embrace tightened briefly before he let her move and rested his hands on her hips again.

"I'm also surprised you let me restrain you," she murmured. "It was symbolic, obviously. But still. You're always in charge."

"Listen, if you tell me to sit back and watch you have your

wicked way with me, then I'll buckle up and enjoy the ride any damn day of the week."

His face lit up in a smile, and her eyes dropped to that gorgeous mouth. She absentmindedly traced the outline of his lips, starting from the left side and swooping across the bottom along the curve of his happiness.

"I remember the first time you started doing this." His lips moved underneath her fingers.

Her fingers stilled as she realized what she was doing and she moved them to his chest instead. "You do? I don't even remember how that started."

A wistful look sparkled in his eyes. "It was that time we went camping."

"¡Ay! That trip was the *worst*." She pretended to gag, but Hawk just laughed and kept going.

"Most of it was. Especially when it poured and our—"

"Tent leaked." Hannah shook her head with a grin. "At least it didn't rain the rest of the time."

"That's how I convinced you to sleep out in the open in our combined sleeping bag."

"You didn't have to twist my arm that badly. The view was gorgeous. No light pollution so the nights were bright by the moon and we could see the whole Blue Ridge laid out before us like a blanket under the stars."

"That next morning we made love as the sun rose over the mountains."

"*Made love*." Hannah laughed as her cheeks warmed at the term. "Hawkins Black, that sounds so cheesy!"

"Maybe so." He shrugged with a grin of his own. "But what else do you call it when it's the first time you say 'I love you?'"

Hannah sucked in a sharp breath. How had she completely forgotten that part of their story? Her heart filled with emotion as he kept going, remembering details that had grown hazy with time.

"I woke up that morning knowing how I felt and knowing I

couldn't keep it to myself a second longer. I blurted it out like a fool, but you still somehow thought I was charming enough to sleep with afterward. Then we watched the sunrise, and you traced my face with your fingers. You claimed the best way to get a feel for a painting was to *actually* feel the inspiration."

The memory flooded in and she rolled her eyes, just like she had that morning. "You said I was just using it as an excuse to feel you up. But I *swear* it helps me remember later!"

"Then I asked why you needed to memorize my face when your favorite thing to paint is skies over landscapes. Do you remember your answer?"

Her breath caught in her chest and her heart fluttered. His earnest eyes didn't let up until she finally whispered, "That I never wanted to forget *mi cielo, mi amor*."

"My sky, my love," Hawk repeated softly as he brushed her cheek with the back of his knuckles. "I never forgot you, Hannah. You can trust me. I know it's been a long time. But everything I've done... *everything*... was to take care of you. I swear it."

Those words suddenly triggered a spark of hurt in her chest. She frowned, unable to stop her frustration from bubbling up. "Look how that turned out."

His eyes widened and his jaw dropped just as hers did the same. Her hand flew to her mouth.

"I... I can't believe I just said that. I'm so sorry—"

"Shh, it's okay." Hawk shook his head and cupped her cheek. The sincerity in his gaze was enough to make tears prick in the corners of her eyes. "I... I get it. I hate it, but I get it." Hawk sighed heavily, the weight of the world and all the emotions in the helicopter no doubt weighing him down more than the Kevlar safety harness ever would. "I have a lot of proving to do and forgiveness to ask for. All I can say is with the information I had, I thought I was doing the right thing at the time. Hell, I wonder now if the whole shooting on the Braves opening day was rigged."

It was an idea she'd wondered ever since her father threatened her at the scholarship party, but she'd never been brave enough to say it out loud. Before Hawk found her, she thought it was the worst thing her father could've ever done, tricking them into separating by orchestrating a shooting at a Braves game, all just to scare Hawk into submission. But now that she'd heard the whole story, well, a simple mass shooting sounded like amateur status. It was hard to imagine anything he *wasn't* capable of.

That day flashed through her memory of Hawk drawing away the shooters so she and Thomas could be safe. Risking his life for her and his best friend without hesitation while they fled to safety. Not only had they not pursued Hannah and Thomas, but from the way the news reported, her "mysterious hero vigilante" had narrowly made it out alive.

"You almost lost everything that day," she whispered and placed her hand on his heart.

"I lost everything anyway." The pain in his voice knifed through her, making it hard to breathe as she scanned the sorrow in his face and traced it with her fingers.

"Maybe not everything," she whispered.

His cheeks rose in a soft grin underneath her touch. In the dim twilight, the faint, fine lines on his handsome dark-sienna skin were invisible, but she could still feel their presence. They were the lines that had been etched every year they'd been separated by her own father, and her entire being ached for the time they'd lost. For the memories they could never have, for the choices they'd both made that further drove them apart in the end.

But *was* it the end?

A buzzing beneath them broke their focus and Hawk grumbled as he dug for his phone and swiped the screen.

He huffed as he saw the message and the glow of the screen in the dusk light made his small smile bright white before he spoke into the mouthpiece.

"Tell him she'll be down in a minute." His eyes found hers

and his small grin turned sinful with longing mixed in as he brushed her hair off her shoulder. "We had some catching up to do."

He pocketed his cell phone after the voice memo and sat back again.

"I like your hair. The color suits you."

She'd just grinded herself to pleasure against his cock and yet his simple compliment gave her butterflies in her belly all over again. She gave him a cheeky grin as she unbuckled him.

"I'm an artist, Hawkins. All colors suit me."

"Can't argue with that." He laughed.

He gathered her close to his chest and hopped them out of the open helicopter frame onto the roof. They walked hand in hand toward the roof door where he grabbed his baseball glove, tucked it underneath his armpit and enveloped her palm in his again. He escorted her down the stairs to the second floor, but when she went to open the door his grip tightened, stopping her.

"Wait..." He tugged her close against his chest. With his arms around her, his glove lay against her back and she rested her hand over his pounding heart. His eyes had a hint of worry in them and the pain twisting her own chest made her feel the same.

He threaded his hand in her loose hair and pulled her by the nape to kiss him. Their lips pressed long and hard in a chaste kiss that still sent her heartbeat throbbing to her already sated core.

When they finally broke away, she stepped back to see yearning on his face that she knew mirrored her own.

"I just... I needed another moment with you," he explained.

"Was it enough?" she asked with a small smile.

He shook his head. "Never, but I'll take what I can get."

Whatever this was, whether it was backsliding in a moment of weakness or the continuation of an epic love story, she wasn't sure. But her heart was racing with possibility while her mind screamed at her to run while she could.

He'd left her once, and from what she could tell, what he was doing was just as dangerous as when he was in MF7. So what would stop him from leaving her again? She didn't know if she'd make it if she had to go through that heartbreak a second time. If it hadn't been for Tommy, she might not have made it the first time.

The sound of her sullen child snapping at an undeterred little girl filtered through the steel stairwell door.

"I don't *want* to watch a girl movie. I want to watch *Sports-Center*. Mom only pays for streaming shows so I haven't watched it in forever!"

"Listen, little Tommyhawk, you can argue all you want with that tiny tyrant, but you ain't gettin' what you want. Trust me, I've tried."

"Phoe-nik is right, Tommy. I always win. Everyone says I'm the boss."

Hannah snorted at Thea's high-pitched voice claiming the authority of a CEO. Hawk's broad smile stretched over his face as he chuckled with her.

They both took fortifying breaths before she opened the door. Even as she let go of his hand and walked through, the feel of him lingered under her skin. It always had.

*I never wanted to forget mi cielo, mi amor.*

*"I never forgot you, Hannah."*

Those words felt like the start of something big. But there couldn't be a beginning to their story, right? They'd already had an ending.

"Tommy, time for bed," she called out.

Her son groaned about not having enough TV time as he trudged toward their room.

"Hawk, where ya goin'?" Phoenix asked in a singsongy voice.

Hannah turned to see Hawk scowling at him with his hand hovering over the stairwell knob.

"Going to take a shower in the gym," he answered gruffly.

"Would that be a *cold* shower, maybe?" Phoenix taunted.

Hawk's rolling eyes caught hers. He winked, making her core flutter again. She smiled back but before she turned toward her room, she noticed the mixture of hope and fear in his vulnerable gaze. Her heart cracked seeing the swirl of emotions so much like the ones pounding in her own chest. It physically hurt when she finally looked away.

She didn't know how their story would go, but the one thing she knew without a shadow of a doubt was she couldn't go through the same ending. She'd do whatever it took to make sure that never happened, even if that meant walling off her broken heart.

# CHAPTER NINETEEN

## Nine years ago

Eagle quietly packed his bag, trying not to bring attention to himself as he eavesdropped on the argument in the next room.

"So, you're choosing this new team, your career, my *father*... over me?"

The way Hannah shouted at Hawk made Eagle's stomach churn. For some reason, the last accusation about her father sounded more damning than the others.

As far as Eagle knew, Hannah loved her father. Even if their relationship was strained, she'd still never said a bad word about the man—or talked about him, now that Eagle thought about it. Then again, maybe there was more to their relationship than he knew. After all, despite the fact the man had given them this once-in-a-lifetime opportunity to advance in their careers and make a real change in this world, General Smithers was still a ruthless bastard.

"I'm sorry, Han, but you're not safe now that I'm on this new team. What happened yesterday might just be the beginning with me around." Hawk's words were clipped and succinct, but his low voice cracked with pain.

Eagle listened on as Hawk broke the news to Hannah on the other side of the wall. It wasn't right to invade their privacy. He knew he should've given them space. But when he'd come over to the apartment to gather the rest of his things for his move on base, he accidentally heard Hawk cutting it off and Eagle's curiosity got the best of him—like it always did. Hawk was making the right choice, but how he had the willpower to say goodbye was a mystery to Eagle.

Logically, Eagle knew if Hawk took the selfish route and held on to Hannah then he would be putting her in danger. And if he quit MF7, General Smithers would have him court martialed for desertion. With the way he unabashedly hated anyone who got close to his daughter, he might even push for something as extreme as execution, especially given the top security nature of their team and all the information that had been shared with them already.

But Hawk would never tell Hannah her father hated him so much that he didn't care about hurting his daughter in the fall-out. Eagle had heard the way Hawk hero-worshiped his pops. Hawk would never want to ruin Hannah's perception of her own father, even if he was a total dick.

Leaving was what would keep her safe and alive. Leaving would keep her relationship with her father intact. Leaving was the ultimate sacrifice Hawk could commit, and he was a saint for it. If the shoe was on the other foot, Eagle wasn't sure he would have the balls to do it.

"I can't help but think my father is doing this on purpose somehow. That you're choosing him," Hannah hissed.

"Han, it's not like that. I'm choosing your life. Your safety. If you got hurt because of me—"

"Who cares?! I want to be with you! The Braves game could've had nothing to do with this MF7 *mierda*."

"Han," Hawk's voice muffled and Eagle imagined him holding her close. "I love you. I won't have my career put you in jeopardy."

"So quit," she mumbled without any forcefulness behind it.

The lack of fight in her insistence crashed against Eagle's

heart. They all knew Hawk couldn't quit. Desertion wasn't an option.

"I can't, dove." Hawk's whisper felt like the slamming of a door.

The defeat in his friend's voice almost made Eagle ashamed of listening. He'd never heard Hawk so vulnerable. And it was his fault.

Eagle had known when General Smithers asked him to recruit for the team that giving up Hannah could be a possibility. But he hadn't shared that information with Hawk, afraid his friend wouldn't join if he knew the full stakes. If Eagle was honest with himself, though, he would have to admit he'd also selfishly been hoping for this exact outcome.

*And then I'll swoop in like a knight in shining armor.*

He winced and shook his head. His hopes sounded much more evil now that he was having to hear the painful reality. There was no way he could follow through with betraying his best friend like that.

Besides, it was too dangerous for her to be affiliated with either of them. *Hawk* was the knight in shining armor, doing the right thing to save her life. Eagle was just the bastard with an unrequited crush.

"No, don't hug me. I can't, Hawkins. If you're going to leave, I'd rather you do it now. If this is really goodbye then this—*right now*—is goodbye. I won't be able to say it again."

Silence filled the space louder than any bomb that could've dropped.

Finally Hawk's deep voice rumbled, "I love you, Hannah. I'll never stop."

If she said anything, it was too soft to hear. Before long, footsteps thudded out of Hawk's old room. After the front door finally opened and shut, Eagle's phone vibrated. He jerked it out of his jeans, hoping Hannah couldn't hear and pressed the home button to read the text message.

**Hawk: I told her. Fuck this sucks. I'll be staying on**

**base with you guys now. You were right. It's better if we leave her alone.**

Eagle's fingers flew over the keyboard on the screen, quickly coming up with an excuse as to why he wasn't there with the rest of the guys.

**Be there soon, man. Just running errands.**

**Hawk: I'll fill you in tomorrow. I'm hitting the hay as soon as I get in. Shit sucks.**

**I'm sorry, brother. But it's better this way. We'll make a pact. Leave her alone, keep her safe.**

He waited for what felt like forever before Hawk finally texted him back.

**Hawk: Anything to keep her safe... Agreed.**

Eagle's chest lightened and he shoved the phone in his bag, readying to leave, just as a high-pitched keening made him still.

After waiting another moment, the sound happened again. He yanked his bedroom door open and rounded the hallway to get to Hawk's old room. Before he could stop himself, he'd opened the door wide without even bothering to knock.

Hawk's room looked exactly the same, with Hannah's knick-knacks, Braves memorabilia, and paintings still everywhere Eagle looked. Even Hawk's favorite landscape of an Appalachian sunrise still hung over his bed.

It had to hurt Hawk to leave it, but he bragged about Hannah's talent with pictures on his phone all the time, so he at least still had them digitally. With their lifestyle, Hawk could barely carry around more than a duffel bag. What was left in the room was essentially Hannah's.

Eagle almost couldn't tell that Hawk had moved out and made this huge, life-altering decision.

Except for the woman he'd left behind, still sobbing on his bed.

Hannah's black wavy hair spilled around her face. Her eyes were squeezed shut and tears streamed down her olive cheeks. The sapphire on her ring glinted in the low light of the bedside lamp as she rocked in an attempt to soothe herself. It broke his fucking heart.

"Shit." Eagle's chest caved and so did any resistance he might have had. He crawled across the bed and pulled her onto his lap. "I'm sorry, Hannah."

*I'm sorry I'm a selfish bastard. I'm sorry I helped take him away from you. I'm sorry we're leaving you behind. I'm sorry. I'm sorry. I'm sorry.*

She sniffled and wiped her eyes. "Y-y-you did-didn't d-d-do anything."

"I've done enough," he grumbled too softly for her to hear.

"I... I feel... I feel like I'm losing everything," she sniffled against him, soaking his shirt with her sorrow.

"You're not, Hannah. You..." The betrayal was on the tip of his tongue when he leapt over the edge. "You still have me, at least for tonight. Maybe more if I can swing it."

"But..." she pushed off of his chest and wiped her cheeks. Her long black lashes clung together in spikes as she peered underneath them. "But, Hawk said you're both going?"

He shifted underneath her, and decided to feed the jealousy that'd been brewing ever since Hawk came home after their first date, singing her praises like a fucking canary. He swallowed, hoping he wouldn't regret what he was about to do.

"Hawk is... scared of what could happen. But I'm not scared, Hannah. I have to go, too, but if it's safe enough, I can still contact you. He's afraid to even do that."

"If you can still contact me, why can't he? Doesn't he love me?" she moaned.

He held her closer and murmured assurances against her soft hair. His skin tingled everywhere they touched and he focused on that heavenly feeling as he twisted the knife in his friend's back.

"He loves his country more, Hannah." The lie tasted bitter on his lips. "He's more afraid you'll be a distraction."

She gasped and tried to pull away but his arms tightened

around her and he rubbed her back, trying to calm her. If she saw his face at the moment his expression would give away his true thoughts. There was nothing and no one Hawk loved more than Hannah.

"Face it, Hannah, he gave up a professional baseball career for the Army. He says he's afraid for your safety, but yesterday could've just been psychos with guns for all we know. Hawk is already making decisions based on paranoia."

*Lies. Lies. Lies.*

*Hopefully they'll be worth it.*

But her muscles—languid with sorrow—tensed at his words. The keening noise that had first pierced his heart began again, and he rocked her.

"It hurts, Thomas... it hurts so bad." She cried, her breaths heaving nearly to the point of hyperventilation. "I just want it to stop hurting."

"It's okay, Hannah. Cry it out. I'm here for you."

He lay down on top of the quilt and pulled her onto his chest. The poor thing was so distraught she didn't argue with the intimate position. Not until his body betrayed him.

As his cock hardened beneath her, she lifted her face from his chest to look at him, her questioning brown eyes sparkling with tears. Uncertainty furrowed her brow as she glanced up and down, seemingly just realizing how they lay.

"Eagle, I'm sorry, I should get off."

"Don't," he whispered, making her pause. "I've wanted to feel you like this for a long time. But I never wanted to get in the way of you and Hawk."

"I... I had no idea."

"I know, and I never told you because he's always been good to you. But after seeing you like this? I can't hold back anymore. I love you, Hannah."

He looked at her lips, so close to his, and pulled her closer, wrapping his hand around her nape. Ever so slowly, waiting for her to stop him, he gently pressed his lips against hers.

She trembled above him, not pushing him away, but not kissing him back either. When he let go of her nape and stopped, he opened his eyes to see her face had crumpled. She shook her head slowly, and he almost let it all go. He'd told her how he felt, and she didn't feel the same way. There was nothing he could do about it.

"It hurts Thomas. *I* hurt," she whispered, almost too low to hear.

"Let me make it go away, then, Hannah. Just for tonight."

He waited for an eternity until she gave him the slightest of nods. Without giving her a chance to go back on her decision, he embraced her and rolled them over so he was on top of her.

"What about Hawk?" she asked, her voice watery.

"It's okay, Hannah. He can't be mad at us after leaving you like this. I couldn't hear you crying and just abandon you like he did. Let me make the pain go away. At least for tonight."

His betrayal tasted like ash on his tongue and he desperately needed her sweetness to cover up his shame.

This time when his lips met hers, he finally broke through the last of her reluctance. She tasted like sugar, tea, and oranges, just like Hawk had always boasted, but mixed with the salt of her tears.

Eagle took everything he could from the only night he'd ever be able to have the woman of his dreams. Hawk may have sacrificed everything to give her a safe life. But he'd also gotten to love her while Eagle had never gotten the chance.

If they ever made it back home after MF7, maybe Hawk could try with her again and they'd all continue on like normal. Eagle was taking the moment for what it was. His one shot. One night. That's all he'd ever needed, all he'd ever wanted, to sate this craving for her he'd always had.

He hoped like hell he wouldn't regret it.

# CHAPTER TWENTY

## Present Day

Hawk hoped like hell Hannah wouldn't regret their moment in the sunset.

Afterward, he'd showered off in the gym bathroom since his room was taken. He changed into another black Henley and jeans from his locker before going to the war room to meet with Wes. It was getting late, but Hawk wanted to see if they'd made any headway with the information Hannah had given the women.

Hawk's navy-haired friend sat before the wall of computer monitors, his head shaking in disappointment at whatever he saw on the security footage. When he seemed to register Hawk's presence in the room, Wes faced him and raised his index finger with a dramatic flair before slamming it down onto the keyboard. One of the monitors went black with a white **"DELETED"** message stamped across the screen.

"Really? You too?" Wes glared at him through his black-framed glasses and waved his arms around. "I think everyone but Jason has gotten off in front of our cameras by this point."

"Ah, give it time, Wes." Jason's laugh echoed in from the hallway. He walked into the room with red-rimmed eyes and clapped

Hawk on the shoulder before finding a seat and smiling. "Congrats, man, didn't know you had it in you."

"Don't forget who the first was," Hawk teased Jason, referring to the guy's sister, Ellie. Jason's smile flipped into a scowl and Hawk laughed as he turned to Wes again. "Get over it, brother. It was practically PG."

"Oh, I'm over it, alright," Wes groaned as more of Hawk's team filed in one by one. Hawk hadn't formally called the meeting, but his teammates were just as invested as he was in taking down the General. "I'm this close to giving all of you the codes so you can delete the evidence yourself instead of forcing me to suffer through soft-core porn every damn day."

"Hey, I deleted mine myself, thank you very much," Nora boasted with a bow, spilling her purple curls over her shoulder. "You'll never have to worry about Drake and me."

The giant Viking in question grunted his assent as he pulled out her chair for her and sat beside her.

"Aw, poor Sna—*Wes*, getting paid to watch porn." Phoenix came into the room laughing and miming wiping his tears before sitting in the chair on the other side of Nora. "Cry me a river, buddy. There are worse things about this job."

"Don't we fucking know it," Callie muttered as she collapsed in the chair beside Phoenix.

Phoenix and Callie had been through the wringer to say the least. They would have a long road in therapy, but the way those two tackled everything head-on, Hawk had full faith in their recovery.

Devil walked in and glanced around the room. "Am I the last to show?" he muttered as he slid around Draco to sit at the opposite side of the table from the door.

"No Ellie tonight?" Hawk asked.

Devil shook his head. "She's studying for her summer class on her shift at the clinic. Besides, I want her out of this shit as much as possible."

"You know how much she *loves* to be babied," Nora scolded in a singsong voice, but Devil just shrugged in response.

"Okay, so this is everyone, I take it?" Hawk mentally counted everyone in the room.

*Jason, Devil, Wes, Nora, Draco, Phoenix, Callie...*

"Our two other frequent fliers, Marco and Jules, have court tomorrow," Jason offered about the assistant district attorney they worked with and Jules, his fiancée. "Katie-Belle has her first day of day care tomorrow, so Jules'll probably be crying in court. Poor thing's upset about it."

Phoenix poked Jason's flush cheek, just below his red-rimmed eyes. "Looks like she's not the only one upset. Someone else had a little tear here already."

Jason swatted his hand away and crossed his arms. "Shut up."

Laughter rolled through the room as Hawk sat in his normal spot at the oval table and propped his elbow on the wooden surface. Before he even began speaking, his fingers steepled in front of him, a gesture he'd learned from his pops.

"Alright. What have we got?" he asked.

Wes cleared his throat. "Well, speaking of ADA Aguilar. He texted me today. Apparently, Officer Henry Brown got a visitor in jail."

"How is that fucker even allowed visitors?" Phoenix griped.

Hawk was thinking the exact same thing, but he hadn't wanted to say it out loud in front of Phoenix. The team had only figured out just last week that the former officer was a traitor who had been helping the General. The guy had been one of Phoenix's best friends, so the betrayal had stung even worse for him.

"Every inmate has a right to visitors in jail unless they've needed disciplinary action," Wes answered. "But Marco wasn't able to tell us anything more than the name because the visit was in the mess hall during designated visiting hours and wasn't recorded."

"Dammit," Hawk cursed. "What'd you get from the name?"

"Nothing," Wes groaned. "From everything I could find, it was a fake name. I don't know what that means other than it puts even more pressure on us to find these assholes as soon as possible."

"Fine," Hawk gritted through his teeth. "We'll table that for now. What else do we have?"

"Right." Wes pushed his glasses up as he continued. "Hannah was able to give Nora—"

"*Nora* can speak for herself," Nora tsked before clearing her own throat dramatically.

"Sassy little pixie," Phoenix muttered. One glare from Callie in her badass all-black ensemble and sleek, raven ponytail had him snapping his mouth shut.

"Thank you." Nora smiled sweetly at Callie. "Anyhoo, Hannah was able to give us some pretty valuable information earlier today regarding the General's private property holdings."

She tilted her head toward the wall of monitors where Wes had already pulled up screen after screen showing different properties.

"Holy shit, the guy's everywhere," Phoenix muttered as he balanced on two legs in his rolling chair.

"How are you doing that?" Jason asked, his brows furrowed.

"Talent." Phoenix beamed.

Devil snorted. "He broke the wheels off the damn thing."

"Phoenix! These are new chairs!" Wes scoffed.

"Traitor." Phoenix scowled at Devil, who just shrugged and popped a piece of Big Red gum in his mouth.

"Boys, settle down." Nora wagged her finger before continuing. "But you're right, Phoenix. That's kinda the impression we got too. That he's everywhere. Most of those holdings are in different names or companies, so Hannah was huge in connecting those dots—"

"Thanks," a soft voice piped up.

Hawk swiveled around in his chair to see Hannah, her blonde hair back in a loose side braid and wearing the same T-shirt and jeans he'd just had grinding on him less than an hour ago. His cock twitched in his pants at the thought, but he ignored it and scrambled to his feet.

"Hannah, welcome. Here." He pointed at his seat. "Why don't you sit? Sorry, I didn't know you were coming. Not that that's a bad thing."

Hannah's black brow lifted in response and someone else in the room snickered. Her lips quirked in a smile as she passed by him.

"Nora invited me. And I think I can sit in one of these free chairs. I don't have to take yours." She pulled back the empty rolling chair right next to him and settled in.

"Oh, right." Everyone stared at him as he awkwardly took his seat again.

"Smooth, dude. Real smooth." Phoenix outright laughed.

Hawk's cheeks warmed, but he didn't care if he looked flustered. He *was* flustered. He'd left her back at her room because he hadn't wanted to bother her with the meeting. She didn't know the extent of what was going on with her father, and frankly, Hawk hoped she never found out. At the very least, he didn't want her to find out in front of people who were virtually strangers to her.

"Hannah, you didn't have to come if you didn't want to," he hedged.

"I wanted to." A frown formed on her face and she crossed her arms. "Tommy is sound asleep and I want to be in on all of these conversations."

"Right, just... some of them are about what your father has been up to—"

"We filled her in, Hawk," Callie offered.

Hawk whipped his eyes toward her, unable to hide the shock in his expression. "On *everything*?"

Callie nodded and Nora answered out loud, "Yup." She popped the *p* at the end and tilted her head with a smile, challenging him to scold her for their decision.

He trusted these people with his life. But this *wasn't* his life. It was Hannah's, and he'd never trust her safety in anyone else's hands again.

"But... it's her father—"

Nora grimaced and Hannah's soft hand reached for his. He hadn't even realized he was pointing accusingly at Callie and Nora until Hannah brought his hand underneath the table with hers.

"We have a lot to talk about on that front," she murmured.

"What do you mean?" Hawk felt his face twist with confusion.

"There are things I haven't been... open with you about. Concerning my relationship with him."

The edges of Hawk's vision faded at the sight of the shame on her face coupled with the implication behind her words.

He sucked in a breath before whispering, "Hannah—"

"Later?" she pleaded softly. "I'll tell you when I'm ready. I swear."

Hawk nodded once, knowing in his churning gut that he was going to hate whatever it was she had to tell him. The worst came to mind, but if she wasn't ready to open up yet, then he had to move past it for her sake and for the sake of the meeting.

He tapped his lips, trying hard as hell not to let his mind dwell on every conversation he'd ever had with Hannah in an attempt to decipher the signs he'd missed. Instead, he focused on his team and the fact that Hannah's soft hand still held his underneath the table.

He cleared his throat and addressed the rest of the room. "Okay, so what did we learn?"

Wes pushed his glasses up before speaking. "Well, in looking for the General's location, I was able to track videos across Atlanta, starting with surveillance footage that hadn't been autodeleted at the compound. Rookie mistake, if you ask me, by the way. If you have an autodelete sequence or any systemwide commands, then you have to make sure every single camera and device is connected to the coding, or else the whole thing is for nothing—"

"Yeah, yeah, yeah, Snake." Phoenix waved his hand. "Enough with the techno mumbo jumbo and all that blah, blah, blah."

Wes glared at him.

Phoenix at least had the decency to look chagrined and his tan face reddened. "Sorry... *Wes*. Being an asshole is a force of habit. Can't expect a man to change in a week." He cleared his throat and nodded toward their comms sergeant. "Go ahead. I'll shut up."

"Thank you for trying." Wes whirled his chair around to face the computers and continued on, pointing to a specific screen. "You know how we found tire track marks at the back entrance of the General's compound? I did some cross-referencing with vehicles in old footage and the tread pattern and I was able to figure out what the General was driving. You guys won't believe it. It looks like *Vlad* is the one carting *him* around."

"Really?" Phoenix's voice rose at the end.

Wes nodded emphatically. "I know. Weird, right? But check it out."

He pulled up a video of a black van in a gas station with Vlad in the driver's seat and one of his men pumping gas into the vehicle.

"Hold on..." Wes muttered and typed on the keyboard until the image enhanced and magnified to show—

"Is that the General tied up in the back of the van?" Callie asked.

Sure enough, the General could be seen, clear as day, through a small sliver between the seats, gagged and his hands taped up in front of him.

"The fuck?" Draco grumbled. "That Vlad bastard has kidnapped his own boss now?"

Draco and Vlad had a particularly nasty history. The Russian had attacked Draco and Nora almost a year and a half ago. In the struggle, Nora was kidnapped and Draco was shot and fell into a coma. If it weren't for the lifesaving drugs the team had confiscated from the General's enterprises, Draco would still be a husk of the soldier he once was before his coma, or worse.

The "or worse" was what kept Hawk up at night. He hated the General, but because of his team, Vlad was on Hawk's shit list too. Anyone who fucked with his team, fucked with him.

"Does that mean my... um, the *General* has been usurped, in a sense?" Hannah asked. "There was something the hitman back in Mexico said. I didn't understand it then, and in the blur of everything, it slipped my mind. But when I asked him if my—the General was in charge, he said 'everything is different now,' and something like 'everyone under the old boss has to go.'"

Rage welled in Hawk's veins at the memory of seeing Hannah fight for her life. He tapped his finger against his lips, unable to do anything more to get the energy out at the moment.

"Damn, if the General isn't in charge, then who is?" Jason asked.

The not knowing was chilling enough on its own, until a thought crossed Hawk's mind.

"Wait, what if... what if Vlad is really calling all the shots?"

"What do you mean?" Wes frowned.

"Think about it." Hawk pointed to the screen, checking with everyone else's expression as he hypothesized. "Draco, you said before that the men you encountered a few weeks ago back at the Charitable Technologies International building were mostly Russians. What if the General fucked up? What if he relied too much on Vlad as his henchman and Vlad tipped the scale, so to speak, hiring men on his side to make it easier to turn against the General when the time was right? We know most of the lackeys at the Ashland County fundraisers were Russian."

"You could be onto something," Callie pointed out, giving Hawk a burst of satisfaction. "I was underground in that compound for two years and Vlad was the one doing not just all the dirty work, but all the *actual* work, too. What if *he's* behind everything while the General is just the mouthpiece?"

"I doubt the General would like that." Jason frowned.

"Maybe he didn't realize it until it was too late..." Hannah offered, her face tight as she obviously fought to keep her emotions in check.

Hawk couldn't imagine what was going through her head. Granted, if they were sitting there talking about his pops in the same way, Hawk would tell them they were all out of their damn minds. But the relationship between Hannah and her father was obviously more twisted than he'd ever known or could've guessed.

They all watched the screen in silence as Vlad did a hand motion to the man outside of the van. The lackey hopped into the car and Vlad drove off. A snippet of the General appeared in the picture, the whites of his eyes wide with terror.

"Shit, what if you're right?" Phoenix mumbled as the van drove off the screen.

The room grew silent for a few moments as they sat in thought.

Hawk absentmindedly traced his lips, finding comfort in the gesture in the face of so many unknowns. After a few circles around his mouth, he finally spoke again. "The only question I have—"

"You only have *one*?" Jason interrupted.

Hawk tipped his head. "Fair. But I do wonder... why would they still go after Hannah? When Draco and I went to Mexico, she was already under attack... why?"

"Loose ends," Hannah murmured quietly beside him.

"We all heard him say *that* plenty of times," Phoenix pointed out.

"Vlad even threatened me with 'cutting loose ends' when he found me at the party. Before yesterday, the threats I got were more taunts that the General knew where I was and he'd found me once again. This time it escalated. Maybe, it wasn't the

General after me in Mexico. Maybe it was Vlad trying to get rid of me? He already thought I knew more than I did. *Dios mio...* I could've actually died yesterday."

Hannah's olive skin turned sallow with the realization. Hawk ground his teeth and squeezed her hand, hoping to provide comfort. It was one of the few gestures they could do in front of people, but he wished he could do more.

"He won't get to you, Hannah," he promised.

A small smile lifted her lips. It felt good to give her a modicum of relief, but when he turned back to his team, the rest of them had similar sickly looks as they all glanced around the room.

"If Hannah's a loose end. That means we're all loose ends," Wes said out loud and swallowed.

"Good." Phoenix took off his hat and slapped it on the table. "We've been on the General's radar for way too damn long. It's time we take him and his giant henchman off the map entirely. Let's go through the evidence and see what other loose ends there are."

Nora nodded. "You're right. If we find some of our own, maybe they'll lead us straight to where Vlad and the General are going."

Hawk's fingertips drummed on his bottom lip for a long moment. "Anything else to know, Wes?"

"No, that's the most recent footage we have. It's a gas station right before the interstate on-ramp. I lost them after that, the net gets too wide and I'm already pushing our good-will with the FBI." Wes nodded appreciatively in Callie's direction.

"In that case..." Hawk glanced at Hannah with a smile. "Ready to play detective?"

"I've been stuck as the mouse in this cat-and-mouse game for way too long. I'm ready to play any other role you've got at this point."

The curve of her pretty lips had imagery of a completely

different role Hannah could play flashing through his mind before he banished it.

*Now's not the fucking time.*

"Alright." Hawk dropped his hand to the table with a light tap. "Time to put together all the evidence we've collected the past ten years and solve the biggest case of our lives."

"A.k.a., let's end this motherfucking thing," Phoenix whooped.

# CHAPTER TWENTY-ONE

"Psst."

Hawk's brow furrowed at the faint sound. Something in the back of his mind told him to wake up, but sleep lulled his instincts and lured him back in. The team had stayed up for hours putting clues together. Hawk only went to bed when Hannah did so he could ensure she was safe for the night.

But a tap on his thigh had him springing into action, landing in a ready stance, his hand on his holster—

Only to see a wide-eyed Hannah staring at him with her hands up.

"Shit, Hannah." His hand leapt from his holster and his heart rate skyrocketed and plummeted in a split second, making him light-headed. He leaned shoulder first against the wall and pressed his other hand against his chest to keep his heart from bursting out. "I'm so sorry. I didn't mean to scare you."

"What're you doing out here?" she whispered, pointing to the ground where he'd been sleeping the past two nights. Her blonde hair was freshly plaited to the side, and she was dressed in a long blue T-shirt and thin sleep shorts that showed off her thighs.

"Um..." He rubbed the back of his neck to get the crick out, using the angle to downplay the fact he'd been checking her out, and to avoid answering the question. "Uh, you know. Just... sitting."

"It's six a.m." She crossed her arms and pursed her lips with a knowing gaze. "How was your *sleep*, Mr. Guard Dog?"

"Ah... so you already knew, huh?" He chuckled.

She shrugged. "Naomi might've mentioned your sleeping conditions. But what I want to know is *why*? She said there's an open bedroom, and I thought *you* said this place was safe."

"It *is*." He stopped massaging his neck and gripped his nape with his hand instead, letting his arm hang in that bent position as he tried to explain. "It's just... I hadn't seen you in years and my fear for your safety hasn't changed. I left you a decade ago because my job was getting you shot at and I found you in the same situation. I guess you could say I have a complex now." He grinned wryly before tilting his head at her. "And why are *you* up?"

"*Mierda*. Yeah, I can see how that could cause issues in the ol' psyche." She winced and shook her head with a sigh. "I woke up to paint. Twilight starts in ten minutes and sunrise is in thirty. Sorry for waking you. I just didn't want you to freak out if you realized I was gone."

"Oh, no, I'm glad you did. You're painting?" His heart leapt at the thought of her painting an Appalachian sunrise again.

"Yup. I'm using the supplies you got me and everything. Mine have dwindled since we were always on the move." She toed the ground with her bare foot and Hawk couldn't stop staring at its slender arch until she spoke again, "Do you, um, do you want to come?"

"Come? With you?" He couldn't hide the excitement in his voice. "You'll let me watch?"

Her eyes sparkled, and she nodded. "Yeah. Come on. I'll pour us some tea and you can see me work my magic."

She wiggled her fingers like jazz hands and headed toward the kitchen. Hawk fell in step behind her, his heart thumping with pleasure at the opportunity to watch her paint again.

"You get the pitcher. I'll get the cups," she offered once they got to the kitchen.

As she reached into the cabinet, her shorts rode up, showing off the smooth curve of her ass.

"Hawk... the pitcher?"

His gaze darted up to see the amused expression lifting her lips. The cool air from the refrigerator hit the side of his face, making him realize Hannah had just caught him standing there in the open refrigerator door, staring at her ass.

*Busted. Whelp, I've got to own it.*

"Shit, sorry. I guess I got distracted." He smirked and she ducked her head with a smile.

"Yeah, yeah, yeah, just get the pitcher, will you?" She giggled as she placed the cups under the ice maker.

He grabbed the pitcher from the refrigerator and as she set out the ice-filled cups side by side, he poured the tea to the brim in each. Once they were filled, he returned the pitcher to the fridge and took a sip of the sugary beverage from his glass. A light moan escaped him as the sugary flavor with just a hint of orange teased his taste buds.

"Mmm, it's been so long since I've had your sweet tea. It's just as delicious as I remember."

"Really? You guys had all the ingredients already. This industrial aesthetic gives off a bachelor vibe, so I was surprised to see both black tea and orange blossom tea in your cabinets. Plus, all of you are ripped. I didn't think you'd own sugar at all. I wasn't expecting to even find a pitcher, if I'm honest."

"We stocked up recently," Hawk answered vaguely, not wanting to give away that those items had been on his latest shopping trip when he'd gone out to get the paints.

"Let's head up there. I don't want to miss twilight if I can help it."

Hannah poured a red Solo cup of water and carried both the water and her mason jar of tea toward the stairs. Hawk took his own glass and joined her as she entered the stairwell and climbed the stairs to the roof.

"What's this third floor going to be?" Hannah asked on their way. "I peeked in and it looked totally empty? No rooms or anything, just one long warehouse floor."

"We bought this place hoping we could grow into it one day. We all lived out of duffel bags for so long, we were itching to plant our roots together and make lives for ourselves."

"I get that," Hannah replied once they arrived at the top of the stairs. Nestling her cups in the crook of her arm, she carefully gathered some of the supplies she'd stored on the landing. Hawk collected the rest of her materials and balanced his own glass with his elbow before opening the door to the roof. "I would love to make something stable for Tommy. We've been on the run for too long."

His heart twisted in his chest. "Even a day on the run is twenty-four hours too long."

She nodded and tilted her head toward the roof. "Come on."

"Oh, there's no way I'm not following you now." He chuckled and opened the door. Her full, dark-rose lips ticked up at his flirting, making his cock twitch in his jeans.

Once they stepped out onto the rooftop, the summer morning air filtered through the long sleeves of his black Henley. Hawk's eyes scanned his surroundings, making sure all was well. He saw nothing but the spherical turbine vents, their rolling toolbox, and the grill, and no one jumped out from behind the large tool shed when he extracted a folding chair for himself.

Farther down the roof, the helicopter stood austere and untouched in the dawn. Behind it, the sky was a navy hue fading into a lighter blue, promising an end to the night even though stars still twinkled above. There was already the barest hint of red, orange, and pink kissing the tree line.

They padded across the dark roof, her in her bare feet and him in his sneakers, until she brought them to the edge. The guard wall was at neck level for her so she could still see the view over the concrete railing. She set the paints on the ground and Hawk extended the portable aluminum easel he'd bought. Once everything was ready, she picked up the canvas she'd been working on and placed it on the easel.

He could already see the makings of the sunrise that must've inspired her the day before. The red, orange, yellow, purples, and blues were a blended blur, as if he was squinting at a real sunrise.

"I'm not finished yet, obviously," she muttered sheepishly. "This is mostly the color-tone base I'm working off of and then adding the colors on top."

"You don't just paint the view straight on the canvas?" he asked.

"Sometimes I do. But it provides a more rich background if there's a different tint underlying it. And if you leave it off-white, everything that color still looks unfinished and you have to paint over them anyway."

"Ah, gotcha. Well, it's already gorgeous. If you stopped right here, I'd still put this on any wall in the building."

A small smile ghosted her lips before she peered around the canvas and studied the sunrise.

"I got here a little too late for twilight yesterday and I've thought about coming back ever since. I didn't even need an alarm this morning. My body was that excited to see it." She shook her head, a look of awe relaxing her features. "It's perfect."

The breeze fluttered her dark-blonde baby hairs out of her braid. Her rounded cheeks glowed from the brightening sky and the reddish-pink shade sparkled in her brown eyes.

"It is," he breathed, letting her see that all his attention was on her before he looked back at the sky. "*Tu cielo.*"

She startled, and he felt her eyes on his skin as tangible as a touch.

"My sky," she breathed, making her breasts rise and fall underneath her blue T-shirt.

The moment grew thick between them, drawing Hawk into

her like a magnet. She shook her head and cleared her throat before gathering paints for her palette.

"I should, um, get started."

"Just pretend I'm not here," he murmured as he set out the game day folding chair behind her in order to watch her work.

At first, the muscles in her shoulders were tense as she mixed paints and glanced periodically between him, the easel, and the view. He almost teased her about being nervous around him, but he was too excited to see her get lost in her passion. Soon enough, her entire demeanor relaxed as her muscle memory and love for the art settled her into a rhythm.

"The blue mountains create a totally different tint to the sky. The navy mixes so well with the purple here, then transforms into red, orange, yellow, a true rainbow of cool to warm colors blending down to the ground," she murmured to herself. "It's gorgeous. I haven't seen an Appalachian sunrise in ages."

Hawk sat and watched her in silence, taking in her shapely legs shifting from one foot to the other as she worked, her quick hands flicking paint here and there before fanning out the colors to blend them. After several brush strokes on the canvas, she'd finally seemed to have found her groove.

"How was throwing the ball with Tommy yesterday?" she asked, her voice slightly monotone from focusing.

"The little man tried to warn me off yesterday," he joked.

"Oh yeah?" Her lips ticked up in a smile. "Warn you off from what?"

"You," he answered simply as he propped his elbows on the folding chair's arms and steepled his fingers in front of his lips.

Her brow furrowed, and she paused mid-brushstroke. "He warned you off from me? What for?"

"Little man said you're already in love with someone else." He felt his smirk grow at the bewilderment wrinkling her face.

"In love with... *que rico*, what is that *niño loco* talking about?"

"I don't know. Something about *tu cielo*." His head tilted lazily to the side as he examined her shocked gaze.

Her lips parted and her free hand ghosted over a curious, raised circle that must've been connected to a necklace underneath her shirt. Her eyes widened in uncertainty and shock.

"Yeah, that was my expression, too," he chuckled. "But then I realized how fucking lucky I am."

"Lucky?" she asked and turned back to the canvas to paint more furiously than before.

"Yeah... not many people get a second chance with the woman they screwed up with."

"Hawk, I never said I was still in love—"

"I know," he interrupted softly. He didn't want to fluster her, but he still needed to tell her how he felt, if for no other reason than to let her know he was serious about earning forgiveness, even if he didn't deserve it. "But the fact I was on your mind at all these past years, well, that's lucky all on its own. Do you think you'd be able to give me a second chance? To make it up to you?"

"Hawk... I don't know." Her voice was quiet as she slowly dotted a dark-greenish-blue color at the bottom of the canvas, creating the conifer trees the Blue Ridge was known for. "I mean, you left me, sure. But, how could you even want me after..."

"After what?" he asked. His brow furrowed hard enough to hurt as he racked his brain, trying to figure out what she'd fill in the blank with.

"After my father screwed you guys over so royally—"

"Hannah, that wasn't you. That was your *father*. I'm just hoping you forgive me for leaving you for his fucked-up schemes."

"That wasn't *your* fault, either. But I... I slept with your best friend. How could *you* forgive *me*?"

His chest ached at the pain and guilt in her voice. He was on his feet in a second and lifting Hannah's chin in the next.

"Hannah, baby, how could I possibly be angry at you? Sure, ten years ago, I would've been upset. And maybe if I was still foolish and in my twenties, I'd be jealous. But after everything we've both been through..." He shook his head and let his sincere gratitude show through. "My best friend is gone, Han, and after all this time, I was sure I'd lost you, too. Now I have you in front of me and a piece of the best friend I thought I lost forever. You and I have lost so much, dove. Tommy is the biggest blessing we could ask for."

Hannah's eyes grew watery and Hawk brushed her cheek, catching a tear before it tipped over the apple of her cheek.

His heart thudded in his chest as he succumbed to asking the question that had been a constant in his mind, "Can I ask... how it happened?"

Her breath came out in a shudder and she held on to his wrist as she seemed to figure out where to start.

"It was right after we broke up. Thomas was there..."

*He'd said he had already moved out. Why was he there?*

The question buzzed in his mind, but he didn't want to interrupt.

"He must've heard me crying. You were gone and the next thing I knew he was consoling me. Honestly, I don't remember what he said. I just remember being... *devastated*."

"Fuck, Hannah, I'm sorry." His own voice cracked as his heart split in two.

She shrugged and set her paints aside on the small table jutting out of the easel. "He said he had loved me from the beginning. I guess I was a fantasy that'd always been too far away, but when you were out of the picture, he didn't want to hold back anymore."

Hawk cursed inwardly and for the first time since Eagle had died, he wanted to bring his best friend back from the dead solely to knock his ass out.

"I gave in to my grief, and I think he regretted it just as much as I did when it was all said and done. Thomas had always been my *friend*. He thought we could be more, but it was obvious that next morning he believed we were better off as friends, too. We never spoke again after that. He left when you did. And I was all alone. Until a few months later when I realized I was pregnant."

"And we were already gone," the words whispered out on a sigh.

She nodded and blew out a breath. Hawk massaged her shoulder as she continued, "I tried so hard to forget about that night entirely that when I first found out I was late, it didn't even occur to me that my baby could be anyone's other than yours. The thought that he could be Eagle's only came later. Then this precious little blond-haired, blue-eyed baby boy came out confirming it." She huffed a laugh with a slight shake of her head. "There was no way to get in touch with either of you, so I just hoped one day I'd see you again, and hopefully when either of you saw him, you'd love him as much as I do."

"I do," Hawk answered immediately, not a question in his mind. "I didn't realize that was a thing. But as soon as I saw my best friend looking back at me, I fell in love with the kid. Eagle would have, too," he assured her.

A small smile crept across her lips but when she met his gaze again, sadness overwhelmed her features. "I'm sorry you lost Thomas... Eagle. Can I... Can I ask how *that* happened?"

Her mirroring his words hit him harder than it should have, but he cleared his throat and nodded.

"We were on what was supposed to be our last mission of that tour. It was in Yemen. We all thought we were finally going home afterward, but something went wrong. Eagle, Jaybird—Jason—and I infiltrated the enemy compound to disarm the big trafficker in the area. But he somehow already knew we were there. He had, uh... a"—Hawk swallowed and motioned over his chest as he tried to find the words inside the memory—"bomb strapped to his chest."

"*Dios mio*," she whispered.

Hawk shook his head. "I've seen a lot of things, but I've never seen evil and crazy mixed up so well in one expression. That's what stared back at us right before he blew the place up.

Eagle, Jaybird, and I barely got out of there, but when we did, everything outside had gone haywire."

"Haywire?" Hannah asked in a whisper.

"We'd trained some locals to be on our side and to help them combat any future threats they might have after we left, but I guess they were playing us the whole time. Suddenly, we had *friendly* fire coming from all sides."

"No," Hannah breathed, her hand drifting up to cover her mouth.

"One of the local soldiers got a bead on Jaybird and I saw them aim. Eagle and I were able to get to him in time, but Jaybird still got grazed in the head. We made our way back to the helo, but Eagle got hit in the thigh on the way."

Hannah stilled, apparently realizing this was the part of the story where shit got real. Her eyes were already rimmed with tears and Hawk looped his arm around her shoulder to pull her in for a hug. His back was to the sunrise so he focused on the fading blue sky in front of him as he continued.

"I sprinted back to Eagle to carry him into the helicopter. There were guys everywhere, but one had a good bead on me and fired. I thought I was done for, but Eagle pushed me out of the way. He took the bullets instead of me. He saved me."

Hawk rested his chin on Hannah's head and stroked her cheek as she sniffled underneath him. A warm tear spilled over his thumb and he swiped it away as he spoke about carrying Eagle to the helicopter, fighting to keep him alive, but ultimately losing the battle.

He told her everything. Every shitty detail of getting him back. Everything she needed to know.

But what he kept to himself was the fact they now knew from her own father that Eagle betrayed them... for her and Tommy. And what she also didn't need to know was that Hawk might've done the same fucking thing.

When he was finished, her tears flowed freely and a lump of emotion kept him from saying anything more. Instead, he let her cry against his chest. No matter what had happened between them, their best friend was gone. The man who had sacrificed his team for her, and sacrificed his life for him.

While Hannah cried in his embrace, an overwhelming sense of purpose filled him.

Eagle had died for the three of them. The best way to honor his memory was to keep Hannah and Tommy out of harm's way. Hawk already knew he'd protect them with his life, but it dawned on him for the first time that he would do literally whatever it took to keep them safe. A decade ago, he'd sacrificed his own happiness to save her. Now he'd sacrifice everything.

The BlackStone team was going after the General any day now. The man who had stolen his best friend and his relationship with the woman he loved. But if going after the General meant losing Hannah in the process...

Hawk had a lot of fucking thinking to do. There was no way he could leave her again. No way he could repeat the past.

When she'd finished crying, she straightened and withdrew herself from his embrace. Before he could say anything else, her lips found his.

Surprise filled his chest, and he brought her flush to his body. He threaded his hand through her thick, wavy hair, loosening her braid, and squeezed her ass through her soft sleep shorts with his other hand. His cock thickened in his jeans as her plush lips melded to his and her tongue delved into his mouth. But the tears he tasted made him pause.

"Han, you're upset."

"Not so upset that I don't know what I'm doing, Hawk," she whispered against his lips. "I want this."

"Are you sure?" he asked, wanting like hell for her to say—

"Yes."

He put all of his emotions into their kiss, holding her close as his cock grew hard underneath her wandering hands. But despite the fact she said she wanted him, and the way she tugged at his zipper obviously showed she meant it, he couldn't take advantage of her emotional state. He wanted to earn back her trust, and having sex with her when she was upset would be no better than what Eagle had done to her all those years ago. And as much as he loved his best friend, Hawk knew he was better than that.

With a smile curving his lips, he repeated her words from the night before.

"I have an idea."

# CHAPTER TWENTY-TWO

"An idea? But I already like *this* idea." Hannah moaned in protest as Hawk pulled away from her. She felt downright sassy when he whirled her around to face the easel.

"You'll like this idea, I promise." He chuckled behind her and planted her paintbrush into her hand. "I want to see you paint the sky."

"Hawk, please. I don't want to paint right now. I need you." She tried to rotate, only to have his palms land firmly on her shoulders.

It was probably wrong to fix her grief this way. She'd certainly done it once before. But this time, it wasn't just sorrow fueling her decision, there was thankfulness, too. Without Thomas, Hawk wouldn't be here with her now and she wouldn't have her son. She'd mourned her friend deeply two years ago, and with Tommy, it was impossible for a day to go by without thinking of him and Hawk. But knowing now that Thomas had sacrificed his life to save Hawk's helped mend the wound in her soul.

Hawk was *alive*. And, more than anything, she wanted to feel his skin against hers. To feel her soul connect to his again in the dawn light like it had the first time they'd said "I love you."

But the infuriating man's grip wouldn't budge, and frustration made her squirm.

"Hawk," she huffed. "What're you—"

"Paint, dove," he whispered in her ear. He bit her earlobe, and a surprised moan slipped out of her. "Trust me."

Her spine tingled with the feel of his sturdy chest at her back.

"O-okay," she breathed.

Lightly tapping the bristles onto the palette, she gathered a bit of greenish blue. She'd combined the two colors until they perfectly matched the Blue Ridge mountains when the sun peeked over them.

Just as she put brush to canvas, Hawk's wide, strong hands left her shoulders and caressed down her back to her sides. Her skin tingled underneath her shirt everywhere he touched. His chest still pressed to her back, hardly allowing any room between them as he slid over her curves and under her shirt.

His calloused hands were rough on her belly on their way up to her chest. Her heart stuttered at the thought he might feel her necklace hanging at the top of her cleavage, but he cupped her breasts and didn't go any farther. When he caressed them, desire pooled in her panties and she moaned. Her entrance literally ached to be filled and she pushed her ass back into his hardening cock. With his fingers twirling around her nipples, the sensitive tips grew taut beneath the soft cotton of her shirt, sending zings of pleasure to her clit. She tightened her inner muscles, trying to give herself some relief.

"Hawk, please..."

His soft lips kissed behind her ear along her neck while he tweaked her nipples, building a fire in her core. When he got to her nape, he whispered again, his hot breath sending delicious shivers all over.

"Keep painting the sunrise, dove."

His prompting made her realize the brush was poised above the canvas, dripping onto the lip of the easel.

"I'll paint this stupid sunrise if you promise to make it worth my while," she growled.

He chuckled as he kneeled behind her. "I promise I'll make this view one you won't forget."

She swooped the brush downward to depict the light curve of a rolling valley just as Hawk's hands left her breasts and stroked her own curves. His fingers curled into the waistband of her sleep shorts and slid them down along with her panties, leaving her bare to the breeze. After the fabric rounded her hips, he let it fall to her feet and crouched to follow them.

Her long T-shirt drifted against her thighs, but Hawk pushed up the hem. The warm, summer morning air skated over her skin and Hawk's even hotter hands squeezed and kneaded her. She peered over her shoulder to see his hungry eyes staring up at her right as he bit her butt.

"Hawk!" She giggled.

"Get to work, Han." His sensual grin made her pussy flutter. "I'm going to taste you, but while I do it, I want you to watch the sunrise. From now on, every time you see those colors, I want you to remember the pleasure I'm about to give you."

Her eyes widened. "You're going to do *that* while I work?"

His charcoal gaze heated and before she could hop out of his grip, he smacked her ass.

"Hawk!"

"I'll make you come *only* if you paint while I do it. As soon as you stop, so do I." His wink had her clit pulsing, begging for attention. "I want to see progress after I'm done making you come on my tongue. Paint me a pretty picture, dove."

"*Fine.*" She dragged her eyes from the sexy man between her thighs to the stunning sunrise in front of her.

The sky had brightened to gorgeous purples and oranges, with half of the sun cresting bright yellow over the blue-green mountains. She dipped her brush in the color for the trees and returned to paint their boughs while Hawk massaged her ass cheeks and inside her upper thighs. He dropped wet, open-mouthed kisses on the globes of her ass and spread her legs. Loving the direction his filthy mind was taking, she widened her stance for him, letting him pull her back so her hips were forward and her butt was slightly perked in the air.

They both moaned as his finger stroked her core.

"Fuck, Hannah, you're dripping for me, baby."

"Mhmm." She sank her teeth into her lip as he did it again, this time teasing her entrance, spreading her arousal around.

He chuckled against her opening, sending hot breath against her wet pussy and giving even more sensation before swiping his tongue up her seam.

"Hawk!" she cried out and dropped her palette and paint-brush to the easel's table.

"Nuh, uh, uh, Hannah. I said you have to paint."

"*Hawkins*," she grumbled but snatched her paintbrush up with one hand and clutched the edge of the guard wall for balance with the other.

As soon as she smeared color over the smooth canvas again, his tongue was back at her center, lapping her up like her pussy was the most delicious thing he'd ever eaten.

Almost as if he'd read her mind, he murmured low into her opening. "I love your sweet tea, dove. But fuck, I swear to God, your pussy is the sweetest thing I've ever tasted. I could drink you all day."

His words alone were enough to make her inner walls contract, almost painfully without having anything to squeeze. But then he pointed his tongue to get farther into her core, giving her just a hint of relief.

As she struggled to keep her eyes on the view, the purples and blues blended with the oranges, reds, and yellows above the blue-green trees. The striking fusion of color in the sunrise accompanied by the breathtaking way Hawk swirled his tongue through her center brought her to the near brink of explosive release.

"Please, Hawk. I need to come."

"I'll always give you what you need, Hannah."

Without any other warning, he dug the fingers of one hand into her upper thigh, spread her legs and tilted her hips. The angle was slightly uncomfortable, but a thrill rushed through her when she felt him move slightly underneath her and between her legs to get into a better position. His other hand slid two fingers into her core, quickly finding her G-spot. His tongue circled around her clit as he continued to kneel behind her while he massaged her inner muscles. Her pussy sucked his fingers, and the sound of him eating her out made her cheeks heat.

As much as she wanted to relax and soak in the delicious orgasm she was already climbing to, she didn't want him to stop and she knew he would if she dropped her brush. She painted the trees furiously, not giving a fuck if they looked good, only focusing on the way his tongue swirled between her thighs.

"Paint for me, little dove," he hummed his approval and the muscles in her lower belly clenched, readying for release.

"Yes... mmmm... *mi cielo*," she whispered.

His fingers shifted to a feathering motion against her G-spot. She climbed and climbed while clenching the paintbrush and smearing it haphazardly across the canvas. His grip on her thigh tightened as her body tried to squirm away from the impending pleasure.

Even though it felt impossible, she did her best to keep her eyes wide, trying to take in every single detail of the view as the sun kissed the clouds and the tips of the tallest dark-green trees. When her orgasm catapulted higher, her pulse raced with it. The beautiful scene in front of her darkened at the edges until she and the sun finally crested over the peak.

"*Dios mio*, please, please, please, *mi cielo*! I'm coming!"

"Paint it, dove."

She clutched the concrete guard wall and cried out. Her chest tightened as heavy breaths pulsed from her lungs. As if they had a mind of their own, her hips pushed against his tongue, searching for that last final...

"*¡Mi cielo!*" she moaned.

Her eyes slammed shut, making all the colors swirl into their inverted hues, a rainbow in reverse. Hawk's lips surrounded her clit and sucked rhythmically, sending her barreling into ecstasy as her body tightened and released over and over. He never let up on his ministrations, his tongue and fingers keeping the rhythm that brought her steadily down that mountain of euphoria.

When she finally opened her eyes, she twisted around to see burning lust beaming back up at her. Hawk glanced from her to the canvas and his mischievous umber smile, glossy with her arousal, widened. Loving that upward curve, she traced his wet lips until he began to chuckle underneath her finger.

"So that's what an orgasm looks like when it's painted, huh? Seems a little abstract. Maybe it's a river?"

She turned back to see the canvas in front of her. A large stroke of blue green swept up into the violet, orange, and yellow sky. A hoarse laugh escaped her, and she tilted her head for a better angle.

"A river in the sky? Not so sure about that. It is pretty, though. Like a mirage over the mountains. In any case, I can fix it. I'll just paint over it."

"Leave it," he murmured behind her. She turned to face him again and brushed her hand over the soft, short waves in his fade. His earnest gaze melted her heart. "Don't paint over it. Use it to create something new. Something it couldn't have been without it."

As he stood, she wrapped her arms around his neck and got on her tiptoes to kiss him, loving that this powerful man tasted like her.

"It'll be something better," she promised against his lips, her chest alight with hope. "And unforgettable."

"It'll be perfect, dove."

# CHAPTER TWENTY-THREE

## Two years ago

Eagle regretted it. Even seven years later, the memory of that night wormed its way into his conscience daily. An unbidden, unwelcome reminder of his betrayal every time he looked at his best friend.

Almost as soon as he'd left his old apartment the next morning, he'd wished he could take it all back. Succumbing to his feelings for Hannah while she was overcome with grief was the worst thing he could have done. Besides the fact he potentially ruined his relationship with Hawk, it just confirmed that he and Hannah would never be more than they were. Friends. And after all this time, they might not ever be that again, either.

The entire encounter was awkward. Hannah cried the whole time, and he felt like a prick for stabbing one friend in the back while taking advantage of the other. In the end, he became the coward he'd accused Hawk of being. He'd run away after having his tryst and never looked back. Instead of trying to reach out to Hannah again like he'd promised, he'd assuaged his guilt by holding strong to the pact he'd made with Hawk to leave her alone and keep her safe.

All those thoughts raced through his head as he drove to the General's office. It was Eagle's first time back on American soil in he didn't know how the fuck long, years, at least. His team—including their new recruit Devil—were nomads and underdogs in the fight against human trafficking.

There seemed to be no end in sight, despite the fact they'd been picking off supposed ringleaders left and right. The trade was insidious, like the heads of a hydra. Every time they cut off one organization, two more syndicates would crop up.

And now that General Smithers had asked him for a secret, private meeting, it was time Eagle brought his team home, for good.

His friends didn't know his plans, yet. He'd been afraid to tell them prematurely, just in case the meeting blew up in his face. But he was hoping the latest bit of intel would put him in a good negotiating position against the General.

"A little blackmail never hurt anybody," he muttered.

Years ago, pre-MF7 Eagle would've been shocked to hear he was going to go toe to toe against his hero. The Eagle today, however, didn't give two shits about the bastard. Eagle would do whatever he had to in order to get his team home. He hoped to fuck it wouldn't have to come to that, though.

Their missions had become more and more dangerous, to the point that the team had a recurring joke that the General was trying to get rid of them. After what he'd learned during their last job, Eagle was beginning to suspect they were right.

They'd gone after a low-level pimp, rookie shit after the years of training and missions they'd endured, but one of the girls they'd saved had triggered something in his mind.

She'd looked a hell of a lot like Hannah.

He and Hawk had talked about it before, how uncanny it was that a few of the women over the years had looked so much like her. They'd first noticed it a couple of years ago on a job back in the States. But during the most recent mission, the resemblance was too striking to ignore. He hadn't been able to stop himself from checking back in on the survivor.

That's when things got fucked up.

The team worked side by side with the Rahab Foundation, an organization that helped trafficked and abused survivors reintegrate back into society, giving them tools to thrive after everything else had been stolen away. But the more Eagle looked into it, the more he found some disturbing discrepancies.

No matter how hard or how long he'd searched, he couldn't find records on the women they'd saved in the Rahab Foundation's database. Granted, MF7 rarely got a full name, date of birth, and hometown from the women before the Rahab Foundation came to help them. That was the foundation's job. But of the faces and names Eagle could remember—specifically the Hannah lookalikes—he'd only been able to find one woman, and she had just committed suicide in a psychiatric hospital.

Even though Eagle wasn't a genius at computers like Snake, he was no novice. He understood enough coding to hack the foundation's records, and to realize important shit was missing from the files.

Eagle had thought about bringing it up to Hawk. But what if he was wrong? And how the hell would he even broach the subject?

*"Hey brother, I think the women we're saving might be getting sold back into sexual slavery. That's one of the reasons why the trafficking never stops and the kingpins seem to only get bigger and bigger. Oh yeah, and the General? You know, the love of your life's father? Yeah, he tricked you into this shit so he could have Hannah all to himself for some sick reason. Anyway, go USA and go Braves."*

Yeah, no, that would *not* go over well. If he was going to ruin Hawk's world, *again*, he was going to do it with fucking proof. And to be honest, if Eagle got what he wanted for his team without having to blackmail, he could be tempted to just forget his "theories."

What he suspected was more than diabolical. It was treason. So fucking unbelievable that Eagle prayed he was missing crucial components to the puzzle.

For example, the foundation often gave survivors new identities, so maybe their information was wiped from the system afterward. And obviously, there was always the possibility that he and Hawk had been going slightly crazy without Hannah. Hawk especially.

Hawk used to be full of laughs and happiness, all centered around Hannah. Now he was serious, sullen, and rarely spoke. The only time he fell back into the old Hawk was when they watched baseball or drank orange-flavored sweet tea, like the kind Hannah used to make. Eagle's best friend had become a shell of who he once was.

They all had. Spending this much time doing this kind of work would eventually wear down any man's soul. They needed to be done, for good.

That was why Eagle was going to first *ask* the General about coming home and staying home. If that didn't work, there was one final puzzle piece he wanted to gather before he revealed what he knew, and he'd have to wait until after the party that was coming up.

In his research, he'd found that some of the men the General rubbed elbows with went to this shindig in Ashland County. It was apparently the American Southeast's worst-kept secret scholarship fundraiser. People were invited from all over the South to the little Podunk county.

But after some digging, Eagle had realized Ashland County was a uniquely ideal hub for trafficking on the East Coast, and the party was the perfect front.

The area was an easy drive to Atlanta, one of the cities with the worst human trafficking statistics in the United States. It also had its very own inland port and an airport that, even though it was small, had a surprising amount of cross-country flights. Planes regularly flew out to major cities like Miami, Washington, DC, and New York City, all common hubs for human trafficking.

Eagle wanted to see what happened at this party when the men—including a Russian American attorney and the General's half brother—got together. Instead of funding scholarships, were they backing traffickers? Were they buying women for themselves?

If what Eagle suspected was true—that the General led a human trafficking ring of his own—then MF7 had been facilitating the operation by clearing out competition throughout the world. This was all a stretch, of course. Major, next-level paranoid shit, he could undoubtedly be declared certifiably insane if he told anyone.

But what if he was right? What if Ashland County was just the beginning?

In that case, there was nothing stopping the General from using strategically located parties like the one in Ashland County and replicating them on the West Coast, too. The General's trafficking ring could consolidate power in the USA and expand after MF7 caught their biggest fish so far, a Russian organization that was currently using a Yemeni village to funnel victims.

The women were often promised better lives and were tricked into hell instead. Eagle knew firsthand how hard it was to foresee the worst in an opportunity that claimed to make all your dreams come true. Hell, his own team had done the same thing when the General lured them into "ending" the world's human trafficking crisis.

*We were so fucking naive.*

Even if Eagle's crackpot theories were wrong, the sheer number of trafficking operations they'd shut down was staggering, and yet, they hadn't even made a dent. MF7 needed a break.

After Eagle pulled into the General's new security facility and parked, he nodded to the man standing guard outside before entering through the main glass doors. It'd been a shock to find out the General had his own security firm. Eagle had been so out of the loop to anything not human trafficking–related he hadn't even realized the soon-to-retire General had already begun a side job in the private sector.

*Everything about this man is shady, goddamn.*

Eagle took the elevator to the General's office on the top floor. When he got to the large corner office at the end of the hallway, Eagle raised his hand to knock on the door.

"Come in, Captain Greene," General Smithers's voice called through the wooden door.

Eagle opened the door and snapped into a crisp salute out of habit rather than respect.

"At ease, soldier. Take a seat," General Smithers grumbled, not bothering to look up as he set aside two large photographs he'd been studying.

Eagle relaxed a fraction, but his heart still pounded out of his chest at all the things he needed to cover during the meeting. He tried to school his face as he sat down and attempted to act casual.

"How did you know it was me, sir?"

"I run a security firm, boy," General Smithers scowled. "I have my ways."

The man with dyed jet-black hair and rheumy blue eyes leaned back in his chair, his hands resting on his belly. It was much larger than the last time Eagle had seen him, almost four years ago. They hadn't needed face-to-face communication to receive their mission dossiers. Every task and job was sent through encrypted code and letters. Eagle had been shocked when he was ordered to physically meet the man, and even more confused when he was commanded not to tell his teammates.

It'd been tempting to disobey, especially with the wild and crazy theories going on in his head, but just in case something was up with the General, he didn't want to put his team in jeopardy by telling them.

"You asked to see me, sir?"

"I did. Let's get right to it. I understand you know more than you should."

That one sentence had Eagle's heart plummeting to his stomach. He shifted in his seat and cleared his throat. On the inside, he chastised himself for exhibiting the tells he'd thought he'd painstakingly drilled out of his mannerisms.

"What do you mean, sir?"

General Smithers scoffed and shook his head. "I know you figured out the Rahab Foundation. I know you figured out the operation. I know all about it."

*Act dumb, or confess... that is the question.*

Unsure how to play this, he watched the General for a moment just as intently as the man stared back at him. Finally Eagle sighed and bent forward, his elbows on his knees.

"Look, I don't know what you think I know. *I* don't even know what I think I know. You called this meeting, but all I wanted to discuss was the possibility of ending the team's contract." The General tilted his head with interest, so Eagle pressed on, "We're done, sir. We've been at this for years, putting our lives on hold for a cause we believed in once, but we now know there's no expiration date in sight. It's time we pass the baton, so to speak."

The General pursed his lips and nodded as Eagle spoke. When he was finished, Eagle leaned back, satisfied the man was actually taking his proposition under consideration, until the General opened his mouth again.

"No."

Eagle frowned. "No?"

"I said 'no,' soldier. Are those two letters beyond your vocabulary?"

Eagle sputtered, "But *why*? I'm telling you we're done. We can't keep doing this anymore. Get someone else, General. The better part of a decade is our limit. This whole operation has become something we never signed on for. Hell, our contracts are up already."

"And I'm telling you your limit is when I say it is. I've put a lot of time and money into your team and you've proven to be quite useful in my little operation."

Eagle's pulse skyrocketed as he put the General's words together.

*Shit.*

Maybe he hadn't been paranoid enough.

Eagle cleared his throat, trying to figure out how he could word his next argument. If the General was profiting off of the women Eagle's team was "saving," then the man was more than an asshole with a power trip. He was fucking evil.

"Look, sir. I'm telling you that whatever you *think* I know, I don't. And I'll keep *not* knowing as long as you do this for me, if you catch my drift. My team is tired. We deserve to go home, move on with our lives, buy homes with white picket fences, marry, have two-point-five kids and all that shit."

He swallowed, knowing what he said next was against everything he stood for, but it had to be done.

"If you can give us that, then I won't go to anyone. I won't even tell my own team what we've been doing. We'll come home and live life. They'll die happy thinking we helped make the world a better place, and I'll die taking this secret to my grave." He waited for a second, analyzing the General's thoughtful face before continuing. "What do you say?"

The General nodded and hope sparked in Eagle's chest. The man gathered the photographs he'd been inspecting when Eagle arrived and studied them once more before turning one around.

"Funny you should mention kids."

He shoved the paper to the end of his wooden desk and Eagle leaned forward to take the photograph. His racing pulse stopped cold as the blood running through his veins turned to ice.

"What the fuck is this?"

"*That.*" General Smithers tapped the photograph. "That is your son."

Eagle's eyes widened to the point of pain. He couldn't tear them away from the photo. It showed a beautiful, raven-haired woman outside of an elementary school with a canvas bag covered in paint stains slung over her shoulder. She walked hand in hand with a blond-haired boy... who looked just like Eagle.

*Hannah... with my—*

"My son?"

*I have a son?*

The thought made his chest light with pride until that night with Hannah flashed into his mind.

It'd been a while since he'd thought about the details further than the regret that still tinged the memory. He'd been so excited he'd finally get his chance with her that he'd completely forgotten to put a condom on. And then he'd never fucking talked to her again.

*I'm such a piece of shit.*

"Yes, soldier, that's your son. And here..." He pushed another photograph, this time one taken by the angry-looking man in the picture. He sat in the driver's side of a van at an angle that showed a modest bungalow through the window behind him. "Here is a picture of one of my Russian partners. He took this less than half an hour ago and I printed it out for your benefit. You can't tell, of course, but he's sitting outside my daughter's house with a brick of C-4, ready to plant it underneath the brat's Braves-themed bed if this meeting doesn't go well."

"What the fuck, Richard." Eagle spat the General's first name like poison. "That's your own goddamn grandson. How could you threaten him like that?"

General Smithers shrugged. "Quite easily, I assure you. You see, Hannah is my pride and joy. The sweet, innocent girl you and Hawkins Black *defiled*. I created an operation to steal whores from my competitors to fuel my own enterprise, and I used *your* team. Not because you are 'the best of the best' as you pathetically refer to yourselves, but to make sure *my* Hannah could stay just that. *Mine.* You think I would want her to keep your bastard child? Surely, you understand there are no limits to what I would do to protect my daughter from vermin like you. Just ask her mother. Or, I guess you could have... before her 'heart attack.'"

"Her mother?" Eagle asked, swallowing back bile as he choked the information down.

"Poor woman died on the spot. After propofol helped her along, of course."

"You killed your own wife? *Why?*"

He sounded like a parrot, but the General's admission was too much to digest all at once.

"Betraying me, trying to leave me, cheating on me. I poisoned her just like she poisoned Hannah against me, except for my choice of drug was more deadly. Once I realized she planned to steal my daughter away from me, I had no choice but to take care of her."

"You're sick." Disgust tasted like vomit on the back of Eagle's tongue.

He had to stop this, but if he played it cool now, he could tell his best friend. Hawk would know what to do, he always did.

One of Eagle's biggest regrets was lying to Hannah about how much Hawk loved her. Even now, there was no one and nothing Hawk loved more than Hannah, and it killed Hawk not to check in on her. He'd been afraid an enemy would somehow get a hold of that information and retaliate against them by getting to her, like the shooters who'd confessed weeks after the Braves game. Eagle had thought Hawk was overreacting, but now that Eagle had just been caught doing the same thing with the Rahab Foundation, it seemed like Hawk had the right idea all along.

If Eagle had just told Hawk about the foundation, he could've helped. Maybe if Eagle told him now—

"Ah, I know that look. Don't even try it."

"I don't know what you're talking about." Eagle's brow furrowed as he tried to play dumb again.

*Not that it's helped so far.*

"Tell any member of your team, and I won't just stop at your son. I'll come for every single one of them, too. Whenever any of you think you've escaped me, achieved your *happiness* with your 'picket fences' and 'two-point-five kids,' I'll appear like a thief in the night. I will find you and everyone you love, and I will wipe them all off the face of the earth."

Eagle's jaw dropped at the General's threat. No, his *promise*. Because Eagle had no doubt this powerful man would make good on his word. He'd already killed his own wife, he certainly hated Eagle enough to kill Eagle's son. And now it wouldn't be just Eagle's family, but everyone else's, too.

*How the fuck did this get so turned around?*

He'd come in with a plan to get his team out from underneath the General's thumb. Eagle had hoped he was wrong about their role in the General's repulsive "enterprise," as he called it. But the truth was worse than Eagle could've ever imagined.

"You see, you thought you had the upper hand with your information. But as you can tell—" The General waved a hand over the two photographs. "*I* always win, soldier. And when it comes to Hannah and anyone that comes between us? *You* will *always* lose."

"You can't do this," Eagle replied in a hoarse whisper.

"On the contrary, I think you know exactly what I'm capable of and willing to do. Both for this operation, and to ensure Hannah stays mine."

The way he said the last made Eagle's stomach churn. Those words and the way the General said them were unnatural and vile. The sentiment opened up even more disturbing questions in Eagle's mind about Hannah's *father*. But asking them at that moment would only get someone killed.

Eagle studied the pictures a moment longer, trying to figure out what steps he should take next.

He could go back to his team and tell them everything. But with Hannah out in the open—with their *son*—there was no way Eagle could find her and get to her in time to save the boy.

Maybe if he told Hawk, they could work together to find and save Hannah and the boy without tipping off the General beforehand. The four of them could leave and go into hiding, at least until they figured out how to take down the General. But then his team and *everyone* they loved would be left in the lurch.

He was trapped. They all were. The General was right. He would win... unless Eagle played the game.

Eagle dragged his eyes away from the picture of Hannah holding his son's hand and met the monster's gaze in front of him.

"What do I have to do?"

# CHAPTER TWENTY-FOUR

## Present Day

Since Hannah was only in her long blue T-shirt and matching sleep shorts after their rooftop rendezvous, Hawk took her by the hand and snuck her back downstairs to his apartment, just in case someone was up early. As he made a show of checking around every corner, Hannah giggled behind him, making his chest light.

When they stopped by his studio apartment, Hawk drew her in for a scorching kiss. After he reluctantly let her go, she slipped inside to set Tommy up with a summer school self-taught lesson on his iPad and got dressed for the team meeting. Hawk paced the hallway until she emerged and they walked downstairs together to meet Wes in the war room.

"You sure you want to do this?" Hawk murmured under his breath. "You don't have to come. I can give you the abridged version."

His protective instincts were still off the charts when it came to her. He knew he should back off, but it was hard to believe she wanted to be in on all the information they were gathering about her own father.

"Yes, Hawkins. I need to help, any way I can." She cut her eyes at him, her brow raised. Sincerity there mixed with an iconic mom look that said "don't ask me again." It was adorable and terrifying at the same time.

He held up his hands in surrender. "I trust you, dove. Just got to make sure for myself, is all."

"Consider yourself reassured. Your dove can fly all on her own, *mi cielo*." She smiled right before he opened the door.

That grin nearly took him out, and the use of the endearment made his heart full with gratitude over this second chance. The urge to steal another kiss was nearly overwhelming, but Hannah had already walked by him. She took her seat at the table beside his without waiting for him to pull her chair out for her. Pride filled his chest at the sight of her so confidently taking her rightful place by his side.

*My dove can fly on her own.*

Hawk dragged his eyes away from his woman to assess the room. Once his gaze landed on Nora and Wes in front of the wall of monitors, his brows shot up to his hairline.

Nora's head drooped onto the table from exhaustion and Wes's blue hair stood on end like he'd been electrocuted. His black glasses were askew over half-open eyes and his fingers typed furiously over the keyboard, almost like he was in a trance.

"Wes... Nora? You good?" Hawk asked, trying to temper his voice so he didn't scare the shit out of them. "Do you need a few hours of shut-eye, or..."

Nora muttered about Vikings and their longships before her eyes squinted and tried to focus. Finally, they seemed to register his presence and they snapped wide open.

"Oh, hey, Cap'n. Wassup?"

"Our meeting?" he asked, emphasizing each word as he settled his hands on the back of his chair. "We're supposed to be checking in with the team on what you and Wes came up with overnight?"

"Oh... right... I'll let Superman cover this one. I can barely think at the moment." Dark circles bruised her pale skin underneath her eyes and she pressed into them with the heels of her palms before pointing at the pile of paperwork and pictures on the table. "Here's the mess we went through all night. Right, Superman?"

Wes—or Superman, as Nora liked to call him—had yet to peel his eyes away from the wall of screens and his fingers continued to fly over the keys as he typed. With his hair tugged upward like it was, he looked every bit like a mad scientist.

"Superman... Snake," Nora called both of his nicknames before picking up a purple highlighter beside her. "Wes!"

"You don't need to scream at me," he muttered, still not taking his eyes off the computers. Wes was harder to distract than a home plate umpire when he was onto something. "I'm tired, not dead."

"Pay attention, then, Superman."

She threw the highlighter at his head, but Wes swatted it away lazily with a huff, "Dammit, Nora. Warn a person before you throw things at them."

"I *did*," she insisted with a saccharine sweet voice. "We have visitors."

Hawk gave Wes a slight wave just as Draco slipped into the room behind him. The blond Viking placed a gallon-sized coffee container in the center of the table and sat in the chair closest to his girlfriend. Hawk barely had time to register the monstrous drink in his large hand—with its whipped cream peaks and drizzled syrup—before Nora zoomed to the table in her rolling chair and snatched it out of Draco's hand.

"Thanks, handsome," Nora cooed to Draco as she waggled her eyebrows suggestively and rolled back to the computer desk.

Hawk tried not to read too much into how *appreciative* the look was, or how Draco's tan face blushed dark red. Instead, he turned to Wes, who finally seemed ready to report.

"Morning, Hawk, Hannah, Draco. Sorry, I was locked in. This is where we're at..." Wes pulled up several different spreadsheets and outlines on the monitors. He pointed at the screens and the table as he spoke, while Nora slurped obnoxiously on her sugary drink. "We've been poring over all the evidence we've gathered over the past year and a half... not to mention going back in fucking time to our MF7 days to see if there's anything we could find out, or should've seen in any of the footage from CTI, the General's security firm, or the McIntosh Hotel. Needless to say, there are mountains of stuff to go through."

Hawk's gaze darted to the actual hills of paperwork, stacks of laptops, and other technology they'd collected from their various missions over the past couple of years.

"I can see that," Hawk murmured as he walked around the table. "Anything of immediate importance?"

"Yuppers. *Just* about everything." Nora sucked her top lip to get the whipped cream off. A light groan slipped from Draco and Nora gave him a mischievous grin.

"Nora's right," Wes admitted. "We've gotten some leads, though. Some more disturbing than others. Especially those pictures from the General's office. It's almost like they're from his private stash."

Wes's finger visibly shook with disgust as he pointed to the Polaroids they'd retrieved from the General's security firm and underground private headquarters a week ago, after Callie and Phoenix escaped his clutches.

A small gasp made Hawk stop his perusal of the electronics beside the pile. Hannah had stood from her chair and was sifting through the pictures of naked women standing in front of the camera like they were taking a mug shot. She picked up one and seemed to analyze the name, date, and location penned on the back.

"Hannah, shit, you shouldn't see this stuff," Hawk insisted, but she waved him off and focused on the pictures.

"These were from his office, you said?" she muttered as she looked through the hundreds of pictures that had been in her father's filing cabinet.

"Yeah," Wes answered. "Callie and Phoenix found them before setting off the fire and escaping."

"The fire?" Hannah's eyes widened and Hawk resisted the urge to once again tell her she didn't need to know the behind-the-scenes details of taking down her father.

But if she wanted to be a part of this, he needed to respect her decision, no matter how much he hated subjecting her to his life.

"Phoenix and Callie set his old headquarters in Atlanta on fire before they fought their way out," Wes answered simply. He hadn't even taken his eyes off of the monitors in front of him, obviously not registering the impact his words could have on the General's own daughter.

"Oh." Hannah's warm-olive skin took on a slightly sickly yellow hue before she nodded and looked back at the Polaroids. "Got it."

"Dammit, Wes, do you have to put your foot in your mouth every time you talk?" Hawk growled.

Wes finally glanced away from his screen. His eyes widened when they landed on Hannah. "Shit. Sorry. I get in the zone—"

She shook her head and waved away his concern. "It's okay. I asked to be here. I want to know everything."

Wes's lips flattened and his eyes narrowed at her, studying her, before he nodded once and went back to the keyboard.

"Were there... were there people inside when they set the fire?" Hannah asked after a moment more of studying the pictures.

Nora thankfully seemed to monitor Hannah's reaction as she replied with a careful tone, "Yeah... Phoenix is the 'burn the world for his woman' type of romantic."

Wes huffed a sardonic laugh, eyes on the screen again. "Totally swoonworthy until you have to smell the lingering stench of burned bodies."

Their communications sergeant rubbed his nose. Wes had gone into the headquarters with the FBI after the rest of the team cleared it so he could help assess what evidence should be taken and what could be left behind. The odor down in that basement was the kind that never left the nostrils. Wes was likely getting the same phantom whiffs of death Hawk still experienced.

"We looked through all the Polaroid pictures," Wes explained further. "We logged the dates on the back to see if there's any pattern. The FBI secured subpoenas, so we can now look through the laptops and flash drives we've gotten from our investigations along the way. ADA Marco Aguilar also set up meetings with the witnesses and suspects. We pieced all that information together with the locations Hannah gave us—"

"I know this place," Hannah murmured as she bent over the table and pointed at a picture.

"You do?" Wes asked and got up from his chair.

Hawk moved to one side while Wes flanked her other, peering around her shoulder to scrutinize the picture she indicated. Hawk tried to see it through Hannah's perspective, as if he could figure it out before she told him, but there were few details in any of the pictures other than the scared and naked women.

"Yeah... this." She showed them a picture of a woman on a bed, eyes wide in horror, gagged and bound. "You see this headboard?" Hawk nodded. "That's at one of his vacation homes in the mountains of Georgia."

"How can you tell?" Wes asked with skepticism in his voice. "You can barely see it."

"True, but if you put them all together, you can." She grabbed several different pictures and placed them side by side, showing more pieces of the bed.

"And you're sure?" Wes asked again. "There are probably tons just like that one—"

"No," she insisted and tapped slowly at the edge of the headboard. "I... I'd never forget this headboard."

Her whisper dropped like lead in Hawk's gut and he watched her as she opened up to them. "It's closer to Atlanta than here, if I remember correctly. It's, um... this was in my bedroom."

Bile burned the back of Hawk's throat at the implication behind the General keeping women in Hannah's bedroom. Hannah's few words, tense muscles, and the almost childlike reversion of her voice made his skin crawl. All he wanted to do was hold her and hope she'd tell him the full truth she'd kept hidden from him. But his years of working with survivors told him if she was ever ready, her disclosure needed to be on her time, and touch was the last thing she needed at the moment.

So when her hand sought his for comfort, his heart nearly shattered.

He was still home for her. After everything, he was still her safe space.

Hawk squeezed her hand, honored she still wanted him. He cleared his throat and rubbed the back of his head. "We need to put that on our list of places to raid. Maybe tell Marco afterward."

"We're FBI liaisons," Wes pointed out. "He'll probably send us to check it out."

"No doubt," Hawk answered, mentally logging yet another task to their long "figure out what the fuck to do about the General" to-do list. "We definitely want to get in there before the FBI does, though."

A knock on the door made him lift his face from the Polaroids and Hannah dropped his hand. The cool chill of Black-Stone Securities facilities wafted over his empty palm as the rest of his team—Phoenix, Callie, Devil, and Jason—filed in one after the other.

"What's happenin'?" Phoenix asked as he collapsed into a chair, immediately balancing it back onto its rear legs. His eyes widened and he pointed at Nora and Wes, who were both working diligently at a laptop and keyboard, respectively. "Jesus H. Christ, you two look like shit."

"Gee, thanks." Wes chuckled with a shake of his head.

"Watch it," Draco growled on Nora's behalf.

"Well, since you've kindly asked why I look so *tired*..." Nora rolled her eyes before landing a glare on Phoenix. "It's because while you people were able to get some beauty sleep, Wes and I were burning the midnight oil trying to put things together for *you*, lazybones."

Phoenix winced and held his hands up in surrender. "My bad."

Hawk suppressed the urge to chuckle at their antics and decided to really start the meeting, but Nora cleared her throat dramatically and began instead.

"Apology accepted. As for the rest of you, Wes and I were saving this for everyone to be here, but... we think we found the General."

A zing of excitement sparked through Hawk's chest. "Seriously?" he asked along with the chorus of surprise sounds coming from the rest of his team.

"What?" Hannah squeaked as she plopped down into her chair.

"Thanks to you, actually. What you said, just now, helped support my theory." Nora smiled kindly at Hannah before nodding toward the wall of computers where a map of the world dotted in red and blue flags stretched over the screens. "I was able to design a map that shows every property we know General Smithers owned in one way or another, whether through his actual name, pseudonyms, his different corporations, or through Hannah's own recollection."

"Damn, the man has mad money." Phoenix whistled.

"Turns out human trafficking is lucrative, who'd have thought," Callie muttered beside him as she crossed her arms tighter.

"He owned *all* of those?" Hannah asked, her big brown eyes wide.

"He owned all the red flags, you see. Which, admittedly, is a lot of red flags for just one person, pun intended. All jokes aside, Wes and Naomi also noticed something about some of the locations." Nora pointed to the blue flags. "These are warehouses, distribution centers, and locations where Charitable Technologies International has some sort of affiliation. Wherever you find a CTI building, you'll find one of the General's properties close by."

"And they're all near major trafficking cities." Wes pointed at the map. "Miami, Atlanta, Orlando, Washington, DC."

"It's disgusting really. Like, are lawmakers not embarrassed?" Nora's voice dripped with scorn. "One of the cities with the worst human trafficking statistics is where they do their damn job."

The rest of the room agreed and broke into discussion as Hawk stepped closer to examine one location in particular that made his stomach churn.

"Is one of those blue flags in Yemen?" he asked, knowing good and well the answer he was about to receive was one he wouldn't like.

"Yes, it's a CTI distribution center," Wes replied solemnly.

"Charitable Technologies International supplied developing countries with technology," Nora added. "They have distribution centers everywhere."

"And *this* one isn't far from where we had our last mission," Wes confirmed for Hawk.

The men in the room swore. Hawk tapped his lips with his finger calmly, but inside his blood vibrated with rage.

"Practically fucking walking distance," Jason spat, absent-mindedly scratching the scar over his ear. "That must've been where the victims were transferred through."

"Yeah, I think it's safe to assume that's exactly what happened," Wes replied with a defeated sigh.

The air in the room grew heavy and Hawk collapsed into his seat. He scrubbed his face with one hand allowing himself a moment to feel the weight of the General's betrayal.

So many lives were lost, including one of their own, all for this sick bastard's greed and perversions.

Beside him, sadness radiated from Hannah. She reached

under the table and laid her hand on his thigh. He reached for it like a lifeline.

When he'd finally gained his composure, Hawk sat straighter and faced Nora and Wes.

"So you said you think you found the General?"

"I *know* we found him," Nora answered.

"We *think*. There are no absolutes with this job," Wes corrected her with a furrowed brow.

She rolled her eyes behind her rose gold frames. "Fine. We *think* we found him. But once you see the footage, you'll know we found him, too."

Her fingers flew over the keys and mouse until the map image she'd blown up zoomed in farther and farther on the monitors like one big screen. "Hannah, the vacation home you're talking about, is it... here?"

She finished typing with a flourish and pointed to a mountain in northeastern Georgia.

"Yeah." Hannah sat straighter in her chair. "Is that where he is?"

Nora shook her head. "No, but where we think he is, is... here."

She moved the aerial map to show a large building at the bottom of the mountain.

"What's that?" Devil asked.

"It's a CTI warehouse," Nora answered. "According to their former CEO, Gail Haynesworth, and Naomi who used to work for her, the warehouse was supposed to be finished this summer, *but* with the 'PR debacle'—"

"Is that what we're calling aiding and abetting human traffickers these days?" Hawk growled.

"That's what *Gail* calls it," Nora scoffed with yet another roll of her eyes. "That woman is a baton twirling master when it comes to spinning her words. Anyway, thanks to all of us catching their trafficking asses, CTI's operations and new projects have been on hold, including"—she pointed to the monitor—"building this warehouse. In our research, this location seemed like the most likely candidate for nefariousness and Hannah just now confirmed that likelihood since the General obviously used the vacation home nearby."

"Do you *think* he's at the warehouse or are you certain?" Hawk asked, trying to listen between the lines when it came to the creative way Nora delivered news.

"Here," Wes offered and twirled back around in his rolling chair to face his desk. He pulled up a video that took up the wall of monitors. "I was able to assess which buildings around the warehouse would likely have the best view from their security cameras. Conveniently enough, they all use a security company we've worked in tandem with before."

"Must've been an area discount," Jason snorted.

"Probably," Wes agreed with a smile. "Anyway, once I convinced my contact we weren't trying to do anything shady with their clients, they sent me over the videos. Although Vlad must have remembered this location from working with the General, I don't think he knew about the gas station cameras across the street."

"And gas station security footage is." Nora kissed her fingers. "*C'est magnifique.*"

Wes snorted and shook his head before pointing at the screen.

"Check this out, you guys."

A black van that looked like the one they saw on the video surveillance the day before slowly rolled up to park in front of the unfinished warehouse. Hawk had to narrow his eyes to see clearly, but he was able to make out a huge man exiting the driver's side.

"Vlad," Draco growled.

The Russian giant glanced around as he opened the van's sliding door. Another man hopped out of the passenger side and blocked their view. Wes zoomed the camera in to the point that it was almost too grainy, but Hawk squinted to see the two men carrying someone outside of the van and disappearing into the warehouse.

Wes pressed a key on the keyboard and the video froze. "So… yeah. Either they put the General in that warehouse, *or* we have someone who needs saving. Either way, we have a warehouse to get to."

While Hawk still held Hannah's hand underneath the table, he used his other to trace his lips with his index finger. The pressure of everyone's bated breath weighed down his shoulders as he thought.

Whether the actual "bad guy" at the moment was the General or Vlad, if they went to that warehouse then BlackStone could take them both down. It'd be everyone in one place, finishing this shit once and for all.

But what if Vlad was manhandling someone *else* into the warehouse? What if the General was free now? Or was it all a ruse? That meant Hawk would be leaving Hannah all by herself so he could do his job… *again.*

It didn't sit right with him to leave her. Not now. He'd done it once before for her safety, and he regretted it with every fiber of his being.

But before Hawk could make a decision, Nora cleared her throat.

"So, that's all for the *good* news." Her voice turned somber, an alarming departure from her normal singsongy cadence. "Ready for the terrible, horrible, no good very bad kind?"

# CHAPTER TWENTY-FIVE

"What's the bad news?" Hawk asked, trying not to growl his frustration at the situation.

"Well, we also found this on one of the flash drives." Wes let out an exhausted exhale while he typed. "It's pretty damning, but I think the General kept it as blackmail in case his plan went south."

A video of the General in a bland office appeared on the screen. The date on the top right indicated the video they were watching was from two years ago.

"What's this about..." Hawk trailed off as a painfully familiar tall, blond man in fatigues entered the door and saluted.

Hannah gasped. "Is that—"

"Eagle," Hawk finished for her and swallowed. "Were we even in the States then?"

"We were," Wes answered. "It was one of those times we were called back in after we saved Callie's sister, but before we were suddenly called to scope out Yemen."

"Goddamnit, what's he doing there?" Jason asked.

In answer, Wes increased the volume.

They all listened in silence as General Smithers broke it to Eagle that he knew Eagle was onto him. When he showed a picture of Hannah, her grip on Hawk's hand rolled his knuckles almost to the point of pain. Her eyes welled with tears as they watched Eagle find out he had a son.

In no uncertain terms, General Smithers threatened not only Eagle's whole team, but Hannah and Tommy, too. When he confessed to murdering Hannah's mother, Hawk cursed and pulled Hannah closer to him as she wept silently.

"No fucking wonder he turned on us," Jason whispered.

"He what?" Hannah's red-rimmed eyes widened as she pulled away to look at Hawk.

He was about to reprimand his teammate for letting the cat out of the bag, but then Eagle asked the General a question that made Hawk's chest tighten.

*"What do I have to do?"*

The job was simple. Eagle had to inform the locals of MF7's every move so the traffickers working for the General had time to escape.

*"Right before the mission, I'll give you the frequency to a different channel on your radio headset,"* the General explained. *"You'll be able to switch back and forth between air traffic control, the locals, and your team. That way your contact will have no confusion about where you will be."*

"That's why I was able to hear them," Phoenix whispered.

"Hear who?" Hawk asked, his brow furrowed.

"Wes already knows this, but the women... after the bomb blew up, Eagle's headset fell off. I was still able to hear their screaming."

A few of their teammates swore and Hawk shook his head. "Shit, brother, I'm sorry. I had no idea."

Even though Hawk's chest felt like it was caving in, Phoenix waved their concern away and continued, "As the pilot, I had to switch frequencies to listen to air traffic control and the locals. His radio must've fucked up after the explosion, leaving his mic hot on the same frequency I was on. I'd always wondered how I could still hear through his headset when everyone else's was busted, and that's why."

Hawk opened his mouth to apologize again, but Eagle's voice echoed through the speakers, making him pause.

*"So I just tell them when and where we're going? I do that and no one gets hurt?"*

*"No one gets hurt,"* the General lied through his veneers. *"After this last job, you'll be done. I have no need for men who can't stomach the work. If you won't be at your finest, I'll have to get others to do it."*

*"Wait, we'll be finished after this last job?"* The hope and hint of desperation in Eagle's voice made Hawk's chest ache.

*"Of course."* The General waved his hand as if what he'd said went without saying. *"Don't tell a soul what we've discussed today. That means no telling Hannah and no telling your team. If you do, you know the consequences. You just have to be a good little soldier, inform the locals of your whereabouts, and when you've finished taking out the proxy, you can all go on your merry way."*

Eagle admittedly looked skeptical on the screen, but Hawk's heart shattered when his best friend reached over the table and shook the General's hand.

Wes stopped the feed on the handshake, freezing the moment of betrayal in time.

"He... he betrayed you all?" Hannah asked, those tears finally spilling over. *"That's* how Thomas died?"

She turned to look at him, but the accusation in her expression was weak. He knew the feeling. Losing Eagle hurt so much more than the deception.

"Han." Hawk glanced around at the grim faces before he met hers again. "Everyone in this room would've done the exact same thing."

For good measure, he double-checked with his men for confirmation. Every single one of them nodded their heads. At one point, they might've felt differently, but after finding their soul mates, they all understood Eagle's decision.

"He loved us," Hawk continued. "He loved you. He loved Tommy. It's plain to see in the video that he was in a hard spot and did what he thought he had to at the time. And in the end, after everything, I can't hate the man who sacrificed himself to save me."

Hannah swore in Spanish and her hand squeezed the life out of Hawk's as tears streamed freely down her face. "He should've told me. He should've told *you*. *Somebody*. Instead he played along and... and *died* in the end."

Hawk swallowed. "He did. That was his choice, one I would've made myself. I don't fault him for it."

Hannah shook her head. "I just... I can't believe it. I can't believe he would do that."

"To be fair," Wes piped up. "The General's terms were that Eagle would tip off the locals so the target could run away. It sounds like we were supposed to eliminate a proxy. The target had probably made a deal with the General that the women would go to the CTI facility before we got to him since it was so close by."

"Only the target must've gone rogue." Jason sat up as he spoke. "The proxy had a bomb attached to him and killed everyone in there and the friendlies we trained turned on us."

"The proxy went rogue... or the General was trying to wipe us off the map," Wes muttered.

"Loose ends," Hannah whispered and collapsed back into her chair, shaking her head. "You were all loose ends. That's why the friendlies turned on you. That's why the so-called proxy blew himself up. It was all part of his plan. Trick Eagle into playing along and kill everyone in the process," Hannah summed up. "Then he tricked *me* into thinking you guys were dead by sending me that KIA letter along with a dead bird."

"The fuck?" Phoenix blurted out.

Hannah nodded. "A dead hawk. It was right next to the unofficial KIA letter that said your team was dead. It was my father's way of showing me he knew where I was, he was in control, and it was his way of torturing me. He tortured all of us."

Hannah covered her face with her free hand, trying to take the other out of Hawk's, but he refused to let go, instead bringing her in for a hug.

"Guys, I'm so sorry for everything my father—"

"Hannah, if you apologize for your piece-of-shit father, I will slap you," Callie threatened, making Hannah's lips clamp shut.

"She's kidding." Nora laughed nervously. "She wouldn't do that."

"I don't know. She might," Phoenix muttered under his breath.

The back-and-forth had the whole room chuckling, including Hannah, still in Hawk's arms. He couldn't have been more thankful for his team. Hannah was going through a lot of shit, but they were, too. And yet, their dynamic made it so they could deal with it together. Anything that put a smile on Hannah's face, even if it was dark humor, gave Hawk relief.

This woman was everything to him. He'd given her a ring, asked her to marry him, and then broken her heart. And here she was, finding solace in his embrace. He couldn't fuck this up again.

Hannah pulled away with a small grin on her lips and peered up at Hawk beneath thick, wet lashes, as if she felt the same connection he did.

*I'll always love you, dove.*

The words were on the tip of his tongue. They had been for as long as he could remember. He couldn't let her go. Not again.

When Hannah finally sat back in her seat, Hawk turned to address the team.

"We finally have answers. Ones we had a feeling about. Ones we were afraid to hear. And ones we knew we would hate. But they are answers all the same. We've got a solid lead. I'll be here for the planning to help you do what you need to do."

Hawk tapped his fingers on the wooden table before glancing at Hannah. Her gaze was on the team as they all waited for him to finish. He took a deep breath and exhaled before making his declaration, not an ounce of regret in his decision.

"But I'm not going."

"What?" the entire room asked in unison.

He could feel Hannah's eyes stare hard at the side of his face, begging him to turn. But he didn't.

This was his decision, and he didn't want her to think he was making it because she'd somehow implied she wanted it. She asked him to stay once, but there was no guarantee she wanted that again.

That didn't matter though, his own conscience wouldn't let him.

He wouldn't leave her again.

# CHAPTER TWENTY-SIX

"I'm not going," Hawk repeated carefully to the stunned room.

"Cap'n, say what?" Nora asked in a high pitch.

Hannah closed her mouth, realizing when a cool breeze wafted over her tongue that her jaw had literally dropped.

"But Hawk... you're our squad leader," Jason reminded him slowly.

"I am. And as your leader, I'm bowing out this time. You've all done it before, for one valid reason or another. Now it's my turn. I'll help coordinate from here."

"You've already diverted from the mission once for Hannah," Wes pointed out. "This can't wait."

Hannah's heart stilled in her chest as she silently pleaded with Hawk to look at her. "Is that true? You went after me instead of trying to find the General?"

Hawk's gaze finally met hers. "I had to find you, dove. And now that I have, I'm not leaving."

"Why?" Devil rumbled from the corner. His blond counterpart Draco frowned heavily, as if he wanted to ask the same question.

"It's a realization I made after Phoenix escaped the General.

My priorities have been out of whack for way too long. I'm changing that from now on."

"Listen." Nora held up her hand as she spoke. "I know I joke that you're the Idris Elba version of James Bond the world always needed, but you don't have to be dramatic. Spit it out. This team deserves to know why you're leaving them high and dry." Her gaze cut to the blond Viking, making Hannah realize the unusual edge in Nora's voice came from protecting her man.

Hawk sighed. Ever since she'd known him, there'd never been a moment where he struggled to meet anyone's eyes. But this was one of them.

Hannah sat up farther, hoping to catch his gaze because she had a feeling why he was saying no, and if she was right, she wanted no part in it. But before she could answer, Callie answered for her.

"If it's about Hannah, I can stay. I'm a trained FBI agent and I know this place backward and forward now, including the security measures. I can protect her. Your team needs you."

Hawk shook his head. "No. While it's likely Vlad was moving the General into that abandoned warehouse, we're not one-hundred-percent certain. I'm not leaving Hannah and Tommy vulnerable when there's even a remote chance that her father is still out there. He's a wild card. There's no telling what he's capable of and I don't want to leave her here with just one person protecting her."

"I thought BlackStone Securities was safe," Hannah pointed out, proud of herself that her frustration only slightly slipped through.

"It *is* safe, but that's not good enough," Hawk answered, meeting her eyes. "I need to be here."

Anger welled inside her chest and she faced the rest of the room while trying to gain her composure. "Guys? Can we have the room, please?"

The team looked at each other with confusion before settling on Hawk. Logically, Hannah shouldn't have felt annoyed that they would look to him first. He was their leader, after all. But the emotion already building in her chest was only compounded by the way they sought him for the answer.

Hawk nodded once and the team slowly left their seats. Nora was the last one out and she mouthed "good luck" to Hannah as she closed the door behind her. As soon as Hannah heard the *click*, she whirled on Hawk.

"Hannah, listen, you don't have to ask me to stay—"

"What in the hell was that?"

Hawk's jaw dropped. "What in the hell was what?"

"That!" She pointed wildly out to the room, indicating the scene that'd just happened. "You telling the team you weren't going to go with them to take down my father and end this once and for all!"

"I'm staying here with you. What's wrong with that?" Hawk asked, his handsome face contorting with confusion.

"What's *wrong*? What's wrong is you leaving your team in the dust when they need you most!"

Hawk shook his head. "Hannah, I'm confused. I thought you'd be glad I'm staying. I'm choosing you—" She opened her mouth to interrupt, but he held up his hand. "I'm choosing you because I want to, not because you've asked me to."

It was her turn for her brows to furrow and he sighed before resting back in his chair. He propped his elbow up and tapped his lips as he obviously tried to think of ways to explain himself.

He'd always had little quirks like that, but they'd only gotten more pronounced over the decade. Those little idiosyncrasies were so human, so unique to him, a departure from the stoic, almost robotic way he commanded his team. But humans made mistakes, and this was definitely one of them.

"Listen, dove." He finally leaned forward and grabbed her hand. The warmth of his calloused palm holding hers made her temper settle a little. When he tugged her hand so that her chair rolled even closer, she didn't resist.

"My team and I have been through a lot," he murmured. "I

used to be all about the cause, duty, and doing what was required of me. Nine years ago, I was all about you until I realized my selfishness would only keep you in harm's way.

"But now that there's a chance to have you again, I don't want to lose you. I've been empty without you, Han. Life has been eat, sleep, breathe the mission, but I want to eat your delicious home-cooked meals while I drink your orange blossom sweet tea. I want to sleep with you in my arms, and I want to be able to breathe deeply so I can smell your sugary citrus scent on my pillow. *That's* what I want in my life. It's what I've always wanted, and if we can live in a world that's safe enough for me to have it, that's what I'm going to strive for."

Hannah's heart twisted, and she left her seat to straddle him in his chair. "But *mi cielo*, *this* is the time we can make sure that kind of safety exists." Her eyes followed his worry lines across his forehead as she spoke. "If you don't go with your team, that's one less person they'll have watching their backs. What if they go and fail? Then we'll be back at worse than square one. Not only that, but you could lose yet another person in your family while you're sipping sweet tea beside me. You said it yourself, you messed up when you left me. Don't mess up and leave them when they need you too."

He pursed his lips, prompting her to trace them the way she used to during their pillow talks before bed years ago.

"I want you too, Hawk. But I want *you*. The woman I used to be wanted the man who'd burn down the world for her, but you've never been that man—" He opened his mouth to argue, but the finger she'd been trailing over his lips covered them instead. "You've never been that man... and I don't want that man anymore.

"I want the man who plays catch with a kid he barely knows, but loves all the same. A man who puts his friends' welfare before his own. Why would I want the world to go up in flames when I can watch love burn bright instead? *Mi cielo*, I don't want the villain who destroys the world for me, I want the hero who saves it so we can *live* in it, happily ever after."

His frown finally lifted at the edges, but worry and concern still wrinkled his brow.

"What if something bad happens and I'm not here?" he asked, his deep voice hoarse with emotion. "We're not one-hundred-percent sure whoever they were taking out of that van was the General. What if he's still out there?"

She shrugged. "Odds are, that was the General and you know it, Hawkins. I get that you're scared for Tommy and me, but I'm stronger than I was. These past two years have been hell, but running away from my father while he stalked and taunted me made me a fighter. I've learned a lot and I can handle what's thrown at me. Not to mention the fact that since Callie offered to stay, I'll have an FBI agent guarding me. Nora will probably be here too, right? She seems like she can handle her own."

Hannah tried to smile but Hawk's watchful eyes made her squirm. When he finally opened his mouth, she wasn't surprised by his question.

"Can you tell me what your father did to you, Hannah?"

She inhaled deeply and exhaled a fortifying breath before she nodded.

"When I was younger... I didn't realize the way my father treated me was... wrong. And when I wanted to tell my mother..." She swallowed back bile. Her father had murdered her own mother, but she didn't have time to fully process that yet. She'd have to grieve later because his team needed him *now*. "When I wanted to tell her, he warned me that I could be taken away from them if I ever told."

"Did he..." Hawk swallowed. "Did he..."

Hannah winced. "Honestly, the memories I have are very fuzzy. Like my mind is protecting me from my past. The things I do remember are wrong enough, but I don't recall anything more than, um... touches. But I've always had a deep-seated feeling there was more. When I saw the headboard—"

A flash of a memory she desperately wanted to pretend was a nightmare blinked across her mind and she shook it away. Hawk squeezed her closer, and she breathed in his pine, leather, and spring morning scent that had always reminded her of happiness.

"Anyway... with what he's capable of, it's easier to just go with what my mind *knows* rather than torturing myself with hazy images. Putting those together might create the puzzle that breaks me, and it's not one I need to see to live my life."

Hawk nodded, outwardly calm, but his rage radiated from within. As much as he tried to portray himself as unshakable in front of others, Hannah had always been able to sense his emotions vibrating through him when he embraced her.

"Everything you're feeling right now, I've felt toward him, too. But I was always too afraid to do anything about it. Now *you* can. I don't want your fear for me to get in the way. When you get back from saving the world, I'll be right here, ready to live that happily ever after we deserve. The one you *fought* for. Okay? No matter what, I'll be here waiting for you."

Hawk's eyes searched hers. Before she could stop herself, she lightly pressed her lips against his. He went stone still, as if she'd caught him off guard, but only half a second into the kiss, his hard muscles softened underneath her.

His hand delved into her hair while his other arm wrapped tightly around her waist. He kissed her fiercely, the way she craved, with all the adoration and passion he had burning inside him. When his tongue sought refuge in her mouth, she opened freely and let him in, loving the way he tasted. Her nails scratched the short waves in his fade as she rolled on top of his thickening length.

There was a finality to the kiss, and whether that was because it would actually be their last or it was the end of this horrible chapter of being apart, she didn't know, but she hoped to hell that it was the latter.

When the kiss settled to something sweeter and softer, she pulled away and found his gaze again.

"It's time for you to save the world, *mi héroe*."

# CHAPTER TWENTY-SEVEN

The fact that the General's vacation home and the CTI facility were disturbingly close to Ashland County made Hawk itchy in his blackout gear. They could've driven it, but they'd been able to take the MH-6 "Little Bird"—the helicopter his team had *liberated* from the United States government. The shorter trip made the General's reach seem even more omnipotent.

*Not that international reach isn't enough*, Hawk almost snorted at the thought before resolving to clear his head.

He needed to be on his *A* game. Soon, Phoenix would land them far enough away so their enemies in the warehouse couldn't hear them, but close enough that the team could roll out as quickly as possible.

They'd all been trained by various branches of the military, and their stint in MF7 had only honed their abilities. But being in the private sector was a dream compared to any military service they'd had, so Hawk hoped their muscle memory would kick in to make up for anything they'd forgotten.

His gaze drifted over his teammates, each one in their own respective headspace to get in the zone before the mission, but his eyes landed on Draco. The man had just come out of a coma two and a half months ago. The lifesaving miracle drug the team had stolen from the General had kept Draco alive and quickened the healing process once he woke up. Compared to civilians, he was in tip-top shape, but compared to the caliber necessary for MF7, or even BlackStone Securities, Hawk worried for his safety.

Even though the team had been preparing since that morning and waited until the middle of the night to approach the facility, they had no idea what they were going to be walking into. They'd assessed the blueprints Gail Haynesworth had on her laptop, but without going inside the building themselves, they didn't know who they were up against. Even with the blueprints, the building was unfinished, so it was unlikely they had the most updated building specs.

"LZ's clear, no cows. Taking her in," Phoenix reported over his headset that the pasture they were using as a landing zone was clear.

"Roger that, take us down," Hawk replied.

Hawk's mind ran rampant as Phoenix landed the helo about a mile away from the warehouse.

What if this was a trap? What if Hannah was back at the base getting attacked right now?

"Wes?" Hawk asked through his mouthpiece.

Snake normally stayed on base when they had missions. Tonight, though, they were all hands on deck. Callie was instrumental, but what they were about to do was below board and having an FBI agent, even one who only loosely played by the rules, could result in mountains of paperwork. As it was, Hawk would have to plead the fifth and claim he didn't know what an "FBI liaison" entailed if this mission went sideways.

If it went well, then it wouldn't matter. No one cared what or how things happened, or whether they were above or below board when the outcome was what everyone wanted. But if shit hit the fan, then they were all boned, including the government, and the feds would turn on them faster than their Little Bird could fly away if they fucked up.

"They're fine," Snake replied back, not needing Hawk to

elaborate. "Nora just texted me and said Tommy is happily watching SportsCenter and Hannah is doodling."

"Doodling, huh?" Hawk huffed a laugh.

The woman was majorly talented, one of the best artists he'd ever seen, and it wasn't just his bias speaking. Her originality and vision were no doubt why she was teacher of the year before she had to go on the run. She might've thought it was all a ruse after she was tricked into going to the scholarship fundraiser, but Hawk didn't think so. Hannah earned that title. So if she was "doodling," he couldn't wait to see what masterpiece she'd come up with.

The Little Bird landed with a slight bump, jarring him from his thoughts.

"Let's hope that's the roughest part of the night," Phoenix murmured over the mouthpiece.

"Amen to that," Jaybird replied. The man was nervous, obsessively checking his gun over and over again.

It'd been a while since he was on a true mission. They were all a little off for their own reasons. Hawk just hoped it didn't show when it counted.

"Alright, men. Move out, flying wedge formation," Hawk ordered over his mouthpiece before stepping out of the helicopter.

His team fell into step behind him in a *V* shape like he'd commanded. Their path to the warehouse was one of the few things they'd been able to map out, and despite the forested North Georgia terrain, it was easy to navigate under the moonlight. The entire crew—him, Draco, Devil, Phoenix, Snake, and Jaybird—traversed the mile from the helicopter with little trouble. They emerged from the tree line to see the abandoned warehouse, the grass around it already growing high from neglect.

Hawk held up his hand, giving the signals to stop and cover their angles. They'd approached the rear of the nearly completed structure. It was on the opposite side of the road and entrance, including where the van had entered. The truck bays lining the back wall were cavernous rectangular holes without doors installed, yawning open with inky darkness. The tall, pale, concrete and steel building was lit by only a few streetlights at the edge of the unfenced shipping yard.

Step after step, Hawk focused on his breathing, making sure every move was deliberate and silent. The BlackStone crew crossed the open concrete lot in pairs, taking care to avoid the hazy lights. Once they got close enough to the warehouse, they prowled flush to the wall until an open doorframe came into Hawk's vision. He waited a moment, listening in the night for any indicator that someone was out there.

Nothing. Crickets and cicadas droned in the humid night air.

He peered inside the doorway, but without the moonlight to guide them, everything was pitch black. Hawk tapped his night-vision goggles on the top of his helmet to alert his men that they were needed before he secured them over his eyes.

With everything now cast in an eerie—but much more defined—green hue, he checked again through the empty doorway before breaching into the warehouse. The large room was outlined by steel framing, allowing him to see several rooms away.

As if on cue, his men fanned out into the space, preparing for an attack on any side. He kept his gaze directly in front of him as they traveled through the steel-lined corridors and rooms of the vacant warehouse back offices. His goggles bathed the interior in the vivid green filter of the optics, helping him navigate their way to the entrance Vlad had used.

Nora had monitored the gas station camera while the team got ready. More men had shown up, although, how many, she didn't know. With no other way to prepare, Hawk's team had at least packed extra ammunition, just in case they were outgunned.

Hawk came upon a partly finished hallway with drywall on each side. At the end of the corridor, a slight glow flickered neon green in his goggles. He slowed to a near halt as he silently led his team toward that open doorway on the right. When he was finally inches away, he peered around the doorjamb.

Several men—including the biggest of them all, Vlad—gathered around an outdoor halogen work light glowing in the center of the large room. Discarded construction materials dotted the area, adding darker and brighter green shadows to Hawk's goggles.

Hawk remained still until a bout of laughter erupted from the room. He glided to the other side of the door with Jaybird behind him so their team could flank both sides of the entry. He made the signal to watch for his instruction, and his heart pounded as he waited for the perfect moment to breach the room.

*First, I'll shoot the lamp. That way we'll have the advantage. Then Vlad—*

A sharp clap resounded throughout the building, making Hawk duck away from the door. He nearly snapped at one of his men for opening fire until he realized they were taking cover along with him. The light inside the room winked out with the sound of tinkling glass. Russian shouts reverberated back at them and Hawk tightened his grip on his gun but didn't move from his position.

"What the fuck was that?" Jaybird's stunned whisper came in loud and clear through Hawk's earpiece.

Hawk shook his head and shifted on his feet as he prepared to look around the doorjamb again. "I don't know—"

Another clap reverberated around the walls. Hawk peeked around just in time to see one of Vlad's men collapse right beside the Russian giant.

*Gunshots.*

"We're not alone," Hawk confirmed to his team.

More shots rang out across the large open room, but they all seemed to be directed at Vlad's men, now running like rats searching for cover.

"They're using suppressors, so it's harder to tell where the shooters are located, but I think the trajectory is coming from our two o'clock," Draco observed over the headset.

Hawk watched, absorbing the scene as Vlad and his men used various items in the empty warehouse to try to hide. Whenever they found shelter, they responded to the attackers, shooting haphazardly. Vlad seemed cool, calm, and collected as usual, while his men shouted and screamed. But it was the glee on the General's face that gave Hawk pause.

"They're his men," he whispered the revelation.

"What?" Snake asked directly across from him.

"They're *his* men. The General's. He knows who's shooting and Vlad is defending himself. Check out the General's face."

Snake looked around the open doorjamb before sitting against the wall again. "Shit, you're right. What do we do?"

Hawk shrugged. "Let them kill each other?"

Phoenix covered his snort in the microphone. "Sounds A-fuckin'-OK to me."

"Jaybird, I want you in a firing position," Hawk continued. "Devil, cover our rear. I don't want any surprises and we need you to be fresh in case there are injuries."

Sweat popped up on Hawk's forehead as they waited for the shoot-out to finish, trying to figure out what the fuck was going on. No one seemed to have seen them or cared that they were there. All the focus was on Vlad's men and whoever was there for the General.

"Do you think it's the government?" Snake asked. "The FBI—"

Hawk narrowed his eyes through his goggles, taking in the dark, sadistic green smile widening the General's bright-green jowls before answering Snake. "I have no idea. I doubt it since he's enemy number one to everyone that matters right now, and he looks too fucking excited if he's supposedly getting caught."

Vlad's men got picked off regardless of what they hid behind. Hawk squinted as a burst of fire tore through a bulk container and the Russian behind it thrashed about before collapsing.

"Man, those are heavy rounds ripping through those containers," Jaybird pointed out, his head right above Snake's. "I thought law enforcement couldn't access those."

"They can't," Hawk replied back. "What the hell is going on?"

Vlad's minions fell one by one until silence sat oppressively in the night air.

Several men in full combat gear quietly emerged from behind crates and doorways on the opposite side of the room.

"There they are," Hawk whispered as he counted silently. "At least four of them it looks like, but the way they're operating, I bet a few are keeping them covered. They're clearing the area. Whatever happens, they can't take Vlad or the General. They're ours."

"Can't we just kill everyone? That'd make this shit a hell of a lot easier," Phoenix grumbled.

It was on the tip of Hawk's tongue to give the order, especially after what Hannah had told him back at BlackStone, but they needed to do this shit by the book. For as long as they could stand it, at least.

"Negative," he finally answered through gritted teeth. "We need them both alive for a trial."

Russian echoed through the warehouse as more of Vlad's men seemed to seep from their hiding spots, coming out from behind open doorways on the opposite side of the vast room. The newcomers' weapons picked the reinforcements off one after another as the Russians appeared through doorways, causing bodies to pile at the entrances. The four men continued converging on Vlad and his lackeys like the horsemen of the apocalypse. But when one of them squatted low and broke rank to run toward the General, Hawk gave the signal.

"Fuck, we gotta engage. *Now*."

He and his team emerged from the shadows, guns at the ready. As soon as the first bullet was fired their way, too damn close for Hawk's liking, he made the call.

"Open fire."

BlackStone returned gunshots at the unknown group as Hawk's team spilled from the hallway and into the room, finding their own cover among the materials. Their firefight succeeded in forcing the unknown group back into their shadows. Hawk couldn't tell how many bullets the gunmen had, but they'd already unloaded quite a few in their standoff with Vlad's men.

*Speaking of...*

"Someone get Vlad," Hawk ordered over his microphone.

"Already on it," Draco grunted.

Return fire snapped and cracked by Hawk as he ducked and weaved, taking cover behind whatever he could on his sprint toward the General's location. But before he and his team could converge on their target, one of their new enemies grabbed the General, hoisted him in a fireman's carry, and ran.

"Got him!" a member of the other team shouted.

"Cover and peel! Cover and peel!" one of them bellowed before leveling a massive squad automatic weapon at Black-Stone's positions.

*What the hell?*

"They've got a SAW?" Jaybird shouted from behind a metal barrel beside him. It had already been loud during the gunfight, but the chugging bark of the weapon made hearing impossible. "Aren't these supposed to be trafficking mobsters? Where the fuck did they get that power?"

"No fucking clue," Hawk yelled back. "We've got to go after them—"

As he was about to give the order, the bullets pouring out on them became torrential. Snake and Phoenix fired blindly over the top of their cover, unable to even stick their heads around the metal girders they were sheltering behind. Hawk clenched his jaw, biting back the order that would no doubt get his brothers killed. Instead, he leaned sideways from his position, and returned fire himself.

After what felt like an eternity, the machine gun suddenly cut off, but the semiautomatic gunshots ramped up. Hawk risked a peek over the top of the barrel to see Russians spilling into the room once more from the recesses of the building as the General's saviors slipped away through a door on the far side.

"This must be the rest of Vlad's men," Snake called out over the headset.

"Shit," Hawk cursed as he took cover behind a different barrel that he sure as fuck hoped was filled with something bulletproof. Jaybird followed him and together they shot around it, engaging and downing a number of Vlad's men spilling into the warehouse. "What's the status on Vlad? We can't lose him too."

"Got him," Draco answered gruffly.

"Good," Hawk grumbled just as another bullet *thunked* against the barrel he and Jaybird hid behind.

"These guys are coming out like flies to a corpse," Jaybird griped.

Hawk took aim, fired, and watched as another man crumpled silently. "Yeah, well, they die just as easily. We need to hold. I don't know where those other guys ran off to with the General or if there's more coming."

"Vlad might have answers," Snake suggested through the headset.

They held their position until the Russians were flagging. Hawk gave the assault order, and the team moved in tandem, clearing the room of opposition. The whole encounter took years and seconds at the same time, but they kept shooting until silence erupted around them.

"Hold," Hawk commanded them to wait a few more minutes as they hunkered down to watch their sectors.

It didn't take long for inexperienced or panicked troops to get impatient and show their position, and inexperienced was exactly who they were dealing with now. Not whoever the fuck those professionals were before.

Hawk glanced at his watch, giving an extra thirty seconds just in case the men had more discipline than he'd given them credit for, but there was nothing.

"Jaybird, you, Devil, and Snake clear the area. Phoenix, you meet me wherever Draco is."

"Copy," Jaybird, Phoenix, and Snake replied simultaneously.

"Fifteen meters from our breach point, about eleven o'clock from there," Draco answered with his location.

"Now," Hawk ordered.

They all emerged from their hiding spaces, Snake and Phoenix weren't too far from where he and Jaybird had been hiding, but Devil was nowhere in sight.

"Devil, brother, you copy?"

When he was met with static, Hawk's heart dropped in his chest. Jaybird shifted uncomfortably on his feet.

"Devil?"

Silence.

# CHAPTER TWENTY-EIGHT

"Devil!"

"He's here!" Snake answered. Devil's muffled voice entered the stream as he yelled through Snake's headset. "My radio ate a round, boss. I'm all good."

So much relief flooded Hawk's veins that he didn't even care that Devil had called him "boss."

"Glad you're here, brother. Copy. Over."

It took him and Phoenix no time to follow Draco's directions. He'd taken Vlad to a small room that looked like it would've been a plant manager's office. Hawk's other teammates had already taken off their goggles, so he did the same, shoving them up to see Draco with his flashlight pointed at the Russian, cornered on the ground and weaponless.

"Everyone good?"

Draco, ever the conversationalist, grunted his assent before he tilted his gun at an eerily placid Vlad.

"Never better," Phoenix replied, but his lips pressed in a firm line.

"What about you?" Hawk asked the Russian, but the man's blank expression gave him nothing. "Were you hurt?" Hawk finally asked.

"*Nyet*," he answered, his broad face still emotionless. "I am not hurt."

Hawk nodded and wiped the sweat off his brow with his long-sleeved shirt. "Okay, then. Let's move him out."

Draco nodded, but Phoenix's brow furrowed. "What about those other guys? What if they're still out there?"

"Clear," Jaybird answered over the microphone. Shortly after, Snake repeated the same, finishing with, "All clear outside too."

"Any sign of the others?" Hawk asked.

"No sign of the pros. Just a bunch of 7.62 casings," Snake replied, mentioning the shells the Russian guns left behind.

"Who were those guys, man?" Jaybird asked through the headset, loud enough to echo into the office from the large room. "They looked legit."

"I'm not sure—" Hawk stopped midsentence as the Russian's face finally registered some emotion, a barely noticeable slight ticking up of his lips.

"Something funny?" Hawk asked.

"Only if you are me," Vlad replied in his low voice. "Not if you are you."

"What the fuck's that mean?" Phoenix kicked the man's ribs, making the Russian cough and Phoenix curse.

"Phoenix," Hawk snapped.

"I owed him one," Phoenix growled before swearing again and propping his hand against the wall. "But, fuck, man, the asshole's wearing the General's strong-ass Kevlar like we've got."

"He is?" Draco asked. An odd smile spread across his face before he took a step back, lowering his assault rifle. In one fluid motion, he drew his sidearm from its holster and took aim.

Hawk's eyes bugged out. "Draco, what the—"

Two shots thundered in the small space before Hawk could spur into action, clamping his hand on Draco's wrist and shouldering him into the wall.

"Draco, what the *fuck?*"

"Everything okay?" Snake asked over the headset.

"Everything's *fine*." Hawk gave Draco a pointed look. "Draco just lost his damn mind for a second."

"I'd say sorry, but that felt fucking good," Draco answered simply, relaxing underneath Hawk's hold. "That's for stealing a year of my life, motherfucker."

Hawk turned around to see Vlad sucking in a breath as he covered his chest and side... the two places where he'd shot Draco over a year ago. Hawk let go of his friend, slowly realizing the reason for his outburst.

Draco had been in a coma for over a year thanks to Vlad and while he didn't die, he'd still never get back that time he could've had with Nora.

"I guess I should be glad you didn't kill him," Hawk muttered.

"Yup," Draco answered back, pulling a toothpick from his vest pocket.

"There's still time," Phoenix said, his eyes slightly crazed. Phoenix had been held captive by the General for nearly three months and Vlad had been one of his torturers.

"I pulled the two exact wrong motherfuckers for this job, huh?" Hawk huffed.

Phoenix shrugged. "What can I say? I feel a little murdery today. Especially toward a sadistic Russian *svoloch*." On the last word, he kicked Vlad in the side where Draco had shot him.

Vlad grunted and closed his eyes but didn't give in to the taunt.

Hawk shook his head, but he knew how to pick his battles, and stopping Phoenix from kicking his torturer wasn't one of them. Instead, he decided to take the declaration as a way to incentivize Vlad.

"You hear that?" Hawk asked, toeing the man's boot. "My men want to kill you. What do you have to say about that?"

Vlad's bored, tired expression only infuriated Hawk more. He couldn't imagine what Phoenix and Draco were thinking.

"You do not have to threaten my life. I will answer your questions."

Phoenix snorted. "Oh, I *highly* doubt that."

Vlad shrugged, the picture of indifference. "I do not care what you believe. I have no ties any longer. No loyalties."

Hawk frowned. "What's that mean?"

"It means I, ah, what do you Americans say? I tried to 'shoot my shot'. It did not work. It was a risk to take to get rid of that *durak* of a *Pakhan*."

He spat on the ground. Hawk, Phoenix, and Draco stuttered back but his aim was nowhere near them. The act was more in disrespect for the General than an attack against them.

"Wait, are you talking about taking down the General?" Phoenix asked. "Is that why you kept asking me all those questions about the General during our last little torture sesh?"

"It is," Vlad answered. "I work for great men. I do not work for a *durak*."

"Hate to break it to ya, buddy. You worked for that *idiot* a long-ass time. What gives?" Phoenix asked.

"I come to know too late he is obsessed. Not with doing a good job, you see. Obsessed with job, I could respect."

"What was he obsessed with?" Hawk asked. He had a feeling he wouldn't like the answer and dread pooled in his gut.

"You. Your team. Sex. His daughter. Sometimes it was all at the same time."

Bile rose up Hawk's throat as he responded, "From what I understand, he's been that way for a hell of a lot longer than any of us ever knew. What made you finally lose respect for him?"

Vlad jutted his chin toward Phoenix. "It was in the taking of this one."

"Who, little ol' me?" Phoenix gasped dramatically, pressing his hand to his heart. "Aw, say it ain't so."

"Phoenix, shut the fuck up," Draco grumbled.

Phoenix's smart mouth snapped shut when he saw Hawk's

displeased face. The jokester finally sighed and waved his hand. "Fine. Go on."

"What did taking Phoenix do?"

"He shows me he does not care about his own operation. He cares about fucking women who look like his daughter and—how you say—fucking over you 'BlackStone boys.' The taking of this one"—he tilted his head toward Phoenix—"was a threat to your team. I would get answers and kill him. Those were my jobs. Retrieve. Answers. Kill. I am *good* at this thing."

"You've got a weird set of morals, my dude," Phoenix muttered and crossed his arms.

"It is how I live. But the General does not have these *morals*. He likes to play too much. *He* is a rat."

Every word out of Vlad's mouth made Hawk more and more disgusted.

"So what, you decided to take over?"

"It was my idea at the time, yes. I would take over the operation and go to my country. We have... easy laws. If we have money, we can do many things. My men worked for me already, and taking the *Pakhan* meant I could make him answer questions from buyers that wanted a *durak* American to answer questions."

"You didn't kill him immediately because you wanted to keep him as insurance basically?" Hawk suggested.

"That is the truth. It also make buyers happy rat is no longer king."

"Well that fucking backfired, didn't it, ol' boy?" Phoenix asked, but Vlad seemed unrattled.

"It is the way of these things," he shrugged again. "You take risk. Sometimes they work. Sometimes you die."

"Damn, and I thought I was the morbid one," Phoenix grumbled.

Hawk ignored him. "Do you know who grabbed the General? Do you know where they've taken him? He's our main target, although a canary like you can't hurt. If you sing to the prosecutors, they might even give you a deal."

Vlad shook his head with a frown. "I do not *sing*. I answer your questions. Only BlackStone. No one else has earned more than my silence. As for where he is. He has a home close by where he likes to *play*, as he says. He is either there or somewhere else."

"Detailed answers. We love to see it." Phoenix gave a thumbs-up.

Vlad stared at him with a furrowed brow before continuing, "He likes to play and it is good to know his ways. Sometimes it makes him less predictable. Sometimes more."

"Predictable how?" Hawk asked.

Vlad shifted on the ground with his hand over his chest, prompting all three of the BlackStone men to raise their weapons at him. He didn't seem to mind having three guns in his face and didn't do anything to assuage their paranoia until he settled more comfortably against the wall and answered.

"He asked me to watch his daughter. Cat and rat, we play for two years. He was done with that game when I took Andrew Ascot with your Phoenix. Ascot told him you were looking for women from the party in Ashland County and Officer Henry Brown told him you were looking for H. Smith from the same party. When he found her this time, he wanted me to get her, to bring her to him."

Phoenix swore, "*Henry* ratted Hannah out? That mother—"

"Why didn't you?" Hawk asked, his chest tightening. "Why didn't you bring Hannah to the General?"

"I did not like his game and it was not her time yet. There were other loose ends to cut."

"But you went after her eventually," Hawk pointed out, and Vlad nodded. "Was that before or after you cut other loose ends?"

"After. I took the General, as you call him, and wanted to leave this country. His need for her would have made him less agreeable. And I was not sure what she knew. I wanted to kill her. Of course, you stopped that from happening."

Hawk's heart thundered as realization crept in. "Does he know your plan failed?"

Vlad shrugged. "He was there when I found out you got her. But it was in Russian. He does not like Russian."

"*Fuck*. Just because he doesn't like it, doesn't mean he doesn't fucking know it," Hawk hissed.

"It is no matter to me. I did want her dead. She is not. Now, I do not care. Another loose end in wind."

"We've got to go," Hawk muttered and pressed his mic closer to his mouth. "Everyone, get ready to roll out. Snake, relay to Devil that we need him to carry this asshole."

"Copy that," Snake answered.

"Wait... do you know who took the General tonight, or not?" Draco asked in his rough voice, obviously over the entire interrogation.

"I do. If it was not you, then it was one other. But it is funny, *nyet?*"

"What's funny?" Hawk asked, his brow furrowed as he tried to concentrate past his racing pulse.

"You are so smart, and yet you have not figured it out. I am surprised after all this time, you thought you were the only ones."

Hawk's already rapid pulse was off the charts, but that response made it stop altogether. "What the fuck does that mean?"

"That you were not the only ones. MF7, as you were, did not *end* with the BlackStone boys." An awful grin barely lifted his lips. "You were only the beginning."

# CHAPTER TWENTY-NINE

"Tommy! Come on, *mi avecito*! *¡Vámanos!* It's time to wake up."

Hannah's son rolled over with a grunt making her snort as he returned to his starfish position, his default setting when it came to sleeping.

"Tomás, it's time to wake up. I know it's early, but I promised Callie and Nora I would cook *huevos motuleños* since they were both up all night."

The men left well after midnight, wanting to use the cover of darkness for their mission. Since then, the women had taken only catnaps in order to stay alert, just in case the team needed them.

Nora had monitored security, Callie had been ready to connect with Marco or the FBI at any given moment, and Hannah had felt completely useless sketching beside them, waiting for updates until she'd nearly passed out from fatigue.

Callie seemed to be just fine with her fifteen-minute power naps, but Nora had eaten, drank, and slept in front of those computer monitors. She'd been living in that war room from the moment Hannah had first met with the team there, nearly forty-eight hours ago. If Hannah was exhausted after her fitful rest, Nora had to be dead on her feet.

Getting texts from the men once they'd landed had been both a relief and stressful, because that's all they'd been. Texts. Wes and Nora had worked on a system so they could communicate while the team was out, but once they got farther into the North Georgia mountains, the signal got spotty until it was out altogether.

Hannah had finally succumbed to her body's need for rest and had promised the women breakfast in the morning. Before Naomi and her daughter went back home to the team's mountain cabin, she'd assured Hannah the facility had all the essentials. Turned out the fridge not only had the typical United States Southern breakfast foods, but also had all the ingredients for her favorite hearty egg, chorizo, and tortilla breakfast dish her mother had taught her when she was a girl.

The fact that these men—who hadn't so much as lifted a spatula since she'd gotten there—had every ingredient down to ripe plantains confirmed what Hannah had suspected that first morning while making orange blossom sweet tea. Hawk had definitely done more than just the average shopping trip that night she'd arrived.

"*Tom*-my," she sang off-key. "Come on, *mijo*, it won't be hard. I even did the sauce and the chorizo last night, so we have very little to do this morning to make the dish. And it'll feel good to do something for others, especially since they've been helping us."

Her son groaned and kicked the sheets. "So *you* go fix them breakfast then. Wake me when it's ready."

"Oh no you don't. *Mientras vivas en esta casa, se hace lo que yo digo.* My house, my rules."

"But this *isn't* your house," Tommy whined as she pulled his hands away from his face and tugged him up to sit.

"Ooh, Tomás Hawkins, how I wish I could've seen you talk to your *abuela* like this. She would've had a fit. Come on. Up you go. You either help me make breakfast, or it's boring oatmeal for you. You know the rules."

Tommy groaned but finally began to move on his own. Albeit they were very dramatic, *telenovela*-worthy moves where he crawled toward the edge of the bed before rolling off entirely, but he was moving in the right direction, at least.

She tossed his clothes at him where he now lay on the floor. "Get dressed and shower. If you're not outside and clean in twenty minutes, it'll be a no-TV time, all-chores kind of day."

Tommy's eyes snapped open at the threat. "Yes, ma'am," he muttered before hopping to his feet and taking his clothes to the bathroom.

She smirked and ruffled his hair as he walked past. Once she heard the water running, she stopped by a mirror and fluffed her wavy, dark-blonde hair.

It'd been a while since she'd dressed herself in something nicer than a simple T-shirt. And when she'd realized the bag of outfits Ellie had given Hawk also had makeup inside, she could hardly wait to put it on, too. The tight jeans and blue blouse made her feel more normal than she'd felt in a long time. And the mascara, complimentary eyeshadow, and blue heels were just the cherry on top.

Hawk's favorite color had always been blue. What would he think about her new outfit—

*No. It's breakfast time. When they're back, I can fantasize.*

She'd developed the daydreaming habit as a kid, waiting for her father to come home from being on tour with the Army. Even as a child, she'd been confused at her mixed emotions over his homecoming after several blissful months without him. As an adult, she could now name the anxious feeling. It was one she desperately wished she'd been able to tell her mother growing up.

"Oh, *Mamá*. I miss you," she whispered, swallowing back emotion she'd been keeping to herself for way too long.

With the information overload yesterday, it'd been yet another shot to her soul that her own father had killed her mother. It was something she'd always wondered, like an awful itch at the back of her mind. But before coming to BlackStone, thinking that her father was capable of killing her mother felt like paranoia.

She hadn't been paranoid, though, and it *was* his fault. These were two facts she was going to have to start accepting. Her mother, Thomas, Hawk... aside from Tommy, every person who ever loved her had been stolen from her in one way or another by the man she hated. She wanted justice.

"Hawk is fixing it. He has to," she told herself out loud.

She sighed and shook her head, resolving not to think about it anymore. Her task for the morning was to make breakfast for everyone. That was her contribution to the team, for now. Maybe one day she'd be able to spruce up the austere aesthetic with some of her art. But in the meantime, she would just have to cook while she waited impatiently for the men to come back.

And they would. They *would* come back.

"He has to come back."

Hannah made the promise to herself as she went to the kitchen to scrounge up some breakfast. Twenty minutes on the dot after she told Tommy to come help her, Nora's bacon had finished baking in the oven and the kid—somehow still half-asleep despite his shower—walked out of the room like a zombie drawn to the rich scents of spice and frying tortillas. Hannah could've sworn his eyes were closed as he cracked eggs. When they'd finished plating the *huevos motuleños* and placing the fried plantains around the tortilla smothered in delicious beans, vegetables, chorizo, and eggs, she gave Tommy a plate to eat at the kitchen's bar top.

As he tiptoed up onto the high barstool, Callie emerged from one of the rooms, wearing a black T-shirt and cargo pants from what Hannah was beginning to suspect was an all-black wardrobe.

"*Buenos días*, Callie. How did you sleep?" Hannah asked as she passed Callie a full plate. "When you were able to, I guess."

Once the question had left her lips, her cheeks heated as she remembered she'd been able to sleep, thanks to Callie and Nora staying up to protect her. But if Callie hated the role of babysitter she'd taken on, she didn't show it.

"Great. I'm pretty used to odd sleeping schedules, so last night was nothing. Thanks for breakfast, by the way. This looks amazing."

Hannah nodded with a smile, grateful for the conversation. "I hope you like it! How's Nora?"

"I haven't checked since Wes messaged they'd landed outside of the warehouse. Have they reported back yet? I know the signal was spotty in the mountains."

Hannah shook her head, a spark of worry in her chest. "I'm not sure. I'll find out in a minute. I'm going to take this other plate to Nora now. Do you mind watching him?"

"Mom, I don't need a babysitter. Draco wouldn't even tell me where the weapons room is so there's nothing crazy for me to do except watch TV," he grumbled.

Despite the boy's insistence, Callie huffed a laugh and nodded to Hannah. "No problem."

"¡*Gracias!*" Hannah yelled over her shoulder.

Balancing both plates and two mason jars of tea, she toed the elevator's down arrow button to take her to the ground floor and made her way to the war room. When she got to the room, she called through the cracked door before opening it with her elbow.

"*Buenos días*, Nor-*ah*!"

Hannah jumped as Nora shot up in her seat, her bottle-green eyes wild and her purple curls wilder. Her rose gold frames barely hung on to the edge of her nose and her pale cheeks pinkened as Hannah cautiously walked through the door with the plates and glasses.

"That scary, huh?" Nora chuckled while straightening her glasses and patting her hair self-consciously. "I've never been a morning person."

"You're not scary. It's just the way you sprang up like a

purple-haired spider monkey surprised me, is all. Were you sleeping?"

"Oh no, just wasn't expecting a breakfast delivery this early. But don't you look pretty? Love those blue heels."

"Thanks! I love them, too. I've been in sneakers and T-shirts for too long. It feels good to dress up a little. Or at least not *look* like I live out of a suitcase." Hannah chuckled and set the plate in front of Nora at the computer desk before gasping and jerking it back.

"Oh my god, I forgot. Someone mentioned you're a vegetarian? But wait, no... you asked for bacon—"

"I'm a nonbreakfast vegetarian. Now, gimme, gimme."

Nora lunged from her seat, somehow keeping her butt in the chair as she grabbed the plate. She placed the meal on the desk before snatching one of the bacon slices Hannah had piled onto the plate next to the *huevos motuleños*. After she stuffed a piece into her mouth, she sighed contentedly.

"I love all of Gaia's creatures, but a woman can only have so much self-control. I can't be expected to be a food martyr when godsdamned bacon is involved."

Nora ate another piece of bacon, and Hannah laughed as she moaned like it was the best thing she'd ever tasted.

"Now that hits the spot," she muttered around the slice before her head tilted and she pointed at the plate. "Hold up now. What's going on here? This looks scrumdiddlyumptious. And is this the orange blossom sweet tea Hawk has been raving about?"

"Yup, it is. And the dish is *huevos motuleños*. It's got chorizo, fried egg, fried tortilla, fried plantain, fried beans—"

"Fried before any type of food is my favorite," Nora sang prettily before taking a big bite and grunting her approval. Then she sipped the tea and did a little happy dance. "Oh my goddess, this *is* delicious. I might have to switch out my morning Frappuccino."

Hannah smiled. "They're both my mother's recipes. She taught me when I was a girl before... before..."

She knew the words, but she couldn't get them out.

"Before she, um, passed away?" Nora tried to fill in the blank with a nicer version of the truth, but Hannah shook her head.

"Before my *father* murdered her. I can't keep sticking my head in the sand about him. I had to suppress my feelings about it for so long, but now I know that mindset is getting people killed. There's no way I can keep living like that."

Nora nodded thoughtfully with a slice of bacon hanging in the air, poised to enter her mouth. Hannah used her foot to roll the chair next to Nora out from under the desk.

"Thought I'd eat with you, do you mind?"

"Oh, please do." Nora waved at the chair before speaking again. "How old were you when she died?"

Hannah sighed before taking a seat. "Around Tommy's age."

"So Tommy never had a father, and your mother was taken too early. Dude, that sucks. It's amazeballs you've managed to raise him as healthily as you have." Nora shook her head as she chewed her *huevos motuleños*.

Hannah huffed wryly and moved her own food around with her fork. "It does suck. But we move on, right? One foot in front of the other and all that."

Nora chewed with a thoughtful look. After a moment of silence, she pointed the bacon at Hannah.

"You know, I used to believe that was all emotions needed to be, too. Nothing I can do about it, so I might as well grin and bear it."

"Good motto." Hannah nodded her head, but Nora shook hers.

"Nope. Toxic motto. We can't just put up a front for people and call it a day. You've gotta at least have *someone* to share your woes and blows with. Life ain't peachy keen all the time, and we need people in our corner to help us get through it."

Sudden tears pricked in Hannah's eyes and she absentmindedly twisted her finger into her gold necklace. The advice felt foreign but second nature at the same time. While it sounded nice, it'd been just her and Tommy for the past two years. She'd had no one.

"I've been alone for so long... what if you don't have someone to lean on?"

Even as she said it, her necklace looped around her finger and Hawk's image flashed in her mind. Before he had to leave, he'd always been there for her. Her rock. Could he be that for her again?

Nora's eyes darted to Hannah's necklace before she could put it back underneath her blue blouse. A small smile curved the woman's painted lips.

"I think we both know you're not alone anymore. Not only do you have a sexy James Bond to fend off all your demons, you've got us now, too."

She said it simply, with a shrug of her shoulder right before taking another mouthful of saucy chorizo and egg. But the words meant so much more than her delivery let on.

Hannah's heart squeezed. "Thanks, Nora. I appreciate that."

"Anytime, girlfriend." Nora beamed at her, her alabaster cheeks round with food.

A sharp beep made them both jump.

"What was that?" Hannah asked.

Nora twisted her rolling chair away from Hannah to face the monitors again, a slice of bacon hanging out of her mouth.

"Naht shurr," she mumbled around the bacon. "Hol' on. Le' me sheck."

Hannah snorted at Nora's messy answer, but another beep resounded in the room. The bacon fell out of Nora's mouth, landing on top of the plate.

"Well, shit, that ain't good."

Hannah's eyes widened at Nora's use of an actual curse word instead of a colorful string of phrases.

"What isn't good? What's going on?" Hannah leaned toward the screens, her breakfast altogether forgotten.

"No... no, no, no. Shit." Nora muttered as she typed furiously on the keyboard. "Shit, shit, shit."

Hannah's pulse raced, and she wrung her hands.

"Nora. You're scaring me. What's going on?"

"Wes tried to get in touch with me through the back channels of our communication system. But their service made his transmission spotty, so it's just now getting through the receiver—"

"Nora."

"Yeah, sorry. Mumbo jumbo. Apparently, Wes messaged us a while ago, but for some reason, it only came through just now."

"Okay... what was the message?" Hannah unsuccessfully tried to quell the edge in her own voice.

"Ah, here it is..." Nora bent forward to read before she frowned. "It just says 'be on the lookout.' Well, sheesh, Superman, not very informative, just unnerving as hell."

"Why would he send something so vague?"

"Yeah, you're a painter, right? And I'm a classic worrywart. Doesn't he realize how great our imaginations are?" Nora typed furiously, reading out loud as she did. "You... can't... just... say... that... you cryptic... blue-haired... goober—"

Another beep, harsher than the other two, made Hannah jolt and sent shivers down her spine. Nora paused over her keystrokes. Her frown deepened and she switched to the mouse until the monitors changed to show BlackStone's security feeds.

"Wes updated all the security measures in the building after the attack a few months back. I just need to check... something..." Nora's words drifted off as she searched the monitors.

"What do you see? Is something wrong?" Hannah could hear the panic in her own voice, but she couldn't help it as Nora narrowed her eyes at the footage.

The woman cursed and pressed a button before speaking through a small microphone sticking out of one of the keyboards. The woman's normally lyrical voice sounded strained as it echoed into the war room from speakers in the hall.

"Callie... the viper circles the nest. Take the egg from breakfast and bring it to ground. I repeat, the viper circles the nest."

On a screen in the middle row, Callie lifted her head. Her sleek black ponytail allowed her face to easily be seen by the camera and the small smile she'd had for whatever Tommy was saying at the bar completely disappeared.

She set down her plate and beckoned Tommy to follow her. When he slid off the chair without protest, Hannah half wondered what the magic words were to get him to move so quickly. But when Callie put one arm around his shoulder and one hand on the gun Hannah had somehow missed was strapped to her side, Hannah's stomach dropped.

"Nora, tell me what's going on."

Nora muttered a curse under her breath as she typed and looked at the screens.

"Nora! Tell me right now—"

Movement on the bottom three monitors caught her attention. Nora swallowed audibly as she finally answered.

"Someone's here."

# CHAPTER THIRTY

Black figures stalked across the screens. They crouched with assault rifles swiveling around as they searched the area. It reminded her of the many military films, videos, and movies her father had made her watch growing up.

These men looked well trained, moving in sync with one another. And from what she could tell, they had the building surrounded. At least three men took up the monitors depicting the ground floor of the facility, and one more climbed the fire escape on ropes before dropping the ladder down for his companions.

"They brought *grappling* hooks? What in the underworld is going on here?" Nora lamented. "Who are these people?"

Hannah had the same question, except there was one person she *did* recognize. Her skin crawled as her tormentor sauntered out of a large black van right in front of the BlackStone Securities garage.

She hadn't seen him in years. His hair was still dyed jet black, but it looked slightly disheveled. Come to think of it, *he* looked disheveled in his wrinkled suit. But he still somehow seemed more imposing than the monster from her past, even on the small screen. The face that plagued her waking nightmares from childhood looked eerily the same, frozen in time. Goose bumps rose on her skin as her father pointed and commanded one of the soldiers.

"The viper circles the nest..." Hannah repeated. "How did he get in through the gate? I thought BlackStone was safe."

"It is! Wes changed all the security after Vlad attacked the facility." Nora flicked through scenes on the monitors and groaned. "But I guess that doesn't matter if someone bombs the m-effin' gate. Godsdammit, they have to know the men are gone. They're being way too brazen."

Footsteps in the hallway sent Hannah's pulse racing and her hand fluttered to her chest as she whirled around to face the door.

"It's us," Callie called out before appearing through the door with Tommy in tow and shutting it behind them. "What's going on?"

Her voice sent relief flooding into Hannah's veins and once her son entered the room, she resisted every urge to run toward him, grab his hand, and flee the building.

"*Ven aquí, por favor, mi avecito.*" She beckoned him softly to come to her.

He nestled under her arm and she embraced him as calmly as she could, trying her damnedest not to freak him out.

"Mom, is everything okay?" he whispered, his worried eyes searching hers.

It was on the tip of her tongue to reassure him, even though she had no basis for the promise of safety, but Nora beat her to the punch with the truth.

"We've got *com*-pan-*y*," Nora sang nervously and pointed at the monitors. "But we're safe inside right now."

Callie peered closer and cursed. "Fan-fucking-tastic. Did you tell the guys?"

"Waiting for the message to go through." Nora tapped the phone screen in front of her, but Hannah sucked in a breath as a red "**Not Delivered**" alert popped up underneath it. "Shoot.

Looks like they jammed the system. Clever, clever, Mr. General."

"What does that mean?" Hannah asked.

"They have a device hindering us from using normal communications. It's why Wes sent his vague message through the backup channels. If I had to guess, this team probably used the device at the CTI facility too, which explains why we couldn't talk to the guys then either."

She returned to the keyboard and typed quickly. A black screen filled the center monitor. White numbers and letters scrolled across at speeds that were far too fast for Hannah to read.

"There. I sent a message," Nora said, finishing her typing with a flourish.

"They went to that facility to get the General." Callie shook her head. "How the fuck did he make it here so fast? BlackStone has a helicopter."

Nora grimaced. "Maybe the boys got held up?"

The lilt in Nora's question didn't hide the very same fear Hannah was beginning to feel slicing up her own lungs.

"Look, I'm not sure what happened," Nora pointed out quickly, making Hannah wonder if the careful expression she was trying to keep for Tommy wasn't as covert as she'd hoped. "But they weren't very far away. It was why they were able to take the helicopter in the first place because it could make it in one trip without needing more fuel. They could've been held up for routine things like questioning bad guys or gathering evidence, and these crazies drove here like a *Mario Kart* driver in the meantime."

"Well, what do we do now? Plan *A* was go to the garage, right?" Hannah hated the waver in her voice and the fact she didn't have any skills to help at the moment. All she could do was fight against every cell in her body screaming at her to escape.

Before the party two years ago, Hannah already avoided her

father. She'd dodged calls, ignored messages, and been all around aloof toward the man. But once his henchman threatened her, she was out. She and Tommy had fled every home they'd had for the past two years, searching for a place her father's power couldn't reach, and every time they'd gotten settled, he'd done something to prove she still hadn't hidden well enough.

She was tired, so fucking tired. And now that Hawk was back in her life, all she wanted was to dig her roots in and settle down for real. No more running. Despite current circumstances, BlackStone was still her best option. But even knowing that, her first instinct was to disappear. It was taking everything in her power not to pick Tommy up like she used to when he was a toddler, and run for the hills.

"Yuppers. Plan *A* was go to the garage and take Drake's truck, but—"

An explosion rocked the building. Callie whipped around to face the door, her gun pointed and ready to fire. Hannah's grip tightened around Tommy as her eyes snapped to the bottom right and top center monitors.

"Okay..." Nora's voice pitched higher than normal at the sight of the huge hole that erupted in the garage door. The General waltzed right through with a soldier at his side.

In the top screens, another soldier entered the roof door that was now open. Hannah glanced around the monitors to see nearly every screen had a soldier appearing in it.

"Guess we gotta go with plan freaking *D* since *B* and *C* didn't account for being surrounded," Nora groaned before jutting her chin to the door. Callie tugged the handle.

"It's secure," she replied quietly. Hannah didn't know how soundproof the walls were, but with the garage right across the hall from the war room, Callie obviously didn't want to draw any more attention to their location.

Nora pressed three buttons on the keyboard and another code flashed on the monitor before all the screens went black.

"Come on. I've just entered a kill-switch sequence. Everything in the facility will lock up and shut down in three minutes. Once it does that, we'll have more time to stall before the guys get here."

"What if they have more bombs?" Hannah asked.

"In that case, at least they'll have to use them. Come on. We need to go underground."

Nora stood from her chair so fast it spun around and banged into the desk. She hurried to the wall opposite the war room's door and pulled aside a hidden panel, revealing a keypad underneath. She clicked in another code. When she'd finished, a metal trapdoor stained to look just like the concrete flooring slid open with a pneumatic *hiss*.

"Cool." Tommy grinned with a nod.

"Glad you think so, kid."

At Callie's shaky delivery, Hannah turned to see her audible swallow rolling down her throat in a lump, her focus completely homing in on the hole in the ground.

"Sorry, Callie," Nora whispered with a wince.

"Callie, what's wrong?" Hannah asked.

She peered into the hole to see bright-white lighting shining on a metal staircase. It led to a sterile, steel-walled basement with concrete stained just like the floor above it.

Callie waved off her concern, but the way her dark-olive complexion had become ashen gave her away.

"I-it's fine. Just with the General... going underground..." She closed her eyes and took a deep, steadying breath. When she opened her eyes again, determination filled her gaze and her lips thinned.

Everyone had said they looked alike, and Hannah certainly saw the resemblance. Even then, with Callie's glossy, raven hair high in a ponytail, the hardness in her brown eyes, her all-black outfit, and the way her jaw was set, Callie's entire demeanor made Hannah feel the odd sensation she was looking at her past self, readying for a battle. The sight gave her courage, and she found herself closing her eyes and taking a similar fortifying inhale.

When she opened her eyes again on her exhale, Callie's gaze met hers. Understanding softened her features.

"You ready?" Callie asked with a tilt of her head toward the hole in the ground.

A door opened from beyond the war room, followed by stomping, setting Hannah's chest on fire from the speed of her pounding pulse.

"Ready," she answered with a single nod of her head.

"Good," Nora muttered as she stepped down into the hole. "Because we've got a minute and a half before this place locks up tight. The General either didn't have the code to get to the garage or he likes to make a big entrance. But if he somehow knows how to get into the war room, we can't stop him. Let's go."

Nora hopped off the stairs, and Hannah followed after her so she could catch Tommy if he got nervous. Callie helped him down the stairs and when he fearlessly leaped off the last two rungs, Hannah stepped back quickly to give him room to land. His wide, toothy grin spread across his face and he did a small fist pump.

"Did you see that, Mom? I didn't even need the last few steps."

"*Bueno, avecito.* You did well." Hannah's smile was feeble with stress, but her heart fluttered in relief at her son's resilience. She was a damn near train wreck and here he was finding joy amid chaos.

They'd been through hell together. She'd tried her best to shelter him when she could and be gently honest with him when she couldn't. There were times when his serious nature kept her up at night, terrified she'd screwed him up beyond repair for not being able to have the childhood every little kid deserves. But the moments where he showed her he was still the wild boy she knew gave her hope.

Slowly but surely, Callie stepped down the stairs. Watching the strong, courageous woman tremble as she descended made Hannah's chest ache. She glanced away to take in her surroundings and give Callie some space.

They were in a steel-walled vestibule that opened into a long hallway with a dead end. Along one side were several metal doors with bars on the windows.

*This isn't a bunker... it's a jail.*

Unease filtered through Hannah's mind at the thought of being locked down there while the General was upstairs. No wonder Callie was freaking out.

Callie finally landed on the ground, flexing and fisting her shaking hands. As soon as her feet touched the stained concrete, Nora pressed a button on a wall keypad, similar to its counterpart above ground, closing the trapdoor.

It crept closed, and with every inch, Hannah could've sworn she felt a new drop of sweat beading on her skin.

When it finally sealed with a barely audible *snick*, another loud explosion reverberated through the steel around them, sprinkling dust from the ceiling and flickering the bright fluorescent lights.

She found herself hugging Tommy in one arm and a rigid-as-stone Callie in the other before the light flared back to life. Heavy thumps stomped above as Hannah held her breath and Tommy tensed against her body. Callie shook her off and raised her gun, aiming it at the door above.

"I guess he didn't need to figure out how to get into the war room," Nora muttered.

"How would he know to look here? Has he been here before?" Hannah asked.

"No, of course he hasn't—oh, *fuck*. Henry has, though. It was Henry. It had to be."

"Henry? The officer you guys put behind bars?"

Nora nodded. "Marco said he had a visitor the other day. Henry must've tattled the layout to his little visitor."

Hannah looked behind them to see if there was anywhere to hide other than the jail cells, but the stark hallway was bare and if they went into the cells, they were practically asking the General to make them his prisoners.

A thought occurred to her with another thump above them. If this was meant to be a jail or a dungeon, then...

She whispered to Nora and jerked her chin above them to the trapdoor. "Does that door lock?"

Sweat had sprouted on Nora's forehead as she murmured back, "Not from this side. But if the self-destruct sequence shuts down in time, he won't be able to open it until Wes or I use our phones to reactivate the facility."

"How much longer until it shuts down?" Hannah breathed.

Nora checked her watch and cursed. "Ten seconds."

Hannah's eyes closed in a silent prayer, just as the footsteps stopped... right above them.

# CHAPTER THIRTY-ONE

## Two years ago

After he'd agreed to work for Satan himself, Eagle had been escorted off the premises and driven to the plane that would take his team to Yemen. They'd gotten orders that quickly, so often his teammates didn't even bat an eye at the abrupt assignment.

The journey took a day of hopping through different military bases. Each second had been pure torture, fighting the urge to take control of the plane at every bout of turbulence, every flight change, every time anyone even spoke a word to him. Half his teammates were pilots anyway, it wasn't like they wouldn't be able to figure out how to land the damn thing *anywhere* fucking else besides their destination.

But the General's threat loomed large in his mind, keeping him seated, silent, and compliant.

Once the team had landed, they'd set up their base a few miles outside of a small Yemeni village. Out of respect for the villagers, the team kept to their camp as much as possible, not wanting to make them feel on edge with a more constant presence than the men already had. It didn't matter how friendly the team got with the locals, no one felt comfortable surrounded by men in fatigues, decked out in fifty-plus pounds of military gear and weaponry, not even fellow soldiers.

As time went by, it grew easier for Eagle to forget the role he would be forced to play. Whenever he did have a moment of weakness that tempted him to warn Hannah or his team, it'd hit him that he didn't know where she was or how to get in contact with her. He'd wanted to look for her himself, but getting caught red-handed by the General last time he did his own research was how he'd gotten into this shit in the first place. By the time he'd finally figured out how to trick Snake into looking for the house, it was already for rent and Hannah was in the wind.

So instead, he got lost in training the villagers, convincing himself that though he was destined to let their target go and fail his team, at least the villagers would be left with the ability to protect themselves against the trafficker he left behind. One of the locals they paid as a translator, a woman named Masuma, even became a friend.

She helped the MF7 team help themselves, and along every step of the way, the angry screaming guilt over betraying his team got quieter. During the day, he imagined hanging up his boots at the end of all of this, maybe even trying to pursue things with Masuma. She was a beautiful, strong woman, and reminded him so much of Hannah, but with an *actual* connection this time. Not like the one he'd fabricated in his mind.

Everything was peaceful and perfect.

Until he got the encrypted message through his laptop.

As he deciphered it, knowing it was from the General, he still prayed like hell there would be a different command. That the General had changed his mind. There was no way the madman would *actually* want him to let a trafficker go, right? It was only after he read it a third time that he realized the dire nature of his situation.

*Shit just got way too fucking real, too fucking quick.*

He was going to betray his team. He would have to let a trafficking scumbag go free. And there wasn't a goddamn thing he could do about it.

He sent the message late at night after the team finalized their operation plan and warned his contact when to leave with the target. A proxy would be left in the ringleader's place, one that had vowed to give his life to protect his leader, if necessary, and sex trafficking could continue unhindered in the area. Just like the General wanted.

"It's time, brothers," he informed them as he entered the big communal tent they called their "living room."

The simple prompting was all his teammates needed to kick them into overdrive and gear up for the mission. Draco and Jaybird readied the weaponry. Hawk helped supervise and organize the packs, and Phoenix prepared the Little Bird. After Snake ensured their communications and headsets were a go, Eagle snuck in after him, changing his own headset to include another preset frequency so he could be on the same line as the locals and the target.

It also meant he was on a similar channel to Phoenix, who had to manage multiple frequencies with the Little Bird's radio. He wouldn't be able to hear the target, though.

As long as shit didn't hit the fan, no one would know Eagle had switched his radio, not unless the team's channel somehow got jammed, allowing Phoenix to still be able to hear through Eagle's headset. Thankfully, there was no way these locals had the resources to jam MF7's comms.

*But what if they had help...*

"What're you doing?" Snake asked with a frown as he entered their comms tent.

"Oh, uh." Eagle cleared his throat and put on the headset. "Just making sure everything's ready. You know how I like to triple-check."

Snake chuckled and waved him off. "It's our last mission. We've done this hundreds of times by now and this is an in-and-out job. We'll be back in the States before you know it. No need to stress."

Eagle tried to meet his friend's smile, but when he realized he wouldn't be able to fake it enough to reach his eyes, he dipped his head to busy himself with his headset.

"Good point. It's been good working with you, Snake. I can't wait to see what you do on the outside."

Snake's smile widened. "Hopefully find a nice little IT job. Geek Squad style. Maybe convince a good woman to love me and have a kid or two." Snake lifted the tent flap joining their communications station with their makeshift living room. "What about you, Phoenix?"

At Snake's call, Phoenix popped his head through the canvas with a wide grin of his own.

"Oh, you *know* I've gotta hit the town first. But maybe if I'm lucky, I'll find my own sexy guy or gal who's willing to put up with my crazy ass."

"Hey now, don't forget about that security firm idea you, me, and Hawk had, Eagle," Jaybird yelled behind Phoenix from the other room. "How cool would it be if we figured out how to live together with our families all in the same place?"

"Like a damn compound? That sounds like my version of hell." Devil, their medic, walked past Phoenix into the comms tent. His perpetually sunburned skin beamed at them as he laughed. "And you guys are all in your thirties. You've had your time before you went Special Forces. Military prodigies don't get to sow our wild oats. I've got time before I even need to *think* about getting wifed up."

Jaybird snorted as he appeared beside Phoenix. "Yeah right. Your surly ass will likely get settled down before any of us. Except for maybe me. I've got a girl back home I wouldn't mind reaching out to when I get on the outside. I kind of fucked it up before I left."

Hawk appeared behind Jaybird and clapped him on the shoulder. "I'm sure she'll give you a second chance, brother. I'll be waiting around a while to make sure we're safe back in the States, but if we don't have any traffickers trying to start bullshit, I'm calling my woman up, too. I'm hoping like hell she is somehow miraculously single and forgives me, too."

The hope in Hawk's eyes made Eagle's chest ache. What would happen between them all when Hawk realized he had slept with Hannah? Or when he found out they had a kid together? Would he forgive them? Would Hannah forgive either of them for leaving her behind? Would she let Eagle see his own child, or had he lost the opportunity to have a relationship with his son?

He shook his head, wishing he could shake reality instead. His phone buzzed, and he checked it before stuffing it back in his pocket. It was the message he'd been dreading.

"Everyone ready?" When he got a chorus of "yeses," he nodded. "Alright men... brothers. We're Oscar Mike."

Everyone whooped their respective military branch's war cry at the order that their final mission had officially begun. They jogged out to the helo, leaving Snake behind to control a drone he'd already planted to be their eyes in the sky.

The helicopter ride was the fastest and longest trip Eagle had ever been on. When Phoenix landed it outside of the enemy's compound—or rather, the *proxy's* compound—Jaybird, Hawk, and Eagle hopped out. Leaving Draco, Devil, and Phoenix to defend the bird.

As their medic, Devil did more good staying behind, remaining available if shit went sideways. During his time in MF7, he'd proven more than once he was always ready to be thrust into any situation on the fly. His medical background with the SEALs, coupled with the miracle healing drug the General had commissioned for them, made it so the team stayed in peak shape. As long as it wasn't a deadly wound, and they got the meds quick enough, Eagle's men were basically invincible.

Draco and Jaybird had already surveilled the place the day before on the ground from afar, making sure there weren't any visible charges or bombs they needed to evade and taking stock of where the lookouts were stationed. Of course, there was no surefire way to know if there were IEDs without taking a step first. Thankfully, one good thing about being the General's lapdog meant the target wouldn't booby-trap his boss's own men.

Eagle led the way with Hawk and Jaybird closely behind him in a tight wedge formation. Once they got to the compound, he pressed the wooden door with his hand to assess what kind of give it would push back with when he kicked it in. There'd been one too many times he'd been caught off guard kicking the hell out of a door that would only go down with a battering ram. He was prepared for the same now, only this time, the door drifted open underneath his fingertips.

*Jesus, way to give it away.*

Just as Eagle thought it, Hawk whispered behind him.

"Was that already open?"

"Watch my six." He didn't explain further, hoping if he just moved on, Jaybird and Hawk wouldn't look into it.

"Always," Hawk replied, making Eagle's chest tighten.

The man had been his friend before MF7, but over the years, he truly became a brother. They all had. The team was the only family they could have in these fucked-up situations, but Eagle wouldn't have wanted to stand beside anyone else in the name of God, country, and cause.

Except, the past seven years had been about none of those things. It'd all been for nothing.

Eagle blinked away the truth and moved through the building. The tile underneath them hadn't been swept since the dust storm that morning, and the light layer of dirt made it so their steps were even quieter than normal.

"I thought this place was full of people," Hawk pointed out.

"That's what our intel said," Eagle assured him.

"That's what Draco and I saw yesterday, too. Maybe they hunkered down inside the interior rooms to avoid the dust."

"Then why are there no footprints?" Hawk asked.

Eagle frowned at the observation.

*Why aren't there any footprints?*

As Eagle came upon a turn, he lifted his hand to tell his teammates to quiet behind him. His heartbeat drummed in his chest right before he pivoted to face the perpendicular hallway to see—

Nothing. That's all there was, with every turn going forward, too. A whole bunch of nothing.

*Seriously, General. This is not the way to keep your cover.*

"Maybe they don't use this route," Jaybird offered as Eagle crept through the corridor. "This is an outer hall, easier to penetrate from the outside. The room we're heading toward is in the back. There will probably be more rooms as we go farther in. And we know women are rarely allowed to freely roam these places."

"Yeah, maybe," Hawk answered.

*Why aren't there footprints, though?* Eagle asked himself again, not wanting to bring more attention to it than there already was. *Where is everyone?*

When the General had told him they were going to be capturing a proxy instead, he hadn't mentioned the target would clear the place out of other suspects first. It would make it harder to convince his team they got the right guy if all the other ones had disappeared. There was no way the ringleader would be sitting pretty waiting for his own pair of handcuffs without his guards around to make the team work for it. Surely, the General wouldn't be so sloppy with his ruse.

And yet nothing stirred in the house.

Unease slithered in Eagle's veins, pumping with the guilt already strangling his chest. They silently made their way through the halls to the back room, where their intel had told them their target slept. And they didn't pass a single soul.

*Something's not right.*

"Something's not right," Hawk echoed his internal thought.

"Yeah, stay frosty," Eagle confirmed, telling his teammates to keep a steady head despite the circumstances. His own footsteps felt heavier the closer they got, as if his very bones were begging him to turn back.

"Here... let me..."—static rumbled over the headset as Snake spoke—"drone's... thermal optics."

"Snake, man, your mic's fucking up," Hawk pointed out behind Eagle.

"Yours is, too," Jaybird whispered. "It's all fuzzy over the headphones."

*Shit*, Eagle thought, not knowing what the hell that could mean but knowing it was something fucked.

When they'd finally arrived outside of the faux target's bedroom, having not encountered a single obstacle, Eagle's nerves were at an all-time high. He and Jaybird stood on either side of the wooden door and Hawk got into position to kick the damn thing down.

"Heat signature... people... target's bedroom—" Snake's speech broke as he informed them. "—no one... in building."

Alarm bells rang in Eagle's head and his pulse hammered in his ears as Hawk and Jaybird got into ready position.

"Three... two... one..." Hawk counted off in quiet grunts, but those Mayday signals sounding off in Eagle's head became unbearable.

*What if this is a trap? What if I'm leading my teammates to die—*

"Wait—"

"*Breach!*" Hawk yelled right before he kicked beside the handle of the door, showering splinters and debris into the room as it slammed open.

A chorus of screams met them on the other side, and despite Eagle's muscle memory and training sending him through the door after Jaybird, he stopped point blank at the terrified cries and stood stock-still when they didn't stop.

They were the good guys, or at least they were supposed to be. The General had fucked them over all this time, but his team and the victims they saved always believed they were the heroes.

As he stood in that room, though, there were only petrified women. The ones who weren't drugged out of their mind or sick, stared back at him, huddling away and seeking shelter.

From *him*.

He searched the room for the target and his heart froze in his chest when his gaze caught the scene in the center of the room.

"Masuma," he gasped.

The woman he'd called a friend stood beside their proxy target, a knife to her neck. Tears streamed down her stoic face, and her brown skin was ashen with fear. Eagle wanted to comfort her, to tell her it was all going to be okay. All he had to do was take the shot. But then his eyes fully focused on the proxy.

Their "target" wore a vest of explosives and a deranged smile.

"No," he whispered as the proxy shoved Masuma in front of his vested chest, blocking the shot.

Jaybird raised his gun, but Hawk yelled at him. His voice was deep and sluggish, as if Eagle was watching it all in slow motion.

"No! You'll get Masuma!"

At Hawk's command, the proxy threw the knife to the side and slapped his chest.

The world erupted around them.

Hawk threw his body against Eagle and Jaybird, shielding them both as the room exploded. Women screamed at the top of their lungs and his men yelled over their headsets.

"Friendly fire! I repeat, friendly fire!" Phoenix shouted over his headset as gunshots peppered outside the wall.

"—get... out—there!" Snake ordered them. "—villagers... setting up... IEDs—"

A new screeching wailed into his ears as his comms went berserk with feedback. Eagle clawed off his headset and threw it on the ground, just as another explosion rocked the earth beneath them. The back of Eagle's vest was jerked up as Hawk scrambled to his feet, helping him stand.

Eagle searched the room to find Masuma, but once he caught her deep-brown eyes, lifeless in a nearly unrecognizably burned face, he knew she was gone.

One part of him wanted to help the women, the other knew there were too many and not enough time to assess who could and couldn't be saved. Meanwhile, bombs were going off outside, shaking the ceiling and walls all around them. He had to get his men the fuck out of there.

This had all gone wrong. The General had tricked him and their team into thinking they'd served their time. It was their last mission alright, but the General had never intended for them to go home. Not without body bags.

Bile rose in his throat as he tugged Jaybird up.

"We gotta go," he ordered his teammates and turned to Hawk. The man was attempting to calm down a bloodied and burned woman screaming at him, trying to crawl away.

"Hawk! Let's go!"

"But, Eagle, the women—"

"It's done, Hawk. We have to go. Our men are taking on fire."

A bullet tore through the wall, proving his point and spurring Eagle to push Hawk and Jaybird through the door.

"Eagle, what the—"

"Move, Hawk. Now! That's an order!"

Hawk's eyes narrowed on him and he looked like he was going to argue further when an explosion behind them rocked their feet. The doorway they'd just exited caved in, but Eagle didn't give them a chance to sightsee. He shoved his teammates down the hallway they'd just come through, forcing them to run. With each step closer to the door, more and more bullets *thunked* through the walls around them. When they emerged from the building, chaos reigned.

Draco and Devil fielded shots directed at the helicopter as Phoenix fired it up. Former allies swarmed the hillsides to their right, shooting at their group in an uncoordinated attack.

"Come on, let's go," Eagle commanded, reaching up to press the microphone to his lips, only to remember it wasn't there. "Shit," he muttered, having forgotten he'd tossed it aside. He grabbed Hawk by the vest and yanked him closer to scream in his microphone over the gunshots.

"Prep for immediate exfil!" Eagle commanded through the mic for everyone to evacuate the premises.

"They can't hear you," Hawk countered. "The headsets are fucked."

Hawk turned around toward the helo and made the signal with hand gestures before taking point. Eagle and Jaybird flanked him on each side, creating a wedge formation that protected each of their sixes.

"Fuck!" Jaybird ducked into Eagle and away from a man aiming at his face. "I *trained* you, motherfucker!"

Eagle turned to look at Jaybird kneeling on the ground, holding his hand to his head. When Jaybird brought it away to look at it, Eagle's eyes widened at the sight of the bullet-sized hole ripped through his friend's helmet.

"You okay?" he yelled over the mayhem.

Jaybird's tan face paled, but Eagle couldn't tell whether that was from shock, pain, or impending death. Before Eagle could ask him anything else, Hawk snatched Jaybird by the vest helping him upright on his feet.

"Move, brother. We've got to go. You can do this," Hawk encouraged him, borderline dragging the man back into the formation that would keep them all alive.

Jaybird nodded, his face still stunned and his eyes blinking as he obviously tried to get back in the zone. Once he flanked Hawk's other side, they moved in unison again, with Hawk vigilant on point. Rounds cracked and zipped past them as they returned fire on the enemy positions. The bird's rotors whipped the air, calling to them, encouraging them to move faster, a beacon of hope. They were so close now, only a few more yards.

*Snap.*

White-hot pain tore through Eagle's upper thigh. The scent of
earthy dust and the stench of metallic death and burning bodies
filled his nostrils as he gasped in agony. His rifle trembled in his
hands, but dropping out of the formation meant death for him or
his friends. He limped with his teammates, trying to keep up, but
the formation began to break apart with his labored movements.

Hawk turned to look at him and his teeth gritted while his
eyes flared with concern.

"Keep going!" Hawk yelled at Jaybird before turning back to
Eagle.

In one fluid and practiced motion, Hawk's rifle dropped from
his hands as his right hand drew his service pistol and his left slid
under Eagle's shoulders to give him extra leverage to move.

Once again, Eagle watched the world move in slow motion.
His heartbeat pounded in his ears as a friendly leapt out from
behind a beat-up car, his gun aimed right at Hawk's chest.

*No.*

Without thinking about anything other than saving the life
of a brother, Eagle shoved Hawk aside, knocking him out of the
way and to the ground. But with a bad leg and his momentum
used to push Hawk, Eagle was exposed.

The gunman fired.

Eagle grunted as punch after punch blasted into the steel
ballistic plate and Kevlar fiber in his tactical rig. A stabbing pain
bloomed outward from his lower stomach and through his spine.
He groaned and collapsed onto Hawk.

A spray of fire from the helo cut the man down with a single
shriek.

Eagle lay prone, unable to move from his position, forcing
Hawk to scoot out from underneath him.

"L-leave me," he ordered Hawk.

"The fuck I will," Hawk growled before grabbing Eagle by
the collar of his vest and dragging him toward escape. Jaybird
continued to lay down fire. Blood poured down the left side of

his head, but otherwise, he looked unharmed through Eagle's hazy vision.

"What the fuck were you thinking?!" Hawk shouted as he fired his pistol, haphazardly shooting to keep a clear path toward the helo. His normally deep voice was pitched higher than Eagle had ever heard it.

His lips cracked open to respond, but only a cough emerged, spraying blood out of his mouth.

*Huh, so much for the General's invincible vests. Guess one of those rounds got through the steel and Kevlar.*

He coughed again and looked down at the blood painting his hand.

*Into the lungs apparently.*

"Shit!" Devil yelled above him as he appeared in his vision.

"Hurry, we have to get him to the bird," Hawk commanded, already assuming his position as their leader.

The thought jarred his mind.

*Wait... am I dying?*

"No, you're not," Hawk ground through his teeth. Eagle hadn't realized he'd spoken out loud. "We'll inject you, and you'll pass out and be fine. You're coming home with us, brother. We need you. *I* need you."

The thought that *this* man needed *him*, made a laugh rumble in Eagle's chest. But instead of chuckling, it only served to bring about another painful hacking cough. The blood settled in the back of his throat, giving the awful sensation he was choking. He tried to suck in a breath but all of his inhales were empty and unsatisfying.

"Three-two-one!" Hawk yelled.

Eagle felt weightless and free as Hawk and Devil hoisted him into the helo, almost like he was actually flying. But he landed hard against the MH-6's cabin floor onto his back with a grunt. Jaybird scooted around him to hop onto the MH-6's external sideboard to fire back at the shooters on the ground.

"What the fuck happened out there?" Devil entered Eagle's vision again as he knelt over him.

The normally stoic man's sunburned face was bloodred from exertion and wrinkles of worry furrowed the light freckles on his brow.

"The target knew we were coming, somehow," Hawk answered.

Devil's lips thinned as he pulled his large red medical kit closer. It slipped through his hands as the helo lifted jerkily from the ground. He lifted his fingers in front of him and Eagle felt his own eyes widen along with Devil's green ones at the sight of the slick blood coating his hands.

"Goddamnit, focus and fix him!" Hawk yelled over his shoulder from where he shot out of the helicopter's open cabin.

"He's lost a lot of blood," Devil murmured under his breath, but it blared into Eagle's ears. Hawk set aside his pistol and turned around to help Devil. Together, they ripped at Eagle's fatigues and kit until hot air breezed over his naked, feverish skin, making him shiver.

"GSW to the chest, punctured lung, through and through in his lower abdomen..." he turned Eagle over slightly and cursed low before he laid him back down. Eagle didn't feel a thing as Devil muttered and shook his head, "Bullet in his spine."

The General's drugs they used for injuries were a miracle, but they weren't guaranteed. If the body passed the point of no return before the drugs were administered, there was nothing that could be done. The person would lose consciousness from unbearable pain as his body tried to heal itself... only he'd never wake up again.

*I'm going to die.*

The thought rested in his mind like a blanket, covering all the turmoil, guilt, and pain that'd been plaguing him for years.

The guilt over tricking Hawk away from Hannah so he could have her for one night.

Leaving Hannah to fend for herself.

Trusting a monster to help him save the world.

Never getting to meet his son...

It crashed into him over and over, like the heartbeat thumping in his chest trying its damnedest to keep him alive. Hawk pulled off his own gloves before tugging off Eagle's, too. He bent over him and clapped their hands together. Blood-coated palms made Eagle's already weak grip harder to control, but he tried to put all his strength into it.

"Love you, brother," Eagle whispered through numb lips.

"Don't start with that shit, man," Hawk ordered with all the authority of a soldier who believed he could stop death itself. "You're not going anywhere."

Eagle coughed a laugh until Devil spoke again.

"You can't feel that?" he asked.

Eagle's brow furrowed as he concentrated. "Feel what?"

"Fuck," Devil cursed. He lifted a syringe and popped the cap with his teeth. "He's lost a lot of blood already and it looks like he's paralyzed, at least from the waist down."

"What're you waiting for then? Give him the drugs already!" Hawk growled.

"No!" Eagle garbled through thick saliva.

Hawk's head whirled to face Eagle, his eyes wide and terrified. "What do you mean, 'no?' You're getting the fucking drugs, Eagle."

Eagle glanced at Devil, who still held the syringe. Guilt and pain glittered in his green eyes, but his lips flattened into a resolute line, no doubt seeing the earnestness in Eagle's face. The medic nodded once before capping the syringe.

Eagle flicked his eyes to meet Hawk's gaze again. "I *mean*... 'no.'"

Confusion etched into Hawk's face, but he must've seen Devil put the syringe away out of the corner of his eyes because he jerked up to face their friend with a murderous expression.

"What're you doing? He's obviously out of his damn mind—"

Eagle squeezed with all his might. "I'm not," he choked, bringing Hawk's attention solely on him.

Fear returned to his best friend's expression, and sweat dripped into the creases underneath his helmet down his furrowed brow.

"Fuck, Eagle, take the drugs, man." Tears brimmed in Hawk's eyes but Eagle held firm.

"If I... take those... I'll pass out... right now. Never wake up."

"You'll die without them!" Hawk yelled.

"I'm gonna die with them, brother."

The words landed in the cabin as brutally as any bomb. Somber truth leadened the air, but Eagle felt his body lighten as he spoke to his best friend.

"You... were the brother... I always wanted," he coughed.

Hawk cursed through gritted teeth. Eagle could tell the grip on his hand should hurt, that he was practically crushing bone, but he could hardly feel anything at all.

"Eagle..." Hawk shook his head violently as if he was fighting the truth from entering his mind, hoping reality wouldn't catch up to them. "Eagle, you *are* my brother. You saved my life out there, you know."

"Any... time." He laughed, despite the growing sensation that his chest was caving in. He couldn't tell if the weight was due to his collapsing lung, or the realization that this was really it.

His thoughts jumbled together. His past, present, and all the dreams he'd ever had swirled to create one confusing scene. Like his life was a photo album of slightly transparent pictures. Page after page flopped one on top of the other until they all blurred together.

"What will we do without you?" Hawk whispered, bringing Eagle back to the present.

*You'll lead them with conviction... better than I ever could.*

"That security firm... didn't sound... so bad. You... and Jaybird... could start it... BlackStone sounds better than... Black and Greene Security... anyway." His snort ended in a moan.

"Fuck, don't hurt yourself more than you already are," Hawk scolded him.

Eagle wanted to retort but all the important things he never got to say bombarded his mind all at once, with one coming to the forefront.

"Protect... them..." he pleaded, unsure whether his fingers were squeezing Hawk's hand still or not.

"Of course, brother. I'll protect this team with my life."

Eagle tried to shake his head, but his neck muscles didn't respond, forcing him to stare straight up.

His vision grew hazier and hazier at the edges. Instead of the ceiling of the bird, Hannah and their son splashed in front of him like watercolors.

He'd dreamed of them so many times since that day in the General's office, but this time they weren't alone in his vision.

Hawk appeared too, holding Hannah's hand in his, gazing down at her with the love he'd always shown her, even when it'd broken his heart to leave her behind.

The blurry image made him relax against the metal floor of the bird.

"Eagle?" Hawk's muffled voice filtered through the fog. It sounded like he was speaking through a pillow, but Eagle could still hear the anguish and grief weighing his words. "We love you, brother."

Eagle closed his eyes as his heartbeat slowed. He gave in to the vision, praying for it with every fiber of his being. Peace embraced him as his family found happiness in this broken, fucked-up world.

"Love... you... all."

# CHAPTER THIRTY-TWO

## Present Day

Hawk's pulse raced as the Little Bird flew over the tree line. Because there were no doors on the MH-6 and there was little room in the cabin, Hawk sat on one of the external sideboards outside of the helicopter, hooked to the helo's metal frame so he wouldn't fall out. He held on to his rifle with both hands, squinting at the twilight horizon, trusting the restraint to keep him secure.

Meanwhile, his mind tormented him with nightmarish scenarios about what would happen if they didn't get back to Hannah in time. He'd gone nearly insane by the time Black-Stone's facility finally came into view.

"Any word?" he asked Snake for the millionth time.

"No," he grumbled, just as anxious as Hawk was. "I sent a warning as soon as I figured out Nora didn't receive my text, but I still haven't gotten anything from her."

"What about your app thing on your phone? Can't you access the cameras?" Phoenix's voice sounded worried even through the headset, but Hawk was thankful as hell he was able to keep his head on straight enough to pilot the helo.

"Negative. Whatever is keeping me from sending a message

through the normal channels must be jamming the CCTV frequencies on my app."

"Fuck," Draco cursed into his microphone.

"I've contacted Marco and told him the situation," Snake continued. "He's getting a team of FBI agents to come to the facility to pick up Vlad."

Hawk's gaze flicked to the Russian, cuffed, bound, taped, and buckled up in the center of the helicopter. Phoenix and Jaybird sat in the front, in the cockpit, and even though Hawk and Devil sat on the external sideboards outside of the helo, the small cabin was still crowded with Draco, Snake, and the big Russian. The giant had been silent ever since he dropped the bomb that MF7—or at least, Hawk's team—hadn't been the only team the General had in his arsenal.

As for the rest of what Vlad had said concerning the General's crazed, sick obsession with his daughter, Hawk was afraid the psycho's perversions had driven him to send his new team to BlackStone to kidnap her before he fled to cower away in one of his vacation homes.

The moment Hawk had voiced his concern and made the plan to go back, Snake sent out the message to Nora to be on high alert. They'd hopped into the helo shortly after and headed to the facility, but they still hadn't heard anything from the women.

"What if he's not at the facility at all?" Jaybird asked. "What if the women are just asleep? It's the ass crack of dawn. He could very well have slinked off to his vacation home. Going to the facility could mean we lose him again."

"I don't care," Hawk growled, glaring at the back of Jaybird's seat. "Hannah and Tommy are at the facility and we *don't* know where the General is. If you give me a choice, I'm choosing them every fucking time, got it?"

Jaybird's eyes lifted to the mirror on the overhead switch panel and he held his hands up in surrender. "Listen, man. I get it. I do. Just putting it out there."

"Yeah, well, put it right back in there because we're going home. Snake, do you have camera feeds? Audio from Nora? Anything? Let's not go in blind."

Snake began to tap away at his phone. "I've got a drone on the roof. It's on a totally different channel than the communication lines for the facility. Maybe I can access it."

He unbuckled his seat belt and hooked himself to the frame of the helo before hopping out onto the external sideboard in the makeshift seat beside Hawk. Snake scooted closer to show Hawk his phone screen.

The drone's camera played on the screen, making Hawk feel like he was walking the roof himself as it hovered out of its storage cubby and flew over the roof's asphalt. A large man in black fatigues stood in stark relief against the sky's brightening dawn backdrop. He turned around, but Hawk couldn't see his face past the high-tech helmet he wore. There was no mistaking his intentions though when he raised his gun and fired. The screen went gray and fuzzy until it went black altogether.

Snake cursed. "Well... I *had* a drone on the roof."

"And we *have* a fucking enemy on the roof," Hawk growled. "Stay frosty, team."

"Fuck," Draco swore again.

A black notification banner popped up on Snake's home screen. He clicked it and typed several codes before white letters in a typewriter font scrolled across the black background.

**Nora: We've got company**

"Little late, Nora," Snake groaned.

"Dammit," Hawk muttered.

"Did Nora text you? What'd she say?" Draco yelled without bothering to listen to Snake's answer, "Fuck, pick up the pace, Phoenix!"

"If you think I haven't been putting the pedal to the goddamn metal, you're out of your damn mind. My girl is in there, too, y'know."

"How many of the General's men did we see back at the CTI warehouse? Four? Five?" Jaybird asked, keeping them on task.

"Hold on, I've got another drone on the grounds." Snake answered for Hawk. "Let me activate it and I'll scope the outside of the whole facility."

Hawk's feet wiggled in the air from nerves as he waited impatiently for Snake to mobilize the second drone. Once he had it pulled up on his device, Snake leaned in so Hawk could watch the footage filling the screen.

"This one is stored on a small ledge nailed into a tree on the outskirts of the facility's property line," Snake explained.

In seconds, the drone's camera showed the inside of the forest surrounding BlackStone before it lifted up and provided an aerial view of the facility. It was surreal to watch the tiny trees whiz by on the small screen while monstrous treetops stabbed the sky beneath their feet.

Draco unbuckled himself and hovered over Snake's other side. After a moment of watching, he pointed at the screen.

"Looks like they blew through the gate. And there—shit. Get closer... You see that black van on the grounds... Fuck, they're setting up charges outside of the garage!"

"Christ," Devil growled through his replacement headset. "After the bombing, we redesigned the facility to camo the garage. Outsiders can't even tell it's not like every other wall on the facility. How do they still know our weakest point of entry?"

There was a brief silence before Phoenix cursed.

"Goddamn Henry motherfucking Brown," he growled. "Marco said he had a damn visitor. Betcha a million dollars whoever that was worked on the General's team. Fuckin' *A*, dude, I should've killed that son of a bitch traitor when I had the chance."

"We needed him for the case," Snake replied.

"Fuck the case!" Phoenix yelled. "If that cocksucker gets my girl killed after all she's been through, I'll break into the jail myself and burn that motherfucker to ashes in his shitty cell."

Hawk bit his tongue, quietly agreeing with every damn thing Phoenix said.

*"I don't want the villain who will destroy the world for me, I want the hero who saves it..."*

*Well, dove, I might just have to be both*, he thought while his grasp tensed around his rifle grip.

A blast detonated on the screen. Panic shocked down Hawk's spine and his pulse skyrocketed. He squinted at the phone to see one of the garage doors in pieces.

"Snake, how many are on the roof? Can I land?" Phoenix asked. "Hell, I'll land on them for all I care. Never seen someone get caught up in rotor blades before. Could be fun."

"Looks like there's three on the roof trying to breach the stairwell," Snake answered. "And three more just entered the ground floor with the General after taking out the garage doors—"

On the screen, a flash erupted in the middle of the roof where the stairwell exited. Smoke billowed up in the air with the single explosion. The flames quickly lessened to embers, revealing the concrete and steel structure that had once housed the stairwell. Now it had rubble for a door.

He looked up from the screen to see the smoke rising from the roof. It physically hurt to be close enough to see his home get attacked, but too far away to defend it.

"Fuck." Hawk punched the helo's metal wall. "We have to get down there, *now*."

Unable to just sit there watching his home smolder, Hawk shoved his rifle onto his back and twisted around, straining against the strap securing him to the Little Bird's frame. He reached for the rope they used to rappel out of the helo, wrapped his arm around it once and tugged, making sure it was tight on his forearm. In his next move, he unhooked the restraint connecting him to the helicopter. When he shifted to face outward again, he unholstered his pistol, now ready to either fast-rope out of the helicopter, shoot his way down, or both.

"I don't know if any others got inside." Snake shook his head. "Or how they got on the roof in the first place."

"Fire escape?" Jaybird suggested.

Snake pressed a button on his screen to fly the drone around the back of the facility before nodding. "Yup. Fire escape. The one on the back is down."

"That shows us for being proactive about fire," Devil huffed.

Hawk shook his head. "Get us on that roof, Phoenix. There're six of us. We can take on those three."

"Copy that."

"Remember, men, this team could be as ignorant as we were working for the General. Try to keep them alive, but if it's a matter of us or them? Do what you have to."

As they cleared the tree line, Hawk's fingers clenched tighter and tighter on the rope the closer they got to the rooftop. His other hand loosely held his pistol in his lap, ready to pick up when they were—

"Within firing range," Phoenix reported.

Just as Hawk raised his gun to aim, a bullet pelted against the Little Bird's fuselage.

Hawk shot haphazardly as he leaned forward on the external sideboard, knowing he was likely too far out to do much other than show intent. Snake pocketed his phone and fired his assault rifle at the railing that was protecting their opponents, throwing up concrete dust at the impact points. Jaybird aimed from the cockpit while Devil and Draco returned fire from the other side of the helo.

The three men on the roof were hunched over, their guns aimed at the helicopter, but when Hawk's team flew closer to the landing pad, the men immediately fell back to take cover elsewhere on the roof.

"That's right motherfuckers, run away! This is *our* house," Phoenix whooped.

The crew kept firing even though their adversaries had hidden behind the industrial AC units, the turbine vents, and the shed near the stairwell they'd blown up.

Phoenix flew over the roof, giving them the height advantage over the men, but they ran back and forth from one hiding spot to the next, snapping back return fire from everywhere they could seek shelter, including within the stairwell.

*The open stairwell.*

"Quit fucking around and land us," Hawk ordered over their headset. "We're getting nowhere like this and we don't know what's going on inside."

"Copy that." Phoenix began to land the Little Bird as Hawk's team successfully kept the enemy back to clear their landing pad. Every second of their back-and-forth in their helo felt way too fucking long.

"Jump zone ready," Phoenix called over the headset. "Less than ten feet to landing."

"Read my mind," Hawk grumbled and clutched the rope.

"I'm with you," Devil shouted behind him, telling Hawk he was jumping, too.

They wouldn't have time to actually fast-rope, or rappel hand over hand on the rope to get down, but they wouldn't need to at that height. Hawk rolled his shoulders, loosening his muscles so his arm didn't jerk out of socket and held on to his gun.

"Cover me," he called over his shoulder before jumping off the sideboard and swinging the rest of the way out of the helicopter.

Jaybird and Snake fired off rounds as Hawk cascaded toward the ground. He barely had enough time to think before he was already landing and rolling onto the asphalt.

As soon as he was righted, he holstered his sidearm and slid his rifle around his body to aim in front of him. Devil flanked him on his left before they split in opposite cardinal directions to find the three men on the roof.

"My right!" Devil called out.

Hawk fired left at his own ten o'clock, sending the man Devil had warned him about back behind the large air conditioning unit in a shower of sparks.

One of the enemies poked his head out from around the spherical top of a roof turbine vent, but Hawk fired before he could raise his gun.

Without turning, he heard the helicopter land behind them and trusted that the rest of his team would hop out of the helicopter and join him.

Once the rotors slowed down, Hawk called to their adversaries.

"Come out! You are on our property. Come out now and we won't shoot!"

Silence answered. Hawk looked to the side to see Jaybird close by, taking cover behind their six-foot-long toolbox, his gun ready. When their eyes met, Jaybird shrugged.

"Come out now!" Hawk repeated. "Come out and we won't—"

The crack of a gun resounded in the air. Hawk dropped to the ground and rolled behind their toolbox. He sprang up to kneel on one knee, rifle tucked to his shoulder, his back meeting Jaybird's to cover the angle he couldn't. Devil and Snake nodded to him across the roof from behind two turbine vents.

Hawk narrowed his eyes and mouthed, "Draco?"

Devil tilted his head toward the grill and mouthed back, "With Phoenix."

Hawk quickly peeked out from behind the toolbox to find the back of Phoenix's helmet.

With all his men accounted for, Hawk decided to lead with a different approach. Hand signals flashed between the group as Devil and Snake rose from their crouching positions, mirrored by Draco and Phoenix on the other side of the roof.

"It doesn't have to be this way!" Hawk tried one more time. "There's six of us and only three of you—"

Another shot rang out and sliced through the toolbox he and

Jaybird were uselessly trying to cover behind. His brown eyebrows rose in shock below his black helmet.

"Guess this sucks as a hiding spot," Jaybird snorted.

Unless the team emerged from their hiding places all at once, they could potentially be picked off like flies. He peered around the toolbox but surmised what he already knew. There wasn't much fucking cover.

*I can't die. Not now. Not when I've finally got Hannah again.*

They couldn't just sit there and wait anymore. Their opponents were using high-caliber rounds. Hawk and Jaybird were sitting ducks.

"I'm not dying behind a fucking toolbox," Hawk growled.

"They're stalling, they know we've got six to their three," Jaybird replied with a wicked smile. "Ready to give 'em hell?"

"Ready," Hawk answered.

He motioned his teammates to get ready to storm the rooftop. After taking a fortifying breath, he held up his gloved fingers and counted off.

*Three... Two... One...*

He chopped his hand through the air and BlackStone jumped out of hiding. They blitzed in full force, firing off at every corner of the roof to drive the other men farther behind their shelters.

In Hawk's periphery, Devil and Snake circled a turbine vent to attack the pair of gunmen sheltering behind it. They were ready for the onslaught, though, and weapons fired on both sides. Devil and Snake were too fast and too close for their adversaries to fire back effectively, enabling them to quickly disarm their opponents.

Simultaneously, Phoenix and Draco found the third man near the stairwell door. With two on one, he smartly dropped his weapon and raised his hands.

Devil and Snake kicked and threw their opponents' guns to the side, but their adversaries didn't go down without a fight. Literally. The men sprang to their feet, resorting to fists and knives in a sparring match that became a brawl within seconds.

"Jaybird!" Hawk called as he pointed toward the combat between Snake, Devil, and their counterparts. Hawk's boots slapped against the pavement of the roof as he pumped his legs, trying to get there before one of his men got hurt.

*Fifteen meters...*

*Ten...*

*Five—*

Three black-clad men darted onto the roof behind the unarmed man that Phoenix and Draco had cornered. Their new foes had their weapons at the ready, their posture perfect for quick firing. Four against two. Hawk only had a moment to decide which direction to go, but at a dead sprint, his body and muscle memory made the choice before his mind could catch up.

He gained speed and kicked his right foot out to skid on the asphalt—keeping his left leg bent underneath him like his T-ball coach taught him years ago—and aimed for the group from the side. He barreled into the newcomers' ankles like he was sliding into home base and knocked them down before they could fully assess their surroundings. Grunts, curses, and yells punctured the air as their adversaries crumpled on top of him.

A second thud followed shortly behind his, with Jaybird having taken Hawk's wordless cue, tackling the men the rest of the way to the ground.

Fists crashed, clothes tore, and weapons clattered to the pavement. Their melee splintered into singular battles, each man one on one with his counterpart, seeking an advantage.

Hawk bounced to his feet and stood, finding his opponent directly in front of him. He was big—almost as big as Devil—and decked out in elite military garb, just like the rest of his team. Focused, deep-green eyes shone back at him from under the man's tactical helmet.

*Use his size against him. Don't lose your head.*

The man lunged for Hawk. Meaty fingers managed to clench a section of Hawk's vest, yanking him off balance. Instead of fighting the momentum, Hawk used it to jerk the man down to the ground with him. Pained gasps wheezed from them both as they collided against the concrete roof. Not giving them a moment to catch their breaths, the man charged again, but Hawk rolled to the side and landed on his knees.

As his opponent pulled back for a punch, Hawk grabbed the wrist the man was balancing on and snatched it out from under him. The man caught himself while Hawk's other hand slid his combat knife out from its sheath. Hawk couldn't remember ever moving that fast, but the knife was at the man's throat in an instant.

His opponent froze.

Hawk tightened his steel grip on the man's wrist and pressed the blade into his neck, forcing the man to slowly stand with him. Once they were on their feet, Hawk moved closer to the large man's side, twisting his foe's arm behind his back and keeping the knife steady at his neck.

The summer's rising sun was already beginning to heat the air around them. Sweat dripped off of his brow as Hawk flicked his gaze around the rooftop, where he found similar outcomes to the individual combats. But his teammates hadn't won every battle.

Phoenix had his man at gunpoint as he writhed on the ground, holding his groin. Devil's grip around his opponent's neck meant he could break a few vertebrae with a bit of force.

But the others...

Draco was pinned on his stomach, a knee against his back and a knife against his throat. Whether he was wheezing from exertion or injury, Hawk didn't know, but neither was good. Snake's eyes were bleary and blood dripped from his mouth as he knelt in surrender, his hands clasped behind his head and the muzzle of an AK digging into his temple. Jaybird thrashed and cursed angrily on the ground with his hands zip-tied behind his back. His opponent angrily swiped at the blood pouring from a cut beneath his already blackening eye before he tightened

Jaybird's zip tie out of spite, eliciting more curses from Hawk's teammate.

*It's a standoff. We know the FBI has people on the way. Just stall.*

He didn't dare lower his knife as he yelled loud enough for everyone to hear. "Who are you?"

His captured man spoke through clenched teeth, no doubt cautious of the knife at his throat. "Better if you don't know. But I'm sure we can figure out a better resolution than this."

Hawk glanced at his teammates and the gunmen, hoping to find some sort of leverage. But the teams had fought to a standstill. Evenly matched. Too much for his comfort to insist on fighting.

"Listen, the FBI is on the way. You'll be outmanned. Surrender and we'll make sure you're treated fairly," Hawk stated matter-of-factly, hoping he came off more confident than he felt.

The man holding Snake at gunpoint answered, but blood rushed in Hawk's ears as a thought screamed into his brain.

*We're evenly matched.*

*But if that's true then...*

The realization came agonizingly late as the cool steel of a gun's muzzle kissed the back of his head.

*They still have their seventh man.*

Hawk's knees threatened to buckle as the pain of losing Eagle, and now potentially his entire team, crashed into him.

"Now who's outmanned?" the guy asked mirthlessly as he circled in front of Hawk, still aiming the barrel at Hawk's forehead a few feet away.

The new man's black balaclava covered most of his face, revealing only serious blue eyes, with his lightly tanned skin creased at the corners. Hawk used all of his willpower to focus on the man's gaze rather than the pistol still aimed at him. This seventh man had the power to end them all, but focusing on the weapon wouldn't get them out of this. Hawk had to appeal to him using a different tactic.

"You're MF7," Hawk replied, his heart thundering before he

made the difficult decision to lower his knife. It clattered to the concrete as Hawk stepped backward, away from his opponent, with his arms up. "Aren't you?"

"Hawk, the fuck dude, what're you doing?" Phoenix hissed.

In the corner of Hawk's vision, the guy he'd just set free went slack-jawed, looking like he wanted to ask the same question.

"You are, aren't you?" Hawk asked, not letting his focus stray too far from the man with the gun trained on him. "General Richard Smithers team?"

His opponent's steady gaze didn't reveal a change in his expression, but the man Hawk had just released tensed beside him.

"You are," Hawk answered his own question, kicked the knife away, and took another step back, putting a couple of meters of space between them, hoping the added gestures of surrender would hit home.

*It would if it were me.*

"What does that mean to you?" the seventh man asked finally. From the way his teammates looked at him for direction, he must've been their team lead.

*Their Eagle.*

Hawk's heart pounded at the risk he was taking. But if these men were anything like his team, there was hope for them all, yet.

"We used to be you," Hawk explained and tilted his head forward to indicate the rest of his teammates. "MF7."

"Bullshit. You're nothing like us," the man wrangling Jaybird spat.

"It's true," Hawk continued. "We began almost a decade ago. And then we were 'psychologically discharged' after a mission went wrong in Yemen two years ago."

"That was you?" the man pinning Draco asked.

"Shut the fuck up, Olsen," Jaybird's guy snapped.

"That was us," Hawk replied. "I'm betting we were peddled

the same shit as you guys were. Stop me if none of this rings a bell."

Hawk slowly stepped forward as he spoke. The leader in front of him didn't stir other than his blue eyes narrowing a fraction.

"General Smithers called a meeting. Claimed you would eradicate human trafficking all over the world. A new, Special Forces unit. Off the books... right? You know, to make sure the bigwigs at the top could be caught, too? Because these things are so rarely ruled by the pimp on the corner. It starts at the top. Am I right?"

With every inch forward and every word, the leader in front of Hawk lowered his gun by a millimeter. When Hawk had finished, the man no longer aimed at his head and Hawk was mere feet away from him.

"Close," the guy in the back answered. "Drug trafficking."

"Olsen, what the—"

"Quiet," the leader rasped low, his lips barely moving the black fabric of his balaclava.

Hawk nodded. "Let me guess. Take out the drug kingpin, deliver the drugs to the rightful authorities. That miracle drug he insisted we take was amazing, right? Too bad it only worked if the wounds weren't life-threatening. We'd still be seven men, too, if it could, you know, actually save lives. Instead it only kept his own private militia healthy for his every beck and call."

"You're that team that went rogue and became traffickers yourselves," the leader accused coolly. "The ones who blew up his security firm so you wouldn't be caught."

Someone behind him snorted. "Wow, did we sound that naive?" Phoenix asked. "Is that seriously what he's telling people? I guess you think we kidnapped his daughter and grandson, then, too."

At the mention of Hannah and Tommy, Hawk's chest tightened and he prayed he could get through to these guys soon. He needed to check on them before it was too late.

The leader frowned. "If that's *not* what happened, then what *did* happen? What went wrong?"

Hawk let his arms rest at his sides before answering. "Our team leader realized *we* were wrong. We'd been taken advantage of and MF7's purpose wasn't what we thought it was. Then he got killed in Yemen after we were ambushed by the locals... under the General's own orders."

That got the man's attention. Whether it was the lack of fear in Hawk's posture or his message, Hawk wasn't sure, but the leader finally lowered his gun all the way. He could still easily raise it to shoot, but the guy would at least have to move more muscles than just the ones in his trigger finger to kill him.

At the gesture, the teams followed suit, each man surrendering his upper hand in unison. If Hawk hadn't known they were all trained similarly before, that act alone—the exact same motions at the exact same time—would've tipped him off.

"Your seventh man... you said he realized your team's purpose wasn't what you thought it was," Eagle's counterpart began. "If your purpose wasn't to end human trafficking, then what was it?"

Hawk released an aching breath slowly from his chest. As his stress eased, he studied the trust already forming in the leader's gaze. Their team's willingness to listen made Hawk wonder if he was only telling them what they'd already begun to suspect on their own.

He nodded once, resolving to trust them, too.

"We've got a lot of shit to talk about. But right now? My family needs help."

# CHAPTER THIRTY-THREE

The percussive explosion from above left Hannah's ears ringing. When the dust settled, she looked up to see the trapdoor that had previously taken up a rectangular slab of ceiling was now wide open to the war room. Terrified goose bumps tingled her skin, raising the hair on her arms. The only thing she found solace in was the fact Tommy was as safe as he could be at the moment.

She, Callie, and Nora had talked about all of them hiding in the jail cells and waiting until the guys came to save them. That idea lasted all of two seconds once they realized the steel doors only locked—and *unlocked*—from the outside. Not only that, but they couldn't count on the guys arriving in time. BlackStone's mission was to catch the General, and yet, the General was now at the facility and the guys were nowhere to be found.

There were thousands of possibilities that could've led to that outcome, very few of which were ones Hannah had the stomach to think about, and honestly, she didn't have the time to entertain any of them. The women had seconds to act and this crappy plan was the outcome.

Nora and Tommy would hide in the cell farthest down the hall.

Callie would sneak behind the door of the first cell to ambush the General once he made it downstairs.

Hannah would be the bait.

And as she stood there, watching his boots *thump* down that steep staircase one by one, every single flaw in their poorly thought-out plan flashed across her mind like a giant warning sign.

*I should've hidden in one of the cells and forced him to find me.*

*But no, then he could've just shot me on sight.*

*I should've walked farther down the hallway so Callie could've jumped out behind him.*

*Then again... he could've just shot one of us on sight.*

*Maybe Callie should've started shooting as soon as the door was blown up.*

*No, because what if the General's team comes down with him? They would immediately... say it with me, class, shoot... on... sight.*

Those suggestions might've actually worked, but for the worst complication of them all. They *couldn't* kill the General. He was too important for the testimony that would bring down one of the biggest international trafficking rings in history. And while they couldn't kill him, he had no such restriction, making it so the women were fighting a perverted, narcissistic madman with their hands tied behind their backs.

*But what if...*

Scenario after scenario splattered across her vision until it began to darken and she felt light-headed. Her cheeks heated and sweat pricked her brow—

*Oh, wait... I should probably breathe.*

She sucked in a breath as quietly as she could. The oxygen did the trick, returning her vision back to normal and clearing her head.

It went against every instinct to stand there, waiting for her nightmare to appear in the flesh. But it was all part of their strategy. There was nothing to do now but commit and fight like hell if something went wrong.

She counted her careful breaths as each one of his steps revealed more of the man she'd tried to avoid her entire life.

*One... two... three... four... five—*

"There she is..." His voice slithered over her like the viper that he was. "Papá's little girl."

Despite the kind words, the sentiment dripped in contempt and revolting sensuality. His pistol appeared next, aimed straight at her chest as he nonchalantly stepped off the staircase.

His evil smile stretched across his face and his eyes leered over her. "You've run for long enough, don't you think, my dear?

"*Papá*," she answered automatically and winced at the familiarity of the name. That, plus the adult revelation of how *wrong* his side of their relationship had been and finding out exactly what he was capable of made bile rise in her throat. Accidentally calling him the endearment from childhood had nearly made her vomit.

It'd been years since she'd seen him face to face. His rheumy blue eyes were the only thing that spoke of his true age and the wear he'd put on his body. He'd dyed his hair absurdly dark, since it was unbelievable he wouldn't have a gray hair on his head by now.

*Stay focused. Play it cool. Stall him. I can do this.*

Even as she tried to center herself, she squeezed her fists tighter, only to realize her fingers had already gone numb from the pressure.

"I've come to fetch you, my dear. One of my business partners has gone rogue, I'm afraid. We need to go into hiding, you and I."

"There's no way in hell I'm leaving with you."

His brow pinched in the center. "Now, now, now, I'm sure Captain Black has probably fed you some frightening stories and all kinds of lies about me—"

Hannah scoffed. "He didn't have to tell me anything. Your actions have already told me all I need to know. If you didn't get the memo the past decade, I don't want to be around you. Leave, *Papá*. I'm not going with you."

His lips pursed and his pale skin reddened. "That... will not do. You see, I have my team here. They'll help ensure you leave with us. And they have no qualms about doing exactly what I say."

"Then where are they?" Callie asked as she glided out of the first jail cell, her gun poised to fire at the right moment.

The General's pistol switched to focus on Callie, sending Hannah's heartbeat into overdrive.

"Don't," she begged softly, her hand up in the air, as if that had ever stopped him.

A deranged, pleased look brightened his face. "Don't worry, precious. I don't want to kill my favorite doll." His gaze turned appreciative as he ogled Callie up and down. "Oh, my little toy, how I have missed you, too."

"*Toy?*" Hannah gagged. "*Dios mio*, you are vile."

Anger squinched his face. Even though she knew she was poking the bear, she couldn't help but feel proud about it. She'd been petrified of him for way too damn long, and had gone from being forced into silence as a child, to being forced into fleeing as an adult. He'd hurt her, murdered her mother, gotten her friend killed, stolen her fiancé, threatened her son... the list went on and on, filling her with loathing. Facing him now was more cathartic than she could've imagined.

But no matter how good it felt, how freeing it was to even stand up to him, the rage in his eyes still spurred a deep-seated fear, one that was innate, as if her body remembered those awful nights more than her mind did.

"You will come with me now, daughter, and maybe I'll be lenient with this one." He pointed the muzzle in Callie's direction, making Hannah's heart surge up her throat. Her shoulders tensed and cool sweat already dripped down her spine underneath her blue blouse. But Callie looked amazingly undeterred.

"Your team?" she asked again, obviously not letting him off the hook. "I asked you where they are."

His nauseating smirk twisted his lips as he stared straight at Callie's thighs. "You look better with meat on your bones, toy. Maybe I should've fed you more. I would've had more cushion for the pushin'."

Hannah gasped. "You disgusting piece of—"

He burst into a laugh in the face of her contempt, but when Callie feinted at him, pretending like she was going to attack him, he tripped backward and slapped his hand against the stairs to catch himself from falling.

Callie took a slow step forward, her gun aimed closer to his heart. She was bluffing—maybe—but the General didn't need to know they weren't supposed to kill him. After hearing the way he talked about her new friend, though, Hannah wasn't sure she cared.

"Oooh. Are you scared, General?" Callie asked, now with a smug smile of her own.

His laugh took on an uneasy edge as he lifted his gun higher to aim at her again. A bead of sweat popped up at his hairline and trailed down the side of his face, confirming his fear, even as he tried to throw them off the acrid scent of ammonia.

"Of course I'm not *scared*. I just enjoy riling you up, toy. I'd be careful about trying to get a rise out of me, though. You think the BlackStone boys will be there to protect you, but I have to be honest, ladies. They've lost their touch." His eyes flicked to her while his gun stayed trained on Callie. "Our business creates enemies, Hannah, and your little Hawk can't protect you. Not like I can. They've been out of the game for too long, but my other team is the *true* best of the best. Come with me and they'll protect us both."

"Is that why they left you to fend for yourself?" Hannah asked, lifting her brow.

The General scowled. "*I* left *them* to fend for themselves. I trust they'll clear the building as quickly as possible, especially since we already know BlackStone isn't back yet." Hannah tried not to dwell on where the team could be while his greedy eyes followed her curves. "Once we get the all clear, a wardrobe change is in order. You're dressed like a whore. Although, I guess it's better than wearing baggy T-shirts all the time," he sneered. "By the way, I've always wondered. Which ex's T-shirts did you keep, little slut? Thomas's or Hawkins's? You can't blame me for being curious since you slept with a *third* of my team."

That morning she'd felt sexy in her tight jeans, blue blouse, and cute heels to match. But now shame had her fighting the urge to cross her arms to cover herself.

"Hannah... don't listen to him," Callie urged.

Hannah nodded and stiffened her arms at her side.

"This is over. Turn yourself in, or get comfortable in one of the cells behind me and have BlackStone do it for you. But know this. Whatever you decide to do, do it far away from my son and me, because I *never* want to see you again."

A vein in his reddening forehead pulsed so thickly it looked like it was on the verge of popping. He lunged toward her, getting in her face, spurring Callie into action. She shoved her gun between them, but Hannah didn't flinch. Pride flooded her chest as she held her head high against her monster.

"I'm not leaving until I've taken what's rightfully *mine*," he hissed.

"She's not yours." The deep voice coming from the jagged hole above them sent a cool wave of relief surging through Hannah's veins.

The General whirled around and pointed his gun wildly at the breach in the ceiling. Callie shoved the muzzle of her pistol into the back of his head.

"Don't you fucking dare," she ordered.

"You won't kill me." The General scowled but didn't turn around. His shoulders remained tense, betraying how uncertain he felt. "You're the *good* guys, remember? You need me for the farce of a trial the government will put on."

Hawk dropped through the ceiling and landed gracefully on his feet with his pistol somehow already trained on his target. The sight of him healthy and unharmed had Hannah's eyes burning with emotion. As he straightened, his serious eyes and chiseled jaw hardened into a fierce glare. The General gasped audibly, as if Hawk's presence sucked the air out of the room, but the safety he promised made Hannah feel like she could finally breathe easy.

A smile lifted her cheeks but she crossed her arms to keep from hugging him. Not only would she have to pass the General to get to him, Hawk was focused on the task, his gun aiming right at the man's head.

"Where's my team?" the General growled.

"*Your* team?" An unfamiliar head peeked through the hole. The blue-eyed man with tanned skin tsked. "We had a chat. Seems like *both* of your MF7 teams have a *lot* in common, *General.*"

The General's cheeks whitened to a sickly pallor, and he shook his head. "W-whatever they told you... it's not true. I can connect the dots for you. If you take care of these two aiming at me right now, I'll forgive this transgression."

The man shook his head. "I highly doubt that. Besides, we've already seen the big picture. My men and I have had questions for a while, and this particular mission set off alarm bells for us. Hawk here showed us where the fire was and I gotta say, General, I've been dying to watch you burn for a long-ass time. If they let me kill you, it'll feel good to know the blood on my hands is finally for a good cause."

"Put the gun down, General," Hawk commanded. "There's no cavalry coming. You have two guns trained on you, and the FBI is on its way as we speak. They've got a nice pair of handcuffs with your name on them." Despite the teasing nature of his last sentence, Hawk's face was serious and his aim at the General's head was unrelenting.

The worry widening the General's dull eyes contorted into hate. His scowl overtook his expression as he shouted at Hawk, "You're all talk, Captain Black, always have been. You can't kill me because the reality is, you need me, and you don't care enough about Hannah to stop me from taking her."

"You have a funny way of 'caring' for people, General, considering you've called your own daughter a loose end and told me to cut her out."

The General smirked. "You're right. Hannah was never a loose end. My little girl is too important for that, but you didn't see it then and left her anyway."

"To keep her safe," Hawk hissed.

"Bah! Keep her *safe*? After that stupid Braves game, it was easy to convince you that anyone could hack into your system and find your loved ones to retaliate. You were so scared, you didn't even start looking until a few months ago when you realized she'd gone missing after the fundraiser! Yeah, that's right, Officer Henry Brown and that fool Andrew Ascot told me all about it. You couldn't keep her safe then, and you obviously can't now. *I'll* keep her safe, Captain, and I won't leave without what's mine."

"I'm not yours!"

"You're my *daughter*. There's no greater ownership."

Oddly enough, the stress in Hannah's muscles eased at his declaration and she shook her head.

"You know, one of the problems I've had this whole time is that I couldn't understand how you acted the way you did with your own *daughter*. As a parent, I can't comprehend it. It's pure evil. But knowing I was just a *thing* to you? That makes the past easier to swallow."

The General's face contorted, obviously irritated she found solace in the revelation rather than fear or revulsion.

"I see you wanted a rise out of me," Hannah pointed out

calmly, finding peace in her courage. "But I'm not going to give it to you. You're the type of man that puts himself over everyone and everything else, at times in the cruelest of ways. You're all about status. You want to be seen and revered in the spotlight, but still get to gorge on your depravity in the shadows." Hannah shook her head. "But you're nothing to me. And soon your secrets will be out. The rest of the world will know *exactly* who you are. I'm done with you, and after you're sentenced for all the crimes and hurt you've caused, the world will be done with you, too."

"You think this is over?" The General's eyes took on a crazed gleam as he glanced between Hawk and Hannah, apparently no longer caring that Callie still aimed her gun at him, too.

His gaze landed on Hawk and spittle collected at the corner of his lips as he yelled, "Don't act like you care about her now. I know what you really want. You *need* me for your so-called justice. Your loyalties don't lie with her. If you ever did care about her, it wasn't enough. All I had to do was trick you at that stupid game and you were gone"—he snapped his fingers, making Hannah jump in her skin—"like that. So fucking predictable."

"It *was* you," Hannah whispered. "You orchestrated the shooting at the Braves game? To make him leave me?" She gazed at Hawk, pain and adoration fighting for her expression. His eyes drifted to hers as she whispered. "You really did end us for my safety."

A small, sincere smile lifted his lips and love burned in his charcoal eyes. "I've always loved you, Hannah. Above *everything* else."

Hannah's chest ached right underneath where her necklace rested, as if her heart wanted to leap out and join the one she loved.

The General's blotchy skin turned a bright magenta as he whirled around to face Hannah.

"You stupid girl! He doesn't love you. He had a choice once

before and he abandoned you! I could've escaped, but I gave up everything to come back for you. With men like Captain Hawkins Black, it all comes down to God, country, and cause. You'll see. Just watch. If we give him the same choice, it'll be the same outcome." His gun waved erratically as he turned to shout at Hawk. "You can't kill me and I need her. So all I have to do is this—"

In the blink of an eye, he snatched Hannah's wrist and tried to bring her to his chest. A shot rang out in the small corridor and the hold on Hannah's wrist disappeared.

She tripped forward from the momentum, but before she could fall, Hawk's strong arm of steel caught her by her waist and tugged her to him.

"I choose her." His voice vibrated in his chest against her cheek before he murmured softer into her hair. "I choose you, dove. Always."

She clung to his chest, holding him tight as he tugged her impossibly closer. Her breaths came in heavy pants, but his assurances settled her.

"It's okay, dove. It's over."

She tried to turn in his grasp, but his biceps and forearms became stone, stopping her from moving.

"No, Hannah. Don't look."

She lifted her chin to see the furrow in his worried brow and shook her head. "I need to look."

His lips tightened but he nodded once and loosened his hold on her. She pivoted slightly, catching Callie's stunned brown eyes before her own gaze fell to the ground. Hannah held her breath, resisting the urge to gasp at the sight of the clean, perfect hole in her father's forehead.

In life, his faded-blue eyes were hard, his face always held a scowl, and his mouth was perpetually ready to remind her that he was in control of every aspect of her life.

In death, vacant rheumy eyes stared unseeing at the ceiling, his slack jaw held no power, and his flaccid body sprawled on the concrete floor, impotent. Blood seeped from the bullet wound in the back of his head, blooming into a shimmering puddle against the shiny stained concrete underneath the fluorescent light.

She turned back into Hawk's chest to find shelter. As he embraced her again, she inhaled deeply and exhaled slowly. Her first breath of true freedom.

It smelled like a spring morning, leather, and pine.

# CHAPTER THIRTY-FOUR

Despite being the daughter of a four-star Army General, Hannah was an art teacher through and through. Everything she knew about the military, crime scenes, and justice came from the *History Channel*, *CSI*, and *Law & Order*, none of which she could stomach for very long, even when their episodes were only an hour in length.

Real life was nothing like that.

When the team covered the General's body with a white sheet, it didn't magically make the aura of death go away. Something thick and heavy clung to the air, and the metallic stench of blood, gunpowder, and urine filled the room. Not to mention it was still painfully obvious there was a corpse underneath.

Thankfully, Hawk insisted on carrying Tommy from his hiding place with Nora up to the war room. Without Hannah having to ask, Hawk had cupped her son's head and secured him against his chest, effectively covering his eyes and protecting her eight-year-old from having to see or smell death.

After that, Hawk led Hannah and Tommy to the apartment level for ice cream of all things. Hannah's mind wrapped around the past few hours—the past few days, really—as Hawk took care of her son. His attentiveness gave her the chance to slump into the couch and quietly process while he and Tommy chatted away about the latest Braves game and their season.

The sight had made her teary with relief. Having someone help bear the emotional burden she'd carried alone as a single mom for the past eight years was like a weight lifted off of her chest.

While Hawk ensured Hannah and her son were comfortable, the mess downstairs was left for his teammates to deal with until the authorities showed up. Devil and the other team's medic had a little patching up to do, but none of the injuries required hospitalization. Once the FBI rolled in, Hannah and Hawk's work began.

Naomi insisted on helping out and left the team's mountain cabin to arrive at the BlackStone facility in record time. She and Thea kept Tommy preoccupied on the residential floor while Hannah and Hawk went back downstairs to speak with the federal agents. Inside the war room was a whirlwind of activity and a standstill all at the same time.

Jules and Assistant District Attorney Marco Aguilar were there, too. The team had been nervous about the legal ramifications of having a dead—previously missing—four-star general in their basement, so Jason had called his fiancée to be their defense attorney. And although ADA Aguilar had been visibly disappointed their lead trafficking conspirator and witness was dead, everyone had breathed easier after he'd promised Hawk wouldn't be charged for murder since he'd done it in Hannah's defense.

Hannah recounted every detail she could remember and answered every question to the best of her ability. The investigators asked about everything, from her childhood to why she thought her father had been obsessed with her, and she couldn't help squirming with discomfort. She'd squeezed Hawk's hand until it had to hurt, but he'd refused to leave her side. Tension had built in her chest again, only releasing when Hawk fielded the most uncomfortable topics. He answered what he knew they needed to know and allowed her to keep other details—ones she'd only just come to terms with—to herself.

After hours of Hannah and Hawk getting mildly interrogated by the FBI, the Bureau's investigation moved to other aspects of the case. The new MF7 team stepped up to the plate for that inquisition, tagging in to fill in the gaps and explain what happened at the CTI warehouse. No one other than the Black-Stone team could crack Vlad, though.

The Russian had stayed compliant, bound, and cuffed the entire time the two teams squared off on the roof. But he'd refused to speak to any of the investigators directly, only answering questions when they came from a BlackStone team member or Callie.

All things aside, it was kind of hilarious to see an FBI agent ask Vlad a question, wait for him to answer, only to be met with a stone-faced reply until a BlackStone teammate asked the same exact question. The scenario played out the same with every query. He'd turn his head slowly and answer the BlackStone team instead, leaving the agent bewildered, Draco and Callie annoyed, and Phoenix with a wildly satisfied grin on his face.

As exciting as it all was, Hannah was dead on her feet. She leaned against Hawk, holding his hand as they stood in the corner of the war room waiting for the next inevitable third degree. The moment Marco gave her the go-ahead to leave, she was beyond ready.

She lifted her head from resting against Hawk's bicep and sighed, weary to her bones. "I need to nap for centuries."

"Don't blame you." His lips were soft against her forehead, and his light chuckle made her lower belly flip.

"Hawkins Black? We have a few more questions," an agent sitting at the conference table called out, beckoning the Black-Stone leader using two fingers without even looking up from his paperwork.

Hannah rolled her eyes on Hawk's behalf and gave him a wry smile. "I'll be right upstairs."

She tried to loosen her hold, but Hawk's grip tightened. When he fell in step beside her, she couldn't hide her surprise.

"Wes, you got this?" Hawk asked Wes who nodded underneath the ice pack on his lip.

"I'll take care of it."

"Thanks," Hawk replied before nodding to the agent. "Whatever I know, he knows. If you absolutely need me, I might be available tomorrow."

The agent's brow furrowed, but Hawk wrapped his arm around Hannah's waist and led her out of the room toward the elevator.

On their way out, Callie passed by them, but Hawk stopped her before she could enter the war room.

"Hey, Callie?"

Callie's sleek, black ponytail flicked over her shoulder as she spun around. "Yeah?"

"Thanks." His voice was hoarse with emotion. "You protected Hannah when I couldn't. I owe you everything."

Callie shifted on her feet, seemingly uncomfortable with the praise before a smirk curved her lips. "I'd say anytime, but how about we just pray it never happens again?"

"I second all of this," Hannah huffed.

Hawk barked a laugh, startling both Callie and Hannah. Her heart warmed at the realization that even in a moment like this, Hawk could still find happiness. He was resilient, like Tommy.

*He would be the perfect dad.*

"Whoa, settle down, girl," she muttered.

"What was that?" Hawk asked as he waved to Callie and turned them toward the elevator.

"Oh, um, nothing. Just talking to myself." Her cheeks heated with embarrassment, but as they kept walking, confusion filtered in.

Was Hawk honestly escorting her to her nap? There were still tons of FBI agents, CSI, the coroner, attorneys, the new team, *his* team. And yet he was walking her to the elevator?

When he pressed the "up" button, she couldn't hold back her question any longer.

"Hawkins, what're you doing?"

He shrugged. "Going to nap with you, I thought? That sounded perfect."

Hannah's jaw dropped. She turned slightly in his hold to point behind her with her thumb. "The FBI agents are still here. You know that, right? They still have questions for you."

He shrugged again, such odd body language for a man who was always so serious and self-assured.

"They'll have questions tomorrow. And the next day. And the next day after that. I've been dealing with the same shit over and over for nearly a decade, and I'll probably have to deal with it for the next few years, too. But right now, my woman wants a nap, so I'm napping with you."

Hannah's chest fluttered. It was something so simple—a nap together—but once again, he was choosing her, and that meant everything.

"All my life, I've felt like a backup plan. Even with how awful my father was, there was still this crazy part of me that silently begged him to pick me over his career. I know it sounds strange—"

"He was your father," Hawk murmured as the elevator doors opened for them. "That's not crazy or strange. It makes sense that a child would hope the best version of their parent would choose them."

Hannah blew out a breath and stepped inside. "And then when you and I were together, you always put me first, until..."

"Until MF7," Hawk finished.

"Until MF7," Hannah agreed before backtracking. "Or, at least, that's what I thought."

As soon as the steel doors closed behind them, Hawk tugged her into his chest and wrapped his arms around her like he was clinging to a lifeline.

"I'm so glad you and Tommy are okay, dove." His heartbeat

thundered against her, making her realize for the first time just how much he'd been holding back until they could get a moment alone.

"We're okay, Hawk. Thanks to you," she whispered against his chest.

"All those years... I couldn't check on you out of fear that our enemies would find you," he rumbled into her hair. "I had to trust that without me in your life, you wouldn't be in danger anymore. When I realized you were missing and I tried to find you, it really hit me that I might never get to hold you again. And to think he was the one behind it all... Fuck, Han, those things he said about not choosing you—"

"I know they weren't true, Hawk," she replied fiercely, hoping he heard her sincerity. "You've always put me first. I get that now."

He pulled away and studied her face before the tense muscles in his back relaxed under her fingertips. Seemingly comforted by her reassurance, he circled his arm around her hip tightly and pressed the button for the second floor.

The air in the elevator grew thick with emotion despite the short ride. Hawk's thumb dipped underneath the hem of her blouse and gently brushed over her skin, making her shiver. By the time they'd reached the second floor, her stomach fluttered with arousal and she was beginning to question whether she'd get a wink of sleep if she slept beside Hawk in his bed. But voices on the other side of the steel doors brought her back to the moment.

As soon as the elevator doors opened, a delicious sugary aroma wafted over to greet them. Once they walked out, Hannah glanced toward the common room to see Tommy's eyes glued to *SportsCenter* on the big screen, and Thea pouting across from him on the *L*-shaped couch, her arms crossed over her green princess dress. Naomi waved at Hannah from the kitchen before setting down a cup of sauce that looked suspiciously like caramel and meeting them in the hallway.

"Hey, how's it goin' down there? Y'all okay?" she asked softly.

Hannah nodded. "Everything's fine right now. I was just thinking of taking a nap. Would you be alright watching Tommy for a bit longer?"

"Oh, yeah, sure, of course." Her chestnut eyes darted from Hannah to Hawk and back again before a mischievous smile lifted her lips. "Take all the time y'all need. I know how... um... necessary a *nap* can be after all that adrenaline leaves your body."

Hannah's cheeks warmed with embarrassment, but her lower belly flipped at the implication.

"Um, what? *Dios mio*, no, um, that's uh—"

She looked to Hawk for help, but his heated gaze told her he was just as excited about the innuendo. He glanced away from her and cleared his throat as he faced Naomi.

"Uh, thanks for watching the little man, Naomi. But a plain old nap is just what we need."

Naomi's smirk proved she didn't believe a damn word he said, but she raised her hands in surrender.

"Alright, fair enough. But like I said. Take all the time you need." With that, she turned around and headed back to the kitchen.

When she was gone, Hannah glanced to Hawk to see mirth glinting in his eyes. Hannah covered her mouth to stifle a giggle, and he gently squeezed her hip before leading her down the hallway. They walked to his apartment in comfortable silence, passing by a room she hadn't seen anyone go in and out of yet.

"Is that the guest room? Or Jason's room, I guess, if he lived here?"

"Yeah, that's the one. Why? You wanna stay there? Don't like my room anymore?" He chuckled, but she could hear the uncertainty in his voice.

"Not me... but if it's available, then Tommy might like it. He hasn't had a nice room in a while, what with all of our moving around, and a boy deserves space to grow, you know? We could move him in tonight, if that's okay?"

Surprise lifted his brows as he opened the door and ushered her inside his room. "Oh yeah? Sure. I, uh, I had a one-bedroom apartment I let the lease lapse on, but you could stay in my room and I can try to rent that out again until BlackStone expands—"

"Or..." she interrupted as he closed the door. "You could stay here... with me."

His palm rested on the frame for a moment before he turned to place one hand on her shoulder and cup her cheek with the other. As he searched her eyes, she grasped his wrists and waited for him to find whatever he was looking for.

*Stay*, her mind whispered, but she bit her lip.

"I've always chosen you, dove. You know that, right? Even when it hurt." He shook his head. "And leaving you? That fucking hurt."

"I know that," Hannah replied and caressed his cheek, her heart aching for the time they'd lost.

His eyes darted to her lip as he murmured low, "Good. Because I'm never leaving you again."

# CHAPTER THIRTY-FIVE

That deliciously deep voice of his sent a shiver of pleasure down her spine. When he leaned toward her, she stood on her tiptoes and met his lips with hers. The kiss was soft and sweet until his hands roamed down her body. He skimmed beneath her blouse and spanned his large palms across her lower back before tugging her close.

She wrapped her arms around his neck to get a better angle for their kiss. When he bent down to grab underneath her legs, though, she clung to him, helping him pick her up. At that new height, she could easily dance her tongue with his. She squeezed her thighs around his waist while he cupped her ass cheeks and carried her to the bed.

"I forgot to tell you I love your outfit." Hawk smiled against her lips. "I almost hate to take it off."

She giggled. "I'd say we could keep it on, but I've already soaked one pair of jeans grinding on you, I need to feel your skin."

On the last word, she scratched the back of his neck, eliciting a rough moan from his chest that vibrated against her breasts.

He climbed onto the bed and laid her out on the quilt. As

soon as she landed on the mattress, she sat up to tear off his clothes, but he stopped her by pressing his hand on her chest. Even under the blouse, her hidden necklace warmed beneath his palm. Her heartbeat thrummed in anticipation as he pushed her to lay against her pillow.

"Patience, dove. You're an artist. You know you can't rush perfection." His lips widened into a sexy smile that made her nipples perk up, begging for his tongue.

His hand left her chest to trail down her torso. She watched his appreciative eyes as he used both palms to glide over her waist before diving under the hem of her blouse. His nimble fingers teased the sensitive skin above the waistline of her jeans before making quick work of her button and zipper. Liquid arousal pooled in her panties at the thought of those fingers stroking inside her, but instead of delving inside the denim, he continued all the way down her legs.

He massaged down her left leg, making her moan at his gentle kneading as he moved along her calves to her ankle. Slowly, keeping his molten hot gaze on hers, he removed her blue heel and pressed a kiss inside her arch. His five o'clock shadow prickled her skin, making her toes curl, and a giggle escaped her.

He tossed the heel aside onto the mattress and transitioned to her left leg to give it the same treatment. Her head fell back as her tired muscles yielded to his touch.

"*Dios mio*, Hawk, this feels amazing."

"Good," he murmured against her arch in a kiss. "But I'm glad this is the first time you've worn these heels. It was hard to resist you before, but seeing you decked out in my favorite color made me want to do all my favorite things to you."

"Like what?" She giggled.

A wicked grin slanted his lips as he bounced the second shoe to join its partner.

"Like this—"

He tugged her jeans off in one swift motion. A laugh shrieked out of her before she had a chance to clap her hand over her mouth. Her eyes widened and shot to the door, but an amused rumble brought her attention back to Hawk.

"Soundproof, dove. Laugh, scream, moan... *come* as loud as you want to. Lift for me, baby."

His calloused fingertips hooked around her panties and she lifted her hips so he could slide the fabric over her curves. A thrill rushed over her, racing after his touch as it left her skin, making her shiver.

After he threw her panties to join her shoes, he scooted back on his knees and nestled between her bare legs. His gaze was entirely focused on the apex of her thighs as he scooped them over his shoulders. One finger slid down her center and he licked his lips as he swirled the digit around her core, driving her mad.

"Goddamn, I've missed this pretty pussy. I got to drink you yesterday, but you've got me hooked again, Hannah. I don't want another day to go by without getting a taste of you." He tapped her clit with three fingers, sending a shock of pleasure to her core.

"Hawk!"

"Mmm, you're so wet already. Do you want me to taste this pussy, baby? Make sure it's soaking for me before I finally get to be inside you again?"

She moaned and nodded, watching intently as he slowly bent lower. His gaze captured hers as he swiped his long, pink tongue up her center. She tried to keep her eyes on him, but her head fell back with a panting moan at the sensation. He pointed that dexterous muscle and twirled it around her clit until she vibrated with pleasure. She reached out, needing to feel him, and caressed the soft waves of his fade with her fingertips.

Not wanting to miss another second of her sensual view, she rolled her head forward again and propped herself up on one elbow. Hannah watched, enthralled as Hawk plunged inside her core and coaxed a keening whimper from her throat. She cupped the crown of his head and began to ride his skillful tongue before she could stop herself.

He drank her in and lapped up her center ending with a swirl around her clit. When he delved inside her again, she whispered encouragement, telling him how much she craved him.

"Please, *mi cielo*, make me come. I want you inside me already."

"Happy to do it, dove."

She felt him smile against her entrance before he dipped two fingers into her core. They immediately feathered up against her G-spot, not making her wait any longer. On the outside, he flicked his tongue over that bundle of nerves at a relentless pace. His free hand gripped her butt as her core tightened. Her fingers dug into the quilt beneath her and her nails scratched his head as she thrust into his mouth, mindlessly racing to the top of the bliss his skilled muscle promised.

When he wrapped his full lips around her clit and sucked, she saw stars and cried out his name. Her ass cheeks tightened in his punishing grip and every muscle in her body tensed, ready for that beautiful moment when...

"*¡Mi cielo!*" she screamed as her body released wave after wave of euphoria.

His fingers never slowed and his lips kept sucking while his expert tongue continued to pulse against her clit. Her muscles contracted and released, squeezing his fingers inside her until the ecstasy ebbed.

Hawk freed her clit and gave it a kiss that made her giggle. He withdrew his fingers and sucked each one before sitting back up on his knees.

"You taste so sweet, dove." He pulled one long finger from between his lips. "Want a taste?"

For her answer, she grabbed his shirt at the chest. He let her pull him down to collide in a shattering kiss and she dove her tongue between his lips, tasting herself on him. His fingers tangled in her wavy hair, pulling her scalp in a delicious mix of stinging pleasure as he devoured her mouth with the same fervor he did her pussy. She bit his lips, seducing a moan from him before she let go. When he attempted to lift the hem of her blouse, she shook her head.

"Not yet. Now, *I* want to taste *you*," she declared, loving the way a spark of excitement lit his charcoal gaze.

Without wasting another moment, he sat on his knees and grabbed the back of his shirt collar with one hand to tug it over his head.

The tempting tapered *V* peeking out of his jeans caught her eyes and her spent pussy fluttered back to life. Her tongue darted out to wet her lips as each one of his lickable, chiseled abs was slowly revealed by his rising shirt—

Her eyes narrowed at his torso to examine the design inked across his midsection. When he shrugged off the rest of his shirt, she looked closer. Recognition crashed into her as she gasped and sat upright.

"What?" Hawk asked, a tinge of worry in his voice as he balled his shirt up in his hands.

Hannah's eyes watered. She pushed his fidgeting hands to the side so she could trail her fingers over the colorful ink tattooed over every inch of his skin.

"*Dios mio, mi cielo*, your tattoo is gorgeous," she whispered reverently. The colors were animated with his moving muscles as he set his shirt aside. "Is it on the back too?"

As he twisted cautiously, his voice broke like he was nervous. "Yeah."

She stroked the peaks and valleys across his spine before he rotated to face her again.

"I never noticed it before. This is stunning work. Why would you cover it?"

"The sun fades ink," he explained, his voice hoarse with emotion. "I didn't want my memory to fade with it."

"Your memory..." She finally took in the image as a whole and sucked in a breath. "It's *my* painting."

The landscape took over the entire top half of his body. From his wrists, up his arms, over his pecs, abs, and muscular back, every inch of him was the perfect tapestry of the sunrise she'd painted for him years ago.

"This is from the morning you told me—"

"I love you."

*I love you.*

Not "loved." *Love.*

Her pulse stuttered in her chest at his use of present tense. She met his sincere gaze with watery eyes before drifting down to study her painting etched in his skin.

His body itself was already a work of art, his sculpted muscles made for easy, defined lines with a brush. Even now, his skin acted as a tinted canvas, making the understated colors seem more alive than anything she could've ever painted.

"I always color tone my canvas before I paint. It adds richness that a regular canvas base could never match. And this... *dios mio*, this is breathtaking, Hawkins. Is it new?"

"I found an experienced tattoo artist in Atlanta during training. I still had a picture on my phone so he was able to finish the tattoo before the team permanently left base and I had to get rid of my personal effects. When we got out of MF7, I called him up again. He still had the picture of my tattoo back when it was fresh and I've been getting regular touch-ups ever since. I never wanted to forget."

"'I could go a thousand nights and never forget your sunrise...'" she quietly repeated the words he'd promised when he'd given her the new paint materials.

The sunrise was painted in deep, warm reds and oranges across his chest. A perfect, hazy yellow orange blossomed on his left pec as it crested over the Blue Ridge, right where the dove flew across the sun. On his abdominals, dark greens and blues blended with his natural tone, completing the masterpiece that made the foggy pine tree-covered mountains. The rolling hills and valleys continued to flow gently across the rock-hard muscles in his lower back.

Her fingers traced every line of the morning she cherished

above all others, forever inked in his skin, forever a part of him. He shivered under her perusal, but she was so lost in feeling the artwork that she didn't stop until her fingertips drifted back up to the dove flying over his heart.

"I thought you left it behind," she murmured finally.

"Never," he whispered fiercely. "I couldn't bear to part with it." He flattened her hand over his heart. "Our sunrises will always be here, where you are."

Her own heart clenched at his declaration. His gaze held hers before he threaded his fingers in her hair and tugged her up for a kiss. She matched his passion stroke for stroke with her tongue against his. When she nipped him lightly, the kiss turned desperate with need.

It was so tempting to pause and take everything in, to capture the feeling of time stopping while the world kept turning. She felt the sensation every time she watched a sunrise, ever since that first one imprinted on her heart just as effectively as the ink imprinted on his skin.

But she couldn't wait. She couldn't hold back with this man anymore, not in any sense, and she didn't want to.

Hannah tugged at the waist of his jeans. He quickly unclasped the button and shucked them along with his boxer briefs, shoes, and socks to the floor, leaving him for her view.

Her mouth watered at the sight of his Adonis belt pointing to his length as it bobbed toward his navel.

"Lie down," she ordered. "I need to taste you."

# CHAPTER THIRTY-SIX

Hawk felt a mischievous grin lift his lips as he obliged. They both knew he was usually in charge in the bedroom, but if she needed to take the reins again for this moment, he was more than happy to give them over.

He lay back against his pillow and propped his head on his hands, anticipation thrumming his veins as he had every intention of watching her.

She placed her slender hands on his pecs and slid them down his chest slowly, sending tingles over every single dip and curve as her fingertips left his muscles. When she got to the *V* below his abs, she lightly followed both lines with her fingernails, ending at the base of his cock. She circled it with her fingers and her eyes kept his gaze as she spat on the head, already weeping with precum. Shocks of pleasure rippled down his spine as she used both palms to spread it from the top down. She kept her gorgeous sweet-tea-brown eyes on his and opened her mouth wide to accept him.

As soon as her velvet tongue laved over his cock, he *needed* to touch her. His abs tightened as he did a light sit-up to thread his fingers through her hair, helping her bob up and down. Her satin-soft muscle curved around his head before sliding down the underside. Both of her hands followed her lips—her wet, viselike grip already bringing him to the edge of coming.

"Fuck, dove." He had so much he wanted to say but those two words were all he could mutter through gritted teeth. His hips jumped underneath her and she moved one hand to his thigh to keep her balance as she put her entire sexy body into sucking his cock.

Unable to stop himself, his eyes rolled back in his head at the sparks ricocheting through him. Without sight, the sensations were overwhelming as her wet, plump lips slid up and down his hard length. When she hollowed her cheeks, the soft muscles were like pillows, and as she relaxed her throat to take him deeper, a thunderbolt of pleasure shot up from the base of his shaft, threatening to combust from the tip. She swallowed his head down, making him curse.

The urge to come had his balls drawing up, ready to explode down her tight throat. His fingers gripped her hair, but he fought the drive to shove deep inside her. Instead, he focused on her satin tongue swirling around his head, concentrating on not exploding too fucking soon. It was barely working until warm metal brushed the sensitive skin of his upper thigh.

His eyes flared open, and he dipped his chin into his chest to see her better. Those dark-rose lips were light pink as they stretched around him and the skin on her knuckles was pulled taut with her intense grip.

But it was the gold necklace caressing his upper thigh, and the flash of blue on the pendant at the end, that stole his attention.

*Is that…*

His pulse thudded in his chest.

He sat up abruptly and grabbed her necklace. His cock popped from her already swollen mouth as she tilted her head in question.

Confusion marred her brow until her eyes widened. She

straightened and her hand fluttered to her necklace, but he refused to let go and tugged her closer to him instead.

The blue sapphire sparkled against his palm. It'd taken him weeks of looking and studying to find the perfect one. Everyone said diamonds, but Hannah had always marched to the beat of her own drum, and he thought the next chapter of their lives should show that, too. His heart thudded painfully in his chest as he slowly realized what it meant to be holding it in his hand again.

His voice broke as he spoke. "Your engagement ring. You didn't get rid of it."

"Never," she whispered low, but her conviction rang through him loud and clear. A small smile lifted her glossy lips as she repeated his words. "I couldn't bear to part with it."

Heat radiated between them, like the building warmth of a sunrise. He slowly released her necklace and threaded his fingers through her hair. With his other hand, he lifted the hem of her blouse. The moment he dove his tongue deep into her mouth, their kiss grew frantic. Their lips barely parted even when they tugged her blouse over her head. He found the hook to her bra, and he flicked it open so she could slide it from her shoulders. Once they could be completely skin to skin, he circled his arm around her waist and flipped her and laid her down on the bed just below the pillow.

Before he could get too carried away, he hopped off the bed to the bedside table.

"What're you doing?" she asked, propping herself up on her elbows.

"It's been a long-ass time so I didn't have any, but Phoenix insisted on giving me these the night before I left for Mexico. Said something about the pregnancy trope being the worst in spicy books." He chuckled and sifted through the drawer until he found the gold wrapper.

When he raised it for her to see, Hannah's eyes narrowed

until he wiggled the condom between his fingers, and she burst out laughing.

"I guess he really was into romance novels all those years ago." She giggled.

"Hey, his hobby is doing us good now." He laughed as he ripped the packet open.

"Wait a minute." Her voice made him still his movements, his fingers poised to remove the condom from its packaging until she asked, "You really didn't have any?"

He shook his head, proud he could give her this answer. It hadn't been hard to abstain. Not only was there no desire for anyone else, his time in MF7 had made it impossible to meet people and it wasn't like he'd ever been the kind of man who was down for a one-night stand. Being able to tell the woman he'd always loved that there had never been another after her made every lonesome night fucking worth it.

He shook his head. "I haven't needed them. Not since you."

Shock parted her rosy lips. "You'd said it'd been a while. I'd wondered what you meant... but I guess I never thought it would've actually been as long as me."

Possessive pride pounded in his chest and he stalked forward, her confession drawing him to her like the sun to the sky. Cool air wafted over his cock as it bobbed against his lower stomach, still glistening thanks to Hannah's skilled mouth. He pumped it once with his hand, readying it for the condom, spreading his precum and mixing it with her spit. Her laughing eyes dropped to his length and turned molten with lust.

"Can I do it?" she asked, her voice pitched low with desire. His pulse throbbed in his cock at the sight of the wanton hunger in her gaze.

"Yeah, baby." He cleared his throat as he handed her the condom still in its wrapper.

She extracted it from the foil, placing the gold on the night-stand before beckoning him closer. His balls jolted as she grabbed his cock and placed the condom on his tip. Circling her palms around the head, she looked up at him before rolling the rubber down his length.

When he was fully sheathed, she sat up on the bed with big doe eyes, seemingly waiting for his command.

*Your wish, dove.*

He grabbed the huge, king-size pillow and folded it in half before tilting his forehead toward the bed.

"Lie down, baby," he murmured, his voice dripping with desire and nearly unrecognizable even to his own ears.

Keeping his gaze, she lay back. Anticipation vibrated the air between them as he climbed onto the bed and crawled toward her on his knees. He settled between her legs to kiss her, loving the way her full, swollen lips met his, and he rocked his hips back, soaking his sheathed cock in her arousal. She moaned into his mouth and he bit her plump bottom lip before making his way down her body.

He tugged her engagement ring on her necklace, still stunned she'd kept it after all these years. She'd only had it for less than twenty-four hours around him, so he hadn't even gotten to enjoy seeing it on her. The gold and blue complemented her warm-olive skin perfectly, just like he thought it would. When he let the ring go, the necklace fell to rest in her cleavage and he changed course to slide both palms over her full breasts, molding them in his hands.

Her pretty, brown nipples were already perked up, begging to be sucked, and his mouth watered to do just that. He swirled his tongue around one and brushed his thumb and forefinger over the other. Switching between the two, he worked them both into diamond-hard peaks, laving, sucking, and nipping at them. All the while he thrived off of every writhing moan she made underneath him.

"Lift up," he ordered as he reluctantly left her breasts to sit back on his knees, unable to do more than short syllable words at the moment. It was taking all his willpower not to pounce on her and drill into her, but it'd been nine years, they both deserved more than a quick fuck and he couldn't wait to make up for lost time.

She put her knees together and lifted her hips high enough for him to fit the folded pillow underneath her. Her legs began to fall open, revealing that gorgeous pink pussy, hidden beneath her dark, trimmed curls, but he caught her left knee. Her brows furrowed as he turned her leg so she was sidesaddle with her heart-shaped ass perched sideways in the air. She was at the exact right height for him, and he soaked his sheathed cock in her arousal, prepping them both.

"I want you, *mi cielo*."

He leaned over her hips and brushed a wavy curl away from her face. "I want you too, dove. So bad that I know I'm gonna come as soon as I'm inside you. But I want to feel you come on my cock first."

As he spoke, he scooped his forearm under her top leg and raised it, allowing more room for his cock at her opening. He gripped her thigh with one hand and held his cock with the other as he eased inside her. His eyes lifted to her face, monitoring her expression, even as he ached to pound into her.

"Damn, you've always been so tight, dove. I've fucking missed this. I've missed *you*."

"Show me how much you missed me, then, *mi cielo*."

Her eyes sparkled at him as he eased inside. With her legs closed in the sideways position on top of the pillow, her channel gripped his cock like a fucking glove. Inch by inch, he fed her soaking pussy his length, stretching her with small strokes, enthralled with the way he disappeared inside her.

When he was fully seated, he was so fucking deep he had to take a few breaths to center himself before his hips began to have a mind of their own. They gently rocked forward and back, enveloping his cock in her core before sliding all the way out again.

Her eyes glittered at him and her bottom lip popped out from under her teeth as she moaned.

"*More.*"

That was all the encouragement he needed.

He gripped her hip with one hand and tugged her leg closer in the crook of his elbow. Her other leg hooked around his waist, pulling him closer with every thrust.

"Touch yourself, dove," he growled.

She listened immediately, with one hand teasing her nipples and the other finding her clit between her closed legs. When her finger found that bundle of nerves, she cursed in Spanish under her breath. Her inner muscles squeezed him and he powered into her harder, his ass tensing and his spine tingling for release.

"Fuck, dove," he moaned. "It feels so good to be inside you again."

"*Mi cielo*, I'm yours."

"And I'm yours," he groaned through clenched teeth.

His eyes rolled back as his impending orgasm built at the base of his shaft. He slowed his thrusts, not wanting it to end just yet, but her heel dug into his lower back and she rotated her hips on the pillow.

His eyes snapped open as a thrill of pleasure shocked through him. "I'm not going to last long like that, dove."

She closed her eyes as he thrust deeper, giving her everything he had.

"Good," she answered finally with a coy smile.

He pulled out and moved her left thigh to spread her legs into a *V* out before him. In his next move, he seated himself between the apex of her legs while she remained inclined on the pillow. Already knowing what they both needed, she curved her legs over his shoulders and clung to the quilt underneath her.

The new angle made the tip of his cock reach deeper than before. Tilting forward, he positioned himself so every thrust dragged the head over that bundle of nerves inside her. On the outside, he applied pressure and swirled his thumb around her clit.

Her fingers dug into the bedding, and he moaned as she

tightened around him. Both their breaths came in heavy pants as they raced each other up that mountain of pleasure. The higher they rose, the harder his muscles flexed and the more her entire body tensed before his eyes. She pulled him closer with her legs and used the quilt for leverage, meeting him thrust for thrust. When her inner muscles squeezed the hell out of his cock, she pushed him over the edge.

He cursed above her just as she keened. Her eyes closed as she got lost in her ecstasy, but he made sure to keep his open so he could see the rush of pleasure jolt through her body in waves. She trembled underneath him, her forehead misted with exertion. Her mouth fell open on a throaty cry of agonizing rapture.

"Fuck, Hannah. You're a damn vision."

As she tumbled down, squeezing rhythmically against his cock, he removed his thumb from her clit to grip her hips, pulling her closer with every plunge. His pace grew wild and frantic until he finally crested.

"*Hannah*," he cried out hoarsely, falling over her, catching himself at the last moment as he continued to pulse into her.

Her nails scratched his upper back and his hard, aching muscles finally grew soft as his strength pumped out with his seed. He silently wished he was bare so it would take root. Now wasn't the right time, of course. They still needed to get to know each other again. But he prayed that one day he would see her round with his child.

He enfolded her with his arms underneath her and held her close, craving the loose, sated way her body molded to his unyielding hold.

When they'd caught their breath, he rolled them over and laid her on his chest, still inside her. He needed to dispose of the condom, but he didn't want to part with her, not just yet. Whether it was intentional or force of habit, her fingers found his lips and traced them. The gentle touch soothed him just like it always had.

She shifted on top of him and lifted up to kiss him once

more. As with every one of their kisses, it grew more passionate, and his cock hardened right back up between her legs.

She moaned and bit his lip before making her demand, "Again. Please, *mi cielo*."

He chuckled. "I can do this forever, dove." He pulled back to meet her sweet-tea-brown gaze and felt grateful when he found hope there, mixed with a much stronger emotion that filled and matched his soul. "And I plan to."

"I love you, *mi cielo*."

His chest squeezed with emotion so tightly he nearly lost his breath, but there was enough to make his promise.

"I love you, dove. I'll never stop."

# EPILOGUE

## One year later

"Is it normal to have a barbecue after a high-profile, international human trafficking case has been solved and several world leaders and hundreds of their minions have been sentenced all over the world?" Phoenix asked.

He cracked open a beer and collapsed into his seat between Callie and Draco near the end of the row of folding chairs. As soon as he settled, he tipped it back onto two flimsy legs in a move Hawk was starting to believe *was* an actual talent.

Draco huffed, "I don't think any word of what you said is—or should be—considered *normal.*"

Phoenix seemed to weigh Draco's critique, then tipped the Atlanta Braves hat Hannah had gotten for him in agreement. "Fair enough."

"Here's your book," Callie offered as she handed him his latest romance novel. "I moved it so you wouldn't sit on it."

Phoenix landed on all fours on the chair and clutched the book to his chest. "Brown eyes, you're my hero."

"Hero, huh?" Jason snorted. "She doesn't look a thing like that shirtless hero on that cover."

"Hey." Jules narrowed her eyes at her husband. "Let people like what they like."

"*Thank* you, Juliet," Phoenix harrumphed. "I always knew you were my favorite FMC."

"Hey! I thought I was your favorite!" Nora pouted.

"Everyone's my favorite after Callie. She's my number one." Phoenix winked at his girlfriend. "But, see, this is why I love 'why choose' romances. There's enough love for everyone."

Hawk laughed with the rest of the team before he pointed out the obvious. "Yeah, see, the BlackStone crew has never been *normal*. And after what we've been through, we deserve all the cookouts, barbecues, and potlucks we want."

"Who wants normal?" Hannah asked.

Hawk looked over his shoulder to see her smirking at his teammates. That carefree cheerfulness was so fucking good to see.

She'd come a long way over the past year. After being constantly on edge and on the run, it'd taken her a while to feel at peace in her new home. Even then, she'd still had to battle the urge to flee, confiding in him that feeling safe in the past meant her father had been just around the corner. Months of therapy, continued freedom, and trusting each other had given them both the security they'd needed.

She caught his eye and leaned over to peck his cheek. Warmth radiated from her kiss and Hawk's eyes glued to her sexy hips as she rounded his chair to sit next to him. Her messy raven braid spilled over the neckline of her sundress. The deep-blue fabric hugged her curves and her blue heels clicked softly on the rooftop's new mural.

She'd just finished painting the forest of trees on the asphalt that month, making the top of the BlackStone facility fit with the rest of its surroundings in the foothills of the Blue Ridge mountains. Thea, Katie-Belle, and even Tommy had the time of their lives trying to find all the animals Hannah had hidden within the forest scenery. There were so many minute details, it'd taken all year for her to finish. Granted, if Hawk hadn't come up there to distract her so many times, she probably could've finished it in half the time.

He'd actually pointed that fact out to her once, but she'd just given him a sly smile.

*"But where's the fun in that?"*

"Here you go." She fitted a cold mason jar in his hand. "Made it fresh this morning."

"Hell yes," he whooped, making his teammates and their women chuckle. "You guys can't tell me Hannah's orange sweet tea isn't the best you've ever had."

"Again, fair," Phoenix conceded.

Hawk glanced around at his team as a comfortable silence rested in the air. His chest filled to the brim with pride as he watched his family get settled in their line of chairs. The kids were either asleep or—as in Tommy's case—watching *Sports-Center* in the residence below.

The little man had been fun as hell to have around and was smart as a whip, as Hawk's pops used to say. A total sponge for all things BlackStone. He was growing into a fine young man, one Hawk couldn't be more proud of.

BlackStone was growing, too. Hawk had stopped sleeping outside of his room the moment Hannah suggested it. That afternoon, they'd moved Tommy into the spare studio, and he'd made it his own with Braves memorabilia in no time. Now they were even expanding into the other side of the second floor to add more studio and family-style apartments.

Life was good. His team was thriving, and they were finally able to take a breath. But it was times like these that made him think about the one brother that was missing.

"What're you thinking about?" Hannah asked, her brows furrowed in the center as she traced his lips in a downward motion. "You're frowning."

He grabbed her hand and kissed it before holding it on the chair's armrest. Her engagement ring caught the light from the setting sun and he squeezed her palm as he met her sweet-tea-brown eyes.

"Just admiring the view, dove. And thinking about the ones who aren't here to see it."

Her lips lifted in a sad smile as she glanced around the roof at his team. She leaned in to whisper low enough so that just he could hear her.

"He would be happy, you know?"

"You think?" Hawk asked, not caring that his voice lilted with emotion.

Hannah nodded. "I think he would be at peace knowing his entire family found happiness in the end. That despite all the twists and turns, everyone found their happy ever after in their own way."

The sentiment made Hawk's chest hurt, and he swallowed back the emotion in his throat as he took in the sight of his family coming together to celebrate.

The past year had been hard and now that the court cases were over, they deserved to celebrate their victory at last.

Vlad had indeed sung like a canary, so long as a BlackStone agent was in the room. He now had a nice little six-by-nine foot home in a supermax prison, one of the most secure prisons in the country. Apparently, he was already making a name for himself as a motherfucker you don't want to mess with.

The second MF7 team had been as forthcoming as they could be without implicating themselves, unearthing even more information about the drug aspect of the General's enterprises. The gut punch reveal of working for the General had been tough on them, but having BlackStone members with shared experiences had helped both teams come to terms. Some of the guys were even becoming friends.

Assistant District Attorney Marco Aguilar was no longer an *assistant*. The public had seen all the hard work he'd been doing and elected him district attorney, a well-deserved promotion the team had celebrated by throwing him a barbecue. They were thrilled for him, even if it meant they saw less of him. Although word on the street said he was busy with more than just his job. He'd also found his soul mate. It was taking some time to convince her of that, but Hawk had full faith the lawyer would be able to sway her to see his side.

Hawk didn't know how the man kept up with everything, really. Marco had been a rock star in the trafficking case and although he'd been stressed about not having the General to take the stand, as it turned out, they hadn't even needed him.

According to Marco, as soon as they'd collected everything from the General's laptops, flash drives, and his various homes and properties, they'd been able to corroborate the evidence with testimony. In exchange for lighter sentences like GPS monitoring, former CEO of Charitable Technologies International, Gail Haynesworth, her COO, Stefan Ricker, and Officer Henry Brown had all taken the stand. Once the news of an impending trial went public, people came out of the woodwork with their own stories about the crimes the General and the rest of his followers had committed. It'd been a lot of hard work, but Marco had claimed that with the amount and strength of the evidence, it'd actually made the prosecutors' jobs "easy."

But no case is "easy" if there are hundreds of people from all over the world who are implicated. They'd even been able to nail down the guy who'd duped Ellie into this mess in the first place. Nikolai Rusnak, Dmitri Rusnak's son—or Benjamin as Ellie and her friend, Sasha, had known him—was the one who'd invited them to the Ashland County Scholarship Fundraiser. Authorities still hadn't found him. Allegedly, he'd run away to Russia, but Marco had assured the team that once they did find him, his case would be an "easy" one, too.

Thanks to Juliet Bellarose-Stone she'd defended Hawk, BlackStone, and the second MF7 team from any and all potential prosecution. Hawk wasn't sure what they would've done without her. Doing all that while also wrangling a toddler couldn't have been simple, but Jules and Jason tackled it together like the team they were always meant to be.

Hawk had always had a soft spot for the couple. They'd reminded him of his relationship with Hannah in the beginning. Even though their middles couldn't have been more different, at least they were all getting a happy ending.

When Jules wasn't busy with their case, she was still able to help survivors at Sasha Saves alongside Ellie, Naomi, Callie, and now Hannah, too.

Ellie was poised to fully take on the role of director at the clinic once she graduated. At the moment, she was having to balance being a college student, her admittedly overdramatic best friend Virginia, and the lifesaving work they did at the clinic.

Devil had been adamantly against her doing both Sasha Saves and school, but everyone knew who was really in charge in that relationship. Of course, that hadn't kept his overbearing ass from hovering. At least he'd been useful as the clinic medic while he ensured that she didn't work too hard. It was undeniable how proud Devil was of his girl. He'd said as much when he'd told Hawk about how he was going to propose after her graduation.

As far as proposals went, most of the team had assumed Naomi and Wes would be the first to tie the knot after Jules and Jason, but they seemed in no rush to get married anytime soon. Considering Naomi had been in a years-long engagement when she'd met Wes, it was obvious she didn't put a lot of stock in them. But Thea sure did.

After watching a movie about a girl who lived in a flower, Thea was now obsessed with the idea of being their flower girl and wearing her princess dress down the aisle. Hawk wouldn't be surprised if they had a surprise courthouse wedding at some point to sate Princess Thea's love for a good happily ever after.

"Is there any more cowboy caviar left?" Nora asked, breaking Hawk from his thoughts.

"Mmm, negative," Devil answered guiltily around a mouthful

of what looked like the last bite.

Nora's painted lips morphed into a line before she sighed and rolled her eyes dramatically. "Okay, then, what about dessert?"

"Here, you can have mine," Draco offered and passed his plate of cookies to her.

"Ah!" she shouted. "Have I told you lately how much I love your sexy Viking butt?"

She danced in her chair and stuffed her mouth full of caramel chocolate chip cookie. A barely there smile ghosted Draco's lips as he bent to whisper in her ear. Her alabaster skin blushed furiously before he kissed her cheek and drank his Icelandic alcohol from his red plastic cup.

Those two had been fun to watch. Now that the trial was over, Hawk was hoping they'd get a chance to travel the world like they'd wanted. Ever since Draco woke from his coma, he'd been living life to the fullest, and they'd planned so much together. Draco had already asked for days off.

Hawk only wished Phoenix and Callie would do the same. Instead, they'd become obsessed with work. Callie officially resigned from the FBI to join the team and since then, every job that required two or more people, they volunteered for. Solo jobs were a no-go, but those two were his first picks for nearly every two-person job.

From what Hawk could tell, Phoenix and Callie always needed to be on the move, doing something, *anything*, even each other in awkwardly public places around the facility, if necessary. They got a little antsy and surly if they went too long between jobs and every time they came back, they were always much more amiable.

One time over drinks, Phoenix had confirmed that work was their release, and he'd opened up to Hawk about therapy. Every successful mission was another "fuck you" to everyone who had ever hurt them. Making the world a better place was their way of fighting back against the pain they'd been through. And seeing them fight the world side by side was a wonderful thing.

"*Dios mio, que hermoso*," Hannah whispered.

Hawk returned his focus to the sunset they'd lined their chairs up to watch and squeezed her hand before looking at her. "It's beautiful. But I'll always love the ones you paint more."

They'd hung the painting from their favorite morning back in its rightful place above their bed. She'd cried tears of gratitude when Tommy had presented it to her from his duffel bag, showing her he'd kept it all that time. Now it hung next to the first one she'd finished at BlackStone. Thanks to their little painting adventure that one sunrise on the roof, the dark-blue-green streak had turned the landscape into a sunset. They were perfect together, side by side.

Her eyes sparkled as she rubbed up his bare tattooed arm. "My favorite will always be this one, *mi cielo*."

Without Hannah, he'd been terrified of losing the memory of the best moment of his life. He'd had the painting tattooed on so he'd never forget, and he'd done everything in his power to keep the ink pristine. With Hannah around, he didn't have to worry about forgetting. Instead, he could show off the tattoo of her artwork all he wanted.

It was perfect timing too, because he'd had to order new shirts since the guys were beginning to complain about the Henleys he always bought the team. It'd all worked out since they'd needed new logos anyway, ones with an eagle emblem that Nora and Hannah had helped design.

"This one is my favorite, too," he agreed, placing his hand over hers.

She bit her lip in a way that made Hawk want to forego the sunset altogether and run with her down to his room, but Nora's exclamation brought him back to the moment.

"Looks like the show's about to begin!"

"Oh! Do you mind letting me borrow those for a minute?" Hannah asked, pointing to his pops's old binoculars around Hawk's neck. "I want to see the definition in the clouds."

"Happy to, dove," he answered and lifted the binoculars from his neck to give to her. They were one of the few possessions he still owned from his pops's storage, but they'd come back in handy for the Braves games he and Hannah had been to with Tommy in the past year.

While Hannah peered through the binoculars in awe, Hawk glanced around at his team as they set aside their plates and drinks to watch the sun touch the peak of the mountains. When everyone had settled, Hawk sat back to "enjoy the show," as Nora had put it.

The red, purple, and blue clouds in the sky mixed with the greenish-blue hue of the rolling Appalachian mountains, reminding him of the painting etched into his skin. His chest filled with emotion as they all watched in content silence until a bird soared through the air, wings outstretched to float effortlessly on a thermal wind current.

Hannah gasped and Hawk sat up slightly and looked at her. "Was that—"

"Yeah," she answered and lowered the binoculars to meet his gaze with watery eyes. "It was an eagle."

"I read online that those were making a comeback around here," Wes murmured. "Maybe he's one of the ones moving back in."

Hannah squeezed Hawk's hand. He smiled on as she spoke to his crew, "I don't think he ever left. Not really."

"I bet you're right, Han." His heart clenched at the thought.

"The best things in life never truly end," she told him quietly. "They change you, imprinting on your soul, and they stay with you even when they're gone."

Hawk cleared the emotion clogging his throat and returned to watch the majestic bird soaring against the backdrop of the setting sun.

"Fly high, brother," he whispered. "Your family's happy."

Hannah kissed him on the cheek and whispered in his ear.

"Happy ever after."

## MEANWHILE

*Meanwhile...*
*They all lived happily ever after.*

———

Keep reading for the 10 year epic-logue!

# EPIC-LOGUE

## Ten Years Later

*Thea*

"Thea, honey, hold on."

Thea turned from the elevator to see her momma catch the rooftop door just in time to open it wide enough so she could talk through the crack. She tucked an errant strand of short, wavy auburn hair back from her face.

"Can you bring the cookies when you come back? I think they've finished coolin' by now."

"Sure, Momma," Thea called out as the elevator doors *dinged* open. "Anythin' else?"

"That should be good, baby. We'll be windin' down after the desserts. The kids have been wild tonight so hopefully they'll sleep good."

Thea snorted as she stepped through the elevator and pressed the button for the second floor.

"You say that every night, you know? What age do kids chill out again?" she asked.

Her mom rolled her sparkling chestnut eyes behind her new green glasses. "T, you're fifteen and you *still* haven't 'chilled out.' Every gray hair I pluck out of my head, I name after you."

"Momma!" Thea pouted and crossed her arms just as the doors closed on her mom laughing like a loon.

"Rude," she muttered and waited for the elevator to take her down two floors.

Once she stepped out of the elevator, it was instantly quiet, something she rarely heard these days with six full families living in the BlackStone Securities complex. Her friends at school joked about her living in a commune, although they sure did come visit a lot if they actually thought it was weird. Thea loved the chaos, but when they had their cookouts on the roof, sometimes she liked to come down here to get peace and quiet. And there was nothing better than the vacations she took with her mom, her dad, Wes, and her little brother.

Soft fur slinked around her calf, and Thea bent to give the cat some love.

"Hey, there, Kittywillow." She laughed to herself over the name her mother had insisted on.

When Aunt Callie had first brought back the crybaby little kitten from the animal shelter, Uncle Feenik introduced her as Pussywillow. Apparently, Thea hadn't been very good at using the cat's full name, and kept yelling "Pussy" at the top of her lungs every time she called the poor thing to come cuddle with her on the couch. Feenik had gotten a kick out of it, but her mom had scolded him and promptly corrected her. The cat had been "Kittywillow" ever since.

Thea gave the little purring machine a few more pats before heading into the kitchen, passing Aunt Hannah's art along the way. The woman was talented as heck, and her flair amid the industrial-style steel-and-concrete aesthetic had brought life to the place, so much so that the entire gang had moved into the building once they'd expanded the second floor.

There weren't any windows on that side of the hallway since the residences lined the far wall. But now there was landscape after landscape of all the places Aunt Hannah and Uncle Hawk had visited with Tommy and their two boys. Thea hadn't been *an-y-where*, so it was fun to see the different sites of the world that *hopefully* she'd get to experience someday.

A tiny bright-red fire truck was parked in front of the refrigerator and Thea rolled it away with her foot into the common room. It hit the back of the black leather *U*-shaped couch and popped into a Transformer, making Thea gasp and slap her hand over her thumping heart.

"Jeez *Lou-ise*," she muttered, mentally cursing her brother for leaving his toys out.

She couldn't get too mad, though. The kid barely had any toys other than electronics and those nerdy science kits their dad always bought him. Her brother was just like him in that he was always eager to study and learn new things. It made him a dang breeze to buy Christmas and birthday presents for.

Thea opened the fridge and refilled her mason jar glass with the backup orange blossom sweet tea. There'd been plenty up on the roof still, but Hannah had made the batch that morning and Thea had needed an excuse to get her moment of peace.

She gulped down a refreshing sip before piling the warm cookies onto a plate to take upstairs. Once she'd finished, she made her way to the elevator and back to the chaos on the roof.

As soon as she opened the stairwell door, said "chaos" jumped on her as a huge mammoth of a dog tried to give her a hug. She swung the cookies and her drink out to the side with each hand, hoping neither of them spilled.

"Chubbs!" Aunt Nora snapped and pointed to the ground. Her magenta hair and angry tone brought out the natural blush in her alabaster cheeks. "Heel!"

But the Alaskan malamute mutt didn't listen until his equally massive father whistled.

"Chubbs, off. Now," Uncle Draco rumbled. He'd grown his blond hair out enough to sport a man bun on the top of his head, and his long beard was neatly trimmed.

The dog happily hopped off of her shoulders to run toward his mom, leaving dog breath and a little bit of drool on Thea's

BlackStone Securities T-shirt. She didn't mind though. The giant wrecking ball of fluff was cute, and the shirt was already a backup after her own brother spilled mustard on her green dress.

"Sorry about that." Nora winced sheepishly. "He's still just a puppy."

Thea chuckled and bit back the urge to correct her. Uncle Jason had no such reservations though as he barked out a laugh.

"A *puppy*? It's bigger than you!"

Nora clapped her hands over the brute's ears and scowled at Jason. "Quiet, he'll hear you! I don't want to give my baby a complex."

"Nora, he's two years old. He's not a puppy anymore. That's just facts." He laughed.

She rolled her eyes, flopping her short curls over her shoulder with her dramatics. "Okay, Mister My Daughter Is One Hundred and Thirty-Two Months Old."

"Listen." Jason's salt-and-pepper brows furrowed as he wagged his finger like he did every time he scolded his daughter. "My KB will always be my little girl."

"*Dad*, I'm not a *little* girl anymore. I'm gonna be in sixth grade." His daughter, Katie-Belle, propped her hands on her hips and glared at him.

"Yeah, right, tell that to the boy I show our weapons room to."

"*Dad!*" KB groaned as they continued to bicker.

She reminded Thea so much of Aunt Jules it was insane, even down to the fact that the girl was obsessed with true crime. Thea had caught her more than once hastily changing the channel from *Forensic Files* whenever she thought her parents were near. They were adamantly against her watching things like that at her age, but they ought to get used to it since KB had already declared she was going to be either an attorney like her mom or an FBI agent like Aunt Callie used to be.

Meanwhile, Thea was still trying to decide between starting her own clothing business or becoming a therapist. On one hand, volunteering at Sasha Saves had made her fall in love with sustainable and secondhand fashion and she'd always wanted to be a CEO, even before she knew what the letters stood for. On the other hand, therapy had kept her sane for the past eleven years.

After everything happened with her bio dad, her parents had insisted on monthly appointments. Once her mom explained some of the things Thea hadn't been able to fully understand as a kid, they'd even pushed for weekly visits until they were sure she was okay with the news.

Thea wanted to help kids like her who'd been through the wringer. Everyone deserves a kind third party to talk to, and she was grateful she had such an amazing support system who believed the same. She wasn't the only one in the BlackStone family who joked about having a therapist for a best friend. The company had practically kept the local counseling center in business.

"T, do you wanna come play?" KB asked. "The boys think they've *finally* found the unicorn in one of the rivers Aunt Hannah painted."

"*Really?*" Thea carefully hid her grin with a fake yawn. "I'm a little worn out, so I'll take a rain check this time. But come find me when y'all find it, alright?"

"Okay!" KB's honey-blonde ponytail bobbed up and down as she nodded enthusiastically before running off to go with the boys.

"When do you think you'll tell her?" Nora asked with a laugh.

Thea shrugged and smiled. "I had to figure it out all by myself. KB can go a little while longer."

The forest mural Hannah had painted was basically a huge "Can you find it" picture, with tons of different creatures. Even after ten years of looking, Thea wasn't totally convinced she'd found them all. But the unicorn was definitely a myth Tommy had made up to get Thea to leave him alone so he could watch ESPN during their TV time.

Realizing he'd concocted the ruse to get her to search the rooftop for hours had taken her *way* longer than she wanted to admit. Once she'd confronted Hannah—who had been *so* confused, by the way—Thea had kept the secret from the other kids. KB, the little investigator, would no doubt figure it out way sooner than she had, but it would be fun while it lasted.

One of Hawk and Hannah's youngest boys shrieked with laughter down on the other side of the roof, and Thea winced.

"So many *boys*, no wonder you got a dog."

Nora smiled. "Yeah, I don't know how Hannah does it. 'Hashtag boymom' seems like a full-time job to me. Draco and I want to see the whole world before we settle down. We may never have kids, but we'll have a good time. Chubbs will make sure of that, won't you, *Chubbsy Wubbsy*." She talked like a baby to the huge beast and he immediately huffed and rolled over to let her scratch his belly.

Thea snorted and lifted the cookies that had miraculously survived the puppy's attack.

"I'm just gonna go put these down."

Nora paused over a wriggling Chubbs before her eyes went wide behind her white square glasses.

"Yasssssss! I've been so excited for those. Devil ate all the damn cowboy caviar again and I've been *dy-ing* for dessert. Can you hide some for me between the vegetable platter and the fruit? The kids will never find it there."

"Sure thing." Thea giggled.

She walked over to the huge spread of food, passing by the empty bowl of cowboy caviar beside a mountain of chips, her momma's home-cooked casserole, and Hannah's *cochinita pibil* taco station. Uncle Hawk and Uncle Jason had gotten together early that morning to smoke some ribs and brisket that was melt-in-your-mouth delicious, and Uncle Devil and Uncle Draco had fired up the grill for hamburgers and hot dogs. It was all so yummy, but her *favorite* food was always Uncle Marco's empanadas. It was too bad his wife couldn't make it that night, especially since there was enough food to feed a small village, which, come to think of it, BlackStone kind of was.

Thea snagged another beef pastry and gave Marco a thumbs-up before stuffing it in her mouth. As he laughed, his warm bronze skin creased around his eyes. It was good to see him smile. Ever since he'd been elected to be a judge, he'd ironically gotten a lot less busy and a whole lot happier.

That last part could've been thanks to his wife. She was amazing, always on the move, traveling the world for the next big story and for her own channel on social media. Even though his wife hadn't been able to come, Thea still wished Marco had brought his sweet, squishy little baby. Apparently, Marco's *abuela* called dibs over the little one for the night and had sent her empanadas as a peace offering.

Thea placed the caramel chocolate chip cookies among the healthier dishes Callie had brought. She then plated two of them and hid them underneath a napkin for Nora to get when she was ready.

"Thanks, hon." Thea's mom squeezed her shoulder. "I made a spot for them at the end of the table, though."

"It was Aunt Nora's request." Thea gave her mom a silly, pointed look.

"Ah, so people won't find them and she can have them all? She's a sneaky one, I'll give her that. Come on over, Devil and Ellie have an announcement."

"Oh, an announcement? *Yes*," Thea sang and followed her mom to the small crowd gathering near the end of the roof.

The last announcement Devil and Ellie had given was to tell the group they were getting married. Devil had proposed to her right after her graduation, not able to wait another second. Thea had been blissfully ecstatic at the news because she'd been a flower girl three times already and was excited to have another wedding under her tutu. She'd already done it for her aunts and uncles—Jason and Jules, Hawk and Hannah, and for her own mom and dad. When it finally came time for Devil and Ellie's wedding, Thea had been a pro walking with KB down the long aisle, tossing yellow rose petals.

Their wedding had been gorgeous, but her own parents' wedding was one she'd never forget. It'd been at the Ashland County courthouse and wasn't at all lavish. That hadn't mattered though. The beautiful moment when Wes had promised her mom he would love, protect, and cherish her forever had made Thea teary-eyed even at her young age.

Feenik, Callie, Nora, and Draco were the only aunts and uncles she hadn't been a flower girl for. Feenik and Callie had never married, and probably never would. The two of them worked harder than anyone she'd ever met, and they loved their careers, Kittywillow, the BlackStone family, and each other, but they didn't seem to need to define their love with a marriage label, and that was okay. There were rumblings they might be trying to have a baby, but Thea didn't want to get her hopes up.

And as for Draco and Nora, they'd had a surprise Vegas wedding when they went to visit a few years ago. Not a soul had known about it until they came back from vacation with the news, merry as can be. Draco might've even smiled, if memory served correctly.

Thea joined the rest of her unconventional family, standing between her dad and mom as Aunt Ellie radiated beside her redheaded giant in the center. Whatever it was they had to tell them, Aunt Jules must've already known. She was practically dancing with giddiness in her skirt suit from work. It was a pretty garnet that hugged all of her curves with matching heels. She looked as gorgeous as ever with her sleek honey-blonde bob, flawless makeup, and bright smile.

"You had a good night so far, Princess T?" her dad asked with a smile.

His laugh lines animated his whole face and the creases behind his glasses were more defined than when she'd first met him. He still had his navy-blue hair, although the silver streaks were natural now.

"Always, Dad." She beamed at him and gave him a quick hug.

Beside her, Feenik whined to Callie. "When are we gonna have a cool announcement?"

Callie's short black ponytail bounced as she faced her partner with her signature smirk. It was one of the few expressions she gave so freely and it'd formed a faint line around one side of her mouth. Her brown eyes sparkled as she answered.

"I don't know, maybe we'll have something to tell them in a month or two."

Feenik's usual joking smile turned soft. His worn Braves hat was on correctly for once, but he took it off to give his girlfriend a scorching kiss, making Thea's eyes widen and her cheeks heat.

Thea quickly twisted away to give them a moment. Their PDA was definitely the worst out of all of them. Each couple had their highs and lows and that was one Thea could've lived without, if she was honest. Her favorite couple, though—besides her mom and dad, of course—was Devil and Ellie.

He was always so sweet and nurturing around her, and from what Thea had gathered, Ellie had gone through a lot when she wasn't too much older than Thea's age. She'd thrived since then and was now the director at Sasha Saves. Devil looked at her the same way he did the night they shared their engagement. It was everything Thea would've wanted for a happy ending.

"Ready?" Devil asked, his normally stern face was light and his smile shone through his thick red beard.

He'd grown bigger over the years, gaining 'pre–dad bod pounds' as Jason put it. Standing beside his wife, Devil was a straight-up giant. Ellie was naturally lithe, but she still ran every day to keep in shape. With her long blonde hair pulled back by a bobby pin, though, Thea could've sworn she'd gained a little bit of weight recently. It suited her new radiant glow.

"Hell, yeah, give us the scoop!" Feenik raised his beer from his seat.

"Well..." Ellie bit her lip before looking at everyone. "We're—"

"We're pregnant!" Devil called out, obviously unable to contain himself.

Cheers went up around the roof as everyone converged on the two new parents. Thea joined them, getting jostled and hugged from all sides as everyone talked all at once. When they finally broke apart, Devil wiped Ellie's damp cheeks, and she hugged him from the side as she told them how far along she was with their baby girl.

"A girl?" Jason burst into laughter. "Oh man, all these years you guys have been teasing me? Just wait. This guy's gonna be *insane*."

Devil shrugged, not denying the claim in the slightest.

"Oh my goshhhh, Devil, you're gonna be the cutest little-girl dad. I'm gonna perish." Nora clapped quickly and squealed before hugging Ellie again. "And Ellie, girl, you look so gorge. I *knew* you were glowing the other day!"

Ellie giggled. "I'm pretty sure that 'glow' was my Southern pregnant woman summertime glisten, but I appreciate the compliment."

The women laughed while the men broke out cigars that Hawk retrieved from downstairs. Thea sipped her tea, basking in the excitement until she realized there was something missing. She frowned until it dawned on her, and she smiled before setting off to find him, knowing *exactly* where he'd be.

Thea walked around the group and made her way to the huge helicopter that took up so much of the rooftop space. Without even checking inside, she climbed into the copilot seat, held her mason jar in her lap, and gazed out at the sunset through the glass, egg-shaped cockpit. After a moment of silence, she finally caved.

"So... whatcha up to?"

Tommy snorted and rubbed the back of his messy blonde hair, just like she'd seen his father do a million times. "Just sitting in the quiet, T. I've been social for hours and I needed a break. No need to analyze me."

She held her hands up in surrender. "Alright, no need to get sassy, either."

He huffed through a small grin while keeping his blue eyes on the horizon. The boy was quiet by nature, always had been. His humor was a little twisted, but he had a heart of gold and he'd been a fantastic role model so far to his two little hellions for brothers.

But he'd been through a lot, too. Thea could see it in his eyes whenever he thought no one was watching. It was the same kind of pain she hid inside, too.

"What're you thinkin' about?"

He shrugged. "Life. College. The future."

"Oh, that's it?" She snorted and loved the fact he chuckled with her.

"Yeah... Mom wants me to keep going to Ashland State, but after this freshman year, I feel like I tried it, y'know? I swear, the only thing keeping me there is my baseball scholarship."

"What do you want to do instead?" she asked, genuinely curious how he'd answer.

"I don't know. I've been thinking about my father a lot—not my dad, erm, Hawk—but... you know... the one that..."

"Yeah," she whispered before making him finish.

The two of them didn't always see eye to eye. She was pretty sure he hated her guts there in the beginning. But when they both figured out they could talk about their fathers together, their relationship had changed entirely.

He no longer saw her as the annoying princess who twirled around in front of the TV during a Braves game. And she didn't see him as the surly butthead that refused to watch—or *do*—anything fun. Instead, they became actual friends.

"Eagle was in the Army like my dad was and my dad started this BlackStone team after. Mom doesn't want me anywhere near this stuff. She says it's too dangerous, but they haven't been on anything really dangerous in like ten years. They've helped people, though. I want to do that, too."

"You don't think you can do that during college?"

He huffed. "I don't need to have people tell me shit in a class-room for four years while I could be out helping people *now*."

"You could volunteer at Sasha Saves," Thea offered, knowing that wasn't exactly what he was talking about.

"Thea, come on. You know all I can do there is basically be a cashier. I want to *do* something." His hands were wide as he spoke, emphasizing his passion.

"I wish I could help," Thea replied honestly. "But I don't know what the heck to do either."

"You're fifteen," he pointed out. "You're not supposed to know yet."

"You're nineteen." She shrugged. "I don't think you're really supposed to know yet, either."

"Hey, son?" Hawk approached the helicopter cockpit on Tommy's side, scrubbing his salt-and-pepper goatee with his hand. His smile made lines crinkle at the edges of his dark-brown eyes. "Oh, hey Thea. Just came to talk to my boy a minute."

"Oh yeah, sure, Uncle Hawk. Do you want me to leave?"

Hawk shook his head. "Nope, not at all. You can stick around. But, Tommy, I've got a proposition for you."

Hannah appeared in the doorframe beside her husband, and Hawk wrapped his arm around her. She'd dyed her hair back to black a few years ago, and now little grays mixed with the glossy raven color in her messy side braid.

"What's up?" Tommy asked, sitting straighter in his seat.

"Your mom and I have been talking." He glanced to his wife who nodded before she continued for him.

"I know you said you're not interested in college anymore, *avecito*, but what if we make you a deal?"

Tommy's eyebrows lifted in interest even while his eyes narrowed with suspicion. "What kind of deal?"

Hawk laughed. "You're just like me, little man. Find out all the facts before you let yourself get too excited. Anyway, I've got a job that could be perfect for you—"

"Really? Yes! I'll take it—"

"*But*," Hannah interrupted him with a pointed finger. "It will *have* to fit in your school schedule, alright?"

"You've gotta show me you can handle the workload we have at BlackStone by killing it in school, ball, and this job. Can you do that for me?" Hawk asked with a raised brow.

"Yeah, of course, I'm in. What's the job? When can I start? What will I be doing?" he asked all at once. More excited than Thea had seen him since the Braves won the World Series.

"You'll be helping out with security at Sasha Saves."

His jaw dropped. "For real? Hell yeah!"

Hawk nodded. "Yup. It'll be simple stuff, at first. Teaching you the ropes you pretty much already know. But it's right across campus, so it'll be perfect to hop on over after class and gear up for the night until the store closes."

"Alright, yeah, I'm totally in. This is awesome. Thanks, Dad."

Hawk broke away from his wife as his son reached out to slap his father's hand. Tommy held on as the older man brought him in for a hug and clapped him on the back.

"I'm proud of you, son," Hawk whispered. "Always have been. You know that, right? He would've been proud of you, too."

The hug lasted a long second before they broke apart, and Thea could've sworn both men's eyes were more glittery than before.

"Thanks, Dad. I love you." Tommy's voice was hoarse with emotion that made Thea's chest tighten.

"Love you too, little man. But remember what I said, alright? Gotta keep them grades up. We'll teach you to kick ass outa school, but you gotta kick ass in school first."

"Deal." Tommy laughed.

Hawk circled his arm around Hannah's waist again before he turned toward the team and shouted. "Tommyhawk's in!"

More military-style whoops and cheers erupted in the crowd and Thea could've sworn the boy's tan skin was blushing.

"Welcome to the team, Tommyhawk!" Feenik shouted, eliciting more cheers.

It was Tommy's good news, but it made Thea's heart soar. Her friend was going to follow in his dad's footsteps. He was figuring life out.

*Now I've got to do the same.*

But Tommy was right. She still had time. For now, she could search the rooftop for the unicorn with her cousins, stuff herself to the brim with barbecue and her momma's cookies, and sit with her friend in a helicopter and watch the sunset.

Once everything quieted down on the outside and his mom and dad walked away, Tommy leaned back into the helicopter. She sat with him in silence as they both appreciated the stunning view.

After a few quiet moments, he cleared his throat. "I've got a confession to make."

Her brow furrowed. "Uh-oh. What is it?"

"It's not bad, I swear. But you know how you used to always watch those dumb girl movies—"

"Hey now, they're not 'dumb girl movies.' Most of them are classics now. Besides, I think you *pretended* to hate those movies, thank you very much. I know you secretly loved them."

He chuckled. "You're right."

"Wait, what?"

"You're right." He nodded at her high-pitched question with a smile. "That's my confession. I secretly liked them."

"Huh." She sat back in her seat as a slow, satisfied smile crept over her lips. "I've never felt so vindicated."

He barked a laugh, and they chuckled together until another comfortable silence rested between them again.

"Do you think this is what happily ever after feels like?" he asked, finally breaking the quiet between them. "Like the ones in your movies?"

Thea nodded at the sunset before meeting his eyes with a sincere smile.

"We're teenagers, so we've got a lot of our stories left to go, but... yeah. If the endin' feels like this? It's gotta be a happily ever after."

"Good." A small smile lifted his lips before they both turned to the sunset again. "I can't wait to see where we end up."

"Hopefully somewhere freakin' cool."

"And hella fun," he added with a snort.

"Maybe even a little crazy?"

"Oh, one hundred percent. You can't be a BlackStone brat and live a normal life."

"True." Thea giggled. "Honestly, though? As long as it's happy, I'm along for the ride."

He bent to the floor of the cockpit and lifted his mason jar of orange blossom sweet tea before nodding to hers in her lap. The sunset sparkled through the beverage before he made his toast.

"Cheers to happy endings."

Thea raised her glass and clinked his. "And all that's ever after."

- The End -

# ALSO BY GREER RIVERS

## <u>Conviction Series</u>

Escaping Conviction

Fighting Conviction

Breaking Conviction

Healing Conviction

Atoning Conviction

Leading Conviction

## <u>Tattered Curtain Series</u>

A series of standalone stories inspired by classic stage productions

### Phantom

A dark, modern retelling of the classic tale Phantom of the Opera

### Rouge

(coming Spring 2023)

## <u>Standalones</u>

### Catching Lightning

An Enemies-To-Lovers College Sports Romance

### A Tempting Motion

An Enemies-To-Lovers, Office Romance Short Story

———

## Thank you for reading!

Please consider leaving a review on Amazon, Goodreads, and Bookbub!

Just one word can make all the difference.

# BE A DEAR AND STALK ME HERE

You can find all things Greer Rivers here:
https://bit.ly/StalkGreerRivers

# ACKNOWLEDGMENTS

Hi! The Conviction Series is in the books! Literally! I started writing as a resolution to myself in January 2020 and to be finished with my first series is such an awesome feeling. This book made me cry, shout, laugh, and tear my hair out, and this series changed my life. It was a catharsis when I definitely needed an escape and it's so very bittersweet to be finished.

If you're new here, this is the part where I ramble on and say thanks a million times and it's still not enough, especially with everyone I owe to finishing this chapter (pun intended) of my life. You obviously don't have to read this, but you can if you want to! Hell, you might even be in it. But the tl;dr version is: if I know you, I am thankful for you, more than you'll ever know.

First, and almost foremost (sorry, the hubs is always my #1), thank you READERS! The dream makers, the spicybooktokers, and the Boss Ass Bitches! I know your time is precious, so to have you spend it on something I wrote is a true damn honor. Let me just tell you that you make an author's world go 'round. Hanging out with y'all is why I do this and I love hearing from readers: good, bad, or ugly, although admittedly I'm always fingers-crossed for good and the bad and ugly make me a sad panda, but it's fine. I'll still love hearing from you and getting to know you! You beautiful words of affirmation people who reach out to me to tell me pretty things: You rock my world with your encouragement and I'm truly so surprised every single time someone says something nice about my words. I wouldn't be able to pursue this dream without y'all so thanks for making my dreams come true!

To Barista Alley and your avocado toast and hot chocolate.

To Marisa at Cover Me Darling: Thank you so much for putting up with me and the hubs! I know I say this every time, but this might legit be my favorite cover! You've been amazing this entire process and I can't thank you enough.

Many thanks to Ellie McLove, my editor at My Brother's Editor, and Rosa Sharon, the Fairy Proof Mother: Y'all have been with me since the beginning of this journey and I'm so grateful for your patience when my schedule is crazy and for your friendship all the time. I'm so thankful to keep working with MBE.

Thank you to my diversity readers: to Renita McKinney at A Book A Day Author Services and Blanca Sanchez. Your insight, help, and guidance with these characters and the book as a whole was instrumental and I am so very grateful!

Thank you Nikki Wein @NikkWeinTattoo for your amazing advice and helping steer me in the right direction! I def need a tattoo now!

Thank you to my clandestine military friend who shall not be named for lending your military expertise when I needed to ask questions about totally made up spec-ops units.

To LC's alpha and beta readers:

A.V., Kristen, Carlie, Carrie, Sierra, Whitney, Janet, Amy, and Pascale

You put up with my last minute BS and I can't thank you enough!! I'm so thankful that y'all have been on this wild ride with me!

A.V.!!! Avie, Avie, Avie you are magnificent. Thank you so much for reading on my crazy schedule and always providing amazing feedback. We started this journey together and I've loved growing with you! I'm so grateful to you for helping me become a better writer, but I'm most thankful for our friendship.

Everyone make sure to read A.V. Asher's Truth and Lies Duet! It's amazing!

Thank you betas for telling me pretty things. I love you all and I'm so appreciative of my friendships we've developed.

Carlie! You're an amazing beta reader, PA, and hype woman and I so appreciate you for reading! I'm so excited for your future!

Kristen! Please never leave! The way you pay attention to doors, and hands, and fingers, and bikes, and phone calls... my stories would be a mess without you! Thank you so much for taking time out of your hectic schedule and the chaos around this book to read for me!

Whitney! Your feedback and insight makes my day. Thank you so much for reading for me and being the bestest ever!

Carrie and Sierra, I've always been so thankful for your constant support. I'm so excited for what's to come next for y'all, too! Carrie, girl, God bless you for lending your home for Vegas! I truly appreciate you!

Janet and Amy! You guys rock. Thank you so much for taking the time to read and provide awesome feedback, even on such a stupidly tight schedule. Your input is invaluable and I'm so thankful!

Pascale! Girl, your insight is amazing. I'm so excited for your future and thank you so much for squeezing me in!

Moral of the story: I've made some great friends with all of you and that means everything.

To Bre! Almost every other day, the hubs and I talk about how amazing you are. You're always there when I need you and supportive when I'm disappeared and I can't thank you enough. Please keep harassing me about manifesting though! I've fallen off the wagon, lol.

To my TikTok author friends: Many of you have been encouraging as hell and also hilariously fun to get to know. Booktok is my people and I'm so glad I joined and met all you other thirsty bitches. This has been such an incredible journey and I am so very grateful to call y'all my friends! I can't wait to hang with y'all near my hometown next year!!! I say breweries on South Slope and wineries at the Biltmore, or bust!

To Kayleigh, aka USA TODAY BEST SELLING AUTHOR: We are wild ones, but I'm so glad to have you as my bestest friend. Vegas is gonna be so fun! I hear they don't even have windows in casinos so we might not even have to squint when we crawl out of our hobbit holes. 100% we need to plot more books and I'm super excited to go waltzing Matilda with you.

To my OG BABs/Dinner Divas: Katie, Sydni, Liz, and Lauren: As always, please never stop hanging out with me even though I disappear and thank you for having a sweatpants and pajamas dress code. Also why don't we do brunch more often?? That was the bomb and Brunch Babes has a nice ring to it. Anyways, y'all are seriously ride or dies and I'm so grateful for you.

Thank you, Katie, my bestie who will HOPEFULLY be living very close very soon *eye staring emoji*. Can't wait to take Goose, Peabo, and Evie to the park together. W I L D.

Thank you, Sydni, my bestie who is had the best bachelorette weekend I've ever been to! It was amazing and I'm so glad we made it out alive lol.

Thank you, Liz, my bestie who I have been stalking the past week to see if Baby Boy has made his arrival yet. #ThanksFind-MyFriends. I'm super excited for this new addition to our little found family!

Thank you, Lauren, my bestie who survived Carolina Beach, Ke$ha night, ten hours in a Fiat, and the wonderland that is Buc-ee's. I had such a great time with you and I can't wait to dance like a fool again at Sydni's wedding!

To my wonderful family, my momma, sisters, BIL, and precious baby angel face niece and the FUTURE precious baby angel face niece we'll be adding soon: Your support means everything. Our lives have been very hectic since the last book. Things were turned upside down and we were faced with something we prayed would never happen. I hate that it did, but I'm so glad none of us had to go through it alone. I swear tho, if someone tries to offer me up an emotional spoon I'mma throw it back at them, lol! BG I'm so proud of you and all the big girl things you're doing with your life! Menee, watching you be a momma is one of my absolute favorite things. I can't wait for the mountains this weekend and I'm sorry I promise I won't make us pick apples during a hurricane. Once again, I *never* expect y'all to read my books, but if you do, I hope you enjoy them!

To Maria: I firmly believe that when everyone is born we should be assigned a therapist and I'm so grateful I lost my mind at the perfect time that I got to have you as mine. I'm so grateful I could up my meetings during this book to every week/two weeks. I desperately needed them.

To Athena, you crazy bitch. You really showed out this summer, huh? Calm tf down, girl. I'm trying my best to get us sleep and I can't be doing that if you're wildin' out all the damn time.

And finally, to the hubs: WE DID IT. I can honestly and sincerely say that THIS BOOK could not have happened without you. The world crashed around me and you lifted me up in the most amazing of ways and held my hand when I thought I couldn't keep going. You are my "Mighty Alpha," first reader, last reader, all the readers in between, business partner, co-owner, co-writer, manager, TikTok approver, cliff jump pusher/catcher, favorite encourager, IRL book boyfriend, best friend forever, and the love of my life. Thank you for reading this book MANY times, helping me write the action scenes, taking care of the entire house when I was hold up in a room all day, babysitting me, and all the little things you do to keep us rocking. I'm super excited/nervous for Vegas and I'm SO excited for our date day next week and the opportunity to just breathe. I'm also excited for the stories to come! When you tell me pretty words, I listen. They fill me up and give me the courage to do all the scariest of scary things in this writing world. Walking and plotting with you are two of my favorite things and quite literally keep me sane. As always, I am so incredibly thankful for you believing in me 100% and taking hugenormous leaps of faith with me. You've saved my life and you've changed it for the better. I wouldn't want to spend a moment of it without you and I'm totally gonna keep you honest about that RV thing you said you'd maybe might do someday. I'm tellin' ya, they'll change our lives for signings and taking on the world! Manifest it, baby! And lastly... thank you for making every day an HEA.

Love,

*Greer Rivers*

# ALL ABOUT GREER

Greer Rivers is a former crime fighter in a suit, but now happily leaves that to her characters! A born and raised Carolinian, Greer says "y'all," the occasional "bless your heart" (when necessary), and feels comfortable using legal jargon in everyday life.

She lives in the mountains with her husband/critique partner/irl book boyfriend and their three fur babies. She's a sucker for reality TV, New Girl, and scary movies in the daytime. Greer admits she's a messy eater, ruiner of shirts, and does NOT share food or wine.

Greer adores strong, sassy heroines and steamy second chances. She hopes to give readers an escape from the craziness of life and a safe place to feel too much. She'd LOVE to hear from you anytime! Except the morning. She hates mornings.

Printed in Great Britain
by Amazon

86840037R00217